GIL JACKSON

THE SEVENTH GIFT

Copyright © Gil Jackson, 2015

All rights reserved.

The Seventh Gift

ISBN: 978-1-8382326-3-4

No part of this publication may be reproduced, stored in a retrieval system or transmitted in any form or by any means, electronic, mechanical, photocopying, recording, or otherwise, without the prior permission of the author and the publisher of this book.

Author's address: **gilvjackson@hotmail.co.uk**

Historical events and names aside, The Tinners Hut is a work of fiction and the product of the author's imagination. All names (excepting two) are coincidental to any person either living or dead.

Cover design, Epaper make-up, and formatting by:
www.hirambgood.co.uk
E-pub2 formatting to industry standards.
HTML and CSS Validated.

DEDICATED
To my wife, Rita

IN MEMORY
Keith Lawrence Jackson 1935-2005

OTHER WORK

FICTION:
The Seventh Gift
The Tinners Hut

NON-FICTION:
Hiram B. Good's
Multi-Drop Training Manual

The London Apprentice

CONTENTS

PROLOGUE

200 BCE

THE WHIRLPOOL OF FIRE reaching into the heavens gave a deafening scream. A vortex of dust drawing upwards around it blocked the light from the sun was likened to a solar eclipse, brought a surreal darkness to the desert.

As if by instinct, a magpie, sensing a manifestation of evil about to enter the building, warned others of its kind away with its hard chattering rattle voice. The half-buried and abandoned single-room stone Tabernacle, its bleached and worn carved Star of David over the doorway, a being formed from the dust. Dressed in a robe, its hair tied back with a strip of Arab cloth, the being eased the lid off from an Ark that was set on a stone shelf inside. Removing the scroll from inside it set to laboring over it with a sharpened strip of wood. Holding the scriber between thumb and forefinger, dipping into a pot of liquid carbon, shaking off any excess as it went, it made additions to the previous writer's abjad script in an identical hand. When it had completed its task it held the scroll toward the light and examined it. Satisfied, it then rolled it up and tied it with cord. Then replacing the scroll in the Ark, dropped back down its lid and turned to leave.

Departing this House of the Lord, fearless now – from a God long since departed – Ahriman disembodied. And, but for the dead bird stiffening from the heat of the sand outside, the sound of thunder echo rolling out across the desert toward Canaan before fading into the distance, there was no other trace that he had been there.

PART ONE

One – 1920s

Give me your tired, your poor,
Your huddled masses yearning to breathe free.
EMMA LAZARUS 1849–87

DARK SHADOWS THAT INFEST THE SOUL, causing our skin to creep while we, in a half world between sleep and death, are the detritus of another creator that sought, indeed still seeks, domination of that dark veil of time and verse humans call life–time. For these shadows are the cohorts of Satan, the one manifestation embedded deep within the human psyche along with all others from time beginning, bringing with them evil that humans are capable of exercising or exorcising as they choose. While the Other, when evil prevails, will turn away, leaving it to the business of man to deal with as and how he sees fit, that he will, choosing the right path, arrive at a greater enlightenment.

In His belief, He had made a fundamental error of judgement.

For this error, not overlooked, rather sought: watched for: came onto the scene one Marco Giuseppi. A promising soul who sought power and wealth; who would bring no baggage when it came to right and wrong to drive forward his ambitions. The seeds were in place. Ahriman would return.

Immigrants in Manhattan's Lower East Side counted the Giuseppi and the D'Sotto family among their kind. For the families themselves, though close enough to pass as fellow countrymen from Sicily, the friendship between their two sons was jeopardizing that relationship. Seeking a better life from poverty and the influence of

Sicilian banditry was something they had hoped to put behind them, but the sons of Sicily had other ideas.

Marco Giuseppi, the older of the two boys by eighteen months seeing opportunities for them both took his friend, Tony D'Sotto along with him. Setting themselves up on a life of serious crime, it was inevitable they would become known to the police. Especially more worrying for their families, with the power to deport undesirable aliens, New York's Immigration Authority. The police, however, Giuseppi could deal with in the medium term, the latter would take longer.

Marco Giuseppi had taken on the role of Godfather, while Tony, that of his consigliere; where a pact of 'easy street' took root and the tried and tested Sicilian methods of protection with menaces became profitable. With that in mind, with the police knocking at their door every five minutes for backhanders, Giuseppi decided that credibility, power, and influence would be an essential asset if they were to rise above bent cops who would inevitably cause their empire to crash when they chose. He looked further.

The union, where desperate men in search of work to feed their families, fell easy prey to those in charge that would exploit them in other ways than by legitimate employment. By keeping wages down and deciding who would work and who would not, nobody was in a position to complain. When it came to the welfare of workers there was not a fag paper thickness between the interests of Uncle Sam, the dockyard board's management, and the union. The first world war with Germany had seen to that. The second had reinforced it. When the death of the sitting union boss created a vacancy, somebody was already lined up to take over. They needed somebody from the dockyard's management team for credibility of fairness. That man was the management chairman. A man with religious credentials.

Giuseppi had other ideas. With paid friends on the inside of the union he made his move.

When the chairman heard he had a rival for the job, he informed the government department responsible for employment that Marco Giuseppi, with possible criminal links to the Italian Mafia, was not someone they should be associated when it came to the workings of an American dockyard. After some deliberations, they agreed. Using Italy's past alliance with Germany during the war as an excuse, they duly informed the board their reasons for turning down Marco Giuseppi's application.

The management chairman had a dark secret though, one that Giuseppi was about to go viral with. Rumor was plural that the management chairman, Matthew Brown, had a peccadillo for young men. For a Quaker elder in a city as corrupt as New York, Giuseppi would be hard pressed to prove this without evidence. And that . . . he determined . . . he would get.

After a tip-off that the haunt the chairman often used to entertain boys was on for that evening he employed the services of a photographer. The subsequent photograph was damning.

With the evidence in his hand, Giuseppi asked to see Brown. The man at first refused, until Giuseppi mentioned to him of what he knew about him. Brown then asked him to come to his office. There, Giuseppi presented him with a fait accompli: that he write a letter to the board's committee telling them that he had been mistaken over Giuseppi's alliance with the Italian mafia; that Marco Giuseppi would be the better man for the job; and then withdraw himself from the running.

With all the respect of his friends within the community of William Pitt House, as well as New York's establishment, Matthew Brown, with the confidence that no one would believe such outrageous rumors from such a two-bit criminal, stared at him, then said: 'Vile gossip spread by those that cannot accept our religious beliefs with regard to pacifism. I don't deal with blackmailers or criminals, Mr. Giuseppi. Thou hast nothing on me. Now get ye from my office.'

Holding his office door open for him, Giuseppi shrugged and walked out. He had offered him a way, and he had declined to take it.

The dockyard board management committee received the negative image glass plate with its accompanying photograph in a plain brown envelope. It showed Quaker Matthew Brown with his pants and underpants around his knees pressed hard into a young boy's naked rear. Smiles before looks of disgust went around the table. The committee had not altogether been taken with the idea of a non-belligerent being in charge of dockyard workers and now they had their excuse not to.

The government commissioner responsible for the commercial sector of the dockyard asked to see Brown in his office. Thinking that the offer of the job was to be confirmed, Brown dressed appropriately in the style of his religion. Rigged out in a long black waistcoat with coat over, turned up on its two side edges, a black brimmed hat in his hands, and under his arm with tooled gold lettering prominent, a copy of his family Bible bound in leather he stood proud. Then he glanced down onto the desk where his eyes were drawn to the photograph that was lying there and his world crashed. Alongside of it the glass photographic plate it had been taken. His lips quivered and sweat broke out on his forehead. He recognized both he and the boy he abused, and the thought of what he had done, the disgrace it would bring on the Society of Friends – to speak nothing of his wife and three children – overwhelmed him. He knew his days were numbered.

The government commissioner coughed gently passing him the letter from the committee. Pushing small rimless glasses back up onto his nose with his hand shaking he read it to himself. The enormity of his crimes was exposed. A sickness God would neither heal nor forgive. He had a dark obsession he was unable to control. God's jurisdiction for what was and was not natural when it came to Satan's world was beyond even His reach. That was for the business of His divine spirit. The second to last paragraph contained the sentences that was to doom him:

> . . . further, that the evidence presented concerning your acts of gross indecency toward a junior member of staff has been passed to the US Government. You have taken advantage of both your position as Chairman of the Dockyard Board and, no doubt, that of your office within the Church of the Society of Friends. You are to resign forthwith, and I will see to it personally, that your church is made aware the reason for our decision . . .

'I am sorry, Matthew,' the commissioner quietly said after Brown had finished reading. 'Your conduct gives us no alternative.'

Brown let the letter fall between his fingers where it fluttered to the ground. He took up the glass plate hitting the edge of it on the desk breaking it in two. Taking a shard of it with him, he left the office and drove to the Brooklyn Bridge. There, he severed the artery in his left wrist allowing the blood to flow until he was at the point of collapse, then climbing over to the wrong side of the bridge rail toppled himself forward into the dark water below taking his Bible with him.

An émigré Jewish boy by the name of David Sutton with similar aspirations to those of Giuseppi and D'Sotto began affecting their regime. Fancying his chances of a take-over, he wandered onto their territory and began trading protection. Giuseppi was not impressed. He had a hatred for Jews as it was, and this one in particular, he was going to have to do something about and quick. He began by giving him some hard advice.

Kurt Runfeldt, a Prussian immigrant, and professional thug Giuseppi had recently recruited, was sent to the pool-room Sutton used as an office. Finding him bent over a table about to take a critical shot, Runfeldt struck him unconscious over the head with a billiard cue causing him to sink the white ball and lose the game, along with several hundred dollars.

Two months later Sutton recovered. Finding out who was behind the attack, he called on Giuseppi at his office with a steaming sack over his shoulder and a knuckle duster in his pocket. Before Giuseppi had time to realize what was happening, Sutton, put the sack down, tipped his desk over knocking him from his chair sending him sprawling across the floor. Standing over him, he picked up the sack and emptied the bag of horse shit over him. He then made the remark that he was a spaghetti bender and perhaps he would like to try it on with him man to man.

Giuseppi lay on the floor spitting splashes of shit from his mouth with the back of his hand. He then got to his feet and with his head down, he brushed the remainder from his clothes, then before Sutton realized it was coming, he hit him so hard and unexpectedly Sutton crashed out through a low window from the office onto the sidewalk outside.

Sutton got up from what remained of the window frame and broken glass and readied himself for Giuseppi as he came out the door.

Both in their twenties, and although Giuseppi gave him a foot in height and a good fourteen pounds in weight, there was the matter of

Sutton being a body builder with ambitions for becoming a pro-boxer to contend with. The odds on Giuseppi winning an all-out slogging match with Sutton did not look good, and the dockyard workers already gathering outside knew they were going to spectate some sport.

Sutton took his shirt off and began shadow boxing exercises. Then coming towards Giuseppi, without ceremony, hit him a vicious blow to the jaw knocking him against a brick wall.

'You stink of horse shit, *schmuck!*' Sutton said. Then sniffing hard he brought up a ball of phlegm, before propelling the green globule through pursed cheeks into Giuseppi's face.

Giuseppi attempted to clear his head from the bang to the wall, but Sutton was closing in on him, and fast. He would need to do something, and quick. Reaching behind him, he put his hand down the back of his trousers and pulled out a stiletto from the sheath buckled to his body belt. With no pretense of formality he stuck the blade into Sutton's side just below the man's ribcage. Sutton had not seen it coming. He staggered backwards but managing to stay on his feet instinctively put his hand to the wound. Blood was seeping between his fingers. Ignoring the pain, he pulled out the stiletto and threw it at Giuseppi. It missed him, pinning itself into the woodwork of the door to his office.

Sutton was like a Spanish fighting bull now. The blade from the stiletto was burning in his side like a picador's banderilla between a bull's shoulder blades. Fortunately, it had glanced off a lower rib avoiding puncturing his lung. Enraged he went for a full-frontal assault on Giuseppi. A southpaw punch caught Giuseppi hard to his nose breaking it.

A '*phew*' went up from the crowd hearing the sound of cracking bone.

Quickly following up alternatively left and right, three, four further blows to Giuseppi's face before stepping back to reappraise the man's defense or potential attack back. Seeing none, he went for the kill. Slipping the knuckle-duster onto his hand from his pocket, he hit him with a single left-handed uppercut to his jaw using the full width of the weapon.

'*Phew!*' Another sound of cracking bone, this time the man's jawbone.

Giuseppi looked at him, his eyes had glazed over, purple balls of bruising had appeared around them, then slowly he toppled forward. Sutton took a last advantage by drawing the duster down the side of his face as he collapsed down. The two thin spikes from the top edge of the weapon had cut deep and parallel into his cheek. Stitches to such a wound would be impossible. Something to remember him by, Sutton thought. A scar for life.

Giuseppi lay a while, then slowly made the effort to get to his knees. Sutton took a further opportunity and kicked him twice in the side of the head. Then reaching down he grabbed a handful of blooded hair raised his head off the sidewalk, then, slapping him hard across the face he let his head fall with a crack onto the cobble edging.

'*Phew!* I felt *that*,' one said.

'*Bastard wop!*' Sutton said then stamped hard on the hand that had stuck him with the stiletto. Quickly looking around at the jeering crowd to be certain that none of Giuseppi's men were about, he stood up. Holding his side from the injury, he shouted at those that had gathered. 'I'm the main man, now. You hear me, not him.' He spoke breathlessly. 'If there's any argument, bring it on.' He looked into their eyes. You're going to need protection from the likes of him and his union. I will provide. Pretenders to the mafia are not welcome around here.' He then spat on Giuseppi's unconscious body and stumbled off clutching at his bleeding side.

The crowd closed in. They pushed and shoved each other to get a better view of the man that had levied their wages. He lay there, the blood from the head wound no longer weeping. Some thought that he must be dead. Others, that he was so afraid of the man that had done this to him, he would spare himself any further punishment by making him believe he was unconscious. But something was happening to him.

Giuseppi was experiencing something weird. He was not sure if he was dreaming or having delusions from the beating. Whatever it was, someone was standing over him. His face was that of a man, but somehow different. He became aware that he was floating in the air looking down on himself. Then there was another. This time a girl. Stupid he thought, but she gave the impression to him of being an angel. He had seen enough of them to know what one was. Icon pictures that hung from the walls of his church in Sicily when he was a boy. Tall women, with vast wings powerfully connected to broad smooth shoulders. At puberty, he fantasized over such images, jerking himself blind.

She was weeping. One of her wings, partially severed, hung awkwardly from her shoulder, then she moved away. The blood from the tear of her wing ran down her arm staining the ground as she went.

A quiet voice whispered in his head, '*You're in the company of princes, old son! Choose.*'

He opened his eyes. He was all but gone, just a name remained. A name for a beast. A worm thought that would live within him forever. That he would take to eternity. Ahriman! *AHRIMAN!*

Giuseppi could count no friends among the crowd that had gathered around him. None, apart that was but one. He had been called. Tall, slim, Tony D'Sotto. Hearing of his brother's dilemma he came as soon as he heard. *Too late?* He leant over him and listened at his chest for any sound of a heartbeat. There was none. He looked up and shook his head. 'Anybody called an ambulance?'

They did not have to. His chest heaved. Then he coughed. He turned himself on his side and began to stand. D'Sotto took hold of his arm but Giuseppi pushed him away. Possessed of a renewed strength, looking through swollen eyes, he looked for the man that had done this to him. 'Where is he?'

'He's in your office, but . . .' someone said, not wishing to say more.

Giuseppi shrugged Tony off to a gasp from the crowd that marveled that a man that had taken such a beating could stand, let alone go back to finish what had already been finished. He went up to the door and tried the handle. Sutton had locked him out. He stood back, lifted his leg up and kicked the door down.

Sutton was rearranging the furniture when the door came in on him. He looked up in astonishment. After the beating he had given him, he was sure he was dead. He knew that to finish Giuseppi now would be a fight to the death, and for the first time in his life, he feared this was going to be one fight he would lose.

As far as Giuseppi was concerned, this Jew-*boy*, as handy with his fists as he was, no longer posed a threat to him. Something had happened to him. He felt possessed of something he couldn't explain. He had an excitement that came from the pit of his stomach that vibrated between his legs. He was sexually arousing, and he relished it. An excitement that he had felt when his father's half-brother had got into bed with him on his ninth birthday and whispered:

'Don't tell your mama or papa – it'll be our secret. When you get older I'll let you do it to me.'

He never got the chance. His father caught his half-brother in the act of fellatio with his son. He went insane. Grabbing the first thing he could lay his hands on he picked up a meat cleaver that his wife had been using in the kitchen and struck him in the back with it as he tried to escape out the door of their house. The angle of the implement severed his spinal column putting him into a wheelchair for the remainder of his days.

Sutton had no choice. If he were to finish the man off, he would need to take the initiative. Looking around him, he picked up his billiard cue propped up in the corner. He knew from experience this was going to hurt him. He brought down the heavy end in the direction of Giuseppi's head, which, if it had struck home with the force intended, the man would be dead for sure. But it was an ill-judged assault that went wildly awry. Giuseppi easily grabbed the cue pulling it from his hands. He snapped it in half across his knees, then threw the two halves to one side and went for Sutton with such violence he could not believe his own strength. Clamping both his hands around the Sutton's throat he squeezed his neck until his eyes rolled in their sockets and his legs gave way.

'*Schmuck*, am I?'

He put his arms underneath the unconscious body of Sutton and in one move, hauled him to his feet. Lowering his own legs, he threw the limp body on his shoulder and walked out of his office. This was the icebreaker for the dockyard workers to begin shouting and cheering. This time it was for him, for they could never be sure where they were where he was concerned.

A brave-heart said, 'What are you going to do with him, Marco? Have you killed him?'

Another said, 'Mind he doesn't wake up and return the favor.'

Giuseppi turned to face them, and with Sutton hanging unceremoniously as a rag-doll over his left shoulder he said, 'He won't wake again in this world! Nobody follows me. Nobody. Understand. They'll get some of what he's goin' to get if they do. I'm still in business. *Tony! Keep an eye on them, I want no witnesses.*'

Giuseppi carried his body over to a dry dock that was filling with sea water. Then lifting him high over his head he hurled him twenty feet away from him out over a stack of large wooden shipping cases where he fell thirty feet down onto a ledge below. The body made a slapping sound as it hit the masses of wet sea weed that had accumulated along the dock wall. Then it shuddered before rolling off, falling a further ten feet into the sea water. The body drifted, slowly at first, then faster as the current took hold, the flowing water carried the dead body through a head gate sluice where it bumped against the sides, before finding direction then drifting out into the Hudson river.

Another filthy Jew less, he said to himself. Then uncontrollably ejaculated into his breeches from an impatiently awaiting evil gift of arousal.

'*Where?* This is important. And you'd better not be wasting any of my time, Stone,' Commissioner Christian Dore said trying to keep his distance from the smell, a combination of alcohol and urine that emanated from the man.

'Honest. The guy picked him up over his head and launched him out there . . .'

'*Out there!* How much had you had to drink?' It was clear to Dore the man, apart from being down and out was distressed. His face was red and sweaty from too little food and too much drink. He kept putting his hands up to his face rubbing his eyes as if he didn't believe what he was saying, then shivering uncontrollably, though it was a warm evening. He began shouting. Dore knew he had been a reporter in a previous life. If he said what he saw, then he was probably right. The piss-head he was could still separate truth from fiction. 'Okay, all right. Take it easy and tell me again.'

He looked up at the detective. He was trying to hold himself together. Stuttering his words at first, he continued. 'I did. Three of them . . . they came right out of that cobbled wall there. *There!* Tearing at each other, they were. He was weird, not like a man at all, and she, least I think it was a she. He was definitely male. Best description, demon and angel and God knows what the other one was. She . . . well she was like one, without ever having seen one, know what I mean?' Dore nodded out of politeness. 'Beautiful she was long flowing hair. You'll never guess what though.' He looked round, then whispered, his breath from drinking meths catching Dore full in the face once again. 'She didn't have any breasts. Oh, yeh, I'm sure about that. Not something a man's likely to get wrong is it? What I mean is, she had the bumps, you know. No nipples!' He displayed cupped hands away from his chest for emphasis. But she didn't have any . . .'

Dore waved his hand past his nose and turned his head to one side trying to get a breath of fresh air. 'Get on with it. Tell me what else didn't she have?'

'Well, it was like, she . . . she didn't have no . . . no *cunt!* neither . . . *all right!* I've said it.'

'*What!*'

Ghosts or spirits coming out of solid stone was hard enough to listen to – but this! This was unreal. But this man's colorful description was that of a journalist and didn't give Dore the impression he was capable of such an imaginative story. Even when he had hesitated, when it came to describing that part of the female anatomy most would skirt round, he followed through.

'She didn't have no—'

'All right, all right,' Dore said. 'I've got the picture. No need to frame it. Can we move onto the other one?'

'Other one.'

'Yes. You said there were three of them.'

'Yeh. A dwarf or an elf. He stared right through me. Best earthly description I have for what I saw. Three feet tall . . .'

A dwarf, Dore said quietly to himself wondering what was to come next. Snow White perhaps.

'Was that one or seven?' he said trying to break down fact from fiction of what this man witnessed.

'*One or seven?* Oh, I get it, you're taking the piss, right? Forget it. Listen, I know what I saw. I was a qualified observer in another life remember. He wore a cloak with a hood over his head.'

'And would you recognize any of them again if you saw them?'

He laughed, 'What like as in an identity parade? That's not going to happen. When it stared at me, when I stared into his face, the darkness went on forever. He's no line-up material.'

The change in the man from bum to rational witness took Dore by surprise.

'I'll tell you this though, Commissioner Dore. If I'm ever asked if I've stared eternity in the face, I would have to confess that I had. And for no more than the briefest of time, I knew, understood even what it looks like and where we're all headed when we're out of this place. But now,' he shook his head annoyed that he couldn't recall its description. 'I've no idea. In a wisp of smoke, as a dream, in the blinking of an eye . . . it was gone. Click and all.'

A chill went through Dore at what he had been told. And that, to him, was unusual in itself.

'All right,' Dore said wondering how he was going to put this down on an incident sheet. He was not sure this man would be a credible witness into the disappearance of David Sutton. If he had been thrown into that basin, and been washed out into the Hudson, for sure he was not coming back.

'All right. Keep that between us. You understand what I'm saying?'

All Stone had wanted to do was to lie down among the sacks of cotton in the shed for the night. 'Don't worry I'm not going to give

Giuseppi the chance to do the same to me. And the two dollars you promised me.'

'*What bloody click?*'

Dore returned to the office. He needed to find a form used for sightings of aliens and the like. There was one apparently. *What were the chances of that?* he thought. *That is one report that is destined for the trashcan*, he thought once more. Licking the flap of the envelope before sealing it down, he took it to the post-room pigeon hole for external mail. He rang the phone number that was on the bottom of the form informing whoever it was that it was there. When he checked the following morning the envelope was gone.

'Yes, Commissioner, a guy came in shortly after midnight and took it. You did say you didn't need a receipt?' Dore nodded. 'He opened it, had a quick read, then replaced it back in the envelope and took it with him. Normally they tear them up and throw them in the bin. Whatever you wrote they must have taken seriously,' Sugden said expecting him to tell him what he did write.

He did. Shortly before Dore died.

Marco Giuseppi took a deep breath and screwed his hand into a fist. Bringing it up level with his head, he crashed it hard onto the wooden packing case that was between him and what he regarded as more than his associate. He stood up. The filthy green leather-studded chair that he was sitting tipped over and hit the wall. The two of its three castors remained in contact with the floor. He sidestepped crablike to the other side of the packing case and faced D'Sotto.

D'Sotto felt his anus loosen; and while he loved Giuseppi – who did not reciprocate, not being a regular homosexual as himself, despite enjoying the occasional blow-job he had given him – he would not be able to console him as a lover would. He concentrated on

Giuseppi's mouth gently placing the back of his hand on the side of his face. The injury to his cheek, that should have scarred him for life from Sutton's knuckle-duster, had miraculously disappeared. Giuseppi was having none of his affection. Not at the moment. This was business. It always came before pleasure. He removed his hand half smiling a look of seriousness replacing it. A spray of mouth-odorous saliva splashed over him as Giuseppi spoke between gasps of warm breath. His cigar-stained teeth in his open mouth revealing a thread of spittle that threatened to break. When it did, it went like an over-tightened violin string causing D'Sotto to flinch involuntarily. He stuttered out the words. 'He's called Fariq Mihalyvich, Mr. Marco. You remember the one that came to you for a job.'

Giuseppi held the menacing stare. 'Is he?'

A slight smile went across his closed lips and D'Sotto risked a concealed breath of relief.

'No sense of loyalty these days, eh, Tony?'

Giuseppi went to the window and looked out onto the docks. Thick with grime, it made the silhouette of distant cranes appear like a painting against the Long Island skyline: the sun having not quite burnt the morning mist off. He turned back to D'Sotto.

'Is anyone else involved?'

'Far as I know there isn't, Mr. Marco . . . if there is they're keeping it to themselves—'

'As long as someone else is prepared to do their dirty work, eh, Tony? Makes our job all the easier. We've only one to make an example of . . . the rest will fall into line.'

D'Sotto smiled and nodded. He knew Giuseppi well enough to know that he would not give another an even break if they crossed him. He also knew Runfeldt would do the business. Not that Giuseppi was above that these days, he was last resort, saving his obvious powers that came from someone up there, or down, as D'Sotto was more apt to think at times. He was happy that Giuseppi was speaking to him as an old friend again.

'As you say, Mr. Marco. The rest will fall in line.'

'What we should do, Tony . . . is . . .' He paused relishing his options. 'Go see Mihalyvich, take Runfeldt with you . . . go see him; explain the way we do business. Carefully, so he understands. Get him on side . . . so he's got it clear in his mind, the Union expects his co-operation and that he has to pay. We all have to pay in this world. Explain that to him, will you Tony?'

D'Sotto shuddered. It was an instruction for them to come down hard and heavy.

'Sure thing, boss.'

He had not answered convincingly. He was not a heavy-weight thug as Runfeldt was. Mihalyvich, on the other hand was somebody in Giuseppi's way. An immigrant as himself trying to make his way in life. A man with a family. Nothing like Sutton. Mihalyvich was a different ball game.

'That, Tony,' Giuseppi said, 'is what separates punks from spunks . . .'

He did not listen to the rest of his speech he had heard before. He was thinking. The matter that had always troubled him with regard to Giuseppi was that he was plumbing depths of depravity to a level that New York's Cosa Nostra regarded beyond the pale, a crime that was drawing in people he thought would have known better. Where on earth had he got the idea to abduct children selling them on for profit?

Fariq Mihalyvich shouted from inside the hold of the ss. *St. Lawrence Seaway.*

'Lower! Lower!'

The hook from the sky-hugging shore-side crane came into the hold. Mihalyvich grabbing at it hooked it to a bale of timber. Satisfied it was secure he called upwards. 'Take it up . . . easy . . . hold it. Okay. Take her away.'

The crane, slowly at first, began to take back its cable. The signalman above him – one foot perched on the rim of the ship's hold – bent forward, his left arm pointed down to Mihalyvich; his right skyward toward the Red Indian crane operator with the name of Ishmael Adams one hundred feet up.

Mihalyvich yelled for care aware of the danger a load swinging out of control if lifted too quickly from off the vertical. For the inside of a ship is a hard place and can do a lot of damage to a soft head. He had seen experienced handlers knocked sidewards to their death across its width – a head smashed open like a hard-boiled egg against unforgiving 2-inch thick rusty-red steel plate.

The signalman waved his wrist energetically to the man in the sky who waiting for his sign throttled the four-liter diesel crane engine wide open. The timber lifted out of the dark as if matchwood, its half ton weight barely making a difference to the tone of the engine as the cable, greased black tension, returned to its windlass.

Taking a moment, Mihalyvich, pulled some paper from his breast pocket placing it between his lips. From another he took a soft leather bear-skin pouch and opened it fingering its contents. He took out enough tobacco for a thin cigarette. Removing the paper from between his lips, he pulled the strands of Virginia along its length and finger rolled it. Subconsciously looking up toward the daylight above him, he ran his tongue along the gum sealing the roll. 'That's it!' he shouted above the noise of the engine. 'I'm outta here.' Putting the cigarette to his lips, he started to climb up the ladder that was his escape. Half closing his eyes against the light he emerged from the hold after a two-hour stint in semi-darkness into the morning light to carry on what would be the remainder of his twelve-hour working day.

The signalman waiting for him cupped a struck match round Mihalyvich's cigarette as he emerged; then lit his own. 'D-Wharf – loada timber to be emptied before tide,' he said inhaling the smoke deeply into his lungs.

'And how many men are they going to give me?' Mihalyvich asked.

The signalman spoke hurriedly. He had had similar conversations on this matter with Mihalyvich before telling him that the management knew of the position regarding safety.

'Half of us,' Mihalyvich replied angrily that nothing had still not been done, 'I told you that wasn't enough to unload a ship onto a wharf the size that one was, sooner or later one of us is gonna get ourselves killed.'

'See your union then,' the signalman answered.

'A lot of use that'll be, Giuseppi will want us to take a pay cut for any additional help we take on.'

The signalman shrugged.

'I'm signalman and overseer. Getting the job done is all my concern. I'm with you at the moment, but I won't be sorry when it goes one way or the other.'

'*Our way?*'

'Like I said, I've gotta consider my position.'

Mihalyvich drew on his cigarette and studied the signalman.

'Yeh, sure.'

Someone shouting distracted them. It came from the other side of the wharf. Both men recognized the voice.

'Here comes trouble,' the signalman said as the man came across to them.

The gang master acknowledged Mihalyvich before speaking to the signalman.

'You'd better have enough men ready. There's a ship waiting to be unloaded and floated on the tide. And I'm speaking the next, so get to it.'

Mihalyvich nodded at him as he turned to leave.

'We'll do it this time,' Mihalyvich said to the signalman so the gang master could hear. 'Okay men, soon as you like. *Gang up, Dee! Move across!'*

Mihalyvich survived another day without a beating. Giuseppi's henchmen had carried out some arm twisting on his men, to remind him his time was close.

He leaped the gap from the ship to the dockside. Littered from the debris from the days unloading, the hards from the warehouses and sheds were more a stumble than a walk. It was late afternoon; Mihalyvich picked his way past the first of the warehouses, his thoughts on what he was getting into with this Giuseppi and his team of Union gangsters that wanted more work for less money. So far, he had persuaded his gang to carry on as they were in spite of threats. The signalman might have had a point. It was all very well having a few men behind him, but how many would there be if Giuseppi got serious. Not many. And that was probably an overestimate. He was passing the rope shop when he saw the first signs of trouble on the horizon. Coming in the shape of a pair of black and white leather shoes and a pair of brown brogues, two men, one he recognized, the other new to him; an oaf of a man with a head the size of his neck, wearing a pin stripe suit that was clearly having difficulty fitting him. They were in his path. He stopped, waiting to walk round them as they, he hoped, carried on their way.

'Nice evening, Mr. Mihalyvich.'

'If you say so, Tony. And with your permission, I'll go home, change and join you for a drink later when you can introduce me to your friend.'

He went to step round but the larger man's hand gripped him on the shoulder.

'Allow me to intro—'

Mihalyvich only heard the first part before a blinding flash went before his eyes as the man caught him a paralyzing blow to the kidneys. He was out for a second or two before he became aware of a flat ringing sound coming from within his head. He felt sick behind his eyes and became anxious as to this sudden trauma to his body. He tried to focus his thoughts and raise himself, only to find someone was holding him down. He was aware of an excruciating pain to one of his knees where it had caught the edge of something sharp as he had gone down, after his legs collapsed from under him. The rest of the introduction came from someone that was clearly a professional hit man, quiet and confident. Someone that knew his business.

'I'm Kurt Runfeldt – your worst nightmare. We shall be seeing a lot of each other in the future, especially if you continue with these, fancy your chances, ideas of yours. Mr. Giuseppi is trying to run a business and you're causing trouble for him.'

'Sorry, Mihalyvich,' D'Sotto added, 'we seem to have been interrupted by my friend here. Kurt tends to be a bit on the impetuous side. Used to be an enforcer for Frankie Yale's Black Hand gang up in New York City before Mr. Marco asked Frankie to let him go you know. Frankie owed Mr. Marco a favour, so here he is. He likes a man with psychopathic tendencies. Do you think he found the one?'

Mihalyvich decided not to respond.

Runfeldt released his shoulder and grasped a handful of his hair pulling his head sharply backwards until he thought his neck would snap. Slowly opening his eyes, he tried to assess the situation to see if there was anything he could do. Two out-of-focus faces were staring at him – he was deluding himself.

D'Sotto whispered into Mihalyvich's ear. 'Well, do you, *punk?*'

He ignored him. D'Sotto put his ear to Mihalyvich's mouth for a second time.

'Sorry didn't get that. Can you hear me I'm closer?'

'My hearing is not what it was a minute or so ago.' He began muttering gibberish.

D'Sotto leaned forward craning his neck to hear what Mihalyvich was saying. Seizing the best opportunity he would have he took a snapping bite at the soft flesh of D'Sotto's ear. 'Have some of this, you *bastard!*' he said between gritted teeth. With a whip of his painful neck, he bit tighter tearing a piece off the corner of it and spat it out. Then to remove the taste of salty blood from his mouth, he spat again.

D'Sotto felt as if a red-hot poker had been plunged into the side of his head, not realizing at first what had happened. A pool of blood was forming on the ground. It was his. Seeing it and the pain he was suffering; he lost any further interest in Mihalyvich. Instead concentrating on his ear, or what he thought was left of it, he staggered sideways reaching into his suit pocket for a kerchief.

Runfeldt released Mihalyvich trying to see what had happened to D'Sotto – who by this time was holding the side of his bloody ear screaming all manner of obscenities. Stemming the flow of blood, he turned back to Mihalyvich who had turned on his side clutching at his knees.

'Wait there,' Runfeldt said going off into one of the rope shops. When he returned he had with him a red-hot rivet in a pair of tongs, a piece of jute and an axe.

'Take hold of his arm. I'll give him something he'll not forget in a hurry.'

While still holding on to what was left of his ear, D'Sotto did what he could with one hand to restrain him. Runfeldt forced open Mihalyvich's hand and placed the red-hot rivet into a cone of pitched canvas. The canvas started to smoke. He put it into his open right hand and forcing it closed tied the bandage of jute, wrapping and sealing the whole tool of torture in a neat oily bandage. Smiling, he shouted over Mihalyvich's screams.

'Mr. Giuseppi feels you've gone far enough. He's not pleased with the way you're undermining his business. He wants more money from all of you, and he wants it by the end of the week. Including you. Are you understanding me?'

Mihalyvich was in a fetal position, semi-conscious, but coming to his senses as the heat passed through the pitched cone onto the flesh. His body went into an uncontrolled spasm from the pain.

Runfeldt leaned over the screaming man. 'Here, take this. A remedy I've used before, should the pain become too unbearable.' He placed a hatchet into Mihalyvich's left hand then turning to D'Sotto said, 'Let's go, he won't be causing us any more trouble, not now. Not with one hand anyway. Oh, yeh,' he nodded in anticipation of what D'Sotto would say next. 'He'll cut it off all right.' He laughed. 'He won't be yanking himself off with that hand again. *Wanker!*'

He then bent down picking up the rivets he had previously dropped among Mihalyvich's knees, and hurriedly walked off after D'Sotto, who, could now concentrate on his ear; no longer hearing the screaming man writhing in agony behind him; struggling to cleave his hand off at the wrist.

Ishmael Adams was a high-crane operator and fearless when it came to heights that the white man suffered sweated palms merely thinking about. Born to the Lakota in 1895 at South Dakota, he was one of scarce few survivors among the 200 men, women and children annihilated by soldiers of the Seventh Cavalry at the Massacre of Wounded Knee. Found by a Mormon family on route to Kaysville, Utah, his screaming for his dead mother's milk, heard by the wife of one of the families, barely audible over the noise of the iron-hoop wheels and horse traces from the wagon-train passing the battle field shouted for them to stop the train. The family, feeling pity for what had happened here, more especially the plight of the child, obtained permission from one Colonel James W. Forsyth the Calvary's commander to remove the baby from the battlefield after first giving his mother a Christian burial. Taking him with them, they looked on the new-born boy with the respect of equality of their faith considering him one out of their own Ten Lost Tribes of Israel, gave him their family name of Adams; bringing him up and educating him until he was fourteen. Then, with a need to finding his own way in the world, he left his surrogate family going to Chicago. Here he learned his trade on the building sites of skyscrapers where he worked as a spider man and crane erector. His line of expertise was cables; the ones that occasionally came off their pulley wheels, where with strong arms and shoulders he would haul himself in their ironwork re-securing them. Moving to New York when work dried up, he found employment in the dockyard as a crane engineer, with these skills, putting them to good use.

It was while on the ground, servicing a crane's windlass, when he mistook the sound of a screaming man from the cable in need of grease coming through its pulley. Noticing it was still howling when he put the brake on he switched the motor off. The screams hit an unknown subliminal memory deep within him. Sounds from a distant past. Of people with medieval weapons trying to defend themselves against fire power from Winchesters and Hotchkiss cannon: from aggressors' intent on Indian ghettoization within reservations. The screams were coming from outside the rope shop. He ran in its direction discarding the tin of grease, coming on a man on the ground writhing in agony. He had smoke coming from his hand that had a smell of burning pitch and flesh. He kicked the axe out from his one good hand he was attempting to sever the other from the arm. It slid across the dockyard cobbles with a clatter. Taking him up in his arms, he ran with him cradled to his chest to the nearest basin-full of sea water and leaped. Leaning forward as both men went through the air to avoid the stepped edges of the dock, their backsides skimmed over the slimy green seaweed covering the last of them. Miraculously avoiding injury, the two men hit the water bomb fashion.

Dockyard workers, seeing what was happening came to help, throwing ropes and buoys after them. Adams, having lost hold of his man from the impact dived down into the murky water trying to get a blind grip on him. The fourth dive, this time to the bottom, he came across two bodies. Not knowing who was who, he pulled the two of them to the surface. Seeing one body alive and the other semi-decomposed half eaten by green crabs, he released him and pulled his man to the side of the basin. Men were down to the level of the step ledge to give him a hand, and one-on-one they managed to pull the two men clear of the water. Adams loosened his arm from round his neck, laying him down where the men cut the jute bandage from his fist, removed the cold rivet from his hand.

Mihalyvich opened his eyes and closed them tightly before opening them again with relief that the agony he had suffered had become no more than painful. He looked at his hand. There was an impression in his palm that looked like a fossil in a piece of rock. It was bad, he thought, but not as that as not having one. An Indian standing over him asked how he was feeling.

He rubbed the base of his spine and smiled, 'I think I must have scrapped me arse on something.'

Two – 1920s

NATHANIEL CLAYPOLE lit his pipe, drew in the smoke, coughed gently, and put his tongue out. Kerosene was getting into everything – his sandwiches, his clothes, and his tobacco. He put his pipe down and adjusted the wick on the stove for the umpteenth time that morning. Wiping his carbon stained hands on a piece of rag throwing it to one side when he was done picked up his pipe. With it puffing contentedly in his mouth, he went to the window of the hut and peered out. Coming through the dockyard gates, he saw the start of two thousand men pouring through to begin their shifts. Among them, limping was Fariq Mihalyvich. He thought the man had been stupid standing up to people that were clearly out of his league when it came to violence. He admired his tenacity to motivate his gang to stand their ground against Giuseppi. It was a pity that not all of them would come out of this unscathed. As for himself and those he represented, well, he had his own agenda, and nothing was to stand in the way of that. As an independent thinker that had his own feelings, he felt duty bound to offer this man some advice. He opened the door of the hut and called out to him.

'Hey, Mihalyvich. Over here.'

Claypole had not been wharf master long. Such an appointment usually coming from someone that had worked his way up through the yard. A person with a track record. In Claypole's case, no-one had ever heard of him let alone worked with him before. As to why the Dockyard Board's management had taken him on was a source of mystery round the yard. That was to say, how did the man manage to wangle such a job? A month ago when he started, and casual questions from men as to where he had worked before revealed nothing. Although knowing what was what when it came to ships' movements he knew little else. Mihalyvich guessed that he might have had something to do with them when America was at war with Germany. Intelligence, perhaps. Everything else he seemed to be picking up as he went along. Mihalyvich had never had any reason to dislike the man for all that.

'How you feeling?' Claypole asked him.

'Stiff!' he replied hanging onto the door frame for support. 'I'll manage.'

He was not convincing.

'You reckon. You don't look as if you will. You got Giuseppi and his men on your case and the word is you've lost the fight.'

'We've got families. Responsibilities—'

'That's as may be, and more reason for them and you to stay healthy. Carry on as you have been, and you'll likely wind up dead. The management appointed him. You can expect no help from them. If you and your people refuse to pay Giuseppi and he brings in others to do the job, what then?'

Mihalyvich shrugged his shoulders. 'The government needs ships clearing.'

'They're queuing up outside to do that; and they'll take less than they're paying you for doing it.'

'Monkeys and unreliables – the best are here, and they know it.'

It was Claypole's turn to shrug his shoulders.

'That may or may not be true. All the government will see is less of a wage bill. Just look out for yourselves that's all I'm saying.'

'Thanks. Where's my gang working?'

Claypole hesitated, 'Don't rightly know. One minute. Umm . . .'

The dockyard siren screamed its end of week blast and 'wedge-up' time as the men liked to call pay day. Coming from the holds of ships, from warehouses, down from cranes, they gathered on the wharf side to meet up with Mihalyvich. He had a plan to end Giuseppi's hold over them. He stood in front of them both hands to his mouth for his message to travel.

'Okay boys, you all know what's at stake here if you're in, this is it. If anyone feels that he can't go ahead with it, I won't hold it against him. It's going to be dangerous; we're dealing with violent men and some of us are going to get hurt. They'll start on the weakest and work their way up until we give in. The trick is to protect those most vulnerable from the start. If we adopt that simple strategy, we can't lose. Anyone got anything to say?'

There was mute mumblings of support for Mihalyvich as they made their way to the paymaster's hut to collect their wages. Waiting for them was D'Sotto with Runfeldt as enforcer, and a collective shudder went through them after what they had seen them inflict on Mihalyvich the week previously. After they had collected their wages, they went with their unopened packets and stood in front of the two men showing no sign that they were going to hand over any. D'Sotto became anxious over this show of defiance, but soon overcame this temporary lapse when he saw Runfeldt looking at them menacingly punching his fist into his right hand. He looked as if he was itching to take the whole bunch of them on. Judging from the look on some of the men's faces, they thought as much as well. All except one.

Adams stared Runfeldt in the eyes. He could see the hatred for him burning out of them. He had seen that look before in the white man.

D'Sotto was worried what Giuseppi would do next if they didn't sort this out today. The fact that Mihalyvich had reorganized the men so soon after the beating Runfeldt had given him showed the two of them that he was not so easily intimidated. Mihalyvich stood forward from the rest of them as if someone had asked for volunteers. He turned and shifted his gaze to the men.

'The wanker wants some more, Tony,' Runfeldt said pointing out the man's right hand to him using his own as a masturbatory example shaking it in a half fist. 'Might need to remove his cock this time.'

This thing with him and Mihalyvich had got personal. He was going to have to try and cool things down. 'If you've any sense,' D'Sotto shouted looking at them for any sign of weakness. Seeing none, he continued. 'Look, okay, listen to me, I can see that you're not happy paying this money. Mr. Giuseppi doesn't want to make things more difficult than they are, and he is trying to negotiate with the management. Pay him this week and I'll get back to him, see if he'll reduce them next week, have we a deal?' He looked round at them half smiling. 'Fariq!'

Mihalyvich knew there was no chance that Giuseppi would honor any arrangement that D'Sotto made. Hoodlums like him do not trade niceties, more, a preference for violence over negotiation.

'Not a chance. I've drawn a line in the sand,' Mihalyvich said. There came a spontaneous applause of approval. 'There's your answer, D'Sotto. Go tell the organ-grinder. And while you're at it, tell him that that psycho of his might want to face me man-to-man, if he's the balls.'

D'Sotto felt his face redden. The stress made his ear painful.

Runfeldt turned on Mihalyvich. His words had hit home.

'Psycho am I?' Mihalyvich smiled nodding his head agreeing with him. Runfeldt stepped forward and pulled down a length of chain that was hanging loose from the corner of a hut. He studied it for a second or two, drawing its length through his hands, then without any warning fetched it across Mihalyvich's head downing him in one.

With the probable view that the man clearly was a head-case, the men stepped out of his way.

Runfeldt looked at them, better for them to understand that he meant business, then thrashed the chain down on Mihalyvich's back as he was getting himself up. His body shook. 'Would have thought you'd had enough of a beating Mihalyvich. It appears not. You're more stupid than I took you for. Perhaps you'd like some more water to cool you down.' He took hold of him by the ankles dragging him to the edge of the dock basin when the Indian stepped forward. Runfeldt seeing him smiled. He would make an example of him instead, he thought. Releasing Mihalyvich he menacingly waved the Indian forward with his right hand, his foot at Mihalyvich's side ready to kick him into the water below.

The Indian ignoring Runfeldt's gesture came forward to help the man on the ground. Runfeldt smiled at this opportunity, then kneed him in the head sending him over onto his side. The Indian lay for a second or two before getting himself up returning to help Mihalyvich. Runfeldt was incensed. Taking up the chain once more, he wound it round his wrist and viciously, with teeth gritted, hit the Indian with all the force he could felling him for what he hoped would be the last time.

'That's enough!' D'Sotto shouted to Runfeldt. 'You've made your point.' This was not going to look good if Mihalyvich or the Indian died, he thought. And in front of witnesses. They could wind up going to the electric chair on a charge of first-degree murder. 'Just leave it, Kurt,' he shouted to appease the situation. 'There's nothing more we can do here, they wanted trouble, and they know how it comes.' He turned to the men making them one last offer. 'Those that want an end to this give me your dues.'

Adams helped to his feet by men fearing Runfeldt might finish him off if he lay there unguarded brushed them aside returned to the limp body of Mihalyvich. He knelt down beside him once more. 'Are you conscious?' he asked.

Mihalyvich's head throbbed, but apart from that, he was surprisingly fine. He guessed he was getting used to all these beatings. His body was beginning to cope with the punishment as a boxer would. 'Just. But I think you might have joined the losing side my friend,' he said pointing watching his gang queue up to hand over part of their wage. He had overstretched himself as the wharf master had said he would. When it came to dealing with the likes of Giuseppi, they were on a hiding to nothing. Some had had enough.

As the two men walked away, Runfeldt turned back to the men and loud enough for the Indian to hear said to D'Sotto, 'Did you see that dirty red-skin cower? Yellow as well as red, I think. Like the rest of his breed.' He carried on walking away still laughing.

Mihalyvich enraged at Runfeldt's comment decided he would have one last go at them. He was hoping that the men, seeing his determination, would join him in running these two men out of the yard getting their money back.

'You pair of bastards!' he shouted after them. 'Why don't you come back here and face me with bare knuckles, we'll see who's yellow.'

Adams stopped him as he got up to go for them.

'No. You not strong enough. You wait here . . . You!' Adams called to Runfeldt.

Runfeldt was smiling pointing to himself. 'You got something on yer mind, filthy Indian?' He laughed. Still carrying the chain he wound it tightly round his left wrist pulling it through his hand once more. He had been looking for an excuse to finish him off and the man had given it him.

The thought of sitting in Old Sparky at Sing Sing's correctional unit – burning from inside while still alive with smoke coming from his body did not appeal to D'Sotto. He tried to stop Runfeldt, who easily pushed him to one side.

The Indian was walking toward him. Runfeldt took hold of the chain and whirled it round his head, faster and faster as he got nearer. With a final swing from it, he wrapped the chain round the Indian's neck. When it loosened, a vicious wheal showed that began to bleed. Runfeldt jerked on the chain once more, he was trying to take him from his feet, but he stood firm and to Runfeldt's astonishment, the Indian was still standing.

Adams had gone beyond the point where he any longer felt pain, with a pull from his short, stocky body turned sideways this time pulling Runfeldt from his feet. He hit the ground awkwardly face first. A sickening crack as he hit his nose on the cobbles could be heard.

'You dirty red skin!' he screamed holding his hand to support the broken bleeding protuberance. Ignoring it, he tried removing the chain from his wrist, but it had snagged. Joined in a common union the Indian commenced to drag him a few yards across the ground. Stopping to adjust the chain, he then broke into a run. He ran Runfeldt over every obstacle he could find, until, at the base of one of the highest cranes in the yard he stopped. Removing the chain from the man's wrist, he wound it roughly round his ankle. Hand-over-hand he then began to climb its iron rung ladder. Runfeldt, semi-conscious, finding himself upside down, with the ground moving away, was coming to realize what the Indian was doing. He began hollering and screaming for D'Sotto to help him. But with renewed enthusiasm, Mihalyvich's men held him back.

Adams slowly, bit-by-muscle-tearing-bit hauled all four hundred and sixteen pounds of Runfeldt up the main frame of the crane. The Prussian was screaming, the blood pouring from his nose, as the ground moved relentlessly further away. Below, the men gathered round, straining necks looking up in awe at this feat of human endurance that would surely put an end to any disrespect that Runfeldt had for Adams. He pleaded with him to stop, but the Indian paid no heed. He kept going.

Reaching the top of the main tower, one hundred and fifty feet above ground, Adams began his climb out onto the frame of the jib attaching the chain to a hanging spare cable. Feeling resistance from the man, who, attempting to stay where he was, was tearing his hands on its rusted metal in a desperate bid to remain secure. With his slowly loosening grip, three of his fingernails came away from their tips.

Adams uncoiled the chain from round his own neck and shoulders and yanked on the chain. Runfeldt gave in to the inevitability of a heart-stopping swing out into space coming off the vertical tower, falling through free space until the cable took up its slack jerking and causing the internal organs in Runfeldt's body temporarily to alter their placement.

Below a collective roar. The sound an audience might make witnessing a trapeze artist slip from his trap at a circus big top that has no safety net. Hands sweated in anticipation of the man falling to earth; bursting body parts open and spreading guts over them from the impact of striking the imported London stone granite the dock was constructed. Instead of which he stayed in the air, swinging as if he was a pendulum from a clock in an arc that spread fifty-five feet at the end of each swing. His hands and arms and his one free leg desperately clawing at the air. Vomit spew from his mouth fell as an evil smelling mist on those below.

Adams went a few more feet out tied the chain off leaving the man hanging and swinging by his ankles thirty yards from the comparative safety of the crane operator's iron hut. He then began his way back down.

Reaching the ground, he stood upright and proud in front of the gang of men that had swelled many times its former size. He was soaked in sweat and blood. The flesh torn from his shoulders and arms was hanging like wallpaper half stripped off a wall in preparation for re-decorating. A sure testament to the man's ability to endure pain. With the screams of sheer panic from the man above them, Adams looked up, smiled, bowing to his audience . . . collapsed.

The dockyard siren did not properly give away its position on the dark misty morning following the funeral of Ishmael Adams. Its banshee-like scream seemed to come from everywhere a head might turn seeking its direction. Mihalyvich went to the wharf master's hut to get his work schedule for the day.

'Bad business with Adams,' Claypole said striking a match and putting it to his pipe. 'Looks as if you and your gang have won the day with Giuseppi gone. How long before the management replace him with another that's as equally corrupt is anyone's guess.'

Mihalyvich nodded at him. 'Where am I working today?'

Claypole turned away and went to the wall opposite. Running his finger down the work list, he came to Mihalyvich's name. Moving his finger sideways, he checked the cargo that was to be unloaded. 'East. That'll be timber. I think it is anyway.'

Mihalyvich turned and shaking his head in disbelief walked out the door. Claypole called after him.

'Look, I'm sorry for what happened to Ishmael, but his death might well have been in vain. Giuseppi might be gone from here,' he said fanning another spent match on his ever-demanding pipe, 'but not from the neighborhood. He'll want his pound of flesh.' He hesitated before going on. 'That man's more than your average hoodlum, he's possessed of an evil not of this world.'

'Possessed! you say. He's another man to me.'

'Listen,' he whispered. 'I shouldn't be saying this, but there's more going on round him than you can possibly imagine. People are watching him. I like you and I wouldn't want to see anything happen to you. Go take care of your family. Move away if you have to and forget all this and what I've told you.'

'You haven't told me anything that makes any sense yet.'

'That's all I'm saying. Me, I've to move on anyway.'

'You're leaving. Coincidence, or for purpose?'

'What do you mean by that?'

Mihalyvich had suspected something odd about this man, of who he was, and what he was doing in a job he had clearly shown no real knowledge. 'The same time as Giuseppi gets kicked out, you're telling me that someone is watching Giuseppi. Are you perhaps moving from wharf master to watchman, Mr. Claypole?'

Oona Mihalyvich was peeling the skin off a rabbit when she heard the click of the downstairs door. She was not expecting her husband, though after the injury he suffered falling into the hold of that ship he had been working she would not have been surprised. She had made up a potion from willow and hot molasses to help ease the bruising and swelling he suffered; remedies for sickness she had learned as a child from her people.

She remembered when she first met him.

Up against a wall outside a fur trading station and general store; with his hands tight round her throat, the Russian seal hunter drunk was forcing himself on her. Other hunters, anticipating an exhibition of fornication shouted and jeered generally encouraging him. Coming out of the store, hearing her screams seeing what was happening Mihalyvich took a heavy cooking iron down from the wall of the store fetching it down on the Russian's head. Fearing he had killed him; he took her by the hand and ran. She was laughing, not out of any sense of freedom, more of relief that a man had taken such an action to protect her. She had not done that since her abduction from her family from Kodiak Island. European hunters seeking comfort women took her, as they did many other young girls, to keep them warm in the harsh conditions of Alaska. She heard later that her father, an Aleut Shaman medicine man, along with her mother and sister might have fallen victims to the earthquake that followed shortly after.

He told her his name was Fariq, but not where he came from. She thought he might be Russian and the likely reason why he did not – knowing how hard her treatment was at their hands: they were either drunk, violent, or both – was the shame that he was one of them. He was none of those things and for that; she stayed with him, while he continued prospecting for gold.

One day he told her he was tired of the cold and would she come south with him as he had made his money. This man, for the first time in her life, was giving her a choice, something that was not part of her people. She took it as a token of how much he thought of her. He smiled, and she saw in him a man she could live her life with, and she let him make love to her. After, he had asked her if she would take him for her husband. Again, another choice from that of an arranged marriage that was Aleut tradition. She had agreed, but only if he could find someone that was a Shaman medicine man to perform the ceremony.

The only medicine man he had come across in his travels had fallen to the allure of cheap whisky. Any Shamanism that was within him; with the ability to conduct a wedding ceremony while still standing, would be sparse to non-existent. He did find someone that might suit her though. The man was Inuit, certainly a Shaman. The problem was Russian Orthodox missionaries had converted him to Christianity when a young man. Held up as a good example for their converting a heathen to Orthodoxy, he had been further encouraged by them, going on to become a priest.

'Christianity is not Shaman,' Oona said to the priest.

In his fifties, well educated, the priest had said that he had been born a Shaman, but that no religion can ever lay claim to the whole of a man's soul that has the capacity to take in and understand the dimensions of the universe, if he is to move to the next level when his time comes.

'Apart from that, with all the advantages that Christianity has to offer, you could consider yourself married by one faith, blessed by the other.'

She had been unsure, but with the pleading look in Fariq's face, and with the difficulty of seeing into his soul, she settled, and they were married in a ceremony that neither of them understood.

When spring came, he decided they should leave. Loading up his canoe, they paddled on the first part of their journey to Dawson. She doing her share of the paddling until her condition got the better of her.

She had the issue early one morning in the bivouac he had put up. He had done his part with two bits of cord and a knife. After feeding the baby the following morning, they continued on their way. By noon, she had lost so much blood she had collapsed in the bottom of the canoe. He had nursed her through the next few days, a circumstance she was ashamed of, fearing letting him down. With that in mind, come the night, she took off with the baby intending that mother and daughter should die together no longer being a burden to him. After three days of desperate searching, he found her, half dead out in the open with the baby asleep wrapped in a fur beside her.

'Why?' he had asked when she had recovered.

She had been unable to tell him that Aleut women were as an important part of the tribe as men. If they were not strong, they could not expect others to provide for them whether they had recently given birth or not. She could not be sure he understood. He however did not question it; and as he got to know her further he no longer required any explanation.

Her husband bought them a passage with a wagon-train family that were heading west, arriving in Lower Manhattan after three years. There he bought a small, terraced house from the proceeds from his prospecting in Nome; then looked for a job. As what passed for luck would have it, Mihalyvich chanced upon a fellow prospector from Nome. He suggested to him, he would find a job in the dockyard unloading timber from ships.

'Mr. Giuseppi is the person to see. Top man.'

'Papa coming.'

Oona looked across at her daughter sitting on the old threadbare carpet in front of the log fire. She listened. She could tell the difference in sound between a caribou and black bear padding across the Arctic tundra at two hundred yards; that was not her husband. Two men creeping up a flight of stairs was too easy. Listening intently, while at the same time removing the last of the rabbit skin from its paws, her baby girl started to speak once more. Oona put two fingers to her lips.

'Two men outside the door, mama!'

Her mother startled. How on earth did her daughter know that? She picked the girl up.

'Shh, baby,' she said putting her in a cupboard where she slept. 'You stay quiet while mamma finds out what they want.'

'But mamma, they're bad men,' she slowly whispered.

She kissed her on the cheek. 'Yes, yes, shh, they'll go away if they think no-one is home. You stay in there and keep quiet for mamma, there's a good girl.'

Oona pulled the door closed and crept back to the table where she had been skinning the rabbit and listened. She could hear the faint sound of breathing the other side of door and gently felt for her hunting knife. A formidable weapon, its blade over twelve inches in length with a handle made from the tusk of a narwhal whale; a gift from her father, that no man seeing it, fearing her ability to use it on them, bought their own instead. Grasping it firmly, she eased it forward releasing its hold from the wooden cutting board that was holding its blade by its tip. There came a tap-tap sound on the door and her heart beat jumped as the knife came free. She stood silently clutching the bone handle of the knife's glistening blade to her chest. She breathed slowly waiting for another knock – or not.

Tap-tap-tap.

It came again. This time like a hammer blow to her. She thought that whoever they were would go away if she didn't answer.

'Mamma!'

The call of her daughter went through her like a thunderbolt. They would surely know somebody was here, she thought. Should she open the door? It might after all be quite harmless. Snake-oil salesmen, carpetbaggers. Yes, that was who they were . . . the traveling show . . . come to town, brought all manner of itinerants selling their wares, she had seen too much into that knock. She relaxed and went to the door putting out her hand to the lift-up bolt and raise it when she recalled her baby girl's reaction to the footsteps. What did make her say that? She had instincts of her own. Something was not right. Why should she doubt herself? Did not her Shamanism give her ancient powers? The fight or flight instinct to survive that the white man had lost. Why should she not open the door?

Mihalyvich thought what Claypole had told him. Working in the job he was, though his qualifications were suspect, did put him in a better position to know of the activities of Marco Giuseppi. It was curious the man chose to keep what he knew to himself. What he had said with him being possessed was a strange phrase to use. He shrugged and gently shook his head, dismissing the word. The man probably uses 'possessed' as another might, 'hoodlum', no more than that. In Giuseppi's case he was another man: overweight, slimy, and unpleasant, but a man for all of that. He was convinced they had been right to take the fight to him. What Giuseppi would have made of the police investigation into the matter must have made life uncomfortable for him. It was strange that the one man that could have provided evidence of harassment, torture, and corruption, when the police were looking into the death of Adams had chosen to hand his cards in. The smile changed to the emotional thought for the man that had done so much for them. Adams, bowing and smiling with a round of applause from his fellows, was an image that he would never get out of his head.

Three – 1920s

MIHALYVICH CROSSED THE STREET to his home. A corner house attached to a row of dismal looking buildings. But for the steady influx of immigrants from Europe wanting a roof over their heads they would have been demolished years since. Those that had been fortunate in securing a roof at all; before losing their jobs; becoming evicted out as the depression moved in making room for the next uptake of occupants. Ordinarily when he came home those that couldn't find work sat outside on their front steps making the most of the warmth of what winter sun remained before returning to damp rooms they endured during night-time hours. That evening a crowd of those same people had gathered outside his house.

It had been two weeks since Adams had died; and the last he had heard from Giuseppi since. That thought, and this crowd that had gathered was worrying him. It was the sight of the ambulance and the police cars that done it for him. He did not know why but he began to put together the events of the last two weeks and was beginning to feel uneasy. He ran toward them shouting.

'What's going on?'

He gasped the words between breaths.

His neighbors stopped talking among themselves when they saw him. Staring at him with their mouths open, they hesitated, waiting for someone else to tell him what had happened. There were no immediate takers. He repeated the question, this time with a quieter voice than before.

'Will somebody tell me? Has there been an accident?'

They looked at each other for someone to answer:

'We think it's your wife . . . Oona? They say she's been murdered!'

He did not thank her, instead, he ran up the stairs of his house, the woman's words echoing in his head, straight into the arms of who he supposed was a plain clothed policeman. A red-haired man wearing a bowler hat stopped him from going any further.

'*Oona!* Let me through, let me pass,' he shouted struggling with the man that did not intend to let him do that. 'Oona!'

'Calm yourself and tell me who you are?'

The policeman had him restrained in an arm lock however hard he struggled he could not get away from. 'Fariq! My name's Fariq . . . Mihalyvich. Let me go, you *bastard!*'

'There's no need for that talk, so there isn't. You calm yourself and tell me what business you have here?'

Mihalyvich was in no mood for niceties and worked out the best way to deal with an arm lock by slamming his head back into the man's forehead.

The policeman, not used to seeing stars during daylight hours, having not that day had a drink yet, lost his hold while Mihalyvich, seizing the opportunity, broke away from him and continued up the final few stairs avoiding the wet patches sprinkled haphazardly on the bare woodwork. He stopped at the last stair as it sunk into him that the wet was blood. He went cold and burst through the open door of the room screaming out his wife's name. Lieutenant Frank Weinberg, of the 7th Precinct, Lower East Side Police Department, looked up from the body of the woman lying at his feet:

'*Sergeant!*' he bellowed. 'Get - that - man - out of here.'

'On it, Lieutenant.'

Detective Sergeant Charlie O'Hare, rubbing his forehead, came in grabbed hold of Mihalyvich and pulled him out back through the door, this time receiving a dig to his ribs from the man's elbow for his trouble. O'Hare winced and ignored the pain. Any sympathy he might have had for him had left him. He put him in a regulation neck restraint that he would not easily remove himself. Mihalyvich stopped struggling.

'That's my wife in there! Let me go!'

O'Hare held him tight.

'Right. You. Mihalyvich, or whatever your name is, settle down and let's talk. I'm not your enemy. Just take it easy.'

'Okay! Okay! Just let me see to my wife.'

O'Hare looked to his lieutenant for approval. 'He says he's the woman's husband, Lieutenant.'

Weinberg nodded, 'I heard. Perhaps he'd like to tell us what he's done to her.'

Mihalyvich didn't answer. On the floor, her left arm spread forward with her right hand clutching the hunting knife that had once belonged to her father, she lay. Two bullet holes an inch apart showed on her forehead.

Weinberg stood over him in case he had any other thoughts over making a break for it. 'Well, Mr. Fariq.'

Mihalyvich was not listening. He was on the floor beside her sobbing and hugging her.

O'Hare looked toward his Lieutenant and wiped a single tear from his eye before shaking his head.

'It's Mihalyvich,' he said looking up at the two men. He kissed his wife on the cheek stood up and turned to the man that was in charge. He spoke quietly – there was resignation in his voice. 'Where's our daughter?'

A daughter. They had not found a daughter. Weinberg's heart missed a beat. He feared the worst. He looked round the room. A door to another room was in front of them.

'She sleeps in there,' Mihalyvich said pointing in its direction.

He went to open it, but Weinberg prevented him.

'*Irinushka!*' Mihalyvich called through the door.

'Wait!' Frank said. 'Wait right where you are. Sergeant!'

O'Hare came over, opened it, and went in.

'God! Lieutenant, you'd better come and take a look at this.'

'Is it her?' Mihalyvich said trying to squeeze by the lieutenant.

This time it was Weinberg's turn to put him in a neck lock.

'Can't you do as you're told,' Weinberg said pushing him away, exclaiming. 'My life!' as he looked in the room.

'Is it . . . her? Our daughter.'

Weinberg went up to the body tied to the chair that was soaked in more blood than he had ever seen in his life. Discarded in a pool of it, was a head. Torn from its shoulders. He subconsciously looked into the neck space where the head had once sat. He retched. Stepping back, he caught the man's head with his foot moving it further away from its body. 'Oh hell!' He muttered to himself involuntarily taking a larger step to avoid kicking it further. He looked back at the body for any sign of . . . he didn't know what. It was clear how this man had died; and that whoever had carried out the act had not needed any weapon. A murder that could go down in history as legendary. More so, if the killer remained at large, leaving the district running scared for years with rumours that a monster was on the loose and that the police had been unable to apprehend him.

'Look at the way those arteries have been twisted together. Like a rope, so they are,' O'Hare said relishing the thought that they would forever be recognized in the annals of criminal history as the police officers that had discovered a murder so bizarre they might never need to work again for the re-telling of its story.

'Yes. . . . Thank you, Sergeant. I've eyes enough, if not the stomach.'

'Runfeldt!' Mihalyvich said.

'You know the man?' Weinberg asked.

He held up the palm of his right hand showing it to the two policemen. 'That's Runfeldt's handiwork. Have you ever heard of Marco Giuseppi?'

Weinberg looked at O'Hare. 'Have we?'

'Only in passing, Lieutenant.'

'Well, that's one of his men, or was, and he's responsible for that, and this,' Mihalyvich pointed to the heavy cut bruise to his wrist, 'is where I tried to remove my hand with an axe. And it's clear, and I'm telling you, the man responsible for murdering my wife and abducting our daughter is Marco Giuseppi. And you'd better arrest him before I get to him first.' He sat down on the edge of his daughter's tiny bed and put his head into his hands. The thought of her being in the hands of such a man sent his body into a tremor.

The two officers were stunned. It was not every day you saw a man cry in front of other men. O'Hare wondered what people would resort to the violence tearing someone's head from their shoulders. They would surely not draw the line at hurting a little girl, would they?

Frank cleared his throat. 'Well. You've eyes to see, your daughter's clearly not here. Perhaps she's with one of the neighbors.' He called to a policemen standing outside. The man came in and Weinberg spoke quietly to him. The officer nodded, clumping his boots down the bare wood stairs as he left. Weinberg turned to Mihalyvich while at the same time speaking to O'Hare. 'Better get a surgeon down here, lock the door and get someone to stand guard outside. This is a crime scene I don't want any of what has happened here to get out into the neighborhood. In the meantime, we'll put a search out for . . . Irinushka. Did you say that was your daughter's name?' he asked Mihalyvich.

Mihalyvich nodded.

'Don't worry, we'll find her. In the meantime, you'll have to come with us. We'll get you a bed for the night.'

Mihalyvich stood up. 'What? In one of your cells, downtown? Forget that.'

He moved close alongside O'Hare then grabbing him round the neck caught him off guard, in one move, removed the gun from O'Hare's shoulder holster pushing him away then pointed it at him.

'Well I'll be damned!' O'Hare said looking down the barrel of his own gun. He put his hand out to him. 'All right, we know you've had bad news, give me back my gun before anyone else gets injured.'

Mihalyvich waved it toward the body of his wife.

'You will be if you try to take me in. She'll want revenge for what's happened here. Blood. And me to spill it. I've told you who's responsible for this, and I'm going to deal with him – my way. Move away from the door. Both of you!'

Weinberg did not intend to allow Mihalyvich to walk out of here, wandering the streets looking for the man he thought responsible. He moved between him and the way out. 'I can't do that, Mr. Mihalyvich. Our job demands I hold the line. I understand what you're going through, but you've got to do it our way. Please, give me the gun.'

'That's right, Fariq, you're in no mind to reason straight, do what the lieutenant asks,' O'Hare added.

'Reason straight! What's reasoning straight got to do with any of this? Orders from Giuseppi have had my wife murdered and our daughter abducted. You reason it if you can, and while you're doing that, get out of my way.'

'We understand all that,' Weinberg said, 'but the law is the law. You've to leave it to us. We'll go and bring Giuseppi in and see what he's got to say. Until then, well, you'll be safer with us.'

O'Hare held out his hand for Mihalyvich to hand over his weapon, but Mihalyvich was having none of it and put the barrel to

O'Hare's forehead. 'I'm not playing games, Sergeant. I've nothing to lose here. I loved that woman and the child she bore us.'

The man had a look of determination, but O'Hare had other ideas. He put his hand round Mihalyvich's wrist, looking him in the eyes for compliance. Seeing none, he started to worry. Mihalyvich cocked the revolver.

Weinberg could not let this game play out. He spoke quietly to O'Hare. 'Best let him have his day, Sergeant.' He knew that O'Hare would be prepared to try to take the man down, but one of them had to show restraint, and it was down to him as senior officer to do it. Apart from which, he had got used to O'Hare and his ways and not keen on losing him over something he had the power to prevent. He raised his voice.

'I said, Let him go, Sergeant! That's an order.'

O'Hare looked back into Mihalyvich's face and for a moment, Weinberg wondered who was going to give way first. The sound of a gun going off played in his mind. To his relief O'Hare slowly removed his hand from Mihalyvich's wrist.

Mihalyvich nodded. He was gone. Back down the stairs. The same way he had come up ten minutes before when he thought he had a family. Stepping out into the street, through the crowd of neighbors, seeing Mihalyvich waving a gun in his hand, parted screaming in panic. D'Sotto sat on a chair behind a screen in the hospital. He had gone through a bad night with his arm the way it was. With pain he could stand no longer, at the risk of arrest, he sought medical attention. He had a cut inside of his arm from elbow to the wrist. A single gash that had severed two veins losing him a good deal of blood causing him to wonder at the time if he would bleed to death. The doctor attending him remarked the wound looked like someone had tried to skin a rabbit. He had hastily added that he didn't think D'Sotto was a rabbit after the man glared at him.

He didn't care what anyone thought; he wanted the pain to go away. He had winced when the doctor dabbed antiseptic on the cut and when he asked what had happened, he replied that he had caught his arm on a piece of jagged metal.

'Did your ear go the same way?' the doctor asked. 'Only—'

D'Sotto gave another intimidating look.

'Sorry, Mr. Soames, none of my business . . . good as new,' he said smiling running his hand down the newly bandaged arm.

D'Sotto got up to go and staggered against the trolley the doctor was using to fix him up. He did not intend to stay any longer than he needed to. The police could be on to them and with all that blood on the stairs of Mihalyvich's house; they could have put two and two together. The hospital might be the first place they would come looking.

'Steady on, Mr. Soames,' the doctor said stopping him from going right over. 'I suggest you sit yourself down for a while, you've lost a lot of blood.'

D'Sotto brushed him aside, 'I said I'll be okay!'

'As you say, Mr. Soames. Any problems though, you come straight back, you hear?'

He nodded and walked out of the hospital in a state of shock from the injury that he'd sustained at the hands of Mihalyvich's wife, confused as to why Runfeldt had not come to the hospital to meet him. *So much for putting frighteners on a woman*, he said to himself. There had been no call for Runfeldt to hit her the way he had. In front of her daughter as well. It was not part of the deal. She looked as if she had fallen on her knife. He hoped she was still alive. He was going to have to find him and get their story straight. Perhaps he should have gone back this morning. Got to think straight, he thought. Duchies. I'll go there first. Get some coffee. Sort me head out.

He continued to walk, crossing the park and out into the center of the town. The doctor had been right, he was feeling weak and his arm was throbbing. What he needed was to lie down, but the calling from the newsvendor at the Greyhound bus station caught his attention:

'WOMAN FOUND SLAIN ON LOWER EASTSIDE!'

The newsvendor's bellow hit him like a bombshell before he reasoned that killings were taking place every day in New York; another one, like that, could be no more than coincidence.

'Give us a paper!' he shouted impatiently at the vendor throwing a coin into an old tin the man used for money.

The vendor shoved a roughly folded edition into his hands before continuing his oyez:

'ANOTHER YOUNG CHILD ABDUCTED!'

Her daughter? he thought.

What blood he had left in his body drained from his face. He was feeling so bad that he had to guide himself along the street using the walls of buildings for support. Falling through the door of Duchies, with his head swimming, he managed to stagger to a table.

Hearing a crash of furniture the owner emerged from the ranch style doors to the kitchen behind the high counter of the greasy eatery. Standing beside him, wearing a red and white checkered kitchen cloth round her waist, sweating, overweight from her eating too many leftovers: his wife. She looked at her husband and sighed:

'Haven't you paid them this week? That's D'Sotto. He's drunk. Get him out of here before he upsets what few customers we have left.'

Dutch smiled uneasily. He heard what his wife had said. A member of Marco Giuseppi's protection racket, he had a reputation for violence. He had been witness to D'Sotto striking a man trying to get onto Giuseppi's patch with such force under the bridge of his nose it had rendered the man useless and screaming in agony. He had only used the edge of his hand. Dutch was not looking to upset him.

'Shut-up you stupid woman,' he said to her quietly.

His wife returned to the kitchen not bothering if he had heard what she said:

'Mafia! Huh! He wasn't old enough to remember what they were in the first place,' she muttered to herself out loud for him to hear.

Dutch came round the counter wiping his hands on a similarly colored kitchen cloth his wife had round her waist. 'You alla righter, Tony, you looka as if you've seen Al Capone paying his taxes, whata caneye get you?'

'Cut the wise cracks, Dutch. Has Runfeldt been in?'

'Haven't seen him all day, Tony, youa maybe looking for him.'

'Why would I have asked? Idiot, get me a coffee.'

Dutch shrugged and went back behind the counter. He worked up the steam from an old chrome and steel Desiderio Pavoni espresso machine that had seen better days – but not in this establishment. Burning his hand on the steam that was leaking from its sides he managed to pour a cup of coffee and milk, sugared it, wiped the spills from round the cup with his cloth and returned to D'Sotto placing it on the table in front of him. D'Sotto ignored him. Dutch made nothing of it until he noticed the bandage round his arm leaking blood, while at the same time noticing the front page of the paper he was reading. He caught its headline and shuddered. He went back behind the counter quickly leaving D'Sotto's business to himself.

D'Sotto continued reading the front page. If it was her . . . well . . . he hadn't actually murdered her had he? He had left Runfeldt after she had attacked him. Leastways, he thought it was her, the light was not good. Definitely a woman though, who else would it have been. If she had been murdered it must have been him that done it. Sweet Mother of Mary! Why would he have done that? Giuseppi had said to put the frighteners on her, not murder her. The police would be looking for them. Giuseppi would not need that for attention. The bandage round his arm was showing his blood. He let it hang down by his side trying to hide it, but he saw that Dutch and his wife had already seen it.

'What're you two staring at?'

'N-Nothing, Tony, couldn't help noticing your arm, that's all,' Dutch said nervously.

'Yeh, well let's keep it at nothing eh, otherwise, well you know, Tony's problems could become Dutch's, follow me, now fuck off back into the kitchen and take that scold with you!'

'Anything you say, Tony, no offense.'

Mrs. Rossi jabbed her husband in the side with wet fingers from her chopping up onions. 'Eh youer. Maybe youer not takin anymore shit from hisa kind much alonger, eh. Maybe youer get on the blower to the police, tell 'em, eh. That there's a woman murderer in our establishment and youer want him outta 'ere, eh . . . Mr. Rossi. Anna maybe, when he goes to the electric chair, we're payin' no more protection to Mr. Giuseppi!' she said spitting out his name onto the floor for emphasis.

'Sshh, you perhaps want for him to overhear and come over and kill us you mad woman.'

D'Sotto looked across at the commotion and saw the look on the scold's face. Dutch shrugged politely and smiled at him. He, not in the mood for trouble if the scold carried out her threat got up from the table pushing his chair aside. He threw a coin down without finishing his coffee – most of which he had spilt from shaking. He had read more than enough of his newspaper to realize trouble would come soon enough with or without her help. Outside he went across to a telephone booth, dialed a number, and waited for it to answer. Giuseppi was going to have to give him cash to get away. This was not a question of keeping low, no, more of clearing off a long way away, and for a long time. Back to Sicily maybe. He would need money for that and Giuseppi was going to have to help – after all – his partner.

'Look! I've got a murdered woman, a dead man – whose head's been torn from his body – a missing four-year-old girl whose father's looking to take the law into his own hands; and you're telling me someone on high has told you to drop any further inquiries into all of this when I've got one Marco Giuseppi that I'm interested in questioning in connection with it.'

Commissioner Harry Rivers looked up from the report he was reading.

Weinberg could see that he was not going to get anything more positive than that out of his superior and the man lately promoted over him. 'So who is it in authority that's telling you how I should be doing my job?' he asked annoyingly.

Rivers looked up at him, 'No-one's trying to tell you how to do your job. We have information of the person likely responsible, that's all.'

'With no evidence . . .'

'He was there! Go book the slob. Rake up whatever you need later. What's your problem . . . you'll have a result, and everyone will be happy? That's all, Lieutenant. Close the door on your way out.'

Rivers smiled at him carried on reading. He appealed to him once again.

'Commissioner! Tony D'Sotto. Come on, the man couldn't drink a cup of coffee without spilling it. And the missing girl, eh. That'll be, what, seven in the last year. None of them found. The public's going to wonder what the hell we've been doing all this time.'

Rivers made a good job of covering his annoyance at this insubordination. Weinberg had touched a nerve. Speaking quietly he said, 'The missing girl is not seven, she's one. Investigations into the other six – as far as we know – showed that they were all, likely reunited with their families that they hadn't told us. Probably because they'd moved on. Why would we investigate people's movements?'

Weinberg was fuming. 'That's an assumption, Commissioner. We had an obligation to follow those cases up. Something's going on here; and it's looking more and more like a cover up. What's more the name, Marco Giuseppi keeps cropping up in the district and that's worrying me.'

'Well, I've been told otherwise. When Giuseppi first took over Union management of the dockyard for its Board an investigation showed him to be squeaky clean. He only resigned his position after the death of some Red Indian; because he felt he was responsible, having a duty of care toward his members. Doesn't that tell you something of the man?'

'Oh, yeh. Funny that. How he left shortly before I went into investigate the death of a crane rigger and got told I couldn't interview Giuseppi because he had government immunity. What's that all about? He probably felt his world was coming down round his neck, that's why he left in such a hurry. Further, information has since come my way that when he was a young man, he, along with Tony D'Sotto, had fines and several jail sentences against them for a string of petty robberies and muggings. He was once a pimp, you know. And to date, is still operating protection rackets.'

'Well . . . yes. But nobody's perfect are they? Let him who is without sin—'

'And do you know what, Commissioner. Not a single mugshot of him on file. Was, according to Sugden. All removed, probably destroyed by the same people that are telling you how to conduct ourselves with this case.' Rivers raised his hand to interrupt. Frank Weinberg continued, 'Think about it. An act looking like a bungled hanging from a British gallows could not have been carried out by him—'

'Equally so, Tony D'Sotto.'

'Far as I'm concerned he's our man. Murdered the woman severed the head from his partner with her knife. Did you see the size of that thing? More like a sword than a knife. I want him brought in; that's an order, Lieutenant.'

Weinberg came out of Rivers's office and hurried down the corridor of the precinct block. He shouted to his Sergeant who he could not see, but guessed would be in hearing shot, 'O'Hare!'

His sergeant shouted back immediately, 'You called, Lieutenant?'

Frank caught him by the arm as he came round the corridor. Pulling him to one side he spoke quietly to him. 'Go find Mihalyvich before he goes out of his depth and bumps into D'Sotto. Bring him in.'

'What charge?'

'Oh, I don't know. Shooting Nicholas the Second and his family, holding an Irishman up, anything. Use your ginger head. We've got to keep him out of trouble.'

'And D'Sotto? Sounds like Rivers has decided it's an open and shut case against him?'

'You've big ears for a Turk, Sergeant.'

'Yes, sir. I'll go find this Mihalyvich?'

'Yes please, Sergeant.'

State Governor Fray Brent was on the phone in his office.

'We don't want any police officers assassinated thank you Marco. We had a deal. I don't interfere with your business, and you don't interfere with my police department.'

'You've a couple of loose cannons that could cause me and you a whole heap of trouble. Get rid of them.'

Brent snapped back at him.

'Harry Rivers will deal with any problems on our side; it's not for you to involve yourself.'

Giuseppi hissed down the telephone.

'This is a big operation, Brent. A lot of people are involved – yourself and the Commissioner included – big people, who look to me for protection; and I shall provide it if you can't, and when I say my operation is under scrutiny by officers under your jurisdiction I expect something done, and if that includes hitting them, well, it won't be the first time. The elevation to commissioner of Rivers is testament to that. What you want is no longer part of the equation.'

'Marco, I can assure you Rivers have his men under control. As far as the officers on the case are concerned, it's over and done with. By the way, another matter I wish to speak to you.'

'What?'

'Your man. Tony D'Sotto.'

'What of him?'

'You do realize that he's likely to cause more trouble than a couple of police officers. He's running scared and the investigating officer is no fool. You'd better be sure there's enough evidence for the murder of that woman and the attack on Runfeldt against him.'

'I'll do no such thing. Tony and me, we go back a long way. And I'll take care of him, nobody touches Tony, you understand?'

'Bu—'

'There's no, *but* Brent. If you know what's good for you you'll do as you're told.'

'I've still to go through procedures. Rivers has issued a warrant for Tony's arrest, if he goes back on that suspicions will arise. Fortunately, the investigating officer doesn't believe it's Tony, it could be an open and shut arrest. You do have friends on the inside even if they are unwitting.'

'Good. And make sure Rivers disposes of Runfeldt's body. I don't want headless corpses examined too closely, especially when they once worked for me. It's bad for business.'

'It wouldn't do our business much good either. People get nervous. They begin to think monsters have landed from another planet and are running amok – unless you want to own up to it being your work.'

Brent waited for an answer, but it was clear he was hanging on a dead line. Weinberg switched the interrogation lamp on, adjusted it into D'Sotto's face, and waited for his pupils to stop dilating.

D'Sotto shuffled his feet nervously under its glare feeling curiously at ease and relief at his arrest. With an alibi from Giuseppi, he didn't have to worry unduly. Weinberg was looking out the window as he spoke.

'Explain to me how you tore the head from your partner's body, Tony?'

What kind of a fool question is that, he thought.

'My partner? His head. You got that wrong, Lieutenant. I don't know anything about a head. He's not dead, he . . .'

'Hasn't got a head anymore. Your partner is dead, murdered in Mihalyvich's house along with the man's wife and the abduction of their daughter. And you . . . well . . . my boss believes you're responsible for the killing. Personally, I don't think it's your style. But . . . long as we got somebody for it, well . . . Old Sparky's not bothered one way or another.'

The blood drained from D'Sotto's face. The thought of his execution in an electric chair loomed in his mind once again.

'And while we're on the subject of the disappearance of the Mihalyvich girl. Any ideas as to what became of her? Only we can prove you were there see – the police doctor has said the cut to your arm matches that of the knife we found on the floor. Oona Mihalyvich's hunting knife.'

D'Sotto had not heard him properly. He was thinking what it might feel like sitting in an electric chair waiting for execution.

Weinberg came away from the window, going up to D'Sotto, he grabbed him by his jacket lapels and hauled him to his feet. 'What's happened to her? Forget everything else for the moment. Where is the little girl? I'm interested in hearing what you've to say over her disappearance. Is that something to do with Giuseppi?'

He held him tightly and D'Sotto started to choke.

'You've gotta believe me, Lieutenant Weinberg, I'm all confused. Giuseppi sent me and Runfeldt round to Mihalyvich's home to put the frighteners on his wife. It was her; she attacked me with a knife. I left in a hurry. I don't know what else happened; I was in hospital having my arm fixed up. I didn't see any daughter.'

He released him.

'My life, there's a thing. She tries to defend herself and her child from two thugs, and you're surprised she attacked you with a knife. How inconsiderate of her,' he stared into his eyes, 'what the fuck did you expect her to do, bake you a cake? You moron!'

'But I didn't kill her, I didn't. It was like I said, after she attack– cut me with a knife, I was in so much pain and bleeding and all, I wanted out, so I ran . . .'

'Leaving her and their daughter in the hands of your partner. The kind of *arsehole* shrinks have in mind when the words, psychopathic disorder personality is written down.'

'What disorder?'

'Oh, yes. I saw what he did to Fariq Mihalyvich's hand. Not the person I would use as a baby sitter. But enough of him. Let's get back to the whereabouts of the child.'

Tony went white.

'But I'm telling you, there wasn't a child. Unless she was in the back room. If she was, I didn't take her. And I didn't kill anyone neither. You gotta believe me, Lieutenant, honest, I didn't. Giuseppi must have taken her, he—'

He stopped himself saying anymore.

'You were going to say?'

'Nothing.'

'Tony. This is serious. Has Giuseppi got the Mihalyvich girl?'

'I can't say anymore.'

'If you know something, like, Giuseppi and missing children; Mihalyvich's daughter in particular, you'd better speak up. She wouldn't have been the first to go missing in Manhattan. There's an on-going investigation as we speak.'

'No I don't, Lieutenant, honest.'

Weinberg released him and dusted down the man's lapels mockingly. That slip of the tongue told him that he knew something; and not very palatable; the man may not have been responsible for murder; likely that was Runfeldt; but the abduction of the child, along with others, he thought. He would press home that line of inquiry.

'Did Giuseppi ask either of you to abduct the Mihalyvich girl? What does he like? Tell me, Tony. When did you last see the man with a woman?'

D'Sotto was shaking. The Lieutenant was hanging him out to dry.

O'Hare burst into the office.

'Mihalyvich has disappeared from the face of the earth, so he has. Have you got anything out of that fuck-rat yet?' he said pointing to D'Sotto.

'Give me ten, O'Hare.'

When Frank heard, he was going to get an Irish–American as a partner – and a Catholic to-boot – he had not been keen, telling Commissioner Dore at the time of his reservations. Not that he had anything against the Irish, a Catholic even. Any more than he had issues with Blacks or Puerto Ricans. It was his own half of the partnership being Jewish that would leave them wide open to ridicule within the criminal underworld round the speakeasies of New York that worried him.

O'Hare had made the stunted remark: *A Catholic and a Jew walked into a bar* . . . the likely future comment played out in his head. O'Hare hadn't finished the punch line. He assumed it had one.

A matter of O'Hare's father having been a Tammany ward boss. Although Weinberg didn't necessarily subscribe to the proverb, Sins of the Father, a demand for loyalty from any of his extended family might jeopardize their effectiveness as officers when it came to arrests. He need not have worried. Detective Sergeant Charlie O'Hare was as straight as a die when it came to law and order (keep those dies coming straight, he thought). As to those remarks, usually accompanied by laughter, of the two men's faiths as they entered a bar, that didn't last long either. Word soon got round the criminal fraternity that O'Hare and Weinberg were not of the frame of mind to having the piss taken from them with cheap cracks as to their opposing religious beliefs, especially after O'Hare dropped one or two of them with single blows to their solar plexus's, less so. A useful attribute he had clearly picked up from his father; that served both officers well in the districts round Manhattan on more than one occasion. The only other problem that Weinberg had as to O'Hare's credentials when he first applied to become a detective was his entertainment value. A reason their partnership may not work, he had put to Dore: was he capable of taking the job seriously enough?

He was thinking of the time he was passing through East Houston Street in a police car on his way to a trial he was the arresting officer for when the traffic came to a standstill. A power cut affected the traffic lights putting them out, and a young officer in – to sort it. He did not know him it at the time (made some inquiries later), but he was on O'Hare's beat. In the meantime, with nothing better to do, he became mesmerized by the young officer as he walked with confidence to the center of the road to begin his performance. It was not so much him directing traffic as orchestrating it. Swinging his arms and moving his body, he was a one-man dance act. So entertaining was the man that people got out of their cars to watch him. They joined in clapping and applauding until, he supposed, the music in his head had stopped. When O'Hare realized he had an audience he noticing them, put his fists on his hips and shouted, 'Move It! Move It! What are you waiting for, *Jimmy Cagney*?' Then rocking with laughter, carried on directing the traffic clearing the freeway.

'Your keenness for the job preventing you from knocking, Sergeant?' Weinberg said after the allotted ten minutes had past.

O'Hare stood at Weinberg's office door.

'Come on, sit down. You know, sometimes O'Hare, it pays to follow your instincts and throw some wild cards onto the table.'

O'Hare pulled the chair out and seated himself, leaned across the desk and stubbed his cigarette out in his ashtray.

'He's as good as admitted that Giuseppi is involved in child abduction.'

O'Hare was puzzled. 'Wasn't Giuseppi the same man that Rivers told you to lay off when you first mentioned missing children?'

'He asked me if I had any evidence for making such accusations. He didn't like my mentioning of it. Not one little bit. But having spoken with your, "fuck-rat", it's beginning to look like I'm onto something.'

'Sounds like a superior officer we can have confidence in. What's he up to, Lieutenant?'

'Like you don't know. Anyway, forget Rivers for the moment. You said you've had no luck finding Mihalyvich.'

'Hasn't been seen anywhere. I've had half the force out looking for him. I must admit when we lost him I didn't expect him to go to ground for quite so long. With all that he's got on his mind I'd have thought he'd had handed himself in.'

'That's because he knows we've got D'Sotto. Perhaps we should do something. Go get some coffees in Sergeant, we're going to go out on a limb.'

Weinberg needed to think. Something was going on here that he didn't like. He had been in charge of homicide four years and O'Hare had been with him the last two of them. When Commissioner Dore was to retire, he was to be his successor. Overlooked; it had nothing to do with him being any less capable than Rivers. He was Jewish. Jews were not particularly popular, even if this one was a Lieutenant. Apart from that, Governor Brent would not have been able to manipulate Weinberg like he could Rivers; and Dore come to that, and he certainly would not be able to move Brent's spirit trucks round so freely. The pair of them had a nice little number supplying half of New York's speakeasies with illicit liquor, with the good Mrs. Rivers, having her name on the door, for the both of them. She, with her brothel, and him with his new found appointment as Commissioner-of-Police – they were fire proof. He determined he was not going to let that continue. Everyone knew what they were up to, only Weinberg had thought seriously enough to put his job on the line to bring the two men down by indicting them for corruption. He had had to bide his time. If Giuseppi were involved in child abduction, as God made little apples, Rivers and Brent would know of it. It had been O'Hare and his Tammany connections, telling him to wait. Good advice as it turned out. Weinberg was, to date, mulling over that advice what with O'Hare being in a position to know these things better than he did. With a little bit more sniffing round, he might get what he wanted. And with it coming from Giuseppi's direction, he knew what he had to do.

O'Hare, carrying two cups of black coffee while at the same time working the door handle with his backside, pushed it open, coming in backwards placing two chipped mugs on Weinberg's desk and sat down ignoring his boss's response that once again he hadn't knocked, sipped at his coffee with an air of nonchalance.

Weinberg, having never been one for superior formality, had inadvertently reprimanded O'Hare more out of his frustration than pulling petty rank on him. This business with Commissioner Rivers was getting to him and he could see no proper police procedure he could use to nail him. This was New York and he would not have been the first policeman to fall the result of exposing corruption. If he were to secure his own reputation as a person that was straight, he had to move ahead of Rivers – catchy monkey-style. Whatever he came up with it was not right for him to involve O'Hare. He picked up his coffee and leaned back in his chair.

'I can't carry on proper lines of inquiry with all this that's going on with the Commissioner. He's causing us . . . me . . . a headache full of problems. A bit of moon-shining and bootlegging is one thing, but his interference where child abduction is an issue . . . well . . . that's a different ball game altogether. Whether that's his intention, or it's an inadvertent side issue for his covering up something else more personal to him, I can only hazard a guess.'

'I did wonder how long you'd be putting up with the way things were, perhaps it was my fault for telling you to tread carefully.'

'Well, I think I've trod carefully long enough, don't you? That last conversation I had with him has convinced me. The fact that he has warned me off using the pretense that someone on high has told him to tread carefully where Marco Giuseppi is concerned has got to me. They may well have done, but that's not the point. Children have gone missing and it needs proper investigating. That slip of the tongue by D'Sotto revealed more between the lines than I think the man realized. He's faded silverware. The magnifying glass is going to have to come out. Something else we're supposed to ignore. Heads coming loose. Not that I would necessarily shout that incident from the roof tops. I've no intention of being the author of a Jack the Ripper-type horror story in New York.'

O'Hare could see that Frank, not normally a man to worry, seemed so. They had only ever had experience of ordinary crime; ordered to back off from a man that may have the answer to missing children was something else entirely. He would agree with Frank on that score. They were about to move up a league, and that gave him some cause for concern. A concern he was happy to live with until he mentioned what he did.

'Look, Charlie. There's no need for you to get involved in any of this. No need for the both of us to go down for my stepping out of line. This investigation into child abduction needs support from my superiors. Support I am clearly not going to get. My immediate thoughts are with the missing Mihalyvich girl. So I am letting you go. Take a holiday. Go to Ireland – you've family there. Get drunk. Just get away until I've cracked it, or . . . well you know.'

O'Hare knew when Weinberg had said, 'go down' he sensed he was thinking of something more permanent than losing their jobs. The thought entered his head of the suspicious circumstances surrounding Commissioner Dore's death. 'Listen . . . my father didn't bring us to America to turn our backs at the first sign of trouble. We're used to trouble where we come from and if you think I'm going to leave you up shit creek without a paddle, well you can think again.' He leaned across Weinberg's desk. 'Try to do anything without involving me, and I'll personally shop you to the Commissioner,' he said with a serious smile on his face.

'That's blackmail, O'Hare.'

'That's loyalty, Weinberg.'

The wind knocked from his sails by someone made up to detective from the shop floor. Most would keep their noses clean. Do as ordered; concentrate on keeping their pension intact. This man was something special.

'I'm moved, O'Hare . . . saying such a thing. I'm not used to a Catholic expressing loyalty to a Jew like myself.'

O'Hare looked at him and quietly whispered:

'Put up with Protestants, so I can with you, *moisher*. It's all only a matter of faith, you see—'

'. . . and the bar tender said, *What goes on here, is this some kind of a joke . . . ?*' Weinberg said recalling a line.

'What?'

'Never mind, Sergeant.'

In the darkness he watched them silently waiting as if for a movie to begin. For that was what it was. A private picture palace. With its pitched floor that would ensure a perfect view of what was about to take place. An atmosphere of perverted anticipation pervading the darkness was that of rotting flowers; the best he could do to cover the stench of what he was, and of where he had emerged. Unchained and freed from a dimension that hitherto it (for angels, fallen or otherwise occupied no species gender), was normally only able to exert influence from, he (for the purposes of recognition never took on a living gender before: man would provide that for him), for the second time in 600,000 years, the legend that he alone was the fallen angel, was among them using a Host that had sold out his soul big-time.

Masqueraded dealers: a Bloodhound, a Bull, a Clown, and a Goat had plundered the pantomime costume department, not so much with a relish for the papier mâché heads as for ladies' over garments and underclothes in the belief that children would comply more favorably with them if they showed their feminine side. He watched them experience a rush of blood to their genitalia from their body-shaping. He laughed at their admiring reflections in the mirrors of this circus that was ridiculous and dramatic with the actors seeing themselves for the first time – if any considered their perverted sexuality as mere fantasy – in a world of reality. As far as he knew, all but one of them was in the market to become the loathsome charge of the child paraded before them. To do with as he chooses. These circuses brought together for the pleasures of men and women that had reached depths of depravity beyond understanding saving that of himself demanded identity concealment. A concealment of which he was well versed, his stock-in-trade. Whether it was clothing, personality, or his ability to become animal, vegetable, or mineral in those respects he outshone God. He had to. As master deceiver in a world that rated evil from zero to ten against the supreme Creator's zero for everything he had more than an edge. He was magical in both his presentation and their mechanics for souls: not as easy as it might seem since access to heaven required only sinners to repent at death. But God the Father has an alter ego (*Filioque*). Third in line of the Trinity, after Him, and the Son – the Divine Spirit. When it comes to God's team, one of Jesus's top disciples, St. Peter – whose legendary position as keeper to heaven's gate would be no more than that of a glorified janitor up against the Divine Spirit's sway for who was to enter the abode of the blest or not. The one transgression He had overlooked, taking ultimate extinction as read, would come down to the Divine Spirit for judgement. His was the business. Man's interpretation of a large swinging board hanging alongside those pearly gates surrounded in white mist with the legend, No Entry to the Following, signed in red lettering, with further instructions at the bottom, Please Make Your Way to Hell, underlining the next port of call for its transgressor. Hell, with its gatekeeper, His Satanic Majesty becoming your 'future master', putting you beyond divine influence for all eternity. No redemption, no forgiveness, no mercy – *no money return'd.*

But who considers what will happen after one's own death? Taking the gamble that when you go, that's it. 'Ill judgement, if I have to own up to it myself,' Ahriman muttered adding, 'and good reason for my existence.'

D'Sotto could not wait to get out of 7th Precinct headquarters. He went straight to Giuseppi's office in the dockyard – but it was deserted. He had packed up and gone. He toyed with the idea of asking round further but guessed he wouldn't be all that popular. Night-time, he took a cab home.

The front door to the multiblock house was open. Thinking no more than that some other tenant had forgotten to close it D'Sotto went in. He climbed the stairs to his room. Getting his key out, he hesitantly inserted it into the lock and pushed the door open. Something was not right. He went in and reaching for the light switch he was immediately drenched in cold water.

He lay on the floor panting. His heart racing with the shock and the pain from the muscular spasm trying to free itself from his chest. He tried to work out what had happened. The light from the bare bulb in the ceiling had been but a flash, but it had been enough to show that he was not alone. His assailant was tying him down using large metal staples nailed to the floor.

Where's our daughter? the voice in his head said from the darkness of semi-consciousness.

Turning his head in the direction of the sound, he felt something puncture the side of his neck. Letting out a yell his head instinctively went the other way. The same happened again. This time to the other side. His brain passed a message to his neck muscles not to repeat the exercise.

'Is it you, Fariq? I didn't touch her, honest! I told Lieutenant Weinberg that, and he believed me. It must have been Runfeldt. Lieutenant Weinberg said he was murdered. Someone cut his head off. He was the last person to see your daughter. It must have been him. I needed a doctor. I panicked. After your wife attacked me I ran.'

The burning pain from each side of his neck was making it difficult for him to concentrate. He could feel the blood trickling out of him. In his mind's eye, he could see himself in a pincer arrangement of two knives. The pumping of his heart was emptying his body of blood from the ruptured arteries. He felt himself fading away.

'Me and you finished playing games, Tony. The tables have been turned and there's no-one here to help you. Tell me, before you die, who's got our daughter?'

Mihalyvich said the words quietly. He was in no hurry quite prepared to watch him die.

D'Sotto was beginning to panic. Some of the blood draining from him had found its way to the back of his throat. Salty, it was choking him and making his eyes water.

He whispered. 'Giuseppi has her. Please . . .' He had lost his voice and wondered if Mihalyvich had heard him. He was dying. He had a final request from his captor. 'Please . . . I beg of you. A priest.'

'Where? Where is he holding her?' Mihalyvich whispered once more.

'*Algonquins Grave.* He lives there. Priest . . .'

He was gone.

Mihalyvich satisfied that D'Sotto thinking himself about to die to the point of needing to make peace with his God had likely spoken the truth. He pressed his thumbs hard against the arteries in D'Sotto's neck, stemming the flow of blood, held the pressure for ten minutes until the blood clotted. He bound a bandage round his neck; leaving the man's fate in the hands of the person, he called on the phone. A message for the 7th Precinct Desk Sergeant to pass to Lieutenant Weinberg, before setting out to find *Algonquins Grave* and the man that held what remained of his family. His baby daughter, bearing Oona's mother's name.

O'Hare walked into Dutch's eater with a hand-full of claypipes sticking out of the end of a neatly packaged brown paper bag with the company advert printed in green on its side that read, Jack Ho Chinese Tobacco Emporium N.Y. He was to attend a family friend's wake later that day. At their usual table, Weinberg was eating a breakfast of gefilte fish and carrots, with an accompaniment of Ma Cohen's best beet horseradish on the side; all being washed down from a large jug of coffee. He pulled a chair up, sat himself down, put down his pipes and tobacco and helped himself to a cup of coffee, then waited for Weinberg to look up from his newspaper.

'D'Sotto turned up at death's door last night.'

Weinberg looked up, and looked down at the sports page of the newspaper made the comment:

'Word is . . . Mihalyvich is searching for Giuseppi.' Weinberg pushed the last of some motza bread into his mouth, flicking off a piece of carrot from his suit lapel. He picked his cup up, took a sip, and continued reading. 'Mihalyvich has more concern for his fellow man than some have for him. Only half killed D'Sotto before patching him up and calling us, saying we might need to bother with an ambulance.' He carried on eating, emptying his mouth continued. 'See the Yankees beat the Red Sox at the Polo last evening. You missed a good game by all accounts. Reckon a crowd of over a million.'

'Heard a bit of it. It's all right, but hamburgers don't taste the same when you're listening on the wireless. Mihalyvich didn't kill him. I would have. Sugden told me how they found him. That right he told Fariq that Giuseppi has his daughter and that he was going after him. Have we an address?'

'Place called, *Algonquins Grave*, wherever that is. Sounds spooky. According to D'Sotto, he moved recently, we're checking it out. Whether we'll find it before Mihalyvich does is another matter. Oh, yeh. Something else . . .' Weinberg folded his paper up. 'About those other missing children . . .'

'The six.'

'Try eighteen, Lieutenant.'

'How many?' Weinberg's voice raised the heads of several other diners having breakfast. Seeing them looking up, he smiled at them, lowered his voice to a whisper. 'Eighteen!'

'Six in the last two years. Twelve in the previous three,' O'Hare said.

'But the file only mentions six, how come?'

'Another file that Commissioner Dore had been working on before he "retired". Sugden happened to mention it when I got talking to him about the missing Mihalyvich girl. He went to find it to show it to me. And guess what? Never mind – I'll tell you. It's missing.'

'So how come Sugden knew about it?'

'We're talking Sugden here, Lieutenant. The walking filing cabinet. Anyway, he told me what it contained. Eighteen girls ranging in ages from four to six. All immigrants. Plus, he said that Dore discovered that several six to nine-year old's had turned up in New Jersey and Pennsylvania with their necks broken. He had written statements, photographs, evidence *etcetera* from the departments involved. Pictures showing them dressed to kill, for want of a better expression, wearing ball gowns, court shoes, make-up. And there's more. Everyone that was involved with those cases at the time has since either retired, or in Dore's case, died; likely murdered far as I'm concerned.'

'God forgive us,' Weinberg said clearly shocked by O'Hare's revelations. 'And did Sugden suggest a name for who was thought responsible?'

'No name from New Jersey or Pennsylvania, but yeh, he was sure a young guy by the name of Marco Giuseppi had some involvement somewhere. So sure was he that he sent a file to the Department of Justice asking them if they could carry out an in-depth inquiry into the man using officers from the Bureau of Investigation. He was concerned that some of his own people at the top might be in league with him and would tip him off.'

'So why didn't they – the Justice Department I mean – act on his request?'

'Sugden could only guess at that one. The enormity of the crime; Marco Giuseppi's involvement with the Dockyard Board. Listen, I'm not trying to teach you how to suck eggs, but, Tammany connections and all that, it doesn't surprise me one bit that this doesn't go on. You must remember, America was trying to build itself back up to strength after the war in Europe. Still is. Giuseppi was helping them do that – he reckons that what Dore told him about Governor Brent being closely involved himself, he had the evidence intercepted before the eyes of the Department of Justice ever came to seeing it. He used the excuse to Dore that someone wanted to scrutinize the case further before allowing it to come to prosecution. In the meantime . . .'

'The case notes get fucked about . . .'

'A file is returned that bears no resemblance to the original. All salient evidence removed. To use his words, "There wasn't enough of a case to prosecute him for playing with himself, let alone abducting children". Of course, as commissioner, Dore hit the roof and complained to on high, but he hit a wall. Sugden filed what remained of the case; and with it gone all we have is Sugden's word for what was in it. Which of course, is *nihil ad rem* in a court of law.'

Weinberg's mind was in over-drive when O'Hare continued.

'Something else Sugden mentioned Dore told him. Although, he made light of it.'

'Go on.'

'A boxcar tramp, by all account that had been a reporter in another world, told him he had seen a paranormal event take place after Giuseppi threw a man into one of the dockyard basins after some argument . . .'

'Nice man.'

'Quite. Well, the point is, about this paranormal thingy. You know those special report forms for recording unusual occurrences?'

'Not off hand, no.'

'Well, there are apparently, and he sent one in, though the storyteller was high on meths. I won't go into what he was supposed to have seen. It's not important; no doubt Sugden will tell you if you want to know—'

'Might be as well.' He stopped to think before continuing. 'So Rivers may have been right when he told me that other people higher up didn't want Giuseppi brought in for questioning?'

'The real question is, why should they . . . why would they? I mean, if what he said was kosher about those girls, this all goes beyond a bit of racketeering,' O'Hare said.

'It would certainly answer the question we asked ourselves recently.'

'Which one was that?'

'Dore getting himself run down and killed. Makes you wonder if it was the accident they said it was.'

Weinberg's concerns for O'Hare's career being in jeopardy helping him on this case might well bring about more than their being kicked off the force. But for his mention of loyalty to him, he would have found some reason for having him suspended.

'Do you want the rest of this coffee, sergeant? Christ! *Eighteen children.*'

'Don't keep saying, *Christ!* Lieutenant. To the best of me knowledge your Messiah hasn't arrived on earth yet. More's the pity. He may have prevented such crimes happening in the first place if he had.'

'No, he hasn't . . . that's wishful thinking, I don't believe He'd have done anything much about them if He had. Sometimes . . . I'm of the opinion, Charlie, that God allows Satan to run his course to remind us of the consequences by allowing him too much slack.

'And what're you doing with all those clay pipes, Sergeant?'

Four – 1920s

LOCAL PEOPLE knew *Algonquins Grave*, the house in midtown Manhattan, as *The Grave*. Once a settlement for Algonquian Indians, later used as a burial ground for them, it had become derelict and unoccupied for years until Marco Giuseppi bought the property unsettling residents, both living . . . and dead.

O'Hare, wearing a large brown checked suit, a bowler hat, sporting his regulation broad grin, sat perched on the wall that surrounded *The Grave*. In something less loud alongside of him, with an altogether different sense of humor, sat his Lieutenant.

Easing himself silently off the right side of the wall, Weinberg landed on the damp grass ten feet below; the wrong side of the law. He crouched listening for sounds that did not belong to the night, before calling for O'Hare to follow. Still grinning, O'Hare obliged. Hitting the ground awkwardly, he lost his balance pushing Weinberg into a hedge where his bowler hat chased in after him. He struggled out from the bush and brushed himself down. Giving O'Hare a less than friendly stare whispered that he had all the attributes of Stan Laurel. O'Hare's grin was about to turn into a full-blown laugh at the thought of the man until Weinberg showed him his fist. He waited for his eyes to accustom themselves to the dark before moving off in direction of the house, leaving O'Hare to retrieve his hat that had rolled out from under the hedge, seemingly with a mind of its own. O'Hare followed him and breathlessly knelt down beside of him.

'Just hope to God Mihalyvich hasn't beaten us to it,' O'Hare said as he shuddered at a thought. 'So many dead beneath our feet, this place certainly has the right name.'

'Can you see any lights in the windows?' Weinberg whispered purposely ignoring his reference. 'Go over the other side behind that glass thing, see if anyone's home.'

'Cold frame.'

'What?'

'It's called a cold frame.'

But Weinberg hadn't stopped to listen.

'Where you going?' O'Hare shouted to him in a whisper.

He was at the front door. 'Round the back of the property. Meet me there if no-one comes out.' He lifted the large knocker on the front door and let it go before melting away into the darkness.

O'Hare froze at his act of bravado. 'What in *hell's* name do you think you're doing?'

He was talking to himself. Not having the time to think what he should do if someone did answer the door, he waited for the time it might take for that to happen before leaving the security of the 'glass thing' and following Weinberg into the darkness, accidentally taking out a stack of flower pots propped up against it with his boot on the way. '*Sweet Mother of Jesus!*' he whispered to himself at the same time putting his fingers into his ears praying for the clatter from the clay pots to die away, and that no-one else had heard them.

Weinberg did. Not knowing what caused it he stopped stock-still before realizing that it must be O'Hare. Seeing cars parked at the back of the house, he went up to one of them.

O'Hare looked at his watch and waited. A minute went by he followed. Coming to the back of the house, he saw Weinberg with his head inside the hood of a car. Emerging with a smile on his face and a rotor arm from its distributor in a greasy hand, he threw it up into the air with his left hand catching it with a snatch in his right as it came down, an air of satisfaction on his face. 'Let's hope it's someone we know, eh, Charlie! Come on. Keep it moving. That window, it's hanging off. Give me a hand-up,' he said lifting it from what remained of its hinges placing it on the ground.

O'Hare put his closed hands together. Weinberg stepped into them and pulling himself up onto the ledge, over did it, disappeared head first through the empty window frame landing on a bare floor. O'Hare waited anxiously below the window wondering what had happened to him when his face appeared right way up rubbing the top of his head. Reaching out to him, he indicated that he would pull him in.

'I'll be thinkin' oylle be goin in feet first if it's all the same to you, Lieutenant,' O'Hare said smiling. The image in his head of his Lieutenant in a crumpled heap on the floor made him feel better after the noise he had made over the flower pots. The floor was seven feet below the window ledge and O'Hare got his leg round and gently lowered himself to the floor. He flicked his torch on. Weinberg was still rubbing the top of his head.

They looked round. There was the usual trash that people put in basements. Weinberg noticed a small flight of stairs leading to a door. He went up them, banging his head on an old yellow lamp bulb hanging from an older length of cable. He tendered his head once more. 'See if you can find a switch,' he said with resignation.

O'Hare looked round and seeing an old porcelain one hanging off the wall with exposed wires obliged. The yellow lamp flickered came on. They switched their torches off. 'You don't think this is going a bit far, what with us not having a search warrant an all?' O'Hare asked.

Weinberg had had reservations when he first suggested it to O'Hare. They could be in a lot of trouble over this and one of the reasons he had not wanted his Sergeant getting himself involved. After all, they did not have any real evidence that Giuseppi had abducted Mihalyvich's daughter. Only supposition. Would they have been granted a warrant if they made their suspicions known to Rivers? Unlikely. He would have a field day with their careers if this all goes wrong. What was going to be more of a problem would be what Rivers would do if it did turn out that they were right about Giuseppi after what Sugden had told O'Hare. Weinberg took these thoughts and put them into something more constructive. 'We're here to rescue a six-year-old girl in danger of her life – shove the warrant, we'll worry about legalities after we've found her – alive. Let's concentrate on that shall we?'

O'Hare nodded his agreement. 'I'm with you on that one, Lieutenant.'

'She may not be, but I'll bet my badge that the man that lives here knows where she is.'

'And I'm hoping that he's not the same bastard that tears heads off bodies – had you given any thought to that, Lieutenant?'

'No I hadn't, not until you mentioned it,' Weinberg said wishing his sergeant would keep minor incidentals to himself.

'Sorry. Just a thought.'

'Tell you what though . . .' O'Hare listened. 'If whoever was responsible for popping heads off manages to get his hands round my neck and you think that it's him that done it, you have my permission to shoot your gun up his arse.'

'And if you're facing the other way, Lieutenant?'

'Up mine, O'Hare. *Up mine!*'

Feeling the door edges for some grasp, Weinberg found what he was looking for. He slowly pulled the door open with his nails and fingertips. He looked through the gap. No light coming from the other side. He opened it further. 'Come on,' he whispered, was gone.

The damp atmosphere of the passageway the two of them found themselves had the faint whiff of perfume, and not a pleasant one at that. They looked at each other. It was as if a lid to a sewer had been left off somewhere. Making their way along the unpleasant smell turned into something else. A horror that neither man had expected to see and the reason they had broken into someone's house uninvited became justified. O'Hare spoke first, at what confronted them.

'*Sweet* Mother of Jesus, won't you look at all of this.'

Weinberg did and his brain sent a message of chill down his spine that erected the hairs on his arms. His eyes watered with the imaginative complexities of a brain that could conjure such deviation. He stared at O'Hare not knowing what to say.

O'Hare had hoped his lieutenant would make nothing of what was before them – that it was something that was perfectly normal and acceptable. Something not to be taken too seriously. He would be disappointed. Round the wall, hanging on pegs were dresses. Not adults', or children but grown women's clothes made small. Gowns hanging, cabaret dresses, wedding dresses and fancy dresses that would have made a whore proud. Alongside were long black cloaks (adult size), with hoods, presumably to hide the identity of the wearer, O'Hare thought. He saw whips, knives, pliers, and . . .

Weinberg controlled a flash of anger . . . *wire brushes!* What does anyone need those for? He put his hand to his mouth feeling the bile from his stomach rise up to the back of his throat as he saw further down the corridor. A horror he took control over.

'Help me get him down,' Weinberg said quietly. 'Nothing more we can do for him here. I'll get an ambulance.'

O'Hare broke their unspoken thoughts. '*Sweet* Mother of Jesus, what the *fook's* this all about?' He was not expecting an answer. His normally red Irish complexion deepened. 'Far as I'm concerned, all bets are off with this and whoever's behind it. I'll stamp on whoever stands between these people and justice. These bastards, whoever they are, are going to have to be taken out, Lieutenant.'

'Come on, let's do it, and hang the consequence.'

Weinberg had hoped that the file that Sugden had recalled to O'Hare had been an exaggeration, a mistake. In that corridor, O'Hare had spoken the word that he had not wanted to think let alone hear. Torture. Involving children in some bizarre rite. Medieval in origin – sacrificial in practice. A left over from an age of darkness and depravity. Religious even. No religion that he had ever heard of indulged in practices like those displayed here. Sex and torture. Satanism. Too many definitions that end in the same conclusion. Pain and confusion to young minds until death.

'*Lieutenant!*' O'Hare had gone on ahead. Coming to a room off a corridor, he put his ear to the door. 'Someone in there, listen.'

Weinberg put his ear to the door. He shook his head and tried again. He could hear nothing.

'See if it opens,' O'Hare said turning the handle.

It creaked. They both looked in. Darkness. They went in closing the door behind them. O'Hare sniffed. The remains of a cheroot were burning in an ashtray.

'Did someone hear us and leave in a hurry?' Weinberg said.

'Well that is what I heard, a clicking, and its coming from that contraption,' O'Hare said.

When beams of colored lights burst from it going through a slit in the wall, both of them startled.

Weinberg looked through the aperture. Below in the gloom, an auditorium with seats arranged in rows. It was dark but he could make out an audience seated in front of the stage. The colored beams of light were catching the side of his head interfering with his view. He turned away and blinked to clear them. 'Come and take a look at this. What the hell are those people dressed in?' O'Hare put his face to the opening and looked down. 'Careful they don't see you,' Weinberg said.

'Couldn't rightly say, two of them are wearing women's clothes though. Do you know what Giuseppi looks like, Lieutenant?' He had never seen the man before. He guessed he would have Latin features. Not that you could see anyone's face. They were all wearing masks. Although, he figured, the man standing on the center of the stage, the way he was strutting about, dressed as a Ringmaster from a circus, would be as safe a bet as any that he was their man. Standing on his own as if he were about to present a show. Strutting across the stage with a top hat on his head wearing a black drape evening dress jacket and, to O'Hare, the most ridiculous waxed mustache with curled up ends on his top lip that he had ever seen. Perhaps he was about to burst into song, although, after what they had seen, this was no musical extravaganza. He pulled his head back, moving so quick that Weinberg did not have a chance to move out of his way.

'*Careful!* You stepped on me foot.'

'Sorry, Lieutenant, but I think, they might have seen me. What'd we do, react? Get out of here, or go blast their heads off their shoulders?'

'Hang on, let me see.' Weinberg looked. 'Well, if anyone did see you, they're not letting on. And in any case, we haven't . . . wait a second though . . . something's about to kick-off.'

O'Hare went to his shoulder holster putting his hand round the grip of his revolver. He slowly withdrew it. Weinberg saw what he was doing out of the corner of his eye. He turned away tapping him on the back of his hand. 'Not yet,' he whispered. 'I want some firm evidence of what they're up to before we do anything.' He stared back down. He could make out the silhouette of a woman with a child by the side of her. Could she be the missing Mihalyvich girl, he thought. He could see she had a rope round her wrist tethered to an adult woman. The projection beam changed from colors to white light, its spotlight making everything clearer. He became enraged at what he was seeing.

It did not matter if it was Mihalyvich's daughter or not. Whoever she was, she was somebody's daughter and in danger.

She wore a small wedding dress ten years before she was of age. A white dress over-laid with flowers. Her face was in full view of him. Her keeper took her forward to the front of the stage for the audience to take a closer look at her. He felt sick. Someone had painted her up as a harlot. Red lips, blushed cheeks; they had managed her hair. High up on her head, bouffant style, he could see it all, along with the audience participation. The Bloodhound and the Bull were becoming agitated. They were shouting and nudging each other; urged the girl's keeper to turn her round so that they could take in a better view of her. But not the two masked as a Clown and a Goat, they seemed to him spectators overseeing the event. A semi-circle of mirrors he had not noticed before showed the little girl multifaceted to infinity. Weinberg studied the girl for any noncompliance. There seemed not to be any. Any more than was distress. She was not smiling. Her face was without expression, it was as if she had been hypnotized, possibly drugged.

'That's the Mihalyvich girl,' Weinberg said turning to O'Hare. 'I'm convinced of it. And if it isn't, well, it's all the same to me.'

'Time for some *shillelaghing*. And none too soon.'

They went back down the way they had come. Weinberg, taking several stairs at a time, drew his gun and with no sense of formality shouldered the door to what he surmised must be the entrance to the auditorium. It stayed firmly shut as he bounced off it. He rubbed his shoulder. O'Hare shouted at him to stand aside.

Having the bigger frame of the two of them the Irishman launched himself sideways at it. It would have opened with half his force; he went through the doorway desperately trying to regain his balance. The masked audience, seeing him turned and panicked in different directions at once. Weinberg had them covered and fired a warning shot in the air over their heads. A second shot, when one looked as if he were about to make a run for it. He would have liked to put a bullet into each one of them where they stood. And, but for his professionalism, he would have.

O'Hare still trying to overcome his forward momentum further confused them as to where he would finish up. He crashed headlong into them scattering them as if they were nine-pins. Weinberg was waving his gun about for best advantage, but with O'Hare in the firing line, it was next to impossible.

The woman keeper seeing that an arrest was imminent took the opportunity to make good her escape. Dragging her charge after her, she went through one of the mirrors that opened as a door.

Weinberg fired once more, this time into the ceiling for order:

'Get your hands above your heads and stand still. You're all under arrest!'

They stood arms in the air. Weinberg could not help noticing that the Bloodhound was shaking. He guessed fear of identity. He kept them all covered looking sideways at what had happened to O'Hare. 'You all right over there, Sergeant?' he called across without taking his eyes off the Bloodhound. O'Hare was struggling with the Bull that had him round the neck trying to wrestle him to the floor.

'Right with you, Lieutenant,' he said, jamming his elbow into the man's ribcage before kicking him between the legs dropping him to the floor unconscious.

Weinberg smiled, snapping a pair of handcuffs on the wrist of the Bloodhound attaching them to the ironwork of one of the seats, nodded. 'Very good, Sergeant. And you! Stay put, or I'll put a bullet in yer knee-cap.' He turned his attention to what was happening to the girl, shouting out to the Ringmaster. 'How do I get to the other side of that mirror . . . *Barnum?*' The Ringmaster spat an answer, 'Find out for yourself . . . *Yid!*'

O'Hare guessing who it was that had insulted his lieutenant lost it. In a rage and with super-human strength, he ripped up one of the seats screwed to the wooden floor, held it over his head, hesitated, launched it into the mirror door where it exploded into a million slithers of silver. The Clown and the Goat standing with their arms over their heads dropped to their knees to protect themselves from the shards that were raining down round them. O'Hare leaping onto the stage intending to go through the remains of the door frame, but another explosion of glass stopped him; one he was not responsible this time. He put his arms up to protect his eyes as the second of the mirror doors collapsed. With his eyes partially covered, he made out the woman that was the girl's keeper come through, the tether once attached to her wrist dangled free. The woman's head contorted backwards at an angle snapped a vertebra. The vicious blow from Mihalyvich's fist into her face its obvious cause. She did a neat unplanned backward roll, ending up flat on the floor lifeless in front of O'Hare.

The Ringmaster, taking advantage of the diversion, jumped down from the stage to confront Weinberg. He struck his fist hard into the side of Weinberg's wrist sending the gun from his hand away across the floor. Weinberg tried to recover it. He ran forward and kicked him viciously in the side of his head sending him over between two rows of seats, stepping forward, pulled his own gun, turned, let go four rounds at Mihalyvich who was coming straight for him. Hitting him in the shoulder with his first shot, it spun him round so fast it reduced his target width to the point that the second and third bullet sailed harmlessly passed him before he fell stunned at his feet. He put the barrel to Mihalyvich's temple and squeezed the trigger.

O'Hare seeing this attempted *coup-de-grace*, jumped off the stage hit him hard across the throat with his forearm, knocking the gun from his hand sending that one across the floor. The Ringmaster recovered from the blow slowly lifting his head to face him. The face was no longer what it once was. He was altering his appearance in front of his eyes. At any other time an illusion, such as this would have been an impressive show stopper and he comfortable knowing it to be no more than a magic trick would not have been in fear of his life. But as it was, this ability of the Ringmaster to do this sent the fear of God through him. His natural reaction was to strike out at him, but the punch was feeble. The demon he had become (for that was O'Hare's later best description), with his black drape evening jacket torn at the back due to the increase in mass, easily took hold of O'Hare's clenched fist squeezing it as if a grape. O'Hare yelled out in pain as the demon lifted him off the ground. His arms and legs flailing in the air trying to make a connection with the demon's body were useless. The demon casually threw him across the auditorium as easily as if he were a dead cat instead of the Irishman, whose fighting mass was that of a mid-heavyweight boxer. He came down across a row of seats on his back with a sickening thump and like the dead cat, without a bounce, put his frame grotesquely out of alignment.

Weinberg seeing what had happened to his sergeant shouted out to him. Seeing the crookedness in his body that had fallen the way it had, he was not expecting an answer. With his spine likely broken, he looked like a rag doll picked apart, its seams all ripped open. If his sergeant was not dead, he figured it was only a matter of time before he was.

He wondered how a routine investigation could have gone so badly wrong. *Routine* – he mulled the word over. It was hardly that. He had deliberately disobeyed a directive from his superior by going after Giuseppi and not for any reasons apparent. They were paying the price for something altogether different. If he survived this, if it turned out that O'Hare had not suffered a fatality instead permanent disablement, the next best he could look forward to would be his dismissal from the force. He would have been responsible for the death on duty of a serving officer of a lower rank while under his orders. Whether the man had been a willing participant or not, his eyes being wide open to the consequence of his actions at the time would be no defense for himself. And Rivers would have got rid of the only officer showing him for what he was: a corrupt policeman in a position of authority in New York. A city that had too many.

The demon turned his attention toward Mihalyvich who was trying to get himself up off the floor. The pain from the bullet to his shoulder apparent. The demon put his foot on him and pushed his arching back down to the floor. He let out a pained, *Agggh* scream. Reaching behind him, Mihalyvich pulled a knife and struck out at the demon's leg with as much force as he could in this position of being face down on the floor. The point snapped making no impression on what should have passed for flesh. The demon leaned down snarling, taking hold of Mihalyvich's head, twisted it until his neck broke. A crack of bone, silence.

Irinushka Mihalyvich walked out onto the stage commanded a hush by all those still alive and conscious to see her. Standing with a backdrop of broken mirror glass, the small lonesome figure, confused and frightened, for this had been the first time in her young life that she had not had the love of her mother and father to protect and comfort her. She had not only seen her mother shot in the head, her understanding of Oona lying on the floor in their house unable to move, never to get up again would have been devastating. She had witnessed her father with his head hideously twisted by something that came from the pages of a fairy tale book her mother sometimes read to her, of a peasant and a demon. And this particular demon turned his attention toward her, and she heard someone shout at it, 'Leave her alone, you *filthy fucking bastard!*' She began shaking as it came for her and she wondered if he was going to eat her all up as giants and trolls do to little girls.

This pathetic child and all those that had gone before her at the hands of this *thing* and his filthy trade were all that Weinberg cared about. God alone knew what pit he was spawned. Wherever it was, he resolved to send him back if it was the last thing he did, 'Leave her be, I said!' The demon turned and faced him. With a presence of mind he never knew he had he leaped at its chest feeling the strength of its arms about him; knowing, ironically, he never had a chance in hell of taking it down. The demon threw him across the auditorium as easily as he had his Sergeant. He prepared his body for major injury knowing it was unlikely he would get away with it unscathed. Unlike his Sergeant's situation though, he was still right way up and conscious after landing alongside of him. Seeing O'Hare's gun, half out of his shoulder holster he took hold of it. With determination, he fearlessly walked toward the demon. It, for the moment, seemed to be figuring out what he was about to do gave Weinberg the thought in his head that it was no longer up for the fight. Getting as close as he could he fired off two rounds. The first went into its neck. Weinberg watched the projectile sink into his flesh as if in slow motion. The flesh round the bullet hole expanded, before closing round what should have been a fatal wound. But no blood. The second went into his head with equal uncertainty that it would kill him. It staggered backward, and he thought he had it. But it was not to be. With both wounds healing before his eyes, he sensed the game was up. Whatever this thing was, he was powerless against it and could only imagine his fate as he laughingly thought of the reference he had made earlier to O'Hare to shoot him up the arse if whoever were capable of tearing his head off had their hands round his neck. He looked back toward the girl to see if there was anything he could do to help her before he shook the hand of fate. She was standing over her father, and he could only watch as the demon ignoring him, turned on her putting his hands round her throat at the same time turning to face him as if performing an act of emotional torture against him before it was his turn. Hands invasive to her young flesh inspired him to make another bid to save her when an ear-splitting crack of thunder struck the air round him. The whole house shook from the ferocity that made Weinberg bring his arms up to protect himself from what he thought would be the certain collapse of the building. Crouching down two more thunder cracks came with such ferocity he expected to see the night sky where the roof had once prevented that.

At the far end of the auditorium, leaving the Goat and the Clown to fend for themselves, the Bull getting himself up from the floor made a move to escape. With O'Hare out of the way, he figured he would easily be able to take Weinberg down get the hell out of this place. He shouted at the Goat to follow him not noticing his predicament. With his wrists handcuffed to the seat stuck his foot out tripping him over before he could make the door they had come in, 'Get these things off of me first.'

The Bull took a bunch of keys from his pocket, inserted a regulation police skeleton into the restraint lock releasing them.

The Goat rubbed his wrist, cowered.

A spinning, screaming, vortex of fire burst out from the floor between the seats in front of them. The three end rows flew up into the air splintering before crashing back down disappearing into a crater that smoked before them. A woman came out to hover in front of the both of them, her hands together in prayer. Turning on an invisible axis away from them, settling her attention on the demon that still had its hands round the girl's throat, and threatening to throttle the life from her. The girl tried to scream but all that came out was a choke. The woman went in enveloping the demon in a pillar of blue force that poured out from the palms of her hands, shaping itself about his hideous body. The blue flickered and burnt away leaving him disorientated. Irinushka broke free and ran to her father who, was coming round, weakly getting up on his legs.

The Clown smiled inside his mask. The proof before his eyes of what the Order of the Most Divine Third Circle had been saying; waited two millennial; seeing it first hand, knowing it to be true; and that it would be possible to bring this about again would leap-frog man's knowledge beyond anything gone before making all other obsolete.

Weinberg hardly had time to draw breath. He removed his hands that were protecting his head intent on studying as rationally as he could what in hell was going on in this place. He was witnessing a paranormal event; one that Sugden had mentioned Dore had seen. This woman, whoever she was, appearing from nowhere was keeping Mihalyvich's daughter from the harm he and his Sergeant had failed so miserably. As far as arresting these perverts was concerned, that had become secondary to events that were taking place here. The demon collapsed. And Weinberg's thinking that what seemed to be an electric magnetic wave force bolted from the ends of her hands, through her fingers, had finished him off. Unfortunately, the lightning wave, that in ordinary circumstances should have felled a sequoia tree, had not entirely disabled him. Whatever magic that woman had conjured needed to be a lot more powerful than that. The demon broke free slowly rising to his feet screamed out.

A snarling spitting scream, a near sneer that came from a hideous mouth from an even more of an odious face and body. Its tongue, brown and long, was flicking in and out as a lizard. The impression was of body parts of plague victims freshly buried and exhumed after several months to have their identities checked out. Dr. Frankenstein would have been rubbing his hands together with glee if he'd built this thing, he thought. And not a stitch or bolt to be seen. He was drawing energy. A different energy from hers, that came by way of a wind with an ever-increasing power that caused the hair on her head to flow backwards and he was using it against her. She leaned forward against its strength until its violence increased to the point it lifted her from her feet. Tumbling backwards, out of control, she hit the wall opposite sliding down onto the floor. Unless either had something else in their armory they appeared to be a match. She shook herself and floated up into the air. Bending her head forward she flexed her neck muscles as if checking herself out. Apparently satisfied she held her arm forward directing the palm of her hand at him. Layers of white light with the intensity of burning magnesium wrapped itself round him. It was consuming him. Finally.

Frank had to turn away from the glare that was burning his eyes. He feared he might lose his sight if he continued looking. The demon with his hands positioned as if he still held the girl's throat between them was burning alive. His body was shriveling away, and it reminded him of the story of Dracula having a stake driven into his chest with a lump hammer. And like him would hopefully soon be dust blowing to the four winds. It surely would not be that easy. For a beautiful woman with long hair to turn up out of nowhere; putting an end to a demon's aspirations whatever they might be was not in his experience of crime and bad things happening the way of the world. With events turning he would not be wrong in that, for the heap of dust that had been the demon was re-forming into the loathsome creature it was. Obviously, fresh blood from a virgin had soaked into him somewhere down the line, revitalizing him, he thought. He wondered what he had planned for the woman, for he was clearly not going to lie down and disappear. But something else was going on. Another had entered the fray. The demon back off the floor, having escaped the winds and the metaphorical dustpan and hand brush, stood erect – if *erect* in the context for a heap of excrement was best description, with the scorch marks from the burns evaporating from its body it sensed this new arrival. The demon stopped and looked up. It worried. It had a duty to protect itself and that time had come. It melted away leaving the body of Giuseppi collapsed on the floor, his top-hat beside of him before he too evaporated away.

'It is come: *There shall no man see me and live . . .*' the Goat said under his breath smiling. 'We'll see about that, Lord. *In the* fucking *beginning* . . . ha! . . . Methinks you miscalculated. Your math is not up to this any longer.'

A paralysis came upon Frank that took him by surprise. As if what had occurred so far was not bizarre enough, he had something else to worry about, he could not move. His muscles had seized. His eyes moved but that was all. Surely, he thought, they had muscles. Whether anyone else was experiencing the same, with his limited field of vision, he could not tell. Not that he was particularly concerned about anyone else. With O'Hare dead no-one else mattered much. Except Irinushka.

It had occurred to him that he had hallucinated all of this. Now, he wishes he had. He had been frightened – *more* – scared. For some reason, the fear of what he had seen had left him. A hypnotic sense came over him, he wondered if death was imminent. God's gift to His chosen people that allowed Jews to depart the world without distress. If it was, it was all right with him. He hoped that O'Hare had felt the same before he died. A ridiculous idea. He was Catholic.

These thoughts, these meanderings; like those of a sick person, demented, continued as perspiration rolled off his forehead and down his face. Unable to mop his brow he could feel drips of sweat gathering at his chin. When what he could only describe as the clicking came, for best description it sounded as if planets were colliding coming unstuck (where had he got such a thought?), his head fell forward as the muscles tight with tension released allowed his body to relax unexpectedly. He was on the point of collapse when his brain kicked in sending thousands of messages a second to the appropriate parts that required the immediacy of attention for balance. He put his foot forward to stop himself from falling and looked at where he thought the sound was coming.

A weirdly strange form came through the auditorium fast. Two feet tall, black and white at the same time with a hood. It resembled a small monk from some medieval monastery. Goblin was too harsh a word for something that instilled both a mixed sense of well-being and terror into a soul in one throw. He tried to look at its face but all he saw was darkness. Straining his brain for an understanding of what it was he settled on Death minus scythe and hour glass. He immediately collapsed from what he later reckoned to be an insight into a world that no-one had any right to see, the overawing experience sent him into a white oblivion of nothingness. He expected at any moment to be standing at the entrance of a tunnel many others that had 'died' before spoke of. Seeing friends or relatives at the other end waving for them to come through. In his case, he did not have any that wanted him. Surrounded by an all-round white softness with a sound that was difficult to describe going on in his head. How long it went on, he could not tell. It was only when he became aware that someone was calling him back from the 'dead' did he begin to reason that this was not his time. He did not want to return but found he could not help himself. He reacted positively to a voice he heard by looking round. A curious idea came into his head that he recognized the person but could put neither name nor relationship to him. A man that resembled himself, like the ghost of an ancestor, or . . . more . . . a . . . *descendent?*

The Clown, having all the information he needed, shouted across to the Goat that it was time to make steps.

Sergeant Charlie O'Hare was in the process of re-birth. No longer lying out across a row of picture house seats, he became conscious and rolled off onto the floor fit and ready to carry on where he had been rudely interrupted in taking child abusers down.

The Goat and the Clown near a way out door, seeing him, the Goat shouted to the Bull, *Kill him! We can't afford to be taken! Kill him!* The Bull cursing the Bloodhound for tripping him got to his feet and pointed his gun at O'Hare; and was about to pull the trigger when O'Hare went for his own gun. His heart sank. His shoulder holster was empty. His mouth gaped open as the Bull laughed out. A shot rang out, it was the sound of his gun but in the hands of Weinberg, and although missing him, the Bull took a second opportunity to turn and run for the exit. He was gone. The Goat followed; the Clown was still running for the same door when O'Hare reacted with his strength fully restored:

'You're mixing it with the *Irish*,' O'Hare shouted after them. 'And *your* days are numbered, *Old Son*,' he shouted to the last man as he running rugby tackled him to the ground. The momentum taking both men on a journey sliding across the floor and into a wall. The Clown turned in O'Hare's direction shouted out to him:

'Let me go, Sergeant. *We're both on the same side!*'

O'Hare confused, looking back at Weinberg for some lead seeing his Lieutenant going into a fit before collapsing, '*Frank!*' With that and the man he had taken down with this surprise admission, he took his eye off the ball. The Clown kicked his foot back into O'Hare's head temporarily knocking him unconscious; was gone out the door.

Outside, the Clown, minus his mask, dropped a metal bar into the door slots locking it. 'What about that? Well we know the truth of it, but what the hell was Giuseppi thinking . . . ?' The Goat sat in alongside of him, removed his own disguise. 'Abducting Mihalyvich's daughter was asking for trouble. Weinberg was bound to come looking for her here. *And* for her father to turn up. Incredibly sad.' He turned the engine over, over again shaking his head as he did so. 'You better cover that door; in case someone smashes it through while I sort this thing out.' He got out and lifted the hood. He was not a mechanic, but he could see that the distributor cap was off, and that the rotor arm was missing. 'Great! I certainly underestimated that pair of clever *bastards*. Fuck Giuseppi and his personal vendettas.'

Neither man could afford to hang round to answer any awkward questions in spite of his letting the cat out of the bag for the second time that evening. First calling Mihalyvich's name out when he saw him coming through the mirror. And to say what he did to O'Hare about them being on the same side. A rather unfortunate admission, but it gave them the second they needed to make good their escape. He was going to have to leave his car where it was. Get someone to pick it up later. Like, in a year or so time, maybe. He was annoyed at the inconvenience those two detectives had caused him. Giuseppi should have taken more precautions where security was concerned. Fortunately, he had plans that would put things right on that score. They knew too much and the decision as to their futures, if they were to have any, was for others to decide. He slammed the hood lid shut and they both hurried away from the house.

'We know those other two guys?'

'Oh, yeh. And as witnesses to what's happened here, they are dead men.'

'And Weinberg and O'Hare?'

'Not our decision to call.'

'*Frank!* Can't you hear me? For God's sake, answer me. Lieutenant . . . I know you're alive, I can see your eyelids moving.'

O'Hare wondered if it was his nerves reacting giving the impression the man was still alive when he was in fact dead. Should he have shouted at him? It seemed irreverent given the circumstances. He decided that a volume change in his voice would be of no great disadvantage to the man's health one way or another.

'*Frank!*' he screamed once again this time shaking him. ' *Frank! It's all over!*'

Weinberg stirred. He opened his eyes and looked at him. '*Son?*'

'I'm flattered you should think so, Lieutenant, but Sarah has two weeks to go yet and any son on that score could turn out to be a daughter.'

'O'Hare! Is that you? Did you call me, "Frank"?'

'Yes, Lieutenant. Sorry about that. But never moind aboot moi state of health, what d'you thinks you're playing at frightening me like that and calling me son?'

O'Hare had a habit of disappearing into the vernacular when annoyance gave way to relief. He helped him to his feet, 'Feel as if I've had an attack of the heart. What about you? Your neck was broken—'

'I wouldn't go that far,' O'Hare said rubbing it. 'Bit on the stiff side, so it is, but that's all. Whatever gave you that impression?'

'Nothing.'

O'Hare looked at the devastation round them. 'Would you believe I dreamed what caused this you know? Leastways, I think it was a dream . . . where are you going, you should sit down and take things easy?' O'Hare said as he walked away from him.

He went across to the stage area, picking his way through broken glass and plaster. He was looking for something. Anything that would put flesh on the bones of what had occurred here. *An illusion?* He knew a broken neck when he saw one. He had seen one of those before. Not one that had fixed itself like his Sergeant had though. He saw a foot protruding from part of one of the mirror doors.

He pushed it aside. It swung away easily before dropping from its hinges onto the floor with a crash breaking what remained of its mirror. He startled. Irinushka's minder was on the floor in front of it, the cord still attached to her wrist. A loop at the other end free of the little soul. He turned her over with his foot and looked into her face. She had a fist mark to the side of her cheek. He guessed it was where Mihalyvich had hit her. He felt sick. He saw her exposed petty pants under her skirt that had ridden up. Saturated in fresh blood that was exuding from her he murmured, '*That's a gallon if it's a pint.*' He swallowed hard, '*You can do this.*' Feeling that he was about to faint, he took a deep breath looking closer at the shard. An icicle proudly standing up out from her inguinal region had done it for her. His forehead broke out in beads of sweat. He wiped it with the back of his hand. Blood was never the favorite part of his job, guessing that the object in question had probably severed the woman's femoral artery. He sucked his lips into his mouth and murmured to himself once more, '*My life, there's gotta be a better way to go than that . . .*'

'You all right, Lieutenant?'

He went to turn to O'Hare, but something caught his eye. Reflected in the piece of shard, of an indiscernible size, certainly no more than a quarter inch high, he thought he saw something vanishing into the wall opposite. He looked up but saw nothing. Wiping his eyes with a kerchief, he removed the bile residue that had built up in his mouth with what he had seen.

'Did you see a goblin go through that wall?'

Of a translucent white appearance, as that described in the Christian Bible (New Testament); an anathema to Judaism; the Book of Matthew, Weinberg, was once again at a crossroads. Not for the first time had he had doubts, not only of his own born faith; but also of all others. This experience, the fact of an appearance he supposed (and that he personally had witnessed, along with others), that fitted in with an event 2000 years before bearing similarities to that legend was convincing. Paranormal (in its religious connotation takes on pnormality when faith becomes a truth) or otherwise, to his mind, what they had witnessed was proof that something greater than man existed, which would be both a blessing and a curse, with the emphasis on the word, *Curse*.

Opinions from a faction had divided some of his own 'people' causing the birth of two 'children', Christianity and Islam, and with-it condemnation by them of their 'mother' since. The Jewish race carried the burden of blame for putting to death a 'Messiah' by the entire world, whether Christian or Muslim, whenever it suited, was wrong. He was not alone in shouldering that responsibility having suffered discrimination from an early age. Carried forward generation after generation the burning question was: if their Jewishness of 4000 years standing was not enough after what some had witnessed in the tomb of Arimathaea on that day, why should his? Antisemitism was a siren call to every lunatic in the world to discriminate and kill that followed in the belief they had God's blessing for the murder of His Son may or may not have been the reason for that conversion. He personally doubted it. Jewish–Christians facing wild animals and certain death in the Roman circuses stood their ground in acts of defiance of their new faith, showed otherwise.

He was Jewish from a Jewish mother and nothing would alter that, but Judaism being the exclusive faith of Jews was changing. (Questions of it being a religion rested on a contradiction that some Jews did not accept the doctrine of a Jewish religion; and those that are secular.) Some were beginning to question the stories in Genesis and Exodus – that of Moses being the writer of the Pentateuch. He could see a time when secular Judaism where Jesus is the Messiah was on the cards. A following of Messianic Jews that accept they can retain their Jewishness, yet believe He was the Messiah; and without going all the way with Christianity. The exclusivity of Judaism by Jews may well have to ride alongside other faiths and beliefs within their communities in a changing, questioning, and scientific world.

'*A goblin though?*'

Detective Lieutenant Frank Weinberg, the man, of the 7th Precinct, Lower East Side police department had a dilemma. A written report of events he and his Sergeant had witnessed was going to be difficult. If not impossible. An appearance on earth of a demon, an angel, and a hooded goblin; and whose side they were fighting for. Smoking mirrors. Certainly, a possibility. But how the hell could they explain the disappearance of a small Latino boy hanging from a rafter they had taken down dead from his injuries? Not to mention the disappearance of Fariq and his daughter.

With all that in mind, Weinberg sought the advice of a local man he knew. The son of a Rabbi of the Zion synagogue that he happened to attend (he wasn't lapsed, yet). Ehrich Weiss had been a cross country runner before a change of name and profession becoming a magician specializing in escapology. He had debunked stunts the like of those he and O'Hare had been witness to. Known as ethereal suspension, performed by Indian Fakirs and the like, it was impressive to watch. Except, according to Weiss was, 'No more than a platform hidden under the clothes of the performer supported by a metal rod disguised as a bamboo pole.'

So good so far. That had answered the first part of the equation. But how in *hell* does someone do that while moving three dimensionally before disappearing out through a solid wall, he had asked? Harry Houdini was impressed and said he would have a think about that one; and that he would get back to him when he had worked it out. To date, Houdini had not been in touch with either Weinberg or O'Hare. He died October 31, 1926 from acute peritonitis secondary to rupture of the appendix leaving his promised escape from death yet to materialize, and the solution to that illusion thus far, unanswered.

Five - 1920s

I

POLICE COMMISSIONER HARRY RIVERS massaged his ribs. He was sporting a substantial bruise from someone's elbow. He had mixed feelings for the man sitting opposite him; but he had caused him a major problem; something in other circumstances he could have him dismissed the force; but without an admission that he was in that place, at that time, he was stuck with him. Weinberg's report cited Marco Giuseppi for murder and child abduction. A crime, for the moment, he was in no position to come out in the open to investigate. As to any arrest of Giuseppi, well happily, that was out of his hands. Other reports previously written on Giuseppi's activities: altered, destroyed, or removed elsewhere. The eighteen murdered or missing children highlighted in those reports, chiefly by those of his predecessor, Dore, Rivers had been happy to write off knowing those reports would never be found. An alteration here or there put Giuseppi in the clear. He was sure he could convince the most persistent of inquisitor that with five thousand immigrants a year descending on Ellis Island. A missing child hardly amounted to a can of beans; nothing on the scale Weinberg was suggesting. He and O'Hare were two maverick detectives – incapable of obeying orders – taking the law into their own hands. When he had finished with them, they would be the laughing stock of New York's Police Department. As for any *Bureau* investigation, well, they can shove that where the sun don't shine and recommend the trouble-makers that instigated it be dismissed for insubordination. For himself, being an employee of the New York Police Department, he was not answerable to the Bureau, only its Justice Department.

Weinberg releasing Tony D'Sotto, after those injuries he had suffered in an attempt to get him to confess to the murder of Mihalyvich's wife had clearly shown he was innocent. As to who did murder Oona Mihalyvich, well, he would not be bringing in Giuseppi for questioning over that either. His instructions had been explicit. Marco Giuseppi would be untouchable when it came to any criminal investigation.

Her daughter (need to find out her name before any Bureau get here asking fool questions – I have a Christian duty), however, probably frightened by what was happening to her mother likely wandered off to seek help. That left the mysterious decapitation followed by the removal of the top of the head of one of Giuseppi's heavies. A Cosa Nostra hit perhaps. He shuddered at the thought. For the time being he would clear the air with Weinberg, see that they understood each other, and remind him that he was in line to be the next commissioner when he retired in two years (no chance of any recommendations on that score he thought). He would point out that they should relax in each other's company. Put past animosities behind them. Maybe involve himself in what he was about. Become part of the Weinberg and O'Hare legend that was fast becoming a no-nonsense crime-busting team. They had certainly gained respect among the run-of-the mill criminal fraternity in Manhattan's Lower East on that front that would do his reputation no harm at all.

II

Frank Weinberg had never hit it off with Rivers. He was a cop on the take who had made their job difficult. He hadn't minced his words when it came to telling him. He had been a constant source of frustration to both him and O'Hare over these abductions having it thrown in their faces whenever they arrested someone that Rivers would get them off if the money were right. Those that benefited from his generosity were not above admitting they had Rivers in their pockets, challenging the two policemen as to what they thought they could do about it. He smiled to himself. The thought of him and his Sergeant taking it in turns made him smile. To give one or the other of them a good shillelaghing, as O'Hare tended to delicately put it, 'To balance the books, so it does'. At least those that were paying Rivers off wore the sign of those that, 'Must have fallen down the stairs judge', a dodgy black eye badge – earned while the other had his back turned. Word soon got out, Harry Rivers might be on the take, but sure as hell, Weinberg and O'Hare were not, and what's more, were not of a mind to having the piss taken out of them for it. Not that Rivers was on the take with everyone, he was selective. Currently it was Giuseppi. Murder was bad enough, but the abuse and torture of children was something else. With the mysterious disappearance of the Latino boy, he had no hard evidence against Giuseppi, but if ever men needed hanging for such a crime, if it were the last thing he did, he would bring them to book. In the meantime, he would have to settle to see Rivers indicted with conspiracy to ignoring crimes of such magnitude right under his nose. He had not understood why he had been so reticent, a bit of bribery was one thing, but surely child abuse, when it comes out into the open would leave Rivers exposed to ignoring evidence of his officers. Could he be that stupid?

Like a persistent nightmare, he had kept coming back to that bust. A rainless storm, a white figure, and forks of blue flames. Had it all been a dream? Could he, a rational thinking cop believe the incontrovertible evidence in front of his own eyes? O'Hare, an Irish cop, hard drinking, hard fighting, just getting up from a snapped third vertebra like he had, as if nothing had happened to him. The report he submitted to Rivers had to have parts missing. He did not have a choice on that score. But he had written a true account that O'Hare was aware of. That would stay with them. Their reputations would have gone right out the window, along with their careers and pensions if they told what they had reported they had seen were to see the light of day. But it was how it was. O'Hare had asked him if he was sure he was doing the right thing. *What choice do I have?* he had answered him. O'Hare had misunderstood his personal motive for that as an answer.

'*Neither* of us, Lieutenant. Any more than a Catholic.'

III

'The department's got a bit of a dilemma, Frank. Nothing we can't deal with if we all pull together, I'm sure,' Rivers said. He looked into Weinberg's face for any signs of approval to continue, seeing none he went on. 'Frank, we know each other well enough to put the reputation of the force first before what we might think of each other.' He looked into his eyes this time. 'Fact is, there's a government inquiry into missing children; fact is, they're sending a couple of guys from the Bureau of Investigation down—'

'That's going to be a bit awkward, Commissioner. Dore's original files have gone missing.'

He ignored his comment, deciding to take it more as advice than criticism.

'Nothing I can't handle, Frank. But I would appreciate some assistance. Look let's cut to the chase. We agree we should have handled the Giuseppi involvement with Mihalyvich and his family better, I can see that, but it's water under the bridge, gotta move on.'

'That's rich, Commissioner. I told you what was going on and you did nothing about it. Nothing to do with water under any bridges, it was your lack of will to act against Giuseppi. Whatever you've got going on with Giuseppi . . .' He stopped himself continuing.

Rivers's face went red at his Lieutenant's accusations, but he wasn't going to comment on them further. 'You still had no authority to break into Giuseppi's house on the off chance that Mihalyvich's daughter was being held by him. And may I remind you, your report makes no mention that it was her. Only a girl with her mother.'

Frank's face remained expressionless. 'I said a woman. Her minder. I didn't say it was her mother. She had her tied to her with a cord for God's sake. Parading her in front of perverts for their gratification. And whether it was the Mihalyvich's daughter or not, she was still a minor in a dangerous situation needing our help.'

Rivers resumed a friendlier tone. 'Look, okay, fact of the matter is, if there has been any misunderstanding . . . well, what more can I say? As you know, I shall be retiring in a year, maybe less, if Mrs. Rivers has anything to do with it (he laughed), I won't have any trouble recommending you as my successor to the State Governor. Support me in this investigation and I'll promise you'll make commissioner in twelve months. What do you say, um?'

'Depends what you want in return, Commissioner.'

Rivers nodded. 'I see no reason for you to mention Marco Giuseppi in any of this in any more of a light than incidental. He was a man trying to run a union on behalf of the government. You didn't know what man he was, or that he were involved with anyone else politically. You can take it from me that he wasn't. As for washed-up children found in the Hudson, well, we are not the only precinct to have dead immigrants on our doorstep; the waters round Ellis Island are turning them up daily. Giuseppi is not responsible for that.' He nodded his head rapidly up and down as if to cement the statement as fact. '*What!*'

Weinberg's expression had changed, and Rivers saw the look of a man that recognized the rights of those less fortunate – niggers he shouldn't wonder. But he was a Jew, and it was that about him that had him worried. 'Look, okay, Frank. I've the same compassion as yourself, the point is . . .'

'The point is, Harry, you want me and Sergeant O'Hare to withhold vital information from the Bureau on a known pervert that's house was stuffed with enough evidence to leave no doubt to a blind man that he was interested in nothing more than allowing children to suffer for an audience – not their welfare.'

Rivers became incensed, he could see that he was going to get nowhere with this man.

'You're a typical Yid Frank. If you and your kind can't have any of the action, you don't want anyone else to have it. There'd be more trouble if the likes of Giuseppi didn't exist. Strikes, sabotage, communism getting a grip. There's a need for the Giuseppi's of this world whatever they get into.' He stared at him waiting for him to say something when he didn't he continued speaking calmly. 'I'm disappointed in you, Frank. I think you should take some leave while this investigation is taking place. In fact – I insist upon it.'

'And how are you going to explain that to the Bureau, Commissioner?'

'What, you taking some leave? Pressure. Your judgment's blown. You're taking unnecessary risks causing the department embarrassment. They won't have a problem with my explanation for your absence. I would have liked to have acted in a manner, *kosher*, isn't that what you say, but I shall have to act in another. With you out of the way, you won't be able to embarrass anybody. I'll put the case papers over to another officer. Now, get out of my office.' Rivers smiled in a satisfied manner as he got up to leave.

'Very neat, Harry.'

'I think so. You could have played ball, instead of which, well, *Barnes*.'

He barked out a name. Working in the office next to his, with only a glass pane between them the smartly uniformed young officer, hearing everything, came into his office. Weinberg knew him. Even encouraged him when he had first joined the department. An affable man that had shown potential for the straight and narrow until falling under the influence of Rivers's brand of police work, and who he had not altogether yet given up on.

'Yes, sir?'

'Lieutenant Weinberg is taking a holiday break. He is not well. Kindly escort him from the building and see that he doesn't collect anything from his office other than his personal belongings. And Barnes, he speaks to no-one.'

'Yes, sir.'

'Frank . . . I think your badge and revolver if you wouldn't mind.' He held his hand out to receive them.

Frank stood defiantly, looking as if he were about to strike him. Barnes restrained him. Rivers told him to release him.

'Go on Lieutenant, hit me if you dare.'

Frank pulled himself from Barnes' grip and thought there might be a better way out of this situation than cracking his Commissioner in the face, though offhand, he could not immediately bring one to mind. He placed his badge and gun on Rivers's desk. In one last act of defiance, he leant forward across to Rivers to frighten him. Barnes stepped forward to protect his boss.

'Sorry, Lieutenant. This way please.'

Frank looked back at Rivers. 'One small thing, Harry . . .' Rivers ignored him not bothering to reply. Instead, going through an act of arranging some paperwork on his desk. 'It was me that informed the Bureau.'

'Police Commissioner Rivers, how do you do? I'm Agent Johnson and my colleague here, Agent Sullivan. We've come to speak to you on a matter of missing children, may we sit down?'

Rivers released his hand from Johnson's greeting and saying nothing gestured them to the two chairs that he had put out for them. Johnson seated himself. Sullivan remained standing. He smiled awkwardly. 'Certainly, I'll help you all I can, but I think you're on a wild turkey chase. Can I get you a coffee, Mr. Johnson?'

'That's fine.'

'And you Mr. Sullivan?'

Sullivan was preoccupied looking first at the ceiling, the walls, before settling his eyes on a filing cabinet. On the top was a photographic portrait of the Commissioner in full dress uniform. Seeing him looking at it, Rivers felt slightly embarrassed at his display of vanity and wished he had taken it down before their arrival. Johnson pulled open a leather case and without looking up said:

'Agent Sullivan doesn't take coffee.'

Rivers was not used to someone walking round his office while engaged in conversation. It unnerved him. Perhaps that is what they intended. He sat and gathered himself together. Johnson pulled a sheath of paper from his brief case and started to read it. Rivers shuffled uneasily in his chair; the silence seemed to go on forever. He was in no particular hurry. 'It's Agent Johnson, Police Commissioner.'

Rivers felt his face glow red. 'Yes, of course, I'm sorry. *Agent* Johnson.'

The agent continued reading.

'Going back to why you are both here I can assure you that investigations into missing children have been fully investigated to the best of the department's abilities given the lack of proper records from the Department of Immigration.'

'A word on that, Commissioner,' Johnson said stirring his coffee with a pencil sipping the end of it. 'I should remind you that this is a government inquiry. We are looking into not only child abduction, but also this precinct and your ability as a police commissioner to carry out a full and proper investigation into certain cases. As to the recording of information from the people involved with records at Ellis Island, we've found those to be of a most immaculate order, as befits a government department of the United States of America. Pass the sugar, please.'

Rivers was dumbfounded. He felt that he was showing signs of nervousness at this extraordinary exhibition of interview tactics that were firmly closing doors before they moved on. His original preconception of these people being failed police officers pushed to one side was to say the least, awry. These were professionals through and through. If he were to come out of this with his career intact, he was going to have to keep his guard up and keep his cool. 'Of course I was not suggesting—'

Johnson looked up from the report interrupting him. 'I shall need in the course of these inquiries to speak to officers Weinberg and O'Hare. Would you make them available to me?'

Rivers felt he was beginning to show that he might have something to hide. He wished he had not been so hasty over Weinberg. 'I'm afraid that won't be possible, Agent Johnson. Lieutenant Weinberg is on leave.'

Agent Johnson continued reading, then looking up said, 'Nevertheless.'

Rivers had had enough of this and felt the need to put his own stamp on proceedings. 'I've been conducting my own inquiries, Agent Johnson, and it's my considered opinion that Lieutenant Weinberg was not one of those officers that you would cite as an example of someone with good governance you seem to hold so dearly. A government department, whether it's law enforcement or keeping records of immigrants, are one and the same as far as I'm concerned, and the record will show that I uphold those same principles as yourself. I cannot say the same for Weinberg or my predecessor, Commissioner Dore. Both men seem to have treated paperwork and evidence as something ephemeral. Much like the Department for Immigration.' He hoped that this would be enough to satisfy the man.

'Your comments have been noted, Commissioner.'

Sullivan in what might have been a well-rehearsed double act with his partner interrupted from deep inside one of Rivers's filing cabinets.

'Still, Weinberg and his sergeant must be made available to us.'

Before he could gather himself together to answer the man, Johnson interrupted.

'Who have you got for the abduction of Mihalyvich's daughter and the murder of his wife, Oona?'

Rivers had never heard of Mihalyvich's wife by name before and had to ask him to repeat it.

'Oh yes, of course.' He moved a folder on his desk uncovering a piece of paper with a name he had written earlier. 'Here it is, Irinushka's mother,' he said glad he'd found out her name. 'Why, I've nobody, not since – inquiries were to begin afresh after Tony D'Sotto, Marco Giuseppi's partner, was allowed to return to Italy; with Lieutenant Weinberg's recommendation I hasten to add, not mine. He reckoned he wasn't the suspect and that it was a guy named Kurt Runfeldt that done it. I personally wouldn't have D'Sotto released. But it was Weinberg's case, and he was.'

Again, the agent was engrossed in the report, this time referring to it.

'Why did you then? You're commissioner. You have rank authority. Never mind. It says . . . that over the years, there have been numerous cases of missing children. This report alone mentions nine. Can you explain that to me, Commissioner?'

Rivers shrugged, 'Immigrants in the main. Look, there have

been 200-odd thousand people through Ellis Island this year alone. I've said this before. Children get separated from their parents from time to time. They wander off. Abandoned by parents without means to feed them. Nine missing children is no great surprise to me, records by the Immigration don't account for numbers that small.'

'Well, again, I will disagree with you on that point, the case for government records being immaculate; we'll leave for another time. However, it does go on to say that, the parents in at least five of those cases did report their children missing. They said they had no satisfactory response by the police. How do you answer that Commissioner?'

'Well I wouldn't have known that; my predecessor was in charge. Commissioner Dore must have had his reasons, I guess.'

'We'll come back to that at a later date, Commissioner. Were you aware that Lieutenant Weinberg and Sergeant O'Hare visited the premises belonging to . . . Marco Giuseppi as part of their inquiries into the abduction of the Mihalyvich girl? Were you aware of their intent to do that?'

'*No, I was not!* That's another one of Lieutenant Weinberg's procedural problems. Insubordination. Going his own way. He and O'Hare are good at disobeying orders.' The room echoed his words. He felt he had shown his true feelings against the two detectives.

Johnson, with the hint of a smile asked, 'Even though he might have good reason to believe that Mihalyvich's daughter was being held. Strange to me that he never mentioned that to you. Or had he? Can you think of a reason why that should be so – was it perhaps you would not have sanctioned such an inquiry because of your, um hum, business involvement with Giuseppi? Your involvement with the man that Weinberg had his suspicions. None of them savory. All seemingly involved with the man you are protecting.'

'That's a preposterous accusation, Agent Johnson. It's as I said.

Weinberg always went his own way when it came to police work. He and his sergeant were both as bad as each other. Why should I have trusted him on this one? His reasons must be his own. Ask him.'

'Except he is not here, is he!' Agent Sullivan piped up.

To Rivers's annoyance, Johnson again looked down at the report. He felt he had acquitted himself well enough in answering their questions thus far, what was he looking for? The worry for him was, were they about to ask what his business dealings with Giuseppi were? But that wasn't Sullivan's next question.

'What are your personal views on the sexual interference of children, Commissioner?'

His face went red. 'What damned fool question is that, I don't understand, you've as well to ask me my views on crime?'

'Nevertheless.'

He stammered an answer. His annoyance was plain. He made no comment.

'Sexual interference of children is a crime. There are views on that question and there are specifics, Commissioner. Agent Sullivan's question is straight forward enough. Have you a view on the sexual abuse of immigrant children? In other words, do you differentiate between them and children of the populace that are American nationals born and bred?' Johnson followed up.

'*What!* It's against the law . . . look, I fail to see what these fool questions have to do with me, child interference, I've no experience of, immigrant or otherwise. I find your line of questioning abhorrent.'

'We have firm evidence to the contrary, but, forget the law, what is your moral standing on the issue?' Sullivan asked angrily.

'What firm evidence? I'm not going to answer that.'

'With evidence pointing in the direction that you condoned it by allowing others to engage in its activity.'

'I say again, *what* evidence?'

'Marco Giuseppi,' Sullivan replied. 'You appear to be profiting from your relationship with that man by turning a blind eye to his activities for financial reward.'

Rivers got up from his desk, went to his filing cabinet, opening it. Rifling through the contents he produced a sheet of typed foolscap, slammed the drawer shut and went to the other side of his desk. He sat down and placed it in front of Johnson with an attitude of self-satisfaction.

'I'm not about to demean myself by answering that question. Read that though. The report on the Mihalyvich enquiry carried out by Weinberg. Tell me anything in that document that refers to my profiting from the sexual interference of children.'

Johnson took it up. He pulled a similar typescript from a brown folder in his attache case. 'This is a copy of that same report, Commissioner. Allow me a minute to digest it.' Reading through it, he came to the signatures of Weinberg and O'Hare. Rivers was right it made no mention of any sexual interference of children that gave Rivers any financial reward. 'Who typed this report?' Johnson asked holding the type written sheet of paper to the light.

'Lieutenant Weinberg.'

'Himself?'

'Far as I know – yeh.'

'Is that usual?'

'It's not unusual. He types. Saves time waiting for one of the office juniors getting round to it. Why the interest?'

Sullivan leant over and took the copy from Johnson. Placing one sheet over the other Sullivan held the two sheets to a window pane.

Rivers was nervous. 'What're you doing?'

'Top paragraphs match. The remainder do not,' Sullivan said.

'Well, Commissioner. It appears the copy you have differs from that of ours,' Johnson said. 'Have you an explanation for that?'

'That's not possible.'

'I'm afraid it is. You see Weinberg's report on the activities of Giuseppi in the abduction and selling of immigrant children for sex along with the abduction of Mihalyvich's daughter are not in the copy of that report. Neither are events running up to that abduction. Nor any of Mihalyvich's involvement that led to it. But it does in this one.'

'If it's the same report why doesn't mine say the same? And what would Mihalyvich have to do with any of this?'

'Revenge – plain and simple. Mihalyvich had got himself involved in trying to prevent Giuseppi's wage scam at the dockyard. He paid them back in the old tried tested ways using terror and harassment,' Johnson replied.

'It's the same report all right,' Sullivan said still looking through the two sheets. 'However, this top one's been tampered with if I'm any judge. Granted typed on the same machine, an Oliver Visible. A standard government office issue. A Model Seven Downstrike by the look of it.'

'That's ridiculous. One typewriter's the same as another. That report could have come off any machine.'

'No it could not,' Sullivan interrupted. 'They are not all the same. Typewriters have their own identities. Each character, each space, has a slight misalignment of their characters. These two reports came off the same machine. Lieutenant Weinberg's typewriter, the lower paragraphs in this one have been altered, and I bet a year's salary if we dig deep enough in your records we'll find other reports, from your predecessor, Commissioner Dore, altered in the same manner.'

Rivers stared at the two men before him. They were right. He had one more trick up his sleeve.

'Gentlemen . . . I have considered this revelation of yours regarding typewriters. As far as I'm aware, your speculation of the peculiarities of one machine over another is just that, not science admissible in court. It is untested. Not evidence against me by a couple of flatfeet that are not engineers. I think the Oliver Visible Typewriter Company might have something to say over your slanderous accusations. That they are not capable of manufacturing a product with consistency.'

'Well, of course, you are absolutely right. However, Oliver has recognized such differences in their machines. And it does not in any way detract from the quality of their product any more than one Ford motor car differs from another, would affect theirs. We will of course bring in experts from Oliver who will confirm what I'm saying should it become necessary,' Sullivan replied.

Rivers shook his head in resignation.

'However, before you say anything further; and in your own interest; I advise you to seek out a lawyer. In the meantime, it is my duty to relieve you of your, and, pending . . .'

Johnson held up his hand to stay a protest from Rivers.

'. . . further inquiries and investigations into these matters. I am arresting you for the abduction of children for sale in the sex trade, further, conspiracy to alter official reports to hide those crimes; and also for your own protection.'

Rivers burst like a boiled container of water.

'You can't do that . . . I protest . . . I'm not employed by you, you do not have that authority, and what's with this protection. By you? From you? Apart from that,' he leaned forward speaking quietly; 'and this is confidential. I am under instructions from my own people not to involve this department with Marco Giuseppi and any of his business activities.'

'We do know about that; however, I recommend that you contact your lawyer. I am relieving you of your duty as Commissioner-of-Police of New York.'

'I repeat, on whose authority.'

'On the authority of the President of the United States of America, Mr. Woodrow Wyatt. You can go quietly, say you're sick, make whatever excuse you like. We've no interest in embarrassing you as you leave the building,' Agent Johnson said.

Rivers sank back into his chair. He was trying to think that Johnson must be wrong. That he did not have the authority to do this to him; that procedures for such eventualities were not as simple as Johnson had suggested. So this was how the Bureau of Investigation worked. He tried his last card, quietly and assuredly.

'Your conduct and intrusive manner will be the subject of an official complaint by me, in the meantime, if I'm forced to accept what you are telling me, fact is, I've first to put my house in order, speak with my own people as to who will temporarily take over and—'

'That will not be necessary, Commissioner. You will not go to prison. We're not that heartless. You are to be constrained under house arrest until your trial. Let's go.'

He stammered. His voice had lost connection to his brain. 'But this is completely irregular, the department cannot run itself.'

'Absolutely right, Commissioner. I wouldn't presume that the Precinct ran itself, and you are as good as the next man in that regard – that's why, my orders are to take the reins from you. I am that next man,' Sullivan said with the confidence of someone that could do the job standing on his head.

Opening a drawer in his desk, he took out a bottle of gin and a glass, poured a large measure and sat down. He picked up his phone and dialed out. A woman answered.

'Afternoon, this is Harry Rivers, Police Commissioner. I need to speak with Art Ambrose as a matter of urgency.'

'Hold the line, Commissioner; I'll see if he's available.'

'*Hold the line!* Didn't you hear me say who I am?' He was beginning to have difficulty holding himself together. With his breathing laboring, he wondered whether they heard his gasps at the other end of the line. A man answered.

'Harry, how are you? Long time, no hear.'

The voice was hesitant, as if he were embarrassed to be speaking with him. 'Art, we need to speak – *urgently!*'

Arthur Ambrose had had a telephone call from the Bureau telling him that his client was under arrest and that he was to expect a call from him. They had spelled it out for him, an indictment of abuse of power in a public office. Ambrose knew instinctively by the way they spoke he was beat before he had started. Personally, and although a client, he had never particularly liked Harry Rivers, far too cock-sure of himself. He had always acted as if the department was his own personal fiefdom; he had heard the rumours of his running with the hound and the hare; but of course, client confidentiality and all that, he had kept it to himself. He was his lawyer more out of family obligation than choice. Family that was a joke. His wife! My sister! With her, you never needed any other business; the pair of them would keep you going till you knew the constitution inside out. Little wonder that there were so many amendments to it. Still, it had made him a wealthy man for as long as it lasted. By the sound of it, that was all about to end. The gravy train was leaving the station, he thought to himself. He would be done with his brother-in-law for good and all. 'What's this all about, Harry?'

Rivers's voice was heavy and cracking. 'You haven't heard? It'll be all over the city by day break.'

Art Ambrose played dumb. 'What are you talking about, Harry? You sound terrible. Whatever's the problem?'

'I'm suspended. That's the problem.'

'*Suspended!* he said feigning surprise. 'You're Commissioner; they can't do that to you.'

'Look, Art. I can't talk here. Needs to be face to face. Urgent like.'

'Busy Harry. There's Fishman, one of our associates, good boy, he'll take care of you. Sorry can't do anything personally, handling city litigation with the Railroad Company. Did I say litigation? Writs falling like confetti. You know what they're like. Anyway, Fishman. As I said, good Jewish boy. Shall I get him to call you?'

'No. I said it's got to be you. You'll have to come here, I can't, I'm under house arrest.'

Blast the man, Ambrose thought. If it hadn't been for him being who he was, he would have disowned him years since. 'Okay, Harry. If it's like you say, I'll be right over.'

Ambrose stared at his receiver, shrugged, then replaced it. If the Bureau of Investigation were on his case, he couldn't afford to be seen involved with someone protecting a child abuser. Too many important clients on his books for that. In fact, had he had anything to do with it he wouldn't have given him the satisfaction of thinking that he was any more than his brother-in-law leaving business out of their relationship altogether. However, she is my sister. If they kick him out, he'll have to live on half pension and the immoral earnings of her brothels, and they would have to live with the world knowing that; and himself by association. A police commissioner that had been upholding law and order for New York being corrupt would have difficulty finding anyone to defend him.

'A *fooking* dream come true, so it does. Only wish that Dore had been round to see it. Still he'd be laughing, he was sure of that, wherever he is, *dear boy,*' O'Hare said to himself remembering his catch-phrase of endearment.

O'Hare assured Weinberg it wasn't he. Going on to say he'd never heard of the Bureau of Investigation before any of this, which left Weinberg with a dilemma. He was winding Rivers up when he said he had informed on him. Still, a photograph some kind staff member had posted on the notice board of the Commissioner wearing his dress uniform with the words, RELIEVED OF DUTY typed under showed that his popularity must have been un-unanimous. As for the Bureau agents themselves, they certainly hadn't messed around, he thought. They must have been sure of themselves, but *where* had they got their information? As if they wanted rid of him. And they want to speak to us. Not role models in the world of law and order. Rivers had been right about them in one respect. Playing by the book had not been their forte. He laughed to himself at the thought of him and O'Hare sitting inside Coleman's Pledge the pawnbrokers one evening. A tip-off that its front window, with its display of jewelry, had come to the attention of a local smash-and-grab merchant by the name of Jack-the-Cat put them on its stake-out. O'Hare was getting cramp sitting in the shop (hardly surprising after being in the same position for three hours). Standing up, after deciding to relieve himself, he found the first thing to hand to piss in. A collapsible opera hat. That same moment, the man in question, let go half a house brick through the front window. If O'Hare hadn't been wearing his derby bowler that night his injuries would have been a lot worse. The look on Jack's face when he reached in to snatch a tray of gems was a sight to behold. O'Hare, hat dented and askew, trying to stifle his dick from pissing any further down his trousers, at the same time trying to stuff it back into his pants, splashing the inside of his leg in the process, 'Oh, *fook-it*,' he had said. His face took on a deep ruddy complexion whenever he lost his dignity. With his pants, still half up he grabbed Jack's wrist snapping handcuffs onto them, while Jack seeing something hanging from his trousers called him a 'dirty bastard'.

Jack-the-Cat. A technician in the world of cat burglary where he acquired his name and reputation had fallen three floors from a window ledge trying to get into Webster the Jeweler without coming in the front door. Sustaining both multiple broken bones and terminal vertigo, he had turned his hand to doing odd jobs for a living, such as throwing bricks through shop windows. He had already that week had a run-in with O'Hare over some spilt beer in a local bar. Standing in a pool of O'Hare's piss, he now saw his life play out before him.

'What's funny?'

Weinberg brought a degree of seriousness to his face. 'Just thinking, Charlie. Bureau's suspended Rivers, they want to speak to us. So, if it was you that called them in, better to tell me.'

'Like I told you, I've only ever heard of them in passing. Anyway, what've we done?'

Frank gave him an old-fashioned look as if to say, 'Don't come the innocent with me; you know the way we operate.'

O'Hare got it.

'In this instance, the girl had to come first. On this occasion, you were acting under my orders. I'll see you're in the clear. I'll say this much though, I don't think you'll be able to fob them off with any of your Irish baloney. Not these people. They're too cute for that.'

'Do I want to?'

'The way they've dealt with Rivers suggests to me if they didn't know anything about us, they'd have certainly done their homework since.'

'Well, you've been onto Rivers for a proper investigation of Giuseppi for long enough. It's not as if you've ignored anything,' O'Hare said.

'When he spoke to me in his office telling me that Giuseppi had immunity, he may well have been right in his understanding.'

Perhaps they had arrested him, O'Hare thought. Since finding Mihalyvich and his daughter alive. If Rivers had been right about Giuseppi having immunity from prosecution, perhaps the powers that be had had a change of heart. In that, he would not have gone down quietly, taking God alone knows who else with him. 'As I said at the time, I would have had the same trouble trying to arrest priests in Ireland for similar offenses, such was Vatican hierarchy. Much the same here by the sound of it, until now.'

Frank nodded. The telephone rang. 'Come on, whatever, we're wanted.'

A sober looking man beckoned them to come in. They both looked round Rivers's office. Stripped of its wallpaper all that remained was bare painted plaster. Filing cabinets that had once lined the walls emptied, their contents packed into cardboard containers piled next to them. The cabinets themselves dismantled. The panels propped against the wall. The carpet, rolled up neatly and tied, was in the corridor outside. All that remained was the photograph of the Commissioner in full dress uniform standing proudly at his inauguration. The backing card removed from the frame surround was lying on the remains of a filing cabinet. O'Hare closed the door behind them. With the change in air pressure, what remained of the photograph fell onto the floor shattering the glass. All three of them looked round. Seeing what it was no-one bothered to pick it up. The other man, seated, spoke without introduction:

'No doubt word has reached you that Commissioner Rivers has been arrested. Please sit yourselves down gentlemen.'

'What charge?' Weinberg asked eager to know if his assessment was right.

'I cannot say at this stage. However, I can tell you that Mr. Woodrow Wyatt is not happy about the situation and is seeking new order in crime and morality and has appointed a . . . Mr. J. Edgar Hoover to bring on those changes. Mr. Hoover has been given an edict to rout out what the President has called "the unacceptable forces of evil that are pervading American society".' Agent Johnson looked from one to the other of them before continuing. 'In particular, the safety and protection of children, both nationals and immigrants. In that, the Bureau is pleased with the manner that you two gentlemen have carried out your duties in the matter of the Mihalyvich family.'

O'Hare could not believe what he was hearing; and was about to make a comment when Weinberg interrupted saying that he was mindful of their acting on their own behalf, adding that he knew they hadn't especially gone out of their way to help the family, and were surprised that it had reached the ears of any higher authority.

Johnson continued as if he hadn't heard Weinberg's remark.

'You disregarded the specific order not to harass Marco Giuseppi knowing that you could both have been disciplined for insubordination. Probably with a reduced rank, if not your jobs being on the line, and no, Hoover wasn't necessarily looking at the Mihalyvich case, but in the more general moral decline of the nation. You two officers, without knowledge that you had come to the attention of a "higher authority", have been courageous in standing up against that decline, especially where immigrants are concerned; where consensus is that they are not worth bothering with. *Gentlemen*—'

To Weinberg's surprise Johnson stood up and held out his hand to first him and O'Hare. Shaking them soundly, he said that it had been a pleasure and relief that a line in the sand was drawn and that others had better recognize it for what it was. O'Hare's face took on his ruddy Irish complexion. Not out of anger this time, but embarrassment. He sheepishly smiled. Weinberg kept a straight face, not sure of what he was hearing and whether perhaps there was some ulterior motive in Johnson's praise of them. He wasn't wrong. Johnson bade them resume their seats, which they had half raised themselves from in the invitation to have their hands shaken.

'We understand that you've both a reputation for physical fighting.'

O'Hare stared at Weinberg with a look that said, *What's coming now?*

'Well let me tell you gentlemen. That is not the way the Bureau of Investigation conducts itself and I make no apologies for your having to leave New York's Police Department.'

Weinberg was horrified. Dismissal was theirs after all. Given their marching orders after that bull-shit Johnson had come out with. He stood up and demanded to know what game he thought he was playing at, talking morals one minute, dismissing them the next.

'Lieutenant, excuse me, I haven't finished yet.' Weinberg sat back down. 'Both of your positions within the department have to end for your own safety and that of your family's, believe me it's too dangerous for either of you to remain. You have inadvertently acquired too many enemies.' He held up his hand to O'Hare's attempted protestation. 'Listen.' He waited until he had their attention. 'Right. We need people of your grit and determination. Your attitude to crime against minors is sadly lacking. We have no intention of letting you go.' He waited for them to catch up with what he had been saying before continuing. 'Will you think about coming on board with the Bureau? I know it's a bit of a step, but I shall need a decision by tomorrow morning.' Johnson smiled and got to his feet. 'If you'll excuse me now, I've work to do.'

'Of course, thank you,' Weinberg said relieved at this as an outcome.

'Yes, yes. Thank you,' O'Hare added holding out his hand for him to shake it once more. He didn't take it and he couldn't help noticing that Johnson had the hint of a grin and a boxer's nose about him despite his no-fighting talk.

They were halfway down the corridor when a shout came from the office they had left.

'*Lieutenant!* A minute of your time, please.'

'See you outside, Charlie.'

Frank returned to River's old office. Johnson was holding an open palm toward him, 'Between you and me. You can return the rotor arm you removed from my Duesenberg now.'

Rivers saw the woman was moving swiftly toward him. At first she had skin on her head, but it was melting away revealing a skull with long flowing whispery hair. She closed in on him shouting, *Boooo!* in his face. He awoke with a start. His heart was thumping, and his breathing was erratic. He leaned over and looked at his fob watch. 3 am. He massaged the area he thought his heart was taking a sip of water he had by his bedside. The dream was the cause of his waking. He got out of bed and went to the window. Magpies. Their hard chattering, their squabbling, echoing across the lawn surrounding his house. His adrenal glands working overtime were increasing his stress.

Not having been well for some time, and this business with the Bureau, well, he thought, it was not helping. Heart-stroke his doctor had called it advising him to eat more meat and rest. Fat chance. However had he got himself involved in all of this? Well, it was all too late. His career was in ruin. He could see the following day's headlines. New York's Commissioner-of-Police arrested on corruption charges. The newspapers would tear him apart. This was not the first time they had looked into he and his wife's affairs. They would add trafficking of children to what else they had on him. The Cosa Nostra appalled at what he was doing, were nevertheless reluctant to do anything about what they regarded as free enterprise. Meetings arranged as to whether they should get involved never got off the ground, they didn't have the stomach for such depravity. The heat was on them from the government and Internal Revenue, they were not about to look for crime they didn't have any knowledge of that would lead to their excommunication from the Roman Catholic Church. Apart from that, Cuba beckoned as the new natural choice for alcohol and drug smuggling.

None of this was his concern. Something had woken those birds. Whatever had done that was in the grounds of his house. The house for which he had sold so much of his soul had been for he and Connie to enjoy. The sound he heard outside was the snapping of tree branches. He had experience of thieves trying to break in and that was the first give away signal. The white horizontal timber planked building with its clump of chimneys brought together in the middle of its steep gabled roof showed wealth to any two-bit chancer to break in. The diamond-paned windows were difficult for him to see through properly. Even so, he could hear, someone was out there. He stared out, his eyes straining to see beyond the reflection of the moon showing imperfections in the glass. His eyes accustomed to the darkness, picked out the familiar landscape of the grounds and the gravel drive approach. He could see nothing, though the sound of cracking continued to worry him. Sounds that would not give way in the imagination – leaving him to face them alone.

Connie Rivers had left her husband to visit her family attorney in Miami. She was aiming to get into her name as much as possible of the assets her fool of a husband had accumulated and that they were about to lose. She had her head screwed on in such matters. She came from a family that's background lived by the family motto, *Keep Ill-Gotten By Whatever Means*. She had every intention of living up to that legend. Her husband no longer counted in the game and she was planning to leave him to his own devices.

Rivers had lost the feeling in his upper body. He crawled back onto the bed, managing to drag the counterpane over himself. Lying on the bed with his eyes closed he tried to get his breath back. When he opened them, he noticed that his left eye had gone out of focus. Was he having an attack of the heart? A reason his eye might be out of focus. Whilst in the past he was more than capable of dealing with intruders, he was not so sure now. He was finding it difficult to move. He reached for the gun he had hidden in a slit hole in one of the bed supports. Johnson didn't know about that when they had put him under house arrest. The magpies ceased their chattering. Was that a good sign? Or were they waiting for something to occur?

Gathering his wits together, he reached across for his telephone on his bedside table. He removed the stem from the cradle, dialed, and listened for a response.

'How can I help you, Commissioner?' the voice said.

That wasn't his doctor. 'What the devil are you doing in my house?'

'Bureau of Investigation, Agent Sullivan. Don't you remember, Commissioner? We're here to protect you—'

'Great, I ring for my doctor, and what do I get? A *wanker* on the other end of the line. And *protect me* – protect me from what? I don't need protection from shite hawks, I want a doctor.'

'No need to get personal, Commissioner. What's the problem?'

'Get off my phone, Sullivan. You're no medic.'

'Give me his number, Commissioner. I'll get him for you.'

'What am I, a prisoner in my own house? I'm more than capable of dealing with my own affairs . . . hello, hello, Sullivan. Where the *fuck*'s he gone now.'

The telephone slipped from his fingers. The effort from his conversation had exhausted him. On the plus side the confrontation with Sullivan had driven away the fear of what was going on outside from his mind. He felt a sense of relief the way he had handled the man in the way he had. He got angry again. They had no respect for rank. Perhaps the way he was feeling was because they had drugged him. Some muscle paralyzing substance. While he was out of it, using the opportunity to search his house for evidence. He laughed to himself. Did they imagine that someone like him was stupid enough to leave things hanging round, he thought. They would find nothing on him here. And if they were looking for more evidence against him, it could only mean they didn't have enough, which made him feel a whole lot better.

A dying bird, its chattering began and as quickly subsided. An act of subterfuge. Was it all trickery on Giuseppi's part? Rivers had seen it all. As others. A snap of a branch was in his head. A shudder of fear tingled down his spine. When ones worst nightmare sees the light of day; when a creature of darkness has a backdrop of darkness; when hauntings become reality: all come unseen. A blinding flash of light across his eyes came. A slow painful snap of several vertebrae. His new found immortality not able to save him. He did not hear or see anything ever again; and an echo-roll of thunder crossed a black sky.

Six – 1920s

FRANK LOOKED AROUND as the door opened. O'Hare coming in; coming upon the scene; placing his hand to his mouth said, '*Christ!*' As if to change the subject to something more palatable to the scene confronting him added, 'Where did all those dead birds come from? Looks like a whole rookery has gone down with sudden death syndrome out there.'

The police surgeon was attending the crime. A coffee-trolley that he was using as a makeshift postmortem table alongside the bed, partially covered in a bloody white sheet, displayed the grisly tools of his profession. For the sake of prudence, the surgeon was doing his best not to allow too much of the scene to be exposed to his audience. It was bad enough that a section of the man's trachea displayed in a pool of phlegm shot through with nodules of hardened blood – black, he guessed from smoking – displayed in a kidney dish; from the look on Sergeant O'Hare's face, and showing the evidence at the same time was always going to be difficult.

To O'Hare, the surgeon's scalpel left to one side of the dish, cut away from the opening of the body where once it joined up with the lungs was . . . to say the least . . . *interesting*. From the passion of his conversation, he was obviously looking forward to making a proper study of it back in his laboratory.

Frank felt the urge to be sick, or collapse, or leave – anything but oversee this partially opened body with its accompanying odors emanating from its interior. This was the second decapitation; the first, the surgeon in that instance had not been so graphic with his *lecture*, getting the body under wraps as soon as he was able. Having decided that it was not fitting for a lieutenant from the police department to act in such a manner, Weinberg found it in himself to see it through without passing out concentrating instead on other aspects of the crime scene, like the blood-stained bed. Still wet, it had formed into pools where the mattress had compressed from years of use. He looked away to give his mind some temporary respite but saw the blood had not been confined to the bed sheets and coverings. It was on the carpet. Up the walls. Running down the lattice windows. It looked as if a mad axe man had entered Rivers's bedroom going berserk on his body except for one small detail. His head was absent, and no weapon used to carry out its removal.

For some reason, unknown to O'Hare, Frank went down on his knees looking under the bed. What gave him that idea as a hiding place for something that was clearly missing, O'Hare could only guess. Still on the floor, he looked up at him, his hand over his mouth trying to contain what was coming up from his stomach. He pointed to a curtain pull rod on top of a wardrobe. O'Hare, not at first getting what Frank was on about until he uttered, 'Uhgg' whilst pointing once again, this time using manual expressions instead of his previous eye movements.

The surgeon reached up took it down passing it to O'Hare. Frank took it and reaching under the bed, fished a few times, then rolled the head out across the carpet. It was Rivers. Wearing the mask of a Bull.

'Well, now who *he* was,' Frank said to O'Hare before turning to the surgeon, 'better bag it up.'

'Good thinking,' the surgeon replied in an ironic tone; 'it may give me a clue as to cause of death.'

Opening a cardboard medical box, the surgeon gently lifted the head with both hands. 'Would either of you gentlemen like to feel the weight of a human brain pan while I've got it to hand, so to speak?' Both detectives shook their heads. '*No!* Suit yourselves. You may not get another opportunity, it's not every day (the pallor of their faces underlined what the shake of their heads had previously expressed) . . . fair enough.' The surgeon put the head in the box closing the lid on it, pulling his pen from his suit pocket wrote the time and date in the space allocated for such detail on the side.

'Blessed Mary ever Virgin. Whatever he *did*, he didn't deserve to go out like this. This is the *second!*'

Frank looked at him hard. 'Can't you, I can. I won't lose any sleep over someone that ignored a child in need of adult help telling us he didn't know anything about any of this.'

'Yeh, well. A loose thought, Lieutenant, I didn't mean—'

Frank watched the surgeon write notes in his pad. *Head twisted and torn from the neck due to flesh fatigue.* He had wanted another theory as to the surgeon's diagnosis for cause of death. 'Are you sure it wasn't hacked off and the saw discarded? Only it doesn't show any indication of being . . . *torn!*'

To the surgeon it was perfectly reasonable to suppose the man did die from having his head pulled off. 'Don't waste your time looking for any weapon, Lieutenant, I can assure you there won't be one,' he said with relish. 'Look! Here!' He lifted the man's upper torso and pulled it round so they could both get a better view. 'His head's been twisted round three or four times until it gave way. Executed so quickly and powerfully the body hardly moved from where it was lying. To my way of thinking, and don't quote me on this, no man would have the strength to do that. And to put your mind at rest, you won't find that in my report.'

O'Hare screwed his face up and drew breath from between gritted teeth as if he were feeling something painful going on between his legs. 'You've made a fair estimate of cause, Doctor,' adding for his own light relief, 'but it certainly pulls the old scrotum bag tight to the stomach, so it does.'

'The only creature I ever heard of that was powerful enough to do a thing like this was a black bear, and that was off a pig. And a pig's head is well stuck on!' Frank added.

'Would you like me to put down black bear as cause?' the surgeon asked. 'I can if you want. No-one's going to argue with this body as evidence. Trust me – I'm a doctor.'

'No. You're all right,' Frank said with a wry smile.

'Good. I will of course carry out further tests back at the morgue, but I don't think I'm going to add anything more to what I've said,' he said smiling. 'Right, if that's all, if you're both finished with me here, I'll arrange to get the departed taken away.'

Frank took a long last look and hoped there would not be any more deaths on this scale. He was reluctant to use the word murder. Trying to keep them under wraps was difficult enough as it was. The press were getting suspicious over the last body. Rumours in the neighborhood, that the man known as Runfeldt had lost his head, had got out despite their best efforts to keep it under wraps.

'Well, if you do come to any other conclusions, Doctor—'

'You'll be the first to know. New York is not crawling with bears this time of year. By the way, congratulations on your promotions.'

With the demise of Rivers, further questions had come to mind that he needed to confront Johnson. Taking O'Hare with him, they went to the offices of the Bureau, he, asking to see the man that had cheekily demanded the return of his car's rotor arm. Shown into a temporary office that looked like an over-size broom cupboard, Frank, without formality leaned across the man's desk asking him, what he thought he was doing in Giuseppi's house that evening wearing the mask of a Clown alongside one wearing that of a Bull. He went on to say that, the report he had written was lacking in a good witness statement and would he like to add anything to it? Further, that due to the two agent's ineptitude in not protecting their prisoner, they had lost the man, that had Frank or O'Hare put pressure on, might well have fingered Giuseppi. The reason the Bureau had taken it on themselves putting Rivers under house arrest (what was wrong with the regular jail), was a mystery completely irregular.

Johnson quietly listened, drawing on his pipe. He had been expecting this meeting; would have been disappointed had Frank not instigated it, more, needed to put part of the record straight, despite their masters' insistence that nothing, but nothing was to stand in the way of the State's agenda. He tapped at his pipe, looked in the bowl, decided it had gone out, and placed it in his ashtray.

'That was best practice,' adding, 'he was after all, your commissioner and as such entitled to the privilege of being kept out of a common cell where he may have been subject to all manner of abuse from other reprobates.'

'So he could be murdered, instead of having a black-eye? *Bollocks!*' Frank said angrily. 'And the rest of my question as to what you were doing in his house that evening? The body of a boy that had been tortured to death found hanging, did you know of him? Give me one good reason why I shouldn't break your worthless neck. You *damn* well knew what was going on in that place.'

Johnson was nervous. Frank Weinberg was beginning to show his colors. 'I honestly didn't know the extent of his activities, I thought … I was undercover, have been for some time – of course I shall deny any knowledge of it should you pursue my brief. This is a highly complex labyrinth of geometric proportions, that should it be unpicked at any point will lose us the way in. That is all I'm prepared to say on the matter. As for putting pen to paper for what I might have seen, or not, forget it. You're in a different world. However much I would like to, it 'ain't goin' t'happen.' He had hoped that without saying any more than that Frank would have the intelligence to accept it. 'What I said earlier regarding your transference to the Bureau, I meant. You and Sergeant O'Hare are the right sort. And what I said about you picking up enemies over this, it's a warning, well intended.'

'I take it that we will be consulted should any further inquiries regarding Giuseppi crop up?'

'Of course. I need to show you something first though, a subject I would appreciate both your views on.'

After a meaningless attempt by Agent Johnson, at least to O'Hare's way of thinking, which resulted in him later reverting to the likely language of his ancestors after America's blighted potato crop blew phytophthora infestans spores across the Atlantic, infecting Ireland's crop culminating in death and famine; he could see that Frank had something on his mind. He guessed it was the painting and broached the subject tactfully not wanting to hurt any feelings he might have.

'Did you see something in that picture that I didn't?' O'Hare asked.

Frank pursed his lips at the question. 'How old did you reckon it was?'

'I'm no expert. Renaissance? But does it matter, a hundred years here or there? If it were 2000, painted by one of the Man's disciples, well, that could be an altogether different ball game. *Why* should Johnson be interested in a painting anyway? He was there along with us; what did he think we saw that he hadn't. Do you know, I'm beginning to smell blarney here, so I am?'

'The point I'm making was that whoever put brush to canvas had the same models that we saw. I might be Jewish for *God's* sake; but I'm not so grounded in Judaism that I dismiss the Christian faith lightly. At the end of the day, Jesus *was* Jewish. That painting was of an angel. From the thrones in the first circle if my knowledge of Pseudo Areopagite is up to the mark; guidance to a Divine Spirit.'

'I'm impressed, Lieutenant. And there was me thinking more on the lines of artistic license,' O'Hare added with no more than that as an assuredness of its truth. 'Anyway, he was a little short in the height stakes for being divine of anything, I'd have thought.'

'You had a broken neck that mended don't forget. He couldn't have been too non-divine not to fix you up. Anyway, it was an interpretation of Jesus in the tomb after His death with the angel showing him where He lay in preparation for resurrection. If this is not some elaborate charade, then, 2000 years of religious faith has either gone down the plug hole for my lot; and yours is in its ascendancy. Johnson mentioned a "complex labyrinth of geometric proportions, that should it be unpicked at any point will lose us our way in", now there's an interesting off-the-cuff remark if ever there was one.'

'That aside, though, has it occurred to you that the picture could have been painted last week to add to the trick?'

'Why would anyone go to such trouble?'

'Giuseppi trying to cover his tracks. As I said before, it may have nothing at all to do religious interpretations of Biblical events. It's amazing what they can do with mirrors. A thought perhaps.'

'And your neck?'

O'Hare shrugged his shoulders, the palms of his hands upper in expression of statement, '*Alleddy, the man's a doctor, so soon.*'

'All right, cut the Groucho Marx routine, I know a broken neck when I see one.'

'Tell you what though,' O'Hare replied. 'You don't suppose the government has produced a race of supermen that can tear heads off. And one has fallen into the hands of Giuseppi and they want him back.'

'Or Giuseppi is the new Superman.'

*   *   *

A year later, Frank needed to check out a rumor that Giuseppi had perished in a house fire. When he approached his assistant director for permission to question the NYPD, he was told that as he no longer worked for them it wouldn't be a good idea to get involved. When Frank asked for clarification, referencing Agents Nathaniel Johnson and Daniel Sullivan, the Director told him they were not names showing as ever having worked for the Bureau of Investigation.

Found guilty on charges of corruption, ex-Governor Brent received two years penal servitude; released on parole after nine months for good behavior. *That all!* O'Hare remarked to Frank, *Get twice that in Ireland for buggering a leprechaun, so you can.*

On Brent's release, he married his ex-lover of five years, Connie Rivers (there's a familiar name, O'Hare noted when he heard it). She went on the boards as a singer, taking the stage name Connie Lamar. She and Fray Brent made a small fortune from real estate funded by money from unknown sources. O'Hare made a second observation, *Goes to show, you just can't keep a good woman and her bugger down, so you can't, Sweet Mother of Jesus* .

Frank had agreed only up to a point regarding one of the 'buggers'. He had received a tip-off from Sugden, still with the NYPD; keen to keep in touch with Weinberg and O'Hare that they had found a body in a trash container at the rear of an apartment block in Manhattan's Lower East Side.

'The body was burnt beyond recognition; wearing the mask of a Bloodhound melted to what remained of his face. We can't be a hundred percent sure that it was Brent,' Sugden told Frank on the telephone, 'but it's a fair bet from newspaper pictures we have of the man.'

When Connie Lamar subsequently filed a missing person's report, later, establishing that the remains of the man found were that of her husband, she, being next of kin, and beneficiary to a double indemnity life insurance pay-out in the event of his murder confirmed to Frank what Sugden had said was right.

Funny old world, O'Hare remarked once again on the subject after he had finished telling him.

'Can't we go find evidence of suicide? That ought to, *fuck-her-up!*'

Seven – 1925

'ARE YOU GOING TO TRY some of this cake or not, Charlie O'Hare?' Sarah asked with one hand on her hip, the other holding the plate temptingly in front of him.

Charlie stood back from her in mock surprise, 'Oh, I'd better had I suppose. I can see I'll get no peace until I do, so I won't.'

'Don't bother then,' she said pulling it away from him.

'All right, all right, I'll have it,' he said taking the plate before it disappeared back into the kitchen. 'A small piece.'

'You'll have a large slice or none at all,' she said pulling it away from him once more.

He smiled taking the wedge of birthday anniversary cake from her.

'Use the plate,' she said. 'I don't want to have to sweep the floor again. I've already cleaned up after David's party guests.'

The contrast of fruit cake and hard icing made his taste buds salivate and he relished it though he wasn't hungry. 'That's a lovely drop of cake, Sarah, so it is,' he said between mouthfuls adding. '*God!* Is it five years since you married Frank? Where has the year's gone?'

She stroked him gently on the cheek, 'And you were a lovely, best man too, Charlie.'

'Get away with you, you married the best man.'

She smiled at his assumption that she might have married him had Frank not won her first. Although unlikely. He had taken it in good part when she did marry the young lieutenant, though . . . well, Frank could be, a little on the insensitive side at times, not always able to listen to her and her problems. But she had loved him for all that, still did. Charlie on the other hand, she could confide. Not in everything, just some things. When it came to relationship matters of a personal nature between her and her husband that was of course sacrosanct – always would be. It was the little things. The bothering problems outside of marriage she had difficulty. Whether it was because he was not always about, or, when he was, had other more pressing matters like his job to deal with, she could not be sure. Charlie on the other hand, was more down-to-earth, more able to respond and offer advice. She could talk to him without feeling that she was being disloyal to her husband. Indeed, at times, Frank would openly encourage her sometimes saying, *Ask what Charlie thinks. He might have an opinion.*

Her husband was away, and she needed to do that.

The birthday card sent to David was short on signature of a relative. A single message written in ink on the inside front cover. A typically colorful birthday card with its cover emblazoned with *Happy Birthday You Are Six*, with a picture underneath of a boy playing with toy soldiers. A tin drum in the background with a trumpet across it. Sarah had opened the envelope with all the excitement of a mother sharing a happy occasion with her son before seeing it snatching it away from him. The tidings written in the foulest of language cut her to the quick.

Having onetime lived in Oregon with her mother and father and three sisters they would quite often receive newsletters from the Ku Klux Klan suggesting that Jews – like blacks – were not wanted in the State, let alone America. They were usually associated with a crudely hand-drawn sketch of a manacled slave hanging from a tree; with a crowd of the white hooded *witches* standing below, flaming torches in their hands, applauding. This time it was different, no mention was made of their moving. Were they to be murdered where they stood?

Primarily a direct attack on her son. A threat or a promise? Both equally as bad. The question she needed to know. Who was Fariq Mihalyvich's daughter? And what happened to her that the author threatened would happen to David when he came of age? Did Charlie or her husband know what the message referred? And why had they not mentioned it before? Sarah knew nothing of their work at the Bureau. She guessed it might sometimes be dangerous. Her husband spending so much time cleaning his gun: looking down the barrel, oiling its revolving parts, dusting with talcum powder the inside of his shoulder holster better to draw it when needed told her that much. With David's bar mitzvah seven years away, someone clearly had a long-term grudge with her husband. Another reason why she would not ask him; preferring instead to seek out what Charlie had to say on the subject. She looked at him and the smile that had been there all afternoon fell away. She bit her lip and he sensed something serious. She said his name, quietly, yet with a forcefulness of a person that was overflowing with the emotion of fear and the need to express herself so overwhelmingly that consequence would go right out the window. She would no more be able to stop herself than hold back the tide. Throwing her arms round him, she burst into tears. *'Oh, Charlie!'*

His arms automatically reached out to her as she sank her sobbing face into his shoulder. There was a pause, and she lifted her head and faced him. Composing herself, her head slowly moving from side to side in a manner that was saying no to a question that he had not yet put; and with tears streaming down her face she asked:

'Who was Fariq? And, Charlie, please tell me, what *did* they do to his daughter that they have in mind for our David?'

His immediate concern was what he was supposed to say to Sarah. With the woman distressed the way she was, he had to decide. He knew he was on thin ice telling her. Frank may well have something to say to him about a decision that was his business to tell, when, and if the time came right, but not him. But Sarah was at the point of having a breakdown if he did not confide in her. And that *something*, by the nature of the beast, began well enough, but with questions and explanations needing to be gone into from her at the start, middle, and end, the story ended became complete before he had a chance to think about what he was saying. He did however manage to spare her the gruesome details of what they saw. Instruments of torture. And of course, a boy, partially stripped of his flesh hanging.

The insidious odor emanating from corrupted humanity that was in their nostrils, he had forgotten. But not the strange occurrences witnessed by them; that would invalidate any sensible conversation that they might have with loved ones and friends, well before both men had taken the decision to plead Fifth Amendment. If pushed for an answer would reply, *Don't know what you're talking about.*

'And what did become of Fariq at the end?' she asked.

'Last we heard . . . he'd returned to Russia. Along with his daughter, Irinushka. Both alive and safe,' he lied, not knowing the truth.

The first part of the question he was confident in its saying; the second – he kept to himself, as he was still coming to terms with the possibility that Fariq's daughter had become an angel. An angel that occupied his sleeping hours. He smiled at Sarah reassuring her that no-one from that time was still round to cause her or David any threat to their lives. 'If there was,' he continued, 'me and Frank would jump right onto it and put a stop to it once and for all.'

She stared at him not believing a word he said.

Charlie put his hand to his face. It wasn't the sting from the slap to the face that he felt so much, more as to why she had done it in the first place. She stepped back; her eyes full of anger. 'What job are you two in, eh?' she screamed at him. 'A few hoodlums selling bootleg to those happy to buy. Is it worth all this? And where is my husband, eh? In a fire fight, shooting it out somewhere. What is he? What are you? Eliot Ness' Untouchables. More to the point, what are you doing here, taking time out for stress? Have the pair of you so little concern for the feelings of those that love you?' Her voice was breaking.

She went out the door, slamming it, dragging a crying David after her to her bedroom. What remained of his cake was a mess at his feet alongside pieces of broken crockery. With Frank out of town on the Seaburg investigation, he was not sure how long it would take to contact him. The card mentioned that the threat to David was some way off. If Giuseppi was behind the message, written in the way it was it would – although put the fear of God into Sarah today – mentally give her time to prepare for the future. And that was not Giuseppi's style at all, O'Hare thought. He studied the envelope. It seemed ordinary enough in that it had a stamp and the correct address on it. He looked closer at the stamp. It seemed proud of the envelope that a regular licked stamp did not. He picked at the edge of it before noticing that it was second-hand. There was glue underneath. It had been adhered to another envelope first. The card that had the stamp crudely stuck to the envelope was not regular mail. This birthday card delivered by hand told O'Hare that he had to get her and David out of there tonight.

So, the evil bastard had not died in a fire. He had found the Weinberg homestead dropped his evil bombshell at the precise moment a mother – at her proudest – would be at her most vulnerable. Organizing the party with all that on her mind it was no wonder she lost it with him. He had never heard of a grudge by a criminal to a law enforcement officer's family before. Idle threats, for sure, usually made in court after a man's conviction, but they never amounted to a can of beans as a rule. Nothing was ever that personal. He had come across hoodlums that he had brought to book, sent down, later meeting them after their release where they would greet him with a civility that, although not brotherly, was never of a vindictive nature. Most considering their separate professions all part of the same game. In the Giuseppi case, with the file closed, they had always smelled rats. All his business activities, his labor scams, the protection, the stills, all had been nothing compared to the child abuse he had been promoting. His house (or what was left of it after the fire explosion he was supposed to have died), boarded up was a despairing and pitiful abode. It gave people the shivers passing without them knowing what occurred there. And that was in daylight. At night, it took on a life of its own. Local people saying they could hear the muffled cries of children from within. Not that he had much time for mumbo-jumbo, but nevertheless—

There was no doubt in O'Hare's mind that it could not be anyone else other than Marco Giuseppi that had sent that card, and he was about to break into the Weinberg household in revenge for him breaking into his. After what Giuseppi had done to Oona Mihalyvich and her daughter, to say nothing of Fariq himself, he was unlikely to show the Weinberg household any pity and his blood ran cold at its thought.

Weinberg was on the investigating team looking into the Hon. James Walker's affairs. Along with other agents from the Bureau, they had started to pick their way through the scams and misappropriation of city monies in the name of the Mayor of New York. What made the whole ball game more difficult was that the department's own vice squad were heavily involved in their own illegal operations. The whole deal was a long and arduous task headed by Judge Seaburg, an Episcopalian moralist; and no stranger when it came to opening cans of worms. Seaburg had personally investigated a courtroom racket by the Metropolitan Street Railroad by them using their own judges whenever their company came to court for malpractice. Despite pressure, threats from various sources, namely local politicians, dignitaries, and the like, Seaburg kept the line where corruption was concerned. Weinberg admired that in the man and was more than happy to be working on this assignment. Although he was not to meet him personally, he was to be answerable to the head of operations, a fellow by the name of Dan Thomas. And, but for his mutton-chop side-burns and long grey hair, he looked as though he might have been the brother of someone he once knew. A no-nonsense director, he had founded the Bureau's Special Operations Surveillance Unit specializing in infiltrating organizations that might threaten America's homeland security. Weinberg took to the man admiring his easy-going manner. His name was on the letter sent to him as being part of Judge Seaburg's operational management team; and with that in mind he figured he would be as kosher as *kosher* was.

He seated Weinberg behind his own desk, preferring to outline their objectives from the public side, pacing backwards and forwards as he spoke, 'First off let me say that it's good to have you with us, you come highly recommended. You had a partner didn't you? An Irish fellow?'

Weinberg nodded, and went to say he still had, but Thomas wasn't expecting a verbal reply.

'Good. Right, let's get down to the nuts and bolts shall we? The planning of this operation has been going on for some time. One of the important aspects is its security. For that reason, teams of agents will be interchanged. We want no familiarity with those we are investigating, that way we can keep the whole operation squeaky clean. *Right!*'

'Right!'

'As to your part in all of this. You'll be in charge of one of the main busts. Literally. At the front end, staring down barrels of guns, so to speak. A club. We arrested someone earlier for importuning who promised to add to the list we've got of people we are interested in on the evening in question. He didn't take too much persuading. Apparently, the police had been blackmailing him. He'd obviously had enough and wanted payback against them approaching us. He works for City Hall's Finance Department, so he's in a good position to know who's been greasing palms better than most. Makes it easier for us to name names when it comes to public servants and the like that're getting backhanders on the Mayor's behalf. Blind eye and all that in return for information. Names. Big and influential likely revealed. Get the point?'

Thomas fired back at him, after Weinberg casually asked what the guy had been caught doing precisely.

'He was a God damn arse-'ole bandit prostituting himself in women's clothes and was that damn attractive he gave me an 'ard-on.' Frank sheepishly made the comment after hearing this that he, *Was that good was he*— 'Better looking as a woman than a man, that's for sure. Still, you can judge for yourself when you speak to him.' He calmed himself down, coughing gently into his hand going alongside him to get to a filing cabinet. Pulling open a drawer, he took a sheet of paper from it handing it to him. 'That's the list. Guard it with your life burn it when we're finished with all of this. Question him for details. Get him to cough up what money was involved, where it went, to whom and for what. As for the Honorable Mayor Walker, he's getting that confident of what he's got going he's getting slap-dash. When the situation gets that bad you can see why we can trust no-one remotely connected with the police.'

'The club's called, *Tinkerboys*. That right?' Weinberg said seeing a name at the top of the list.

'Mob run. You've two days to sort yourself out before you go in.

Use whatever resources you need. The quicker and harder you hit them, the less chance anyone's going to get killed. We're after Mayor Walker and everything he has had his grubby hands on. Right. It's all yours. I'll leave it with you. Maddox is his name by the way. He doesn't want a lawyer and sure as hell I don't want a cop near him when you interview him.' He ushered him from behind his desk. 'Right, get outta my chair and don't forget, soon as this is over, clear up, clear out, and clear off back to where you came. I'll do the mopping up and reporting. We won't be leaving any agents in this field to be popped off by the mob when it's over.'

Weinberg did not take to Maddox when he met him. He had all the appearance of another, who was also homosexual, he was a Tony as well. Homosexuality being contrary to Orthodox Judaism, he, not being one, although finding it difficult to accept, had not altogether made his mind up regarding what consenting adults get up to in private. Maddox, though, was more than that; he was also transvestite. At least according to Dan Thomas he was. Though looking at him closely this man was wearing women's light make-up powder with a hint of colour to his lips giving the impression of a face recast in plastic. The skin was stretched. He had heard of surgery that made aging actresses younger. He was also aware that it was expensive, not within the means of a finance clerk. He was tall (as D'Sotto) and appeared to look after himself. There the resemblance ended. Rolled-up shirt sleeves revealed bulging biceps. There was the stockiness of someone that worked out with weights about him. Though, how Thomas was supposed to have got an *'ard-on*, looking at the man dressed as woman; built like a half made-up weight-lifter was a mystery to him. But it took all sorts he supposed. A nervous man under interrogation, Frank spoke with him for an hour and a half. His recall was good, and Weinberg kept notes checking back regularly for inconsistencies. There was none. Even the amounts of missing cash involved, tallying. He was not plucking figures from the air. Mayor Walker seemed to have his fingers all over New York's commercial and business world; others would be dealing with that – Tinkerboys was his concern. And if it were mob run, as Thomas had said it was, looking down barrels would concentrate his mind and that of his team. These people armed themselves with Thompson machine guns. Usually they ran clubs for prohibition drinking. Tinkerboys went a stage further. Along with those activities, it openly encouraged all sexes prostitution from which they took a cut. The Honorable 'taxing and blackmailing' in return for keeping the authorities off his back. No-one was going to be happy with what was coming.

Weinberg asked, out of curiosity, why Maddox should prostitute himself when he had a perfectly well-paid job. He said it was to finance a $500 a week bill for shots of arsenic and bismuth to cure his syphilis, going on to say it was rife. Frank was stunned at the kind of money involved. A victim of a choice he freely made. He knew venereal disease was epidemic in New York, he had no idea it was that bad. All he could do was reassure him that they were not in the business of compromising his career or making life any more difficult for him than it was. Weinberg going as far as suggesting that a doctor and a hospital might be a better bet for him.

Frank Weinberg, he muttered to himself. *You're becoming a social worker.*

Frank made up his mind regarding dressing as a shape-changer going undercover into Tinkerboys. That was not going to happen. He had thought about calling up O'Hare, see if he fancied it, but saw that would be stretching their professional relationship too far. The image came to him of a ruddy-faced, curly and ginger-haired Irishman, wearing brown brogue shoes, a black bowler, a green-sequined dress with the merest hint of make-up, tap-dancing and jigging his way into the club before taking everybody out with his fists. He shook his head saying to himself, 'He'd never pull it off.'

From the list of resources Thomas had made available to him, he selected and recruited ten agents with a dozen from Pinkerton National Detective Agency. The plan was to go in heavy-handed with sledge hammers, armed with mob-familiar sub-machine guns. It would not be the faeries or the shape changers that would be the problem when they went in but the heavies in the back rooms waiting ready for a bust they were ever ready for. He was under no illusion on that score – they would be armed and ready for such an eventuality. The real danger was if there had been a tip-off somewhere down the line, where the police might be waiting for them. They could all be mown down with no questions asked. And with them using the excuse to an inquiry that they had not known these men were not another mob in for a wipe-out of the opposition instead of Bureau agents. With that consideration to the back of his mind, he gave orders that there was to be no question that they should get in first. He would shout that order. The excuse that law enforcement officers shot-down by the police saying they were a gang used for the murder of Bureau enforcement officers in the past was not going to happen. Not on his watch; and despite Thomas's confidences.

US Customs and Border Control had made available an empty warehouse to act as a holding center for the estimated 2000-odd 'customers' that were expected the night in question. Beds and furnishings, toilet facilities and screens had been brought in from an emergency war-time facility as well as doctors and nursing staff and equipment in case of any blood-bath. Transport was supplied by the prison service in the form of coaches. Catering was courtesy of DeLuxe. The prosecution witnesses were to be spirited away right from under the noses of the police and anyone else connected with

Mayor James Walker where interrogation at a secret location would take place. He was not so naïve as to think that everything was covered; but as sure as he could be, he gave the order to go.

O'Hare had difficulty getting through to Frank on the telephone. The sensitivity of the operation needed special clearance to any outsider wanting to speak to anyone involved. His explanation to the Coms. Director as to Frank's wife's distress brought on under the pretext of David taken seriously ill did get him through to his partner in the end.

'*Charlie!* How are you? You'll love what I'm on—' His voice trailed off as his mock enthusiasm gave way to anxiety, ' *What is it?*'

Frank put the telephone down. They at least would be safe with O'Hare until this is done with, he thought. Why would anyone threaten Sarah through David? *Anyone,* he thought. But it wasn't anyone was it? O'Hare had spared mentioning him that detail though he guessed. How in hell's name could that man possibly know of her existence, let alone where we live. Unless. He and O'Hare had followed every possible lead they had in tracking Giuseppi down the last five years. The fire was a red herring, no doubt in his mind about that. Something as simple as a tip-off by a 'bent' agent or police officer could direct anyone to where he lived and who his family were. More likely, though, if it were Giuseppi's people, it would have been the result of their own discreet inquiries of the man and his whereabouts. There was a formula: Rule 1, Information you're seeking may alert your enemy before you have become near enough to apprehend them; Rule 2, Gather all the intelligence you can to remain the hunter.

Not easy, O'Hare suggested to Frank when first making inquiries as to the truth of Giuseppi's malaise. *But we can surmise.* He had gone on:

'In this case, it would mean someone, somewhere, in a place on high knows more of the works of Giuseppi than are letting on, putting them in the position of the hunted without them being aware that the switch from one to another had been achieved. If their objective were to rid either of us for what we knew, a high-profile operation like the Seaburg investigation would give them the ideal opportunity in your case. You'd better be mindful of that, Frank.'

'That would involve someone high up?'

'High enough to be able to pass a directive down through the system without questions being asked or challenged. There would not be many capable of that Frank. They would operate under the pretext of the directive of the President, though he was unlikely to be personally involved himself. An unofficial group run by a person that purported to be on their side. Someone like Johnson or Sullivan. Why the denial to us by the Bureau as being on their payroll when we know full well they were? The President would not need to know the details for the running of such a group, neither for that matter would the head of the Bureau, but the person taking the order would have the necessary credentials to kill on grounds of National Security. There would be no questions asked. They would have freedom to stalk the country's inner government as England's spymaster; Sir Francis Walsingham did for Elizabeth I; and no questions asked, nor explanations proffered. The Seal of the Queen in one hand, a rack to torture confessions out of Catholic conspirators in the other. If such a man or men existed, and they were protecting Giuseppi, they would have license to kill with impunity.'

He thought seriously about what O'Hare had told him, and the possibility he may have right made him shudder; though it at least would put him one jump ahead of any Sir Francis's peering from behind heavy drapes, dagger in hand, waiting to strike. The Third Rule: Be mindful the possibility you have gathered enemies round you that would do you harm came to mind.

Wearing chain-mail body armor under their suits, the army of twelve Pinkerton and three Bureau agents sledged and hammered down the locked and chained double back doors that were Tinkerboys night-club. Finding the rear windows and doors boarded and pit-propped, using the wall of the adjacent building, the occupants ran round like headless chickens. For they had been caught like rats in a trap without a weapon being discharged. Herding them into the corner of the club, he had the lights put up. They panicked and Frank shouted for quiet, trying to make his voice heard above the screaming mass. And what a mass, he thought. There was no way of telling their sex, not from appearances at least. Men dressed as women, women as men. Some dressed as they should be, and some half way, provocatively attracting anything they fancied. Some were holding hands; some had been caressing in intimate dark recesses of the club. The police had never raided the place before and it spoke volumes as to why. There were high-ranking military officers, captains of police, a State governor, and a senator, as well as religious people from various persuasions and faiths, judges, writers, artists. All were in various states of having over indulged in drink or drugs, or both. Rooms off the main part of the club found fornicating couples of same sex, with acts of flagellation, buggery taking place, or at the point of.

Above the ceiling of the club, in the rafters, out of eye shot to anyone on the floor below, a small hatch opened. Two men, one prone, the other kneeling beside him were in the darkness.

'That Frank Weinberg?' the kneeling man whispered.

The other looking down through the telescopic sight of his sniping rifle, its crossed hairs moving from man to man searching for the face he would recognize.

'Not yet. They're sure he's here, are they?'

'He's here. He's in charge.'

The viewing man strained through his sight again and thought he caught sight of a face he recognized. Holding the cross hairs an inch above the top of his nose on the man's mustachioed face he gently squeezed the trigger.

'You've seen him. You've got him?'

He breathed out releasing the pressure on the trigger.

'No. He doesn't have a mustache?'

'Shoot the guy anyway; no-one's going to be too concerned. You never know, you might strike lucky.'

He took his eye from the sight and looked up at the kneeling man. He nodded at him to do it. Turning back to the sight he once again squeezed the trigger, but the man, whoever he was had moved. He relaxed and turned round. Sweat was pouring from his forehead in the enclosed space that took all the heat from below.

'We'll have to leave it, he's not down there. Maddox must have it wrong. He's probably directing operations from the comfort of an office chair.'

An hour had gone by before Frank had everyone rounded up. By midnight, they were put on coaches driven to the warehouse allocated for interviewing and questioning. Some were shielding their faces with whatever they had to hand. Perverts was how the Bureau's (Obscene) Section had labeled these people. Third parties making money from them by blackmail was something else though. His first job was to separate those that were victims from those that were abusers; by people sworn to *Protect and Serve*. There were genuine perverts though, the kind that hanged round the city's parks and toilets. Loners that would make a liaison with another man for sex with scarce a word passing between them. Bohemians, poets, actors, all struggling to sell themselves using the excuse that the experience broadened the mind, but what they wanted was the money their acts offered. The population of New York could barely afford food let alone art. The interesting ones, and where his job would be quickly finished for he needed to get back to Sarah, were the face shielders, for these were the ones with highly regarded reputations and professions. Elected representatives, government officials, doctors, lawyers, and the top brass police. For this was where the Mayor made his tens of thousands of dollars.

By midday, the next Frank was finished. He passed his report to Thomas. There were some interesting names. Some closer to home than he would have liked. There was Cardinal Carlos y Xavier from Mexico, an Episcopalian minister; Captain Flanagan from the New York Police Department; Earl Rothbury, all the way from England; along with three high ranking businessmen. An architect working on the new civic amenity complex. A hit-man from the mob that the Bureau had been after for some time. A Borough President and, Frank thought, *It would have to be wouldn't it*. A Rabbi.

The new Bureau of Investigation (section: Obscene); and whose statements and information might be traded in return for some immunity to those who passed names higher up the chain; yet to be pulled into this net. He had accepted Rabbi Michael Levin's reasons for involvement after his story of enlightenment, sympathizing with him, but sent him forward for prosecution anyway. One of many prosecutions that would decimate the New York Police Department and all corridors that led to Walker.

Frank and his team commended on a job well done. With typical brass neck, when the heat was off, the Honorable James Walker stood for re-election. President Roosevelt hearing of it stepped in having a quiet word in his ear. The result of which led the Mayor settling for early retirement back in his native Ireland, taking with him a small fortune from the city coffers, and an Indian girl old enough to be his granddaughter as a bed warmer.

Frank returning to his hotel room at 6 am, pouring himself a glass of bourbon and swallowing it in one. Then, removing his chain mail body armor, his round-rimmed plain glass spectacles, his theatrical mustache, with its accompanying wig, he showered, dressed and telephoned O'Hare at his home asking him to tell Sarah that he would be home the following morning. He turned in.

He had wanted to speak with Thomas earlier, but the man was gone.

The following morning he dressed, breakfasted, packed his bag and checked out. It was a bright sunny Manhattan morning when he walked out of the Belvedere Hotel. He stopped briefly on the top step and looking up at the sky, taking in a deep breath of fresh air, he dropped dead to the ground the result of a sniper's bullet from the window of an opposing building.

An Orthodox Jew with ear locks walking up to the still body of Bureau Agent Frank Weinberg placing a buff envelope into his inside jacket pocket. Standing up, he shrugged to the police officer that came running toward the scene; he walked on.

A device shattering the window of Frank and his wife's house, landed on the carpet, and exploded razing the property to the ground within minutes. Sarah and David were guests at O'Hare's home in Albany.

PART TWO

Eight – 1940–50

And the Lord said unto Satan, Whence comest thou?
Then Satan answered the Lord, and said,
From going to and fro in the earth,
and from walking up and down in it.

JUDAEA–CHRISTIAN BIBLE, JOB Ch. 1, v. 7

WITH THE UNIVERSITY he worked questioning his research into genetics; discovering he was closeting an unrecognized scientific group known as the *Order of the Most Divine Third Circle* – an association of mainly failed academics from differing scientific backgrounds delving into an applied religious philosophy using unproven technology – they gave him an ultimatum. With such affiliations, they would no longer fund him. Effectively unemployed, Dr. Jarvis Raynham turned his back on his academic career; and with America dragged into a European war; lusting for some action, he enlisted with the army.

As a doctor, he qualified as an officer. He trained in sabotage and engineering with the British taking charge of a unit of engineers at sector Easy Green; their duty, to clear a pathway through German mines and obstacles allowing the American First Army to bring landing craft ashore for a final push against a resolute enemy.

It was D-Day minus 1, June 5, 1944.

For the obstacles to be removed it was necessary for demolition teams and combat engineers to go in the night before the day of the main assault. A highly dangerous exercise for those involved; his team being one of the first sabotage units to go in under cover of darkness. Before they had got near to the shore ten of his men from the twenty involved had lost their lives, he being one near close to losing his.

Cracking his skull open from a falling girder he was attempting to cut underwater; he became trapped fifteen feet down with his face pushed hard side on into the seabed; the situation to the rest of his team seeing him there in the murk seemed bleak. To make matters worse his oxygen re-breather bag had sustained a puncture from the falling girder releasing life-giving oxygen into the water instead of his lungs. His unit tried desperately to release him. Repeatedly diving down to him, they stood on the sea floor to gain a purchase; lifting the girder with their shoulders pulled him clear. He had held his breath for two and a half minutes. Still suffering the effects of concussion, he donned another re-breather continuing with the task.

Not returning to America after the war, going instead to Italy, he sought out Sax Stonercrop, a fellow lecturer he had heard was involved in a theory he himself first speculated upon, and one that was to prove the existence of life within the universe as appraised by historical books of faith; not alone, but with this new Order. His Doctor of Philosophy credentials not immediately required; Stonercrop asked him if he were willing to take part in an operation they had in the planning that would require his specialist skills. He accepted, taking it as a rite of passage to learn more of the organization.

Asked if he would return to America, Raynham was to meet one of its leaders with the title, First Congener. He himself had learned his was one of Congener; though the term of address between members was one that was encouraged, rather than demanded, there being no hierarchy within the Order, he would live with it as a nomenclature.

'This man, for reasons we are not altogether clear of why or how, has exposed a window to another world; its light showing us a way forward. The Divine Spirit spoken of in the Christian Bible may well lift itself from those same pages becoming a reality in place of current legend, myth, and faith. His knowledge is within man's grasp, but not for all men. Do you understand what I'm saying? (Raynham nodded that he did.) My name's not important, Dr. Raynham. Of course,' the First Congener continued, 'there will be those that if they knew who I was would bring an end to what we are about. For that reason, I must remain anonymous. As to who our sponsors might be that you asked earlier, I could tell you that we have become self-sufficient, the result of the man in question. Our explorations into the unknown will one day shine like a beacon condemning current scientific knowledge to the dustbin of time. We will not share it with any other organization. We are near to reaching out and taking the prize. The last jig in the puzzle will set a chain reaction in motion. A reaction from the physics that created the universe by those responsible revealed to us. That is where you come in. We might have one of them in our midst: you've heard the name Tempter; but before we can move forward, proof that can be presented to our masters is needed.'

'*Tempter!* What, as in Jesus's tempter?' Raynham interrupted. 'You think that, Satan . . . real . . . is with us. On *earth!* Are you serious?'

The First Congener smiled. Why it was that so many people when it came to the question of good and evil, God and Satan, dismissing the latter of the two as myths, when it was rooted in their religions and beliefs was a question of eternal mystery to him. More especially a man such as Raynham, a man who had spent his young scientific days in the pursuit of a soul he believed was interacting with the base pairs of chemicals within the double helix: a third strand. The soul strand. A scientific theory that may not turn out to be as absurd as first seemed. Anything is possible when it comes to physics outside the boundaries of the known. He shook his head involuntarily at the man's closure of mind before continuing, 'Absolutely, and you are to be honored with his confrontation for confirmation that it is him. There is every chance that a man by the name of Frederik Spannocs is possessed of him. The evil that, as a mortal the man so eagerly grasped with both hands shows all the signs of hosting.'

Raynham had think about what the man had said, answered: 'Assuming Satan does exist, what would he be doing here now? He's not made any personal appearances these last 2000 years.'

'No more, or less, than the influence of God. We believe he is here because of his awareness of a second coming of Christ. Or whatever guise God chooses this time round for the appearance. But if you want further evidence of his existence, we have him on film, and it is our job to make sure we are ready for this second coming if and when. The evidence is there, and his appearance on earth has interested the Order. And that Order you first mentioned; you had not heard of; has existed 2000 years.'

Raynham feeling an allegiance to something as old and as historic as this *Order* gave him a sense of belonging to something important for the first time in his life and was perfectly prepared to test Frederik Spannocs if he could drive its beliefs forward. He told the First Congener if the man were not Satan, then he would be quite prepared to die for the privilege of attempting to prove it, and to face such a being if it did exist. He did not see any of it being a problem, it was after all, what he believed. Another experiment on the road to understanding. As the First Congener explained it would be a difficult operation; but it was Raynham's disbelief at the back of his mind that a man could be possessed by something that was, after all, no more than a mythical entity from the Bible that gave him the confidence to say all of this.

There could be no other way, the First Congener told him, reiterating that Raynham himself might die in the attempt. There had been previous attempts by others that had so far failed to prove the matter settled one way or the other. Satan had cloaked himself using a mortal for good reason. And with what the First Congener knew of past attempts, Raynham may be wasted; and they would lose a man with scientific kudos within the current team.

Raynham smiled, a smile bordering on imminent laughter, which he managed to suppress.

The two men knelt as the First Congener whispered a silent creed while Raynham pondered his chance of surviving this attack on the Prince of Darkness, being prepared to take on the second most powerful spirit in the supra physical world, would, if what he had been told were true, begin with pistols for two; ending with breakfast for one.

'We must maintain possession of any knowledge obtained. I trust you understand that.' Raynham nodded. 'Be under no illusion, Dr. Raynham, we need Satan. Speak with him. Cut him a deal. Anything to bring others to earth. And I speak of the Holy Ghost, or the Divine Spirit, even God. Think of it, the actual author of the book of physics, captured here on earth persuaded to give us the math. America and the *Order of the Most Divine Third Circle* will become masters encompassing not only a New World Order but the Universe and all Verses within.'

Raynham asked the First Congener what special gift Spannocs had that Satan should take him as his mortal Host. He appeared to look inwardly into himself. It was as if he was carrying guilt for something bad – black bad. The question would not draw him for an answer though.

'We shall pray together,' he said quickly taking Raynham by surprise. Seeing a look of wonder as to why they should do that on

Raynham's face, he added, 'For a successful conclusion and your safe return, Doctor. *What else?'*

Leaving Raynham still on his knees the First Congener changed out of his robes and left the building via the subway car park's lift. Getting into his car, he drove the interstate highway non-stop for 150 miles. Approaching Malaka's Corner ignoring the main interstate highway to Washington DC; instead, taking a turn that had no directional signs but which, after a quarter mile, ended at a building boarded in the bright red sans serif lower case lettering of the typeface known as, Venus extra bold condensed, the building's title: administrative (annex ii-38) section pen.gov.

Fading into his own risen cloud of dust and darkness of the subway lot, he stopped his car. Getting out, he went to an elevator gate; pushed a perforated card into a slot pulled it out. Stepping into the opening gate of the arriving elevator, he stepped inside and pushed a button. Getting out at a fifth floor that carried no indicator, he walked the long corridor to his office. For Nathaniel Johnson was the US Government's Sir Francis Walsingham and no-one else, to his knowledge, but three knew it. For himself and his equal of two of the most powerful men in the dark corridors of its government, in a department that had no name, and was as far removed from the *Order of the Most Divine Third Circle*, but *not* its aim, as was possible. He had a dilemma. How many more had mortality? Would there be a need for them to take Raynham out if he were successful in his mission for what he would have learned?

Daniel Sullivan was working through a pile of paperwork smoking a cheroot when Johnson returned to the office. Johnson preferring the more conventional fad of a pipe: the air mix of both their tobaccos, old and new, permeated the office. It had wormed its way into the clutter of books, files, papers, bags, boxes, telephones, the Gestetner machine, and their accoutrements for making coffee. Sullivan looking up confirming to himself who was coming in.

'Give me a second Nathaniel,' he said continuing what he was doing. A telex machine was playing out a ribbon with a clatter from its punch decipher; its ASCII paper tape coming from the perforator carried across a desk making its way onto a broken chair, off, onto the floor, where, when the tangle beginning to resemble spaghetti without the bolognaise, Sullivan pulled it clear directing it into a lead body casket, where a rotor arm embedded in resin he used as a paperweight held it in position. On the wall behind his chair above his head, an old photograph of a policeman in dress uniform with the epigram scrawled in pen beneath: Lost head in line of duty.

Sullivan dragged on the cheroot looking up at him, and took a deep lung full of smoke down his throat, 'Will he do it? You know if he survives, he'll have to be taken out after. We did discuss the possibility. We cannot afford people going round saying they've seen demons and angels. Bad enough the Irishman is still round with the knowledge.' Demons and angels, Johnson thought. Whatever she was, neither man had been able to explain her. She was clearly nothing to do with the other spirits. Appearing from nowhere, thwarting both demon and spirit equally, she had become a complication.

'Wanted some clarity,' Johnson replied. 'I'm sure Raynham didn't believe me when I told him that Spannocs was possessed of Satan. When he finds out that what I said was for real and he does survive, he could well blab it round to enhance his reputation. Whether "taking him out" will be necessary though; Stonercrop may have something to say on the matter. As for O'Hare, well, we do need to keep him round, if for no other reason than if things go tits up, he's the only one that can back us up as to what happened that night.'

'Rather an irony when you think about it. Don't forget Spannocs might get to him first and we need his money to finance this lot,' Sullivan said. 'He may well have had his pound of flesh with Weinberg, but I wouldn't trust him where O'Hare was concerned if he chooses to force the issue. We might have to yield to his desires. By the way,' he said as an afterthought; 'I'm rather worried about this aging thing we seem to have inherited?'

'Are you? How so?' Johnson asked.

'Two things. I need to see my doctor for a routine appointment; he'll see my records, likely wonder how come a man that's sixty looks thirty-five. You must have had similar thoughts yourself.'

'Well in that case we should get them altered. We are, after all, above the department that can affect those changes.' Johnson smiled.

Information regarding two lecturers with the names of Dr. Jarvis Raynham and Dr. Sax Stonercrop, one time linked with the University of Iowa had come to the attention of FBI headquarters in Washington DC passed to Assistant Director Franklin Lomax for his attention. One of the reasons given: communist sympathizers. The other, that they belonged to a group counter to United States National Security called the Order. All routine enough except the suggestion that he use Agent O'Hare for the inquiry. Another aspect of the inquiry he was not surprised at was that no name was on the directive. There was a secretary, but nothing else. He called the office concerned. A woman answered saying that the information he was given was all there would be and that to proceed according to instructions that would be with him the following day. He knew what was at the bottom of all this. He murmured to himself the acronym, COINTELPRO.

A large cardboard box turned up the following day. In it was an attache type case with a combination lock on its flap. Typed on a foolscap sheet of paper were instructions. A telephone number written on the bottom had a directive that it was not to be remembered, recorded, or passed on to any other person; and was to be locked away in the case with all information collected in the field on completion by the officer concerned. (Ignoring to forget would be a good trick, Lomax thought.) As an addendum at the bottom of the page, WARNING underlined in red, typed from an overused part of typewriter's ribbon that no-one could be bothered to change, followed with the usual *covering the government's arse clause.*

> Any deviation in procedure of the National Security Act, 1947, with particular reference to, protection of identities of certain United States undercover intelligence officers, agents, informants, and sources as well as, limitations on handling, retentions, and storage of certain classified materials by the Department of State will render persons contravening them liable to prosecution and imprisonment should they be found guilty of any of the above.

There was no combination number to re-open it should he make a mistake locking it. He was to ring the number informing the person that answered that an important government document awaited collection. A courier sent to collect it from him personally. There would be no receipt given.

Lomax waved O'Hare to sit down. He leaned back in his chair and passed him the sheet of paper containing the notes, 'You were saying you knew these men? Were they involved with anything the American security services might be interested in? I'm curious to know because they specifically asked for you by name to conduct the inquiry. And before you say anything, the fact that you might know either man will not be a complete and satisfactory answer to me. I need to know all you know.'

O'Hare reached over, read the sheet, smiled and dropped it back in front of Lomax. 'Nothing to do with my magnetic personality?' Before it had time to settle, he retrieved it back again. 'As it happens. . . . Wait a minute; you say somebody asked for me in person. Do you know who?'

Lomax smiled. 'It doesn't say. Thought perhaps you might be able to help me on that one, seeing how you happen to be flavor of the month.' He had heard the rumours that flies avoided this man, preferring to settle elsewhere, and he wondered how he had come about that for a reputation. O'Hare was studying him but did not answer. 'I think you were about to continue, "As it happens" . . .' Lomax said his mouth open in anticipation. 'Would you, perhaps, like to elaborate?'

O'Hare said that he had met Stonercrop some years before at university, but not Raynham, adding that Stonercrop and Raynham were colleagues that had not – professionally speaking – got along with each other. Far as he knew, they did not have any political affiliations, if that was what he was asking.

'And the nature of this animosity?'

'I wouldn't have gone as far as say animosity. More . . . an internal wrangle. Matters had been worrying the university on its approach to faith. A touchy subject. They called both men in for advice on how they should approach it from a secular stand point with its students. The meeting between them soon heated up, and to resolve it the university decided to get a broader view from those that would be affected – the students themselves. A debate was organized. Ecumenical Direction v University Responsibility. Stonercrop was for the motion, Raynham against. It was one of those arguments that had Stonercrop been against it, Raynham would have stood for it. Such was the natural mentality of the two men for each other. Anyway, the debate lasted three hours before they called time and a vote taken.

The count gave no direction for the university administrators. 73 against, 71 for.'

'And what were you doing in Iowa? You didn't say.'

'Taking a degree in religion. Stonercrop was my tutor head—'

'You a *student*? Religion?' Lomax asked wondering how the look of the man squared itself with him being – a *theologian*.

'Don't sound so surprised.'

'Sorry. Took me back a bit, that's all. Anyway, please continue.'

'As I understand it, Raynham had something to do with biology. Some theory that an invisible strand ran through the body somewhere. All absurd of course and loosely based on later workings carried out by Crick and Watson. Human genome. Chemical inheritance and all of that. Anyway, Raynham picking up on the idea adding his own piece of theory conned the university into providing him with the wherewithal to begin research into the theory. All went well for him until a drinking session organized by his students one evening, he getting himself pissed saying too much. He openly discussed this research – which at that time was only theory on paper – saying that universities were idiots paying out good money for something so elusive as God, or something on those lines. The university board, hearing about the incident called him in asking to see his research papers to date. With nothing to show but reams of theory, they suspended him.'

'Do you know anything about an *Order* that he is supposed to be involved?' Lomax asked.

'No, never heard of any Order, although, after he had had his funding withdrawn, an organization did approach him with the idea that they would fund his research in return for him working for them alongside other people with similar ideas to his own. He told them, he wasn't interested in science any longer; packed it all in, went and joined the marines or something.'

'Have you heard of any organizations or corporations with groups of scientists working for them?' Lomax asked.

'Are you serious? Pretty well every company in the America worth its salt has research facilities of one kind or another. Soap powder and cleaning products to mention but a few. Not God searching though. Not something I'd particularly think was ground-breaking; I think conventional religion still has the monopoly on that one,' O'Hare said smiling. 'Anyway, what'd you think I am – a walking cyclopedia?'

O'Hare tracked Stonercrop down to the reading room at City College New York. As a visiting religious lecturer, he had been invited to give a talk. Entitled: *The Death of God in Nazi Germany—A Jewish and Christian Perspective*, he was writing up notes. O'Hare stood to one side of him waiting for him to finish a notation, before asking:

'Bet you don't remember me?'

Stonercrop looked up. A man had his hand out to him, 'Sorry. Your face is familiar, can't quite place it though.'

'Charlie O'Hare. You were one of my lecturers from Iowa,' he said taking his hand back unsure that he had the right man after all.

Stonercrop put his hand to his mouth in surprise. 'Well, I'll be jiggered. It is. As I live and breathe, Charlie O'Hare. I remember. You were with the FBI weren't you? Didn't they sponsor you? They had an education program if my memory serves. Of course. Ha! We had one or two drinking sessions, as well. How could I forget you? You're looking well. In fact . . .' Stonercrop studied him closer, 'you're looking, *very* well. You're not still with the Bureau?'

'Shame to say, I am. It's them that keeps me young – that and following an intensive fitness regime. They do tend to keep us on our toes. Especially us older ones.'

'That's good, that's good. Mind you, I never did see you taking up religion as a vocation. But, if my memory serves, you never did have any intention for a career move in that direction, did you? Too much of the no nonsense about you for that. Anyway, I take it you haven't come to see me on matters theological. How can I help you?'

'No, Sax. Although, we could have another drink, some time. There's some great Irish bars springing up in New York. Guinness—'

'Ugh, no, Charlie. I'm a wine man with a drop of Napoleon thrown in for good measure if you'd forgotten. Keep the Liffey water in Dublin Bay where it belongs. But, we can compromise.'

O'Hare laughed changing the subject. 'I wonder if you can help me with some information,' he asked seriously.

'Of course, of course.'

'About someone you know. *Raynham.*'

Stonercrop's face drained.

'*Dr. Jarvis—*'

'Are you still in touch with him these days?'

Stonercrop tried to keep himself calm. Why had this man come to speak to him about Raynham now? Had someone told him the connection between the two of them? After a disconnection, they had spent years fostering. That should not have changed to the outside world. Anyone that was anyone knew the relationship between him, and Raynham had been fractious. Within the Order, they would be something else. His mind thought outside the proverbial box. The sought-after science they were involved depended on secrecy. A concealment that began 2000 years before when the science to unravel the mystery had always remained one step behind. It was within their grasp, men, as in times past, came to question them and their motives no longer with torture and death for holding heretical views, in the present world as dangerous now; where members of fanatical religions were prepared to die to return man to the Dark Age's no-one was any longer safe. Nothing, it seemed to him, had changed. Nescience was still holding court. Not that O'Hare was such a man, but his organization might have other ideas not in keeping with their own. O'Hare was a trained inquisitor and no fool. If he was asking about Raynham, it was likely he was seeking information about him, too. He thought ahead. Did it extend into the world of Frederik Spannocs, and *Oceans Galactica*? Fortunately, there were those controlling events that must know that the FBI were knocking – or to put it bluntly – those that pulled O'Hare's strings, were looking into what they were about, putting the word out on how best to deal with a creeping curiosity that only the security forces of a country can muster. The only comfort he could draw was that 'people' would know of his visit. He swallowed deeply before continuing. 'Haven't seen him in years, Charlie. I assumed he'd returned to lecturing. He was in England for a time you know. In the army. Mentioned in dispatches for bravery and all that. D-Day. Got a medal from the British, last I heard. And that was what I read in the papers. What's he been up to that interests the FBI, cohorting with the Russians or something? O'Hare laughed out loud, and Stonercrop picked up on it. 'So he is. An educated man of action. That wouldn't surprise me that you'd want him. Your people are always looking to recruit others to work behind the iron curtain. Or is it, wait a second, you looking to arrest him under the FBI's Counter Intelligence Program? McCarthyism begat Hoover-ism. Reds under beds and all that. You think that Raynham is a *subversive*?'

O'Hare shook his head, smiling. 'I couldn't say what our people have in mind. We're trying to find him that's all. Are there any organizations that might be interested in his past theories? I did know about his research, although an idea stolen from Crick and Watson might be pushing it a bit far.'

Stonercrop was worried. O'Hare was not a million miles from what they were about, an investigation of Raynham based on a crazy hypothesis that a schoolboy in First Grade would dismiss would be credible enough reason for another FBI section to be interested in him. 'You mean his third strand theory. Ha, ha, ha. Listen; let me say that Raynham was no geneticist, his concepts crossed over the line from known science to pure fantasy. As for any organization that would want to fund that, well, short of calling up L. Ron Hubbard the science fiction creator, I couldn't begin to help you with that one.' His own knowledge of religions and beliefs, with their theoretical ideas, put him in demand on the lecturing circuits of American universities. O'Hare would know that. Unless he admitted to this man's questions, sooner than later when it was found one existed that had been prominent for 2000 years he would look either a fool or someone that was holding something back. The FBI could have him blacklisted for withholding information. They would never have enough on him to send him to jail, but they could certainly make life awkward for him. After all, the Order was perfectly innocent to outsiders. Its outer ring kept those inside secure from prying eyes. Himself for instance. 'There is an organization with the name of Order since you mention it. He could well be involved with them. Not surprised you haven't heard of them; I'd forgotten them myself. I believe they go back to the death of Christ, more scientific philosophy than religion, although they consider themselves the latter. Might be something Raynham would be part of. More prayer and chant than science.' He dismissed them by a change of subject. 'And what with you . . . you were a Roman Catholic I believe, are you still one?'

'With your background you should know better than ask a question like that. A Roman Candle until my dying day, so I am.'

'Not an organization that would suit you then.'

'Where are they based, do you know?'

'Phwww! Not sure. I should imagine somewhere like Italy, or its Austro–German borders – look—'

'Vatican City . . . perhaps Turin?'

God, doesn't he give up. Stonercrop thought to himself.

'You're letting that interrogative brain of yours run away with itself Charlie O'Hare. I have no idea. I tend to concentrate on more mainstream faiths and ideas than those of cranks.'

O'Hare thanked him and promised that they would have that drink sometime.

O'Hare passed details of his conversation with Stonercrop over to Lomax with some noted advice that if he had some understanding of what, whoever it was, wanted to know about these two academics and the Order, they may be worth more than a cursory glance'.

As new appointed Assistant Director of the FBI, Lomax, not yet familiar with O'Hare's way of saying things, penned some notes. He had not figured out that O'Hare needed to know who was asking, and why, before he made any further recommendations. Lomax reading between his penned lines scratched his remarks out with his pencil. He took O'Hare's advice.

An investigation by his own team into the two men revealed nothing further than what they knew of them. Any considerations he might have that the two men were involved in communist activities counter to the country's national security were, he agreed with O'Hare, nothing more than a smokescreen; any investigations from COINTELPRO would need to be 'trumped-up' to secure convictions against them by McCarthy if they were needed out of the way.

Nine – 1950s

EX-CAPTAIN. Doctor Jarvis Raynham DSM, formerly of the United States Army, looked out across the bay through his binoculars. It was early evening. The *Algonquin* anchored off Campeche in the Gulf of Mexico was a yacht built for the wealthy. The First Congener had told him that Spannocs conducts business by radio telephone early evening. With his crew ashore for amusement, leaving no more than a skeleton watch, no-one was likely to see him coming. It was late afternoon when he removed his equipment from the trunk of his hire car. A large hold all containing his dry suit, two Siebe Gorman air-tanks along with their ancillary equipment alongside. He opted for compressed air tanks instead of the more traditional oxygen re-breather he was familiar; but would take one with him should there be a need, where bubbles of air-gas coming to the surface would leave a trace for anyone to follow they may turn out more useful. With a combined capacity of eighty cubic feet of compressed air, connected to a manifold, a Merlin two-stage twin-hose demand valve complete with contents gauge, he connected them together and turned on the valve. The red needle indicated 120 atmospheres, he calculated breathing a cubic foot of air a minute the tank would give him a theoretical eighty minutes of breathing time below the surface; halve that at 33 feet. The yacht lying a quarter mile out he would stay on the surface for as long as possible to conserve air. Aware that he would be breathing heavily from the swim; and with a loaded weight belt to keep him low in the water, he would breathe the first part of the swim through his snorkel, allowing himself an hour and a half to get out to the yacht, screw the limpet mine to its hull, then return to the beach.

He struggled for half an hour putting his suit on. Normally divers helped each other; he was working alone. *That was one bastard*, he said to himself when dressed, the sweat from the exertion ran down the inside. He strapped a Rolex Submariner watch to his left wrist, a compass to his right, and then carried his equipment to the shore line laying out first his air-tanks, then the limpet mine. This to be placed under the main fuel tanks two-thirds down the yacht's length. An MIR-type packed with 9lb of explosive was more than capable of ripping the bottom out of the *Algonquin* taking everyone on board out. An aniseed ball sweet, he had earlier inserted into it, would act as a time delay allowing him to get clear. If anyone on board should be aware of what he was up to and attempted to depth charge him, they would need to bear in mind that the shock waves would suck the nails right out of a wooden hulled vessel.

He knelt on the beach putting his arms through the straps of the air-tanks above his elbows, then lifting them over his head dropped them neatly onto his back. He pulled tight the adjusting straps. He then carefully lifted the mine strapping it to the front of himself. Normally attached to the bottom of ships by magnetism, the *Algonquin*, not being steel, he was to screw a hook into the hull hanging the mine from it. He spat into his face mask smearing his saliva on the inside of the glass to prevent it misting up, rinsing it in the sea pulled it on over his forehead. He pushed his feet into his flippers, leaning behind pulling their straps tight round the back of his ankles. One last look through his binoculars he dropped them into the hold all, zipping the bag closed, burying it in the sand. He pulled his mask down over his eyes, put in his mouthpiece, drew a breath to check that it was issuing air on demand; then removing it replaced it with the snorkel, then lastly strapping on his weight belt containing 22lb of lead, he entered the water. It was 1730 hours.

Frederik Spannocs was waiting for a call on his telephone. He had gone out on deck to enjoy the warmth of the early evening half-light. Finding less hassle and any embarrassment of knowing too many people in American society he had decided that living on board *Algonquin*, combined with his home in San y los Amado, suited as an operational base for *Oceans Galactica*. As for the jungles in the region, well, he thought, what better burial ground for bodies with no questions asked. Sucking on a huge Havana cigar, his man-servant and associate, Tony D'Sotto approached him. The man completely altered by plastic surgery and psychological personality enhancements was striking. The new D'Sotto was now well educated, had a superb locution, was tall, with an effeminate charm. He was as trustworthy, loyal and every bit as dedicated to Spannocs as he had been to Giuseppi, protecting him with a jealous zeal from anybody that got within a mile of him. You could say, love would not have been too strong a word, if Spannocs's understanding among ordinary mortals were as he once remembered. D'Sotto was pointing to the sweep hand of his chronograph. Spannocs standing at the rail of the yacht nodded, his human instinct to tense his body for what was to come took him over.

It was 1830 hours.

The sky lit to daylight luminosity with the heat and flash from the explosion below their feet. *Algonquin*, blown from under them, left, along with the three men, not so much as a splinter of wood to record that any of it had ever existed. Twenty minutes later Raynham came ashore gasping for breath – an exercise successfully completed; and as good as any he had achieved at Omaha in 1944. The man, supposedly possessed of Satan was dead, along with the Order's myth: that Satan was here on earth ahead of the Messiah's Second Coming, was no more than wishful thinking to the First Congener and *The Order of the Most Divine Third Circle*. He laughed at the very idea of it.

D'Sotto approached Spannocs; the sweep hand of his chronograph recording a past time stopped – continued.

'Sir. Mr. Beagle sends his compliments and wishes to inform you he's detected underwater activity.'

Spannocs went through the process of consideration without having to know any more details of what was to happen – have happened. That verse had been and gone. Taking a slow draw on his Havana once again, drawing in deeply, he spoke the smoke from his lungs.

'Inform Mr. Beagle he has my permission to carry on, Tony.'

D'Sotto nodded his head in a sideways salutary manner, turned smartly in his deck pump heeled shoes, a small squeak of rubber from varnished oak heard, walked off. Spannocs resumed his position at the rail of his yacht to reconsider his cigar.

Five minutes after the Avon inflatable swept away from *Algonquin*; and with its bow lifting and dropping, accelerated up to eighteen knots, its hull beat a dent hollow sound of time to the fifty horse power Mercury outboard engine that was pushing the boat across the waves until, a quarter mile away, its engine settled to a sedate tick-over. The yacht's coxswain, clearly seen patrolling the surface with an echo-sounder through the outboard's exhaust smoke. After a time, the inflatable moved off, stopping again after fifty yards where the whole operation would begin anew. Three times more Beagle repeated the operation until he was satisfied.

Spannocs watched the coxswain drop an object over the side of the inflatable. From across the bay a bonging sound echoed, followed a few seconds later by a plume of water that went skywards showering both the coxswain and the inflatable. Twice more he dropped miniature depth charges from the back of the inflatable while maneuvering the inflatable skillfully in a circle. With the tiller between his legs and the inflatable at half-throttle, the boat tilted into an angle that only centrifugal force kept Beagle from falling into the sea. Satisfied he stopped the inflatable, leaned over the side retrieved an object from the water. Dropping a tangled heap of equipment into the inflatable, he accelerated one last time bringing the Avon round before returning to its mistress.

Spannocs was still looking out to sea when D'Sotto gently coughed catching his attention. He turned. D'Sotto, his head limped to one side, held a silver tray balanced on his upturned fingertips. On it a tumbler, half filled with blue liquid.

'Your aperitif, sir.'

Spannocs began sucking strongly and quickly on his Havana taking the glass. He removed the red-hot end, held his head back dropping it neatly down his throat. Taking up the glass from the tray, he poured the absinthe after it swallowing hard. He opened his mouth and eructed a blue flame that turned to a wisp of smoke then replaced the empty tumbler back on the tray. D'Sotto held out a lighter, thumb-grinder a flame from it and re-lighted Spannocs's Havana he held in his mouth toward him.

'Mr. Beagle recovered two air-tanks, Frederik.'

'Very good, Tony. Give Mr. Beagle my compliments.

'Yes sir. Will that be all, Frederik?'

Spannocs turned his eyes towards the sea continuing to draw on his cigar. Removing it from his mouth said, 'I think so.'

D'Sotto smiled. He looked at his chronograph. The sweep hand skipped forward before continuing its circle. It was 1830 hours. His smile faded. He was worried for his friend that possessed of something, he knew not what, that the church would any longer be able to reach out to.

Spannocs seeing his anxiety said, 'No need to be fearful Tony. Everything is in order.'

'Yes sir, I believe so, Frederik. . . . Yes, everything is in order.'

'Very good. Goodnight Tony,' he replied. He turned and looked back out across the sea saying to himself, *Now . . . that's powerful magic!*

Ten – 1950s

'AFTER ALL, it's only a matter of having other strings to your bow,' O'Hare said to Lomax with an impudent nod of his head.

Lomax holding his lower lip between his thumb and forefinger, agreed. The organization could do with some scrutiny. With Stonercrop's reported death in Italy while on vacation; Raynham entering Mexico purportedly taking a similar break; the coincidence of a link between the two men was enough to turn the heads of any department involved with national security. In this case, following Lomax speaking to the Justice Department of O'Hare's concerns, using the argument of Raynham being in Mexico, with Cuba in mind, further mentioning COINTELPRO; not to mention Mafia, it fell to them to investigate, adding another case to Lomax's burgeoning workload. Although he did caution O'Hare that, the coincidence of the rivals did not necessarily mean they were hand-in-glove with the Order. With current Bureau files having nothing further to add to what they knew O'Hare suggested, as a starting point, that they might be a business or charity the Internal Revenue would know of. Being a specialist in organized crime and tax evasion with the FBI, O'Hare suggested that David Weinberg would be the ideal investigative officer to carry it off. Lomax, pulled on his lip once again, reluctantly agreed.

Internal Revenue was eager to co-operate with David Weinberg. If the FBI needed information regarding an organization, it would mean malpractice; and malpractice means loose dollars sloshing round; dollars that sloshed could amount to tax evasion. At least, that's how Gerry Tell saw situations. Twenty-five and eager to make a name for himself within the IR, Tell clung to David as a limpet. The scratching of backs was as important to him as it was between corporate businesses. He had learned that lesson early in life from his father. This would be a coup as far as he was concerned. For the moment, David had said, it would have to remain unofficial as they had no hard evidence that the Order were anything more than a bunch of religious cranks. Even so an unofficial inquiry from an agent of the FBI, well, he thought, this could be the friendship of a lifetime.

David felt at ease with the man that used his first name. It made him feel comfortable. When you want something from someone and that person, one you've never met before begins to do that you know he's going to be super, *super* cooperative, he thought.

'This Sax, *Sax*— Stonercrop?'

'Right. Is he actively corporate or a sleeper?' Tell asked.

'I'm sorry, are we talking of the same organization here?'

'It could take more time to dig into everyone that's involved with a company that size. They have so many strands in their web, for tax avoidance purposes, I don't want a law suit issued against me for making inquiries that are not correct. Sometimes it is necessary to pick at them with a needle as if one were taking meat from a crab shell. It could take time.'

Trying to see the analogy, and still not sure what he was talking about David assumed that when he said 'company' that it was a general term used by the IR applying to both a religious sect and a business. 'Well, do what you have to. Tomorrow be too soon?'

'You don't want much do you? I'll see what I can do. Got to find out if they still exist first.'

The following day David got a call back from Gerry Tell informing him that they were still in existence and a list with over 400 names on it.

'400?'

'About what I expected with an organization that size. It does include all the subsidiary companies connected with them . . .'

'What'd you mean subsidiary companies? *The Order of the Most Divine Third Circle* hardly warrants having a subsidiary; they're supposed to be religious sect.'

'They may well be, but from where I'm standing, they *are* a subsidiary; and of a company known by the name of Oceans Galactica. Didn't you know?'

O'Hare stared up at David, re-adjusted his glasses, and carried on reading down the list of names. He was not to be hurried. David continued studying the wallpaper and was about to count the *fleurs-de-lis* horizontally for the fifth time when O'Hare said:

'Pour me a whiskey, will yer? Me brain's gone numb.'

David sighed. He went to O'Hare's drinks cabinet took out two tumblers poured one for himself and one for O'Hare, then handed it to him. He went to the window sipping his own and looked out for a change of scenery from wallpaper.

'Got yer, yer *bastard!*'

David turned away from watching two drunk men arguing with each other in the street outside and faced him, 'Not you. The one here.' He sat opposite him and looked at the name O'Hare was pointing out to him. 'That is, *Tony D'Sotto*. A criminal that your father and me were very familiar. Please forgive me for repeating myself, but that, *bastard*, is Marco Giuseppi's partner. Giuseppi was involved with child abduction that your father and me tried to bring to book failing; getting ourselves transferred to the Bureau for our so-called devotion to protect children from abuse. Giuseppi was supposed to have burned to death in a fire before anyone could arrest him. We got warned off from investigating the incident when I told them I didn't believe it . . . I should have shot him dead when I had the chance.'

'So what happened to this D'Sotto fellow?'

'Supposed to have returned home to Sicily.'

David became interested in what O'Hare had said about him and his father. He had known that his father Frank had been involved with O'Hare years before but had guessed it was something to do with prohibition, leastways, that was what his mother had told him. He asked O'Hare how his father had died. 'Mother told me he was shot dead caught in a cross-fire, is that right?'

O'Hare looked at him. He had not noticed so much at first, but with his mentioning of his father, he saw him in his eyes. David was his father's son right enough. More so, his mother, Sarah. He had not been there; he could not, in truth answer him; only that he had died in the line of duty. It came to him of the paper that was later found in Frank's pocket, accusing him of being an abuser himself.

'When was all this?'

'Err, let me see. Started about, 1916, 20s. Somewhere round that time. We were all . . . all about the same age as Giuseppi. Mid-twenties. Him and D'Sotto were Italian immigrants. Their families came to the US together. I guess D'Sotto would be about sixty now.' He studied David not knowing where all this was headed. His uncertainties when he heard David was the best man for this investigation had not been for nothing. None the less, he could not help himself saying:

'This is gold-dust to me, David.'

It took David two days to find D'Sotto's name on an FBI file of informants under the alias Philip Maddox. (It had never occurred to O'Hare to check it out.) There was a reference alongside that interested David: (See Seaburg: Written Authority Required). The reference to the filing cabinet had a number. He went to it and pulled on the cabinet handle on the off-chance that it had not been locked. It was. He took from his pocket the end of a broken engineer's scriber, pushed it into the lock and turned it. The lock clicked open. He quickly went through the file dividers looking for anything relevant to his father. A report of the actual event leading up to his father's death would be useful. He noticed that some of them were police files, some old Bureau of Investigation ones. They had been hidden under a sub-section that no-one was ever likely to have stumbled across. They should have destroyed them all if they wanted to bury the evidence, he thought. Someone was making sure that if any of this ever came to light, destroying government files would not be one of their crimes. He found it weird reading through the bust on the club that had the name, Tinkerboys (he shuddered). He read on not sure that he wanted to know the way his father had died. He need not have worried. There was no mention of his father having taken a hit by the mob. When O'Hare had first mentioned the name of D'Sotto, he thought that his alias might have been responsible, but the man had an alibi. He was in police custody at the time. He was also a clerk employed by New York City Hall. That was interesting. He took out an accompanying file card:

```
Tony D'Sotto, Sicilian origin,

b. 1888 (approx.)

Entered America 1905.

No case to answer, file closed)

(Delete all ref. to Oceans Galactica)
```

The card typed: FILE DELETED. Why would they mention D'Sotto and his connection with *Oceans Galactica*? He took all the files marked for deletion putting them into a paper sack. Returning to the cabinet, he pushed the drawer closed, and taking his handkerchief from his pocket wiped his fingerprints away. File deleted, but what were these? Were there others elsewhere? He would come back later that evening when the staff had gone home; retrieve the evidence.

'What harm can it do?' David said to O'Hare when he caught up with him. '*Oceans Galactica* is a registered company in New York; supposedly legitimate.'

O'Hare cautioned him. He supposed with them being the subject of an IR investigation their people would be aware that the Bureau would have been informed 'as a matter of courtesy', so to speak. He reluctantly agreed that he continue.

David found they were not particularly co-operative. Pleasant enough, but Miss Marple, the telephone girl on the other end of the line, said they had never heard of either D'Sotto or Maddox. She agreed with him, when he asked if his name might be on a list held by any of their subsidiaries – the Order, for example. She laughed, saying that the Order was one of the founder's little jokes. A form of stress relief for his executives to use when they needed God, or something more human. It was their code name for relaxation. Wouldn't want to go into what the relaxation consisted. But you know what high-pressure execs are.'

'I see. So they're not a regular organization within your group?' She said no.

'You mention the founder. Is it possible to speak him?' David asked.

She laughed once more, 'I'm afraid you're a little late on that one, he died, what, forty years ago.'

'He had a name I suppose.'

'I'm sorry, Mr. Weinberg, company policy forbids.'

'And how would I contact this Order?'

'Not sure they're still going. It would be as near as impossible to help you on that one. Unless you've a thousand years to spare,' she added for smartness, 'or a court order for corporate disclosure from a judge.' She had a last laugh.

David was annoyed with the woman's intransigence. 'I'll have one with you in the morning, Miss.'

'*Shit!*' Miss Marple whispered from beautifully formed red lips, replacing the telephone onto its cradle. She picked it back up and dialled.

The company list of executives, managers, employees, together with accountants, outside agencies – past and present – obtained from Oceans Galactica landed on David's desk the following morning. O'Hare had got to it first. A manuscript of foolscap pages, worn, with space for further names as and when a new employee taken on. No founder. No Maddox. A list of lawyers with equal voting rights, re-typed over old names. Some painted out, with additional people typed further down. O'Hare made the point that they did not waste paper. There were hundreds of them; some so illegible from time O'Hare had to hold the sheets up to the window to make them out.

'Why should Maddox's name be on one of our files, and not theirs?' O'Hare asked.

'I'm ahead of you there, Charlie. I called Miss Marple earlier to thank her for her efficiency asking to speak to their employment records office. Rather rudely, I might add. They told me that up until 1925 there would have been, but after the fire . . .'

'He likes his fires, doesn't he?' O'Hare interrupted his face buried in the paperwork. David looked puzzled. '*What the—*'

O'Hare's face took on a smile that turned to laughter. He banged his fist several times on his desk.

'What is it?' David asked.

'Ha, they've fucked up, that's what. Look, look at that name.'

David had to pull the sheet from his eyes as O'Hare was holding it too close for him to focus properly. 'What am I supposed to be looking at?'

'That, that there.' O'Hare pointed his finger at an inked-out splurge on the paper. 'Hold it up to the light.'

David did as he was asked. He could not see what all the fuss was about. 'What am I supposed to be looking at? Show me.'

He snatched the sheet from him and pointed his finger at a name barely visible. '*Joseph!* There, there. By the King of the Leprechauns, someone from his outfits fucked-up big-time. As ours have. We've found him.'

'Who? That's not Maddox's name. What are you on about, Charlie . . . *Joseph?*'

He faced David and put the sheet down. 'The founder. Joseph is English for Giuseppi. The M wrapped round it is for Marco. And they told us to forget him. That they would deal with him. He ups and supposedly dies. Not on your life, does he. The founder dead! I don't think so. For Oceans Galactica read Giuseppi. Find him and you'll find D'Sotto sucking on the end of his *cock*. That's how dead those two will be. I thought there was something amiss with what you said about those files. I know. He and his lover-boy are being protected. And I think I know why.'

David had not understood O'Hare's obsession with this man he called Marco Giuseppi. This was supposed to be an investigation into Stonercrop and Raynham. His brief had been to highlight communists that were working on high profile projects in sensitive areas likely to be a threat to America's security. Without realizing, his investigation into that had pulled in other issues changing the game. Names listed from his father, as well as O'Hare's past linked to a corporation. One that had government contracts. The fact they had or did at one time have a pseudo-religious connection, as far as he was concerned, was incidental. He told O'Hare that he would have to speak to Lomax if he wanted him to get any more involved in any of this. O'Hare was annoyed, saying to him that this was to be his own private investigation and it had nothing to do with Lomax. People needed exposing for what they had done. Still doing. He had read the papers. Child abuse had not gone away. If anything, it was increasing to industrial proportions. Unlikely, he had to admit, that Giuseppi was orchestrating all of it. Nevertheless, that particular man, as far as O'Hare was concerned had a price on his head that warranted a sale, 'If there were any possibility he was still alive,' he told David, 'he would go after him, and hang the consequence.'

When Johnson had first inducted him and Frank into the Bureau of Investigation, the same man later denied by the Bureau; as being on their books, should have rang alarm bells for him and Frank. As experienced policemen, they should have known better than to have been put off leaving it for others to worry about. Words suggesting that they were officers rare on the ground for their stand on non-corruption in a city that was rank with it; officers that had the interests of immigrant children that had been isolated from their families, abused, prostituted, sold on by adults whose depraved behavior made Satan look saintly, were what, Johnson said, was what the new Bureau looked for in the new order for agents was looking more like bull-shit. Since it has become apparent that someone somewhere had wanted them both out of the way; that left him remaining. His nightmares since that day. Of events, that he had put to the back of his mind as fanciful haunted him. His feeling that he was possessed was real: the result of a rift in heaven and hell, the likely consequence of what occurred that evening.

He had, for the last ten years, settled on the back-burner of his mind the idea, that he was immortal. The first indication, the simple one, of friends, complaining of back-ache, arthritis, high blood pressure etc, etc; all alien to his own body; putting those maladies to one side, came to terms with the fact that he was fitter, leaner, led a healthier life style, luckier, etc, etc was burying his head in the sand. For so long he had managed to kid himself that those were the reasons that creeping old-age would catch up with him later rather than sooner to redress the balance. But as the years had passed, he no longer believed that. He should not be fit. (Neither by design nor otherwise.) His life style was comparable to his contemporaries. More so in his case. The nature of the job. How many lived with the idea that rising from one's bed mornings; that it could be their last day on earth? A solider on active service, for sure. Getting gunned down for being a law enforcement officer with the FBI was more likely than, say, a footballer. Stresses of duty, people he dealt encouraged all manner of bad habits. He smoked cigars most of his life, drank alcohol more than necessity demanded; and certainly eaten more than his share of crap food over the years. Whether it was those stresses, or he had subconsciously over done those vices in order to prove that he was as mortal as the next man he again, could not say. If anyone should be struck down by premature heart-attack, wasn't it likely to be him. Something within him was preventing that from happening. Had been ever since he and Frank Weinberg had busted Giuseppi's house. At seven-year intervals a sharp pain in his chest struck him down, forcing him to take to his bed for a day or two, only to recover with vigor anew. Doctors had found no cause or reason for his recovery. If he thought too deeply of this immortality, mixed feelings came over him. First a sense of depression, one of excitement that he was going forward into a future that would see such changes and inventions. If it were not for the option of suicide, he would have taken his life years since knowing the despair that awaited him. For those he loved seeing buried one after another, was the thought that sent his depression spiraling down. If Frank were still alive, would he have lived in the same state? And what of Fariq Mihalyvich and his daughter, Irinushka (the jury was still out for him as to whether she was the one that possessed him). Johnson, *Giuseppi* himself even. There could be a new super race of man wandering the earth unable to speak of it for fear of experimental incarceration. Man had sought immortality: an elixir of youth, a sup from the Holy Grail, since he had witnessed the unconsciousness of a loved one believing they would rise from their sleep only instead to rot away before their eyes. If death were a curse, it not occurring to an unbeliever; unlike immortality that he would have to bear for all time. That would be one Road to Perdition signposted: Forward to the Fourth Dimension.

Lomax was not a man to have agents working with their hands tied behind their backs. He told the Research Director that he, Lomax, should be the man who decided who would do what, not them. David was an accomplished agent, but why should they know that? What other good reason had they forwarded his name out of so many other agents? He went on:

'If the higher echelons within the FBI, even the CIA, are up to anything, it was not to be at the expense of the lives of my people. Send your own.' He took advantage of the silence, hurriedly continuing. 'Do you suppose that agents in our field of expertise are interested in some amateur surveillance unit who may or may not wish to exist to prove the existence of space aliens and other crackpot wanderings of the mind to keep conspiracy theorists happy by hiding the truth? No. What this is about is something unexplained seen off the coast of Campeche you believe are the Ruskies building missile silos in Cuba.'

Special Research only got involved when there was something unaccountable that needed investigating. Considered an invaluable department when it came to national security their contributions based on academic research using history as a benchmark was impressively accurate when it came to knowing what an 'enemy' had in mind. An enemy that not all that many years before were America's allies during a European war. The USSR, distrustful after having so many of their people killed by an invading German army the West was reaching out to re-capitalize, lodged in their craw.

The Research Director hollered down the telephone to Lomax, 'There's more to us than seeking out the existence of flying saucers . . .'

'*Exactly!* A Russian first strike. In which case you should own up to it and leave professionals that work within the framework of law enforcement to pursue longer-term unsolved objectives.'

At this point Research lost control telling Lomax that David Weinberg had no need to know anymore other than check-out what was happening in Mexico, citing Doctor Raynham as whether he was dead, alive, or plain switched sides.

'And that's between you and me, Franklin. David will work well alongside the CIA already there. Is that clear enough for you. J. Edgar thinks he's right for the task, why should you know any more than that?'

Lomax's voice took on a cynical tone, 'Oh, well. If Mr. Hoover thinks he's the right man for the job he must be, don't stress yourself asking me.'

The telephone from the Research end clicked. Lomax looked into the dead mouthpiece and issued a verbal adjective as to the marital status of the Director of Research's mother and father. Replacing his phone in its cradle added. 'And up yours, too.'

In the back of his mind was why. How was it that the

Department of Research had been able to single David out? It was not their decision to make; it was his. To say that Hoover was all for the choice, that worried him. It was as if Hoover's name had been subtlety dropped in to override him. The adage, *To kill two birds with one stone*, entered his mind, and he had no idea why.

Information that diving gear found washed up on the shore of Campeche came through on the teleprinter in Lomax's office. He tore it off and passed it to O'Hare.

'That's out of our jurisdiction,' O'Hare said reading it. 'CIA business has nothing to do with us. We're checking out Stonercrop, the two men may come together nicely when that investigation's completed.'

Lomax pulled a face, well aware of the relationship between him and David. He was not sure how to tell him that he was sending him. He did not need to worry.

'They still want us to investigate it, don't they? And you're going to send, David. For God's sake Franklin, hasn't his mother been through enough losing her husband?'

After having cooked dinner for Sarah Weinberg at his place that evening, O'Hare settled down to a whiskey and a cigar.

'David is going to Mexico on an assignment, did you know?' *Did he know?* He'd spent an hour arguing with Lomax as to why he should not send him. Everything about this case was too neat for his liking. Oceans Galactica, the Order, Stonercrop, Raynham, and the names D'Sotto and M. Joseph, all too neat and coincidental for his liking. The threat to David's life when he was a boy was still to the forefront of his mind. He covered those concerns by acting mildly surprised by answering Sarah that David had not said anything to him about it, adding, with a shrug of his shoulders:

'Didn't want to make me envious I suppose. He'll be all right.'

She pursed her lips. She had not understood him saying, *He'll be all right*, but did not pursue the point putting it down to, Something someone might say.

O'Hare was Bible black in the face after hearing what David's brief was.

'Raynham slipped through our net. Reports of him being in Mexico came late. Look, Charlie, it's more than coincidence, but a yacht, belonging to *Oceans Galactica* was blown out of the waters down there; only to re-appear minutes later out from the smoke as if nothing had happened. It has put a spot-light on a sensitive situation. Nothing to do with any strange activity, but it has drawn attention to that yacht and its occupant. The CIA has people down there who have been monitoring Cuba. There is a Russian presence round an area known as Bay of Pigs. Military intelligence has it they are building missile silos in response to what we have in Turkey. At least, that's what President Kennedy believes. Current opinion is that Raynham is spying for the Russians; I've to go and liaise with the CIA, find out any truth in any of it. Events have turned political and I could be in the middle of something that will make history.'

'Trouble with history, it's littered with corpses.'

O'Hare was anxious about a situation David Weinberg was being channeled. David was no longer a boy. He was grown and every bit the law enforcement officer he and Frank had been at their age. He had never got over the gunning down of his father feeling protective of him and Sarah. The threat to his life with that accursed birthday card that had made Sarah confront him the evening before, and to damn her late husband as to the worth of what they were about was uppermost in his mind. An aspect of investigations into child abuse that he had often questioned without result appeared to be rearing its ugly head with familiar names in spite of all this talk of

Russian–American politics that he was damned sure the Kennedy government had well in hand. He played along concentrating his questions to those relevant to what they were currently investigating, that of Stonercrop and Raynham, in the Responsibilities Program for subversives and communists and which David had been first co-opted to work with him. A move, he worried, instigated to draw David Weinberg into a late Bar mitzvah revenge threat. Whether Lomax was privy to any of this, for the moment, O'Hare would remain with the jury that was still deliberating.

'The CIA found diving tanks washed up on the shore near Canún on the Yucatan Channel. The pillar valve torn from it. That suggests either a dodgy thread on the tank's pillar valve, an over inflated bottle, or an explosion from another source. All of which leads me to think that Raynham is likely dead. I'll be back before you know it.'

'Raynham was an ex-military diver wasn't he?' O'Hare asked.

'A specialist engineer, yes. You're right. I'd forgotten that.'

'If that's the case, I think we'll find this particular communist subversive, is very much alive.'

O'Hare continued his argument with Lomax. With the suspicion that he was prepared to initiate an assignment, knowing that it may jeopardize an agent's life because of other factors. He expounded further.

'That of revenge, from a past that he was not responsible.'

Lomax stared at him shaking his head.

The man was unbelievable, he thought. 'Do you honestly think that I would do that, Agent O'Hare? Because if you do, you'd better have a good reason for saying it, and quick.'

He broke his own rule of ever trusting a superior within the FBI by telling him of what he knew of two men, supposedly working for the FBI, Johnson and Sullivan, who had given him and Frank their promotion and who he suspected were behind covering a catalog of child abuses; with the man likely still alive and responsible, are still protecting him, 'That your right hand knows what your left does not. Franklin, am I supposed to tell you something that Research has willfully withheld from you?'

Lomax said he could try, but it was out of his hands.

'Assuming what you're telling me is true. And that's something you only have their word for.'

'What do you expect me to do about direct orders? I've had an earache from Research already when I suggested it was CIA business.'

'Oh, is that all? Well you know why you don't. A dollar to a dime they didn't say to Research we'd like to send an agent, one that's expendable . Who've you got? I know says the other, David Weinberg . . . the *Jew!* He'll do. We'll suggest him to Hoover.'

Lomax waited for him to get it all out of his system.

'Have you quite finished? *Thank you.* More supposition. They'd had got more than, *Up yours!* from me if they had. It's a routine assignment. No more than that. This is no more dangerous than any other operation we undertake outside of the country from time to time. Apart from that we'll have all our resources behind him, *and* he'll be with a good man.'

'The last time anyone I know was recommended for a special operation of no consequence and danger was my partner, his father. After his death – and with nobody in the frame for it, I smelt blarney, and if you don't mind my saying, it reeks of it still.' Lomax listened as he continued his voice quieter. 'Franklin, I don't want to have to go tell that woman that not only did we let her husband down, but her son is dead, because he is a Weinberg. I haven't finished with all that yet. The only way that they're going to stop my inquiries into finding Marco Giuseppi and bringing him to book for what he did in Lower Manhattan is to take me on. Someone within our organization knows something. If you've any inkling David will be in danger, I'll go.'

'If I pulled a field agent every time I had a bad feeling, we would never get anything done. If you don't know that, Charlie, you should have got a job as a photographer. I have to send him. Is that black and white enough for you.'

'Bit late for that now,' Charlie said under his breath.

'Yeh. Well don't push me. You're damn near retirement if you're not there already. Agent Weinberg's going to Mexico because he's the best man for the job, that's all. If there's nothing else, I'll bid you good day.'

'Secret and safe,' O'Hare muttered under his breath without thinking.

'"*Secret, and safe*". What'd you mean by that?' Lomax asked.

He didn't answer.

They had other duties. They were serving officers. Keeping them close, murdering them at their leisure, may have been their mandate for what they had witnessed. Dore, Rivers, Brent, Frank; apart from himself, possibly Mihalyvich and Irinushka – Giuseppi undoubtedly a special case – no-one else was left standing. No more people being witness to it than necessary. Sarah was under the impression that Frank killed in a mob shoot-out was by a stray bullet when he knew it had been a marksman. Telling Lomax of his concerns was not to tell him how to do his job, but to protect those he loved.

This brought to mind another question for him. Did Frank know who the Clown was? Wouldn't he have said something to him? Unless . . . he had kept it to himself to protect him. He remembered that shortly after the incident Frank had searched his memory as well as police files to trigger identification with no outcome. He had tried press libraries, photo agencies that had hundreds of pictures of celebrities and film stars. Nothing had shown up. Yet when the mask of the Clown fell from his face in that skirmish, had he seen enough to recognize him later. The hint of recognition from the both of them, of each other, was to put either one in danger of the other. He might have been mistaken, he himself was hanging between life and death at the time. He had been sure, that the man had shaken his head at Frank as if to say, *Let me go!* But O'Hare could never be sure if it were for purpose or the man was using a ploy. The best chance they had of busting child-abduction rested on Frank coming up with a positive identification. He was not able to. *Or wouldn't.* Some of the files removed from Rivers's office by Johnson would have contained damning evidence against all of them, including Giuseppi; none of which made available to them in spite of knowing it was their investigation.

That evening, O'Hare, halfway through a stout in Doheny & Nesbitt's bar on 42nd Street, clutched at his chest toppled from his stool taking the better part of a pint of Guinness with him. Pronounced dead by his friend, Sergei Bezukladnikov, a Russian doctor studying in America; ordered home by the political commissar, Nikita Krushchev. This was to be their last evening together. As usual, they had argued politics while playing backgammon. On this occasion it was pogroms and purges under Stalin.

Eleven – 1950s

'O'HARE HAD NO IDEA WHERE HE WAS. He could hear voices, but whom they belonged and where they came from, he could not say. Not that he was particularly bothered. He did think that he might be dead though. He was conscious of a ringing rattle in his head that was becoming louder. While one of his senses was wondering that, another was aware of an odor, the same that came from a dentist's operating room. The gas that came out of those half-inflated medicine balls that gave you the whirly pits making you feel like shit – he was feeling like that now, and it was no laughing matter. When the sound in his head ceased, he opened his eyes. The bright light was not the cause of his lack of vision, his eyesight had not yet adjusted to the trauma his body had suffered. A faint image of a face (for all that out of focus), he could see was a woman. A white hood over her head she had her back to the window. To him she looked like an angel from a stained-glass window. Now he was not sure if he was in a church or laid out in a chapel of rest. He could see that she was wearing a uniform; she was tapping him on his arm to get an attention he was already giving.

'Charlie?' she said. Turning to the doctor referring to a clipboard on the end of his bed said to him, 'He's come round doctor.' O'Hare thought that she was being a bit formal for an angel and decided to close his eyes again. He started to float. He was warm and comfortable, and he did not want to open his eyes, but the dizziness forced him. He looked up. Another voice, this time one he recognized, joined the first:

'Is he all right?'

The doctor pulled open O'Hare's bed jacket put a stethoscope to his chest and listened, at the same time looking up at the nurse. 'I don't understand this at all. His heart's as strong as a man in his twenties. An hour ago, I was ready to pronounce him dead. I've not come across a recovery like this in all the years I've been practicing. 'Charlie O'Hare! Can you hear me?'

'Hear you; loud enough to wake the dead, who wouldn't be able to hear that bloody shouting? I might be a lot of things, but being dead isn't the same as being deaf, you know.'

God, I've one here all right, the doctor thought to himself. 'I have a visitor for you, are you up to seeing her? It's your wife. I'll be right back. Mrs. O'Hare. If that's his normal attitude, I would say he's returned to the world of normality – quite unbelievable, he has been – well, you know.'

'Hello, Sarah! Thought I recognized the voice.'

'Try and get him to drink some water,' the doctor said. 'I shall need to examine him again. Along with a second opinion.'

'Hello Charlie,' Sarah whispered. 'What have you been up to, you've given us cause for concern, so you have?'

He smiled at her phony Irish brogue and put his hand out to brush her face. She took his hand and put the back of it to her cheek.

'My life! You're accent's worse than my Yiddish,' he replied shrugging his shoulders and opening his hands palms upwards toward her. 'Where did they find me this time?'

'Under a bar stool. A friend you were with went to hospital with you in the ambulance, apologized for leaving you. Something about affairs of the Russian state and a plane to catch.'

'Sergei. A future president in the making if I ever saw one.' He smiled. 'A bar stool you say. That wouldn't have been a first. Hospital? It never put me there before though. How long?' He tried raising himself from his pillow. Gathering his thoughts and events that led to him being here. His eyes were clearing and could see the end of the bed. Sarah was holding his hand once again.

'Whoa, there Charlie. Lie back down,' she said trying to reassure him that he would be all right and was in safe hands. 'Three days. They think it was a heart attack. You were . . .' She hesitated not wanting to say the word.

'You were about to say, I wasn't supposed to make it and that they're calling it a miracle.'

Sarah gently restrained him as he tried to raise himself once more. 'You must take things gently.'

He closed his eyes in resignation. He felt too weak to fight.

'Sweet Mother of Jesus,' he whispered. 'I feel awful. Heart attack you say?'

'A big one. Big enough to . . . well. Your working days with the FBI are over, that's for sure.'

He gently laughed. 'Not if Irinushka's got anything to do with it they won't be—'

'Irinushka?'

His thoughts were back in Giuseppi's house. And Frank – dear boy. Spirits and the angel they had never before revealed by name. The mention of her very presence marking him insane, putting him into a funny farm for psychological investigation. The government had such places he was sure. He would be categorized along with those 'abducted' by aliens. That believed in Leprechauns. Didn't everybody. Fairies at the bottom of the garden. Mentally unstable. Nutters. What's the difference from those and those beliefs in the existence of God, and Angels – Satan? That small voice in the human psyche that says they do – often dismissed as an irrational thought, replaced with a shake of the head and negative response of, We've only one shot at life. There's nothing beyond.

Irinushka, who had suffered pain at the hands of her abusers, was about to shine a light on a God that recognized His creation would destroy itself if He were made for real instead of remaining an image drawn from faith. She was seeking revenge for what was taking place because He would not. Taking it upon herself to destroy such people was only the start. He knew the danger her interference in the affairs of a world not of her making would bring about. His messenger would be under no allusions as to why he would have to bring her to heel, despite Satan sitting in the wings awaiting opportunities. The gift of immortality that no-one had necessarily sought would reveal to the world the first of half a dozen 200-year-old to walk the earth aiding her in her mission. Unless getting shot dead in the interim prevented that. How fortunate was Frank in that respect. This was no longer a dream that he had conveniently pushed to the back of his mind. There were mad-men out there that knew all he knew. He understood that design once drawn was capable of copy with interpretative modification added to suit the customer. Laws of physics had spilled over onto man and He had moved on leaving His deputy to clear up the mess before mad-men did. The Book of Revelations' 1000 years had long passed; and the demon counting the days down, had reached for the rim of the box, pushed off the lid, and pulled himself out. It was all abundantly clear.

'My working days are only beginning. She has work for me.'

'Who, this Irinushka you speak of?'

He laughed, 'She's an angel that wants to put the world to rights.'

Sarah smiled not knowing why. 'It's as well she remain in God's kingdom,' she replied patronizingly.

'Never left. She's right alongside you.'

Sarah turned round, more for humor than belief. 'Got a whiskey in her hand, has she?'

The doctor returned with a colleague. 'I wouldn't have expected a man a quarter his age to recover from this so quickly – if they survive at all. Come and see. Would you mind if my colleague examines you?' he asked O'Hare.

'If you feel he could do with the practice, by all means, carry on. I'm not one to be standing in the way of medical advancement. Better, do it today though, I shall be gone tomorrow.'

'He hasn't lost his sense of humor that's for sure,' Sarah said.

The senior physician pulled O'Hare's pajama jacket open went through the same routine as his junior. He listened with his stethoscope. He tapped it on the side of the iron bed-end, carried on with the examination as if he believed the instrument were faulty. He pushed O'Hare's sleeve up strapping a rubber band onto his arm. Pumping the rubber ball attached to the end watched the gauge. He put his stethoscope to the enlarged artery and listened for the auscultation. He pursed his lips, Hmm, moved the hearing plate back to his chest.

'Gone! What'd you mean, gone?' Sarah asked.

'Going home, tomorrow . . . what did you think I meant?'

'Is that right, doctor? That he'd be fit enough to leave, tomorrow?'

'Technically he'd be fit enough to leave today, Mrs. O'Hare.'

'Weinberg. My name's Sarah Weinberg. We're not married. I'm Charlie's oldest chaverah.'

'Ah . . . friend . . . right. Sorry, Mrs . . . Weinberg. I assumed . . . I'm sorry, not of course there's nothing wrong, we needed another opinion on Mr. O'Hare's powers of recovery that's all.' He smiled turning to the senior physician for any other opinion.

'Good to go. See no reason why he shouldn't. Nurse.'

'Doctors,' the nurse said nodding at both men as they left the ward. 'I'll be back in later to see you, Mr. O'Hare. For the moment, take things easy.'

'Yes, he will, thank you nurse. Well, whatever that's all about? You can't go home tomorrow, Charlie. You're talking nonsense – good God man, you were within a priest's whisper of absolution an hour ago. Whatever are you thinking?'

He put his hand on hers and smiled, 'I'll be all right, Mrs. O'Hare.'

She pulled her hand away. 'And you can get ideas like that out of your head, so you can. Good Lord, we're both in our sixties.'

'Makes no difference, you're still a good-looking woman, Sarah. And this change in my health means that we will be able to sail into the sunset after all. I still got some years left in me.'

She looked at him. His face had a resolve she had not seen before. 'You are not thinking of returning, surely? Not after what's happened. That was a warning. You won't get many more of them you know.'

'Not the first – definitely the most painful – but not the first,' he said to himself.

She did not hear this self-assessment. 'You're still going after those people, after all this time?'

He noticed that she was still holding his hand. The warmth gave him a sense of well-being. They had never spoken of their feelings for each other in any more than a casual way, yet, as far as he was concerned it felt right for them to be more than – dare he think it – lovers. Man and wife, though it would lead to her being an 'out-woman' in the eyes of her people. Though how he thought he would be able to cope with an emotional commitment he had never had any experience before, he could not say. He would surely fall far short of her expectations so set in his ways was he. So set that he would not only lose her as a wife, but a friend he had always treasured should it all go wrong. The risk to either intercourse would be hard to bear, yet . . . when they came; the words from his lips surprised even him.

Without any conscious effort, and much to his surprise, he did not regret them when they did. 'I love you, Sarah Weinberg. Will you marry me?'

This proposal to her by him, pleasant shock though it was when it came, that one day she knew he might suggest, would be impossible. There was no question in her mind of his feelings for her. And hers for him. But as husband and wife – lovers? It would be an awkward situation for the both of them. Gripping his hand she looked into his eyes, kissed him on the cheek, she said:

'Study the Torah, the Mishnah. Get yourself circumcised, and I'm all yours, Agent O'Hare.'

He could see it was impossible for her. He screwed up his face, drew a loud breath between his teeth replied:

'I'm not sure I can be doin' with all the pain of that reading at this time o'me life, Sarah, so I'm not. But let me think on it a while longer, will yer?'

Twelve – 1950s

LOMAX HAD TWO TELEPHONES. One on his desk, which was black; the other, under it: gray. The black one worked the gray one did not. At least that is what he was told long before he became Assistant Director. A back-up telephone, in the event, of a national emergency; or some other occurrence, the stiff, hair bun-topped matron of a woman in charge of the typing pool had snapped at him, her head shaking side to side as if to set the sentence and the telephone in stone, in case (perish the thought), he had any ideas regarding the touching of it.

When, as a younger agent, he had dared (he thought she was out of the room), when he thought the line might be dead, but wasn't sure (just checking), she came back and caught him. He had not been able to confirm it one way or the other. He made out he was cleaning it, hurriedly putting it back on its cradle. Smiling at her he carried on with what he was doing while at the same time feeling her eyes boring into the back of his neck. Not wishing to repeat the experience he had not done it since.

Over the years – she having long retired, since died – after he had been promoted, that same telephone had acquired a life of its own by way of attracting layers of grime made up from the transference of perspiration, coffee spills, food, flakes of body skin, staff coughing and sneezing, cigarette smoke and ash. All the result of being in some persons way being moved; removed to make space for a file or some other piece of office paraphernalia. His instincts told him it was not connected; never had been. It had never rung. The occupant of the desk at the time of the Second World War told him she had not heard so much as a 'ting' out of it the whole time. As for Lomax, all national emergencies, of which there was one a week, nor had he.

There was the usual yearly office inventory with the standing order for the telephone still on it. [Telephone: Gray #278].

In the event, etc . . . Example: communication from Head of FBI, or the President of the United States of America]. An office organizer, sent in to improve efficiency by the government, said that it needed removing to a more permanent position on a desk. And while they were about it, Would he like to have it replaced for something more in keeping with a 20th-century office? Lomax (out of respect and fear for the ghost of the late matron), politely refused, instead got right up the organizer's nose by re-situating it off the carpet onto a shoe box. Here it continued to gather dust for a few more years (he still hadn't checked if it was operational). It was level, and on the floor with that same shoe box, that Lomax found himself now.

He cursed his embarrassing predicament. Crammed under the desk's leg well wearing his new suit ($60), the pants, to his annoyance – he hated baggy knees – tight from his kneeling was picking up dirt in its weft. Lomax prided himself on being able to recognize voices of people he was likely to come across in the course of his working day. The voice he was hearing was neither the President nor J. Edgar Hoover. On the other end of that dirty old gray telephone that rang and that he found himself answering, in the presence of his office staff that had gathered round, wondering what their boss was doing on his hands and knees under his desk with his arse sticking in the air instead of at his usual one with his feet up on it holding a cup of coffee between his two hands.

David Weinberg took a flight from New York to Mexico City. There he took delivery of a rental Pontiac that would take him into the Yucatan

Peninsula. Lomax had arranged for him to meet an agent from the Special Intelligence Service; and the only contact the Bureau had in Mexico. A man burrowed deep in the South American continent.

Tiber Colsson's office and living quarters was a government-owned hacienda at Campeche with views across the Gulf of Mexico. And although he worked out of the American Embassy in Mexico, or rather, that was his cover base, he was hardly ever there except to take and receive orders from his controller. His primary function was to collect foreign intelligence from Cuba and any other South American country that were potential sites for Russian activity. There was no shortage of tin-pot dictators ready to trade suitable real estate to the Russian's for American dollars.

'So,' Colsson said after he had made David welcome with a tumbler of rather rough local Tequila. 'How can the Mexican Chapter of the FBI stroke CIA assist you?'

David smiled at his use of the word, guessing by the pictures of motorcycles round the walls, a set of leathers hanging from the door and the framed photograph of him sitting astride a dirt bike amidst a group of Hell's Angels, where the 'Chapter' reference came.

'A piece of inside work,' Colsson said seeing David admiring the bikes. 'The powers that be had it in their minds that they might be engaged in subversive activities against Uncle Sam.'

'And were they?'

'Not if you don't count urinating over each other's motorcycle leathers while still wearing them; soaking the stars and stripes with stray piss by way of initiation they weren't.'

David smiled, 'No. Do you still ride?'

'When I can. Doesn't seem to be much time at the moment with the Russian's turning the screws.'

'Can't blame them for that. What they need is a port on the Mediterranean, they wouldn't bother us.'

'No. Europe. This is the Cold War, David. And we're at the cutting edge. Stalin's legacy for a new world order and all that. American and Russian spies everywhere you turn. You know what the newspapers liken us all to?' David shook his head. 'Scorpions and tarantulas all trying to get out of the same bottle. God alone knows how it's going to pan out. With Cuba currently undergoing assaults by Batista and Mafia, it's got to be ripe for a revolution anytime soon. We're watching closely for that one. There are a couple of fellows already on our radar. With backing from Moscow, they could easily take Cuba. Before we know it, the whole of Latin America would come under Russian control, threatening American security. One of the reasons Truman gave Mexico a big wad of cash in '47. Helping the people out had nothing to do with American generosity.'

'So how come you're FBI, *and* CIA?'

'Don't ask me. I get confused myself sometimes. Like, who I'm supposed to answer to. I feel like a mercenary spy. Look, the bottom line is, the FBI has no business here; and as for the CIA, well, denial is the watch-word. Leave it like that. Anyway, enough politics, I understand you're making inquiries into someone?'

'That's right. Jarvis Raynham, a doctor. We had our eyes on him lost him. Apparently he came across the border. Information we have is that you found diving tanks washed up on the shore near Canún. It's a long shot, but we believe a yacht belonging to a company by the name of Oceans Galactica had an attempt on her by someone to blow her up. Trying to assassinate its owner. We don't know who that might be or why. Hoping you can throw some light on it for us.'

'If you spin your head forty degrees to starboard and look out that window you will see a yacht resembling something from the US Navy anchored out in the bay,' he said reaching over for a pair of binoculars hanging on a hook underneath his jacket passing them to him. 'That thing out there. Blocking the sunset. *Galactica I.*'

David took them adjusted the focus screw. There were several yachts out in the bay; only one the size Colsson used for a comparison with a warship. 'The one with the Decca radar dish on its the mast-head?'

'You got it. Money no object there. Frederik Spannocs, he's chairman of Oceans Galactica . . .'

'We've heard of him, got nothing on him though.'

'Well, you may not have, but if your Dr. Raynham has been involved with him, I wouldn't have given him more than five minutes to make a will. You don't go upsetting Spannocs, let alone try to murder him. I'm used to crossing people, but I'd need to make a special effort over that one if it ever came to it. If he's what you're here for, I suggest you say you've found nothing and go home. For starters, the man and his company have clout with the US Government; and apart from that, your Raynham wouldn't have got past his heavies.'

'Well, the yacht's still there. I guess he didn't manage it.'

'And not for the first time I've heard that particular story. There was talk that a large explosion occurred recently out in the bay. I didn't hear anything myself. I was away at the time. Locals said the yacht disappeared. Some said they saw it rise up out of the sea falling back into it in pieces, but that's tequila for you. We do get storms out in the bay from time to time; he probably moved it round the bay for shelter.'

'Any bodies washed up recently?'

'Always bodies, this is Mexico. All criminals. All wanted. All identified.'

'These heavies you speak of, anyone in particular?'

'His personal bodyguard. A homosexual, useful with his hands; and I'm not talking wanking. You won't get past him.'

'Well, I won't go into aspects of what he can do with his hands; but that reference you made to getting past him, how so?'

'Well let me put it this way; they can't do you for being queer down here. But having said that you wouldn't make comments to anyone you didn't know as to their sexuality. Not if you have any sense. Especially round the clubs. You're likely to finish the evening with a knife in your back.'

'So what's that to do with this bodyguard?'

'Some American marines on shore leave took the piss out of him while he was dancing with another man at the *Tropicana* . . .'

'Tropicana?'

'A night club and day bar. Two men dancing together, well, uncommon, not unusual. Though not something I'm particularly fond of myself. I like the feel of a woman's breasts against my chest too much. Know what I mean?'

David smiled.

'Anyway, I digress. Typical marines got themselves drunk on local tequila start upsetting everyone. Normally they'd get away with a good kicking from the bar staff before being thrown out. This night it was different. The bar they were in was mainly men if you know what I mean. Spannocs's bodyguard among them, the same one they were taking the rise out of. As I was saying, these two were dancing when one of the marines decides to cut in on them, getting fresh with our hero. Tries to pick him up. Dances in front of him waving his hands using sexual gestures. He may well have been one himself, I don't know. Anyway, to be fair our hero ignores him and walks off the dance floor going to the bar. The marine though, he can't leave it alone – starts cat calling and whistling – by the way, do you want another drink? I've some Jack Daniels if you'd prefer?'

'Since you ask, JDs fine, can't get on with this stuff. Rocket fuel. No offense.'

Colsson got two fresh glasses from the small bamboo decorated cocktail bar in the corner of his room and poured drinks. 'None taken. *Ice?*'

'Please. So what happened then?'

He passed David his drink tapping the bottom of his glass with the lip of his own. 'Cheers. *Stalin.*' He took a gulp put the glass on a table picked up a packet of cigarettes offering David one. He declined. 'Well I wasn't there, you understand, only what I heard, but apparently the bodyguard hit him in the face, knocking him to the floor. That's when the rest of the marines join in help their mate out. He takes the first two down in a flash. The rest hold back not sure of themselves. He takes another one out while they're standing thinking. This time right across the man's throat.'

'What on his own? They must have murdered him.'

'You'd had thought so, wouldn't you? Used that oriental hand fighting – you know the kind Tibetan monks use. Something to do with them not being allowed weapons.'

'Kung Fu?'

'That what it's called? Yes, well, Kung Fu. Whatever it is, it's effective. Right across the throat. The man never stood a chance.'

'I can imagine. I saw a demonstration recently – they're thinking of training us in it.'

'Useful I'd imagine. Well anyway, he put two in hospital, the other died where he lay.'

'*Phwww.* So what was the name of this guy?'

'Tony D'Sotto. Spannocs's lover-boy and personal bodyguard.'

'*D'Sotto!*'

'You know him?'

'Not personally, but I know a man that does.'

David passed the binoculars back.

'Well, if your Raynham had made an assault on Spannocs and

got away, he wouldn't have got far. He'd have sent D'Sotto after him. When we later found diving gear washed up on the beach, on the off chance there had been an attempt at blowing up Galactica, we informed your people. It was of no interest to us. And here you are.'

'Have you ever heard of the Order of the Most Divine Third Circle? They were connected with *Oceans Galactica*, the company.'

Colsson shook his head, 'They sound a right mouthful – but no.'

'Raynham may be one, we're not sure.'

'So what would Raynham have against Spannocs?'

'That's what I'm here to find out.'

'That's intelligence gathering for you. You never can be sure who's on which side. I'll tell you one thing I did see though,' Colsson said. 'Might have some relevance. When I was in a cafe. One I use from time to time, along the beach. I hadn't seen it in there before. It looked as if it was a left over from the war that had been washed-up. Bit of a coincidence, seeing as we found that air-tank. An oxygen re-breather. It was punctured in several places. The cafe owner said he'd picked it up one morning beach-combing, hanging it on the wall as a souvenir. That might have been his. If it was, it may be another reason he's missing.'

'How so?'

'The puncture marks in it were made by a shark.'

David shook his head. 'No. Army diver. He would have known how to handle them. He would have carried repellent.'

'Might well have done. Shark may not have known what it was though. He'd be breakfast in these waters. They're not known for bothering with cereal.'

'Someone mentioned that the air tank showed signs of being in an explosion. Where is it, I'd like to take a look?'

'Downstairs. Come on, I could do with some fresh air.'

He took him outside along to a store next to the hacienda. He unlocked and opened the door showing David in. He looked round. It was full of old fishing nets and boating paraphernalia. An Indian motorcycle propped against a wall. A sweet smell of dryness, sea, petrol, and paint pervaded.

'I share it with a local fisherman. Here,' Colsson said walking across the dry sand floor. 'Mind how you trip over that old hat, I'm in the process of cleaning it.'

A brass diving helmet was lying on the floor, next to it a tin of abrasive and a cloth, alongside that, an aqualung bottle. One of two. A metal clamp that would have held its twin was still in place. David stood the single bottle up to examine it closer. Its pillar valve was missing. He looked inside, run his finger inside the hole where it would have been screw fitted feeling for any remains. There was none. 'Something's not quite kosher,' he said. He picked the bottle up holding it up to a stream of sunlight coming through a crack in the wooden door. Directing the sun's rays inside the hole he looked in. 'Well, I would say that the valve wasn't so much blown out, more removed. Unscrewed to be precise.' David passed him the bottle. 'Got it?'

Colsson nodded taking it from him. He stared inside the hole. 'What am I looking for?'

'The thread on the inside has either been filed or knocked with a punch to make it look as if it had blown out in an explosion. Look at the thread remaining. Far too clean, in fact, you can see file marks on the remaining thread. A pillar valve blowing out from a bottle normally only happens when too much air has gone in. Or the bottle dropped on its valve causes it to fracture. Neither is the case here. This has been deliberately got at making it look like it exploded from the bottle, giving the impression to whoever saw it that the person wearing it would have died from it going through the back of his neck. I reckon that valve was unscrewed and taken out on purpose.'

'So it *was* a shark that got him as I said.'

'No doubt the shark got at the re-breather, but I reckon Raynham was well ashore before that happened. He wasn't wearing it.'

'Suggesting that he is still alive.'

David shrugged. 'Well my brief is to find him and I'm thinking; if he had taken a crack at Spannocs and didn't kill him he wouldn't want to advertise that he was still alive, taking another pop at him.'

'Well, Spannocs isn't always on the yacht, he's got a place in the jungle. The Pyramid of the Magician, a homely title for a house that most definitely isn't. In fact, it wouldn't look out of place in Transylvania. Your Buster Crabbe could well finish what he started there.'

'Sounds ominous. Can you take me?'

They returned to the hacienda where Colsson poured two more drinks for them.

'I've been told to give you any assistance you need. If that's what you want, you're on, but I must warn you that Spannocs comes and goes in a helicopter to get into its jungle interior. In fact, look at the yacht, you can make out a raised deck with a 'copter straddled and cabled down onto it. He'll be on board but can be in the jungle in twenty minutes. We'll need another means of transport which is going to be extremely arduous taking us considerably longer.'

'Haven't you got one?'

Colsson choked half swallowing the last of his tequila.

'Can you ride a dirt bike?' he asked, wiping his mouth with the back of his hand. 'Hell will freeze over before we get one of those from Uncle Sam.'

A second bike needed, Colsson had a word with a guy he worked with from time to time over borrowing his. The man, no longer able to operate the gear lever owing to arthritis in his foot caused . . .

A British fellow left behind after the war that had not been able to return to Northampton due to a bit of bother with the British military police over some Nazis gold that had gone missing. A German officer's wife – that he was having an affair – and who (the German officer) wanted 'Tommy' (not his real name), garroted, not so much for seducing his Fraulein, but the original theft of the aforementioned gold, was made an offer to be helped to escape to Argentina by 'Tommy'. With the British close on his tail after they had been tipped off there was a Nazi in town; the threat of the hangman's noose looming, the man reluctantly accepted the offer to escape; to leave 'Tommy' still breathing, the gold, and his Fraulein to be left in 'Tommy's' care. With the assistance of a local Mexican government official, who had turned a blind eye to this escape, not so much to save 'Tommy', more, getting their hands on a piece of the action – namely the twenty bars of bullion stamped with the eagle emblem of the Third Reich – from under the noses of the military police. Unfortunately, for all of them, more so 'Tommy', two men wearing white suits with red cross brooches on gray metal shields in their lapels turned up and got to him first. They tied him with ropes to a makeshift cross in his beach store attempted to persuade him to tell them where he had secreted the gold. Hanging in this position, he laughed at their pathetic attempts to extract information from him by this soft method of crucifixion. When one brought out a knife cutting the rope releasing his feet, he laughed even more until the other, presenting two rusty nails and a lump hammer, threatening to make him suffer as Christ had gave him a change of heart. With sweat pouring from his forehead, he told all. While the other man went to get the hidden gold, the remaining one with nothing better to do decided to hammer in a nail to one of his feet anyway, 'To remind you of your Son of God's suffering for mankind and His, some hopes for a better world, *ouch*, that was my thumb.' He shook his hand and screwed up his face in pain, '*Awwh! Phwww!* May Mephistopheles bring a plague of locus down on you for that,' he angrily said giving the nail another thwack driving it home.

Leaving that evening by powerboat under the noses of the port authorities; and with the nineteen ingots wrapped in a hessian sack, they left 'Tommy' to hang overnight; where Fraulein, Olga Murphy, found him the following morning, his throat and voice all croaked out from screaming.

. . . by a rusting nail. All David had to do was reimburse 'Tommy' a crate of Jack Daniels, a box of Cuban cigars: part of a Customs night raid that evening; providing he didn't advertise the fact that the man had a mouthful of gold teeth.

'*And bring it back in one piece!*' he shouted after them.

David had not ridden on any bike, dirt or otherwise, in years, and it showed. It was not so much that he was having trouble riding the Indian. He managed it well enough. Provided he went along with the bike, both man and machine were happy. But the Indian had other ideas not in keeping with his. The Indian rope trick David was finding hard to accomplish was to get the thing to go his way, and to Colsson's frustration, over the following days would put the journey he wished to make next to impossible. If there were a straight hard surface, running between Campeche and Tekax it would not be a problem. But there wasn't and it was ninety miles over rough country and beat-up tracks with the onus on the rider to decide the direction the front wheel had to take and not the bike's.

'It is said,' remarked Colsson, 'that inanimate objects have no brains; but in a straight competition between that Indian, it has to be said, that the latter, has very much the edge over you.'

After his first tentative ride, David brought the bike to a halt after what Colsson was saying, 'Thanks for that.' Promptly losing his balance, he fell off.

'David!' Colsson screamed approaching him on his own bike showering him in sand and dust from the side-on maneuver. 'If you're goin' go to the trouble of putting your foot down to keep your balance, stop pussying with it and get your weight over it. Hold the frickin' thing upright!' Adding, 'You'll find it a lot easier to pull away in first over fourth!' And, 'Back wheel, back wheel! Use your back wheel brake the same time as your front. That bike's going to be fit for the scrap heap time you've finished with it.' Also, 'That's it, that's it. Keep the revs up . . . now . . . change gear. Now! And look where you're going—!' Colsson closed his eyes, opening them slowly saw David in a tangle with the Indian and some painful looking vegetation of the species Texan barrel cactus dangerously near the region known as, Between ones legs.

By afternoon, after several visits to the washroom to relieve his bowels from the burning of tortilla from the night before, and much to Colsson's admiration, for this man was no quitter, there was an indication that he had cracked it. He could accelerate up to forty, brake hard on the back wheel, bring the bike round in the opposite direction; accelerate away again still remaining upright.

David, wearily, with a dirty ingrained sweaty face, bloodied arms and grazed hands asked exhaustively, Why do I need to keep doing this?

By late afternoon, he could drive off a hillock, fly for ten feet, and, provided he landed back wheel first and not front, stay up right. He had concussed himself when he had first attempted the stunt. The front wheel not being in line with the direction of travel, one of Newton's laws of motion coming into play. The one that Colsson remembered as, The bike one way: the rider the other.

David had never before experienced double vision.

Why do I need to keep doing this? he asked not for the first time repeating himself.

By evening, looking like a lone cow-hand that had tried to stop a cattle stampede without a horse, Colsson figured he was good enough to make the journey that . . . Why do I need to keep doing this? . . . he had got tired of listening to.

Thirteen – 1950s

LOMAX'S PRESTIGE LEAPED FOURTEEN FLOORS of the Empire State building on that one telephone call. The President was still alive with the Head of the FBI still firmly in control. His staff waiting with bated breaths. It was an important call, and they knew it. Asked for by name, he had to read 'Little Bo Peep' into the telephone for Bell Laboratories 'Audrey' voice recognition system (on loan to the FBI), to confirm they had the right man. The line kicked into a scramble that only made sense at each end to the participants. The caller said he had the authority of J. Edgar Hoover with direct instructions from the Oval office. He was to recall Weinberg from Mexico immediately. He was not to make any further inquiries of the Order of the Most Divine Third Circle, Frederik Spannocs, or Doctor Jarvis Raynham. All evidence collected by David Weinberg whether verbally, written, taped, or photographed, handed, and spoken to their administrative officer on his return. Lomax was not to mention details of the call to anyone. Issued with a National Security directive he was bound to do as instructed. He put the phone back on the shoebox and stood up, dismissing his staff to their duties with the announcement that it was, *A line test*. No-one believed him. Returning to his desk, he heard the murmuring of voices singing, *Little Bo Peep Has Lost Her Sheep* . With so many *children* to pick on, he chose to ignore them all.

He would not exclude himself from speaking to Hoover directly. His position demanded that. The caller would be aware that he might well call Hoover to confirm. The ordering of an agent by name into a foreign field operation; to withdraw him in as many days without any form of explanation, on the telephone, on that particular one, that he would have expected the caller to inform him that an imminent missile strike by a hostile nation was beginning. That one!

Hoover's office confirmed that he was to follow the caller's instructions. He asked if they had any more information. They would make no further comment. The directive was as it stood. Lomax was in the process of recalling David Weinberg, when, to add salt to the wound, he took a call from O'Hare saying he had received a death threat against someone dear to him if David was not withdrawn from Mexico forthwith.

Lomax in his eagerness to contact David Weinberg had discovered a fundamental problem with the FBI's latest communication system recently installed . When there is no-one at the other end to receive the call it falls down. He was becoming increasingly concerned that the onus to contact David was down to him, no matter the problem. His gut reaction was to send in marines for a rescue mission, but this was another country and liable to cause a diplomatic incident with no guarantees of support for his action from Hoover's office. The CIA was the proper option; though, was not David working with one of them, he asked himself. The CIA had the cooperation of the Mexican Government for being where they were in return for security in the event of a missile strike from the East. That was not the case here. He made the decision to wait a while longer hoping the communication system would kick-in. If David and Colsson have taken the decision to take themselves off without word, it was life and death before he could involve anyone else. The fact that the caller using, gray telephone #278, had not put conditions on David's return other than as an order told him that it was not so much a matter of life and death, more a political withdrawal. He figured that if either man were in that much danger the CIA themselves would be acting. He would deal first with O'Hare and the threat against Sarah Weinberg's life (the spelling out of that particular person's name not required). As long as O'Hare thought he was treating the issue seriously, he would be satisfied. When one of his staff shouted across to him that O'Hare was on the telephone again, he began to lose his temper with the man. He closed his eyes, drew in a deep breath, shook his head and picked up. Before speaking, feeling sympathy for the man, he changed the predetermined tone in his voice. 'Is Sarah okay, Charlie?'

'What'd you mean? I've called to say she's not. What made you say that? She's devastated. Doesn't know which way to turn. Someone's threatened her saying that if David Weinberg is not pulled out of Mexico he's dead meat!' O'Hare said adding angrily. 'That's what I've rang to tell you. Who else did you think it was?'

What's the *fuck's* he talking about, Lomax thought. Under normal circumstances, the Irishman's brusqueness was something he tolerated. But on this occasion, he no longer did. '*Yes!* From you. *You* . . . O'Hare.'

'This is the first time I've called you. What are *you* talking about?'

'Hold the line, Charlie . . . for *fuck's sake!*'

Lomax put his hand over the mouthpiece called across to Sayers, his secretary that took the call first time round. She nodded at him saying, 'As far as she could tell, it was O'Hare. He had used the correct password and everything—' (She was relieved she asked for it on that occasion; she didn't always.)

'Thanks, Louise . . . *Charlie* . . . I didn't take the call, Louise did. She swears it was you. And I believe what she heard would have convinced her. We'll look into what's going on. If it's any consolation, I took a call from head office earlier. They want David out anyway. We're in the process of doing just that, soon as we get in touch with him. What did the letter say?'

O'Hare went through its preamble concerning Jewish mothers'

propagating the race, 'You know the usual bile from racists and the like. Anyway . . . they said the people that killed her husband would do the same to her, unless, well you know the story . . . that enough.'

Lomax breathed a sigh, consoled him, and hung up. He knew two groups wanted David out of Mexico, one likely an impersonator. As to the reference to the same people that murdered Frank Weinberg, *God*, according to O'Hare that was over 35 years ago, he thought. Charlie, with his ravings of the past, may be making sense after all. He called across the desks to Louise Sayers.

She looked up, 'Yes, Chief.'

'I want a trace on that first call.'

David knew what Colsson had always known. The last two bone-shattering miles down a rough-hewn track, would be the worst. The agony of riding the ninety miles to Spannocs's residence in the jungle had been unrelenting. He dreaded to think what it would have been like were it not for all his riding training. His muscles stretched like violin strings played with a blunt razor blade were buzzing. His spine from the neck to the small of his back down was painful to straighten and as far as he was aware, he never knew arse-bones actually existed before. Whichever way he moved on the saddle of that Indian, he could find no relief. The dust from the dry track and the heat from the sun along with that of an engine that seemed to him permanently at melting point added to his riding experience. He had two red marks on the inside of his knees where he was gripping the gasoline tank, testament to his ordeal to stay upright on the Indian. His enthusiasm for motorcycles was not what it had once been. Yet there was a masochistic satisfaction on this last part of the journey. Riding side by side, the two engines reverberating through the vacuum of warm air they had created between them gave him an exhilaration that he wished could go on forever.

Colsson stopped. The track had disappeared. He pointed ahead and David followed his line of sight. They forced their machines through some dense jungle for a hundred yards, out into a clearing, and there it was in the valley below.

The Pyramid of the Magician the locals called it and David could see why. Pointed like a wizard's hat with foliage growing up its walls it looked like a conjuror wearing a long green gown. For all the hotness of the day, a cold chill went through him at the sight of it. Set on three levels, its concrete porches supported by huge porticoes running horizontally for a hundred feet, given other circumstances, would be spectacular. Covered in a trailing growth of creepers with large leaves, it resembled pictures he had seen of the Hanging Gardens of Babylon, except they did not have a fence of range wire surrounding them as this had. On the inside guards slowly walked towards each other. A ragged bunch of Mexican guerrillas, toting automatic weapons and smoking cheroots. They had looked up at the sound from the two motorcycles, but they were too far away for them to make anything of them, probably assuming illegal loggers wielding power saws were at work. They cut their engines. The silence was overwhelming and, except for the whispering sound of insects, was disorientating to David.

'Cicadas,' Colsson said anticipating David's question. 'They're trying to attract mates.'

'Must be worn out when they find one after making that row all day.' He took out his binoculars and scanned the perimeter fence taking in the surrounding area of the property. 'He's got some security down there. Must have upset a lot of people over the years.'

'They won't be a problem,' Colsson said casually shaking his head. 'Bandits, *huh!* They'd sell their mother's favors for a peso *and* charge an audience to watch the show. We'll wait till nightfall. There's something you need to keep on-board regarding this particular brand of Mexican low-life, my fliend. If it doesn't see a need to do a job it'll sleep through it.'

'I don't follow.'

'Well let me spell it out. Those guards are Mexican and certainly related, friendly, or known to other bandits in the area.'

'Still don't.'

'Employment, my fliend,' Colsson said, liking the mock accent first time round and using it again for effect. 'A Gringo like yourself wouldn't know that. Your run-of-the-mill criminal doesn't need guards, he thinks he's getting them, when what in fact he's getting is insurance. No-one's going to break in as long as local bandits are employed.'

'Providing they *are* locals.' Colsson looked at him puzzled. 'Spannocs may not be such a fool. He'd also know that they would have to give the impression they were a raggedy-arse bunch of Cisco Kid look-alikes to make his presence here seem as normal as possible.'

Colsson smiled. 'That's very perceptive of you, David. You've got a devious mind there. You should be spying on the Russians. Except on this occasion, you're wrong.'

'What makes you say that? Have you been here before?'

'No. But they are the Ramos, a left-over from the Seditionistas' campaigns of 1915, on the run from the Texas Rangers, and that's their leader, the self-styled General Pablo Wilhelm Balsal. Wanted by us for gun-running, drug smuggling, rape, murder, extortion, the torching of villages that don't pay him taxes, and double-dealing with the CIA. Not to mention non-payment of his cheroot bill to the local drug store. I wondered where he'd slipped off to.'

'That last bill must have got someone mad. What would this Balsal be doing working for Spannocs seeing how well he's doing for himself?'

'I don't know, but he'll be dead before I've finished business here.'

David looked at the coolness in Colsson's eyes, seeing an assassin staring back.

Lomax bit the bullet. Calling the CIA department responsible for controlling Colsson, he asked for Mr. Moon. Being put through, he immediately apologised to the woman that answered saying, 'Sorry wrong department, I wanted Head of Control.'

'You're speaking with him,' she said sarcastically. 'Jesurus Moon. How best can I serve you?'

Moon, Turkish by birth, had been an intelligence officer with the Office of Strategic Service working out of Istanbul as one of their agents during the Second World War. She went on to become an interrogator for the Nuremberg War Trials, later becoming Head of Operations (Latin America), first with the OSS then its successor, the CIA. She was a hard, no nonsense woman with the tensile strength of steel. An ash-tray full to the brim with Buffalo cigarette butts was testament to her late nights, and never ever more than a coded signal from the agents under her away. Her ability to ascertain a situation and act quickly was legendary. She would call Lomax when she had made contact.

'Given the circumstance of the situation what if you are unable to?' Lomax asked.

'Not, *if*, Lomax. I said, *when*.'

She went on to say she would walk to Mexico personally if there was no other way, asking Allah by way of prayer, that he instill those with such little faith in her that they can be rested and assured in their God that she would find them; putting him firmly in his place. Although Moon did not make anything of what amounted to a cock-up on the FBI's part, she had managed to instill the feeling all the same.

In the event Colsson being, 'out of the office' longer than twelve hours without them being aware, CIA's standing order was, contact the American embassy in Mexico City to shut them down. This Moon did. A holding team immediately sent to secure Colsson's 'workshop', taking all relevant paperwork, before destroying the hacienda, had done the business three hours after Lomax called her. Although the Mexican Government were happy for the CIA to be operating in the area, they were not official guests. A fact not overlooked by the Russians seeking to embarrass America. As far as the Mexican Government were concerned the FBI were keeping a lid on Communism; something that President Miguel Alemán was struggling, in his attempts to improve Mexican kudos on the world stage; being on a par with infiltration of Communism in Eastern Europe to President Harry S. Truman. Moon promised that Truman would renegotiate and reorganize with Alemán at a more appropriate time consolidating America's commitment to the cause.

Colsson had been right over his assessment of Spannocs's security arrangements. The bandit's attitude and devotion to duty was a shining example of what an utter shambles should be when a concentrated effort employed by so many dedicated to its art takes place. Seated in random groups of disorder the Ramos was swigging from bottles of tequila at the same time smoking rocket-shaped panatela cigars. Several were singing and playing guitars – badly. An entourage of women in various stages of undress, the result of their blouse buttons not being able to restrain their more than ample breasts adequately, the Ramos were to David the most unlikely security company he had ever clapped eyes on. The raucous laughter from the display of sexual inhibitions by this band was a clear sign to David that Spannocs was not at home. As for getting into the house, that would be a pushover. They had only to wait for the drinking and fornicating to end, sleep to take over, and they would be in. Assuming Colsson could drag his eyes away from his binoculars long enough.

Colsson studied with professional intensity what was below them. With eyes straining, he was seeking the one thing that David had mentioned; that these bandits may not be what they represented. He had not managed to stay alive in the hostile environment that he operated by misreading what was before his eyes. He never underestimated the subtleness employed by the secret services of the world in the art of subterfuge. It was essential reading in the sophisticated world of the spymaster. And he, well-versed in its techniques, neither trusted nor gave in to pre-conceived ideas of what was before him. No matter the shabbiness of the actors to create an illusion, or their ability to misguide the unwary. Know your enemy was the benchmark by which every successful general operated and if he didn't, his army would be defeated. If David had the sense to have mentioned it, it was as well he make damn sure for himself. Blind certainty could be the death of you. Communism was across the bay waiting for him to make a mistake. He was, to date, ahead of that game, a lesson from an outsider in this one, would be one well learned. David agreed with him that they lie-up until nightfall when they would have a fighting chance of breaking through what passed as security but might easily be a con.

At midnight, David and Colsson made their way into the compound. The snoring from the sleeping gang the only noise in an otherwise quiet night kept them cautious. Frozen into silhouettes against the side of the house both men heard a faint buzz like a humming-bird in the distance. They looked at each other. Their worst fears were soon realised. The Ramos had heard it too and was rising from their slumbers.

A helicopter directly overhead. Headlights slung underneath its belly picked out the area, then quite unexpectedly, rained shining cylinders down among the bandits. There was hardly a choke from David before he realized what they were. Holding the last breath that he had taken in before diving to the ground, he looked up. The plane was one of their own. He could make out the pilot's face. The photographic image matched that in his memory of Adolf Hitler and a chill went through him. The sleeping Ramos never had a chance. Choking they tried to get up; only succeeding in making things worse. Coughing, they were unconscious in a minute or less. Colsson managed to get his jacket over his head seeing the main thrust of the vesicant rolling across the ground on the breeze toward them.

David realizing their chances of survival out in the open being limited saw shelter. He pulled his own jacket over his head. From his prone position in the dirt, he rolled towards a door of an outbuilding. Kicking it open with his boot forcing it open. Pulling Colsson by his collar, he dragged him after him slamming the door shut behind them. The helicopter was still overhead. He could hear the sound of more cylinders dropping to earth. The Ramos gang choked for the last time. The plane having delivered its lethal cargo moved off into the night sky leaving the two of them to cough gently before they too succumbed to unconsciousness.

David opened his eyes to see daylight streaming through the window by the side of the door. He felt like shit. He nudged Colsson hoping for a reaction that would indicate that he was still alive. The man opened his eyes and moved, 'How are you?' he asked. 'This hasn't turned out as planned, has it?' Colsson was clearly not yet with it. David went to the window and looked out. There were bodies everywhere. The faces of those he could see were contorted; green ooze coming from open mouths confirmed to him that mustard gas was responsible. He turned his head to concentrate his hearing. A distant hum was getting louder. The gunships were returning. He looked in the direction of the skyline. Over the trees, low, six in formation. With no formality of introduction, they began machine gunning the ground, spraying bullets among the dead. They ceased, their shells were taking a different direction now, tracing a line to the outbuilding they were sheltering. The helicopters were hovering, firing in bursts they had all the time in the world and were clearly making sure there was to be no witnesses to what was taking place here. The size of the munitions they were spraying purposefully threatened he and Colsson's sanctuary.

'Time to find a way out, I'm thinking,' Colsson said snapping into the world of the awake, too late.

The walls round them collapsed into rubble. Both men found themselves exposed to the elements and instinctively put their hands behind their heads in surrender. A single helicopter hung in the sky above them. Its engine at half throttle, a smell of aviation fuel pervaded, the rotor blades slicing the air with a *phut phut phut phut phut* sound sent a message of imminent death into their minds. The down draught blew clouds of dust choking both men, who were still trying to hold their hands up while rubbing it from their noses and eyes at the same time. Slowly at first, it changed its position in the sky. The engine note altering, doppling. Turning in an aerial axis of its own space. It increased engine revolutions, and moved off, over the trees in pursuit of the rest of the swarm ahead of it.

David took his arms down and moved his legs. Colsson stood up and shouted to him to run before the *bastards* changed their minds and decided to come back and finish them off. David did not need a second invite. He legged-it toward the house. Not somewhere, he wanted to be, but ports in storms and all that, he thought. Body-rolling through the front door previously blown open by cannon shells, neither of them was in any mood to ask the occupant for permission to enter, instead taking it for themselves. With the hinges to the front door still in place they slammed it closed, the echo from it reverberated through the building that would give both men away to any occupant that they were in the house.

Colsson shouted at David before breaking into a fit of coughing:

'So much for a covert night-time operation. Remind me again, whose side did you say you were on?'

David ignored him. He was having his own coughing fit problem. When he got himself together, he replied:

'Well, at least you won't have to bother with the Ramos anymore. And keep your voice down, you'll liable to wake somebody.'

'A marching band wouldn't wake anyone asleep here,' Colsson replied.

'Hey! What's happened to my clothes?' David asked.

'I switched us out of them with two of those poor bastards out there while you were asleep. Might have saved our lives,' Colsson said adding. 'What did you say you were working on? Before you came out here. Because if you didn't, I'd sure like to know . . . perhaps, before one of us *dies!*'

'I don't suppose you ever considered it might be you they were after?'

'Not at all. Unless you've forgotten, this is my working territory. I'm a fully paid up member. They'd hardly take me out, would they? For what reason? Whereas your people . . . well, I don't know who you've been upsetting. You could have a mole that's trying to bury you under the sod alongside that Raynham mate of yours – permanently like.'

'Well you didn't need dust in your eyes to see that they were CIA decals on the sides of those gunships.'

Those decals had concerned Colsson. If those planes were a warning from Spannocs for them to think again about snooping about his place, a show of strength using them would indicate how much influence he had and how bothered he was by arrogantly displaying them. Although, they could have been Russian. If they were, would they display CIA insignia? Rumours of their activities, unconfirmed by his masters, he knew to be true. Russian intelligence networks attempting to infiltrate local communities were stirring up potential revolutionaries. President Miguel Alemán made protests to Washington, leading to Harry S. Truman telling the security forces to be more subtle in their identification and eradication of these networks, perhaps using other methods. If the Russians were playing on that using planes that were clearly identifiable it would lead to an international crisis. Your average Mexican peasant seeing their own people blown to pieces by Uncle Sam were more likely to embrace communism. Who would blame them? The possibility that those planes were on their way to kill and maim innocent people appeared a reality. Not for the first time, when he had seen them, had he said to himself, *Where in hell are our F89 interceptors when you need them most?*

'Well, we're here, and by the look of it we've got the house to ourselves. Might as well get some breakfast,' David said smiling.

'I'll get the cooking pots out,' Colsson said still not sure of David's true motives.

The words were scarce out of Colsson's mouth than a horrifying scream from below hit their ears. They looked at each other and shuddered.

'What the *fuck* was that?' Colsson exclaimed.

Appearing to have come from below ground David opened a door that looked as if it headed in that direction. It did. A flight of stairs leading down into darkness. With a smell of must and damp in the air, David, looking into its gloom, was on his way down. To his relief, Colsson was right behind him.

'That was the scream of a child!' David said looking back toward him with fear in his voice.

Although David Weinberg was an agent for law enforcement, he suffered the same emotions as any other man: that, given the circumstances of their surroundings: being shit scared. The only difference for him in these cases, as an active employee of the Department of Investigation's Federal Bureau of Justice, he did not have the luxury of turning away when another was in danger. Schooled that the bogey-man was only in your head, everything outside of the cranium, reality human, was a match for confrontation and as such capable of being 'taken out'. Colsson looking at him, apparently with the same emotion, said, 'Let's get on with this.'

Pushing past David, he took the stairs two at a time eager to locate the source of the scream. The stairs went from a straight flight to a spiral that seemed to go forever. The air became fouler in their throats as they descended. The walls thick green, slimy wet, concealed to vivid imaginations creatures not of this time; but to those with eyes to see, were the feeding grounds for large creeping invertebrate from another; their dependence on decayed flesh for survival squirmed. They briefly paused on these steps, shuddered, continued down the winds until they gave way to a veranda with a rail round. They looked over into the black abyss below.

'What now?' Colsson asked shining his torch into the darkness seeing nothing.

'*Switch it off!*' David shouted at him.

He had seen more than nothing. Three people. One appeared to be . . . 'Is that a Goat down there?' he said turning to Colsson. He looked again not believing his eyes. 'And a Clown . . . a *Bull!* And look . . . a *Dog.*'

'Let me see—'

'Give your eyes a chance to become accustomed to the dark.'

Colsson stared down. He could see nothing. He turned his head to one side and listened. Still nothing. 'What did you say you saw?'

David returned to the scene. Had he been mistaken in what he had seen? This time though, it was different. This time what he saw sent a chill through him. A child tied to a woman by rope. A girl, judging, from what appeared to him to be wearing a wedding dress. He tried to make sense of what he was seeing. He startled, catching Colsson in the chest with his shoulder. Two men burst in brandishing guns. A fight broke out and for a moment, in the chaos, David could not make out properly what he was seeing. A clap of thunder, which shook the building, accompanied by rapid lightning flashes, gave the phenomenon movement of those above stop-framing those below, until all became silent. As if a safety curtain in a theater pulled down, giving an interlude of darkness and the audience a chance to draw breath, the second act kicked off.

David shouted to Colsson, *'We're being bombed again!'* All Colsson could do was stare at him with incredulity. He had seen nothing, heard nothing.

David leaning further over the veranda better to see, watched a creature come out from one wall, glide across free space, out through the wall opposite (he was later to recount to Colsson the creature to be three feet in height without legs). A clicking sound accompanied it. He looked at Colsson; he was getting angry at the man's apparent lack of observation. 'There! For *fuck's* sake, you must have seen that!' Before Colsson could answer, another explosion, this time the sound of glass shattering. No longer on the veranda, David was down among them. Aware that a man, he guessed was a policeman from the NYPD badge on his jacket, hanging limp across two chairs. Lifting the man down, he laid him on his back instinctively began giving him the Sylvester-Brotsch resuscitation technique. Pulling the man's fully extended arms towards him, closing them onto his chest, he repeated the exercise for what seemed an eternity until the man opened his eyes, coughed, went over on his side. Putting his hand out to help him further, he immediately withdrew it. He was nothing more than vapor. Mist. Something, or somebody, went through him.

'Not past me. Through me!' he later said recounting what he had seen to Colsson.

David was on the veranda once again alongside Colsson. He was screaming and shouting all manner of obscenities at him. His disappearance, less than a second, gave the name Pyramid of the Magician significance Colsson had never contemplated before; and for the sake of both their sanities he needed to get the pair of them out of here and to safety as soon as he could. With the strength in David's legs gone, and needing to get a firm grip of him, while all the time he was struggling, becoming more and more difficult to do that, drastic action was called for. He sat David down on one of the steps and hit him a blow to the chin knocking him clean out muttering, *Sorry about that, old man.* Taking his arm round his neck and shoulder, holding the limp David upright, he dragged him back up the steps and out into daylight and fresh air.

Colsson was still holding David up when he saw a glint of light out across the surround of the Pyramid. He instinctively knew what it was. The sun had caught the rifling inside the barrel of a sniper's weapon, too late for evasive action. A bullet went into his body, releasing his hold of David, his arms went up into the air, and he was down. The second shot, a fraction in time after the one that hit him; spun David round as he tried to regain his balance from the man that had been supporting him, before he too, hit the ground.

The sniper, lying prone with the butt of his rifle pushed tight to his shoulder, pulled his head back from its sight. The ground round him battle-strewn with bodies. Satisfied that no-one alive saw him; he stood up and brushed the parched ground from his clothes. He then removed the military coat covered in medals, took off the bullet proof undershirt and placed it with a gas mask. Looking round, further, to satisfy himself that he was unseen, he removed a wig and several layers of theatrical hair from his face. He went over to the dead body of General Pablo Wilhelm Balsal and laid the man's para-military coat back over him. He carefully put the man's cheroot back in his mouth that was lying in the dust at the side of his head. Taking up his radio-telephone, he spoke into it. '*Sullivan!* You can send me transport now; we're all done here.'

Jesurus Moon telephoned Lomax with the news that they had recovered two bodies. One was Tiber Colsson; she could not confirm the name of the other.

'Are they alive?'

'Cannot say at the moment, communication problems,' Moon said biting her lip. 'It might be as well you don't get too optimistic.'

'*Great*,' Lomax replied replacing the receiver.

He was stunned to the point that he hardly heard the gray telephone ringing under his desk. Sayers hearing it drew his attention to there being someone wanting him again. Second time this century, he thought. He picked it up, '*Lomax*. What now?'

The voice informed him that with the death of another Weinberg wasn't it time that O'Hare poked his nose out of what did not concern him. The line clicked. Silent.

'*Chief!*'

'What is it, Louise?' Lomax asked wondering what O'Hare had been up to that deserved all this.

'That call we took the other day. The one you asked me to follow up on.'

He nodded with a questioning of his forehead and remembered.

'The telephone company traced the caller to the site of an old

Indian cemetery in Manhattan. They said the number belonged to a house by the name of . . .' Referring to her notes she looked up from them and reported the name, '*Algonquin Grave.* Apparently, it was once a property that stood on the site destroyed in a fire round 1920. The number was not re-allocated out of respect for the bodies of mutilated children. Their remains found in its basement.' She had to pause before continuing. 'And none of the bodies, Algonquian, Cheyenne, or Arapaho, Native American warriors the graveyard was intended.'

'*Charlie!* It's Lomax.'

O'Hare replaced his telephone. Mortified. Persuaded by Lomax to leave the passing on of revelations he had received from Moon, he had suggested that their own people pass any information, good or bad, to David Weinberg's next of kin. They were better qualified. What was the CIA thinking sending helicopter gunships into an area to break up bandits for the Mexican Government knowing that they had their own operatives working in its interior? He thought quickly and returned Lomax's call.

'Not yet, Franklin. Say nothing. I've a feeling over the validity of information you've been given.'

'I'll give you twelve hours, Charlie. And I pray to God you're right.'

Oh, Sarah, O'Hare said to himself putting the telephone down with his hand over his mouth.

Fourteen – 1950s

DAVID WEINBERG RECEIVED A LETTER of reply from J. Edgar Hoover, or rather an associate director on his behalf. This despite Lomax asking him to leave things as they were insisting that Hoover, as far as he was concerned, the person that got him out of Mexico politically; it was a woman by the name of Jesurus Moon, who did it for him physically.

'Obviously, I can't stop you writing to the head of the FBI. That is your prerogative,' Lomax said. 'But there is an intergovernmental inquiry going on into what happened down there involving us *and* the CIA. Obviously, that concerns both yourself and Colsson. I strongly ask you to reconsider your decision. You could jeopardize your standing in this matter due to any misunderstandings.'

David told Lomax, with respect, that he – unlike others – had nothing to hide.

The reply read:

> Mr. Hoover sends his regards to a valued
> member of the FBI and is pleased to hear of
> his safe return and hoped him a speedy
> recovery; but had not the time to write to him
> personally. However, as to his investigations
> of Oceans Galactica, in particular, its CEO
> Frederik Spannocs, they were now at an end.
> Assistant Director Lomax has been made aware.

No doubt, you have been informed that Spannocs
may not be who he says he is; that the FBI has
wanted him since the 1920s. Let me cut to the
chase. The matter of Frederik Spannocs being
Marco Giuseppi wanted for historical child
abuses dating from that time, possession of
FBI records show a death certificate in his
name. Born the first of April 1890, died
eighth of November 1921. Further, that Oceans
Galactica headed by its Chief Executive
Frederik Spannocs, is a successful company
that was good for employment, good for
America, and likely to lead to Congressional
or Senate accusations of a witch-hunt if they
were to be investigated by the Bureau on
nothing more than scant information. He has
friends in high places.

Mr. Hoover is also aware that Doctor Raynham
has gone missing and that he had possibly
drowned while on a diving vacation. If you
have evidence that his body had been recovered
and cremated by others, that you suggested as
a possible reason for not being found, you
should present it at the forthcoming inquiry.
As for conversations that Dr. Raynham was
supposed to have had with a Dr. Sax
Stonercrop, that they may be members of an
organization known as the Order of the Most
Divine Third Circle, these had been looked
into and turned out to be tenuous. The
organization is no more than quasi-religious

with harmless scientific beliefs. The fact
that a few egg-heads and celebrities belong
the less said the better.

Mr. Hoover does not want any of his agents
stepping on toes that are true fitted in the
boot of American citizenship causing
embarrassment to the agency.

A standard, unpunctuated third paragraph had been inserted:

I shall expect a report from you during the
forthcoming inquiry on whatever else you may
have that could be useful to the Department of
Justice and wish to caution you that no
attempt to detain or arrest any employers or
employees or agents of Oceans Galactica, or
the religious Order shall be made by either
yourself or any other agent and furthermore
should it be necessary to direct undeveloped
leads to other field officers they be
accompanied by appropriate advice as to these
instructions and the discreet nature of
interests into child trafficking or murder.

The punctuation returned.

Once again, your co-operation with other
enforcement agencies; and the help that you
afforded the Mexican Government has not been
ignored. The disbandment of a dangerous gang
of gun-runners and criminals amidst a
defoliation program by the authorities against

wood wasp can only add to the courage you
showed in an otherwise dangerous situation. We
look forward to your rapid recovery and a
likewise early return to duty.

Regards JEH
pp Clyde Tolson
Associate Director, FBI.

'Good for America, *my arse!*' O'Hare said putting the letter down. 'What did you expect him to say, admit that there's a probable cover-up? He's not going to say that even if he suspects it. This goes on all the time. J. Edgar's straight enough. A bit on the strange side, granted. But honest for all that. He bides his time until one of you goes out on a limb and brings in the evidence.'

'And its tone?' David asked.

'Standard. Plenty of room for maneuver still.'

'What with Ocean? I can't do anymore that would involve the Internal Revenue.'

'No, but we don't need to, we've got enough. With them and our own files. I'm thinking CIA.'

'Would Spannocs be of interest to the CIA?'

'There's a question. A businessman of his stature. With a tie-up in Mexico. You said the CIA were there keeping an eye out for Russian movements. They wouldn't trust anyone with the assets Ocean had in such a region. Spannocs would be no exception to that rule whatever deals he might have elsewhere with the United States Government. His energy business with communism moving into Latin America, we might suggest to them a change in affiliations. They couldn't resist him. Helicopter gunships? Someone's got something to hide. Like Gerry Tell, you can barter information with Colsson. Anyway, how is your Mr. Colsson? I see they brought you in together.'

'He took it in the shoulder, same as me. He saved my life. He's being discharged tomorrow.'

'Whoever hit you, I'm convinced, was either a useless shot or was warning you.'

'Or you. Did you think about that?' He lowered his voice to a whisper. 'Whenever we start to talk to each other, the same doctor is hovering round.'

'Perhaps he's thinking of your welfare, you shouldn't look too deeply into that.'

'Except, he's not doctor to either of us.'

'What does Colsson say?'

'That some of our people are not very bright when it comes to security.'

'Fooking cheek! Get a picture of him. I'll bring in a Minolta. Perhaps we can ID him.'

O'Hare got up to leave.

'Before you go. There's something else with regards to Raynham . . . his disappearance.' O'Hare sat back down. 'When I first made inquiries of the yacht I got nothing but conflicting stories. Of how it was blown up, then it wasn't. And that shortly after the explosion, two bodies were washed up and taken to the morgue for postmortem. An official from the American Government had ordered it along with instructions that they were to be examined by two different doctors. Colsson, not happy, and smelling a rat, mentioned it to his Ops Director who told him that she would arrange for him to see them, with or without authority.'

'And did he?'

'He did. Of course, he had never met the man. But he did say something concerning the bodies. One killed by an assault that had broken his neck; the other, having all the hallmarks about his face of having mistaken a stick of dynamite for a cigar. What either doctor failed to notice, without the benefit of seeing both bodies together, as Colsson had, was that both men appeared identical.'

'Identical! What, as in twins?'

'According to Colsson. They were the same man. Each had a mole on his face. Below and to the side of the right eye.'

'Raynham had a mole.'

'When he told his ops director of what he had discovered, word got out. Someone had the bodies removed before anyone was the wiser.'

'And when did he tell you all this?'

'Yesterday. Yes, I know what you're going to say. He's apologized. But as he said, it was CIA business. Something he was reluctant to tell me, until, he had a change of heart.'

'Didn't you ask him when you first got there if any bodies had been washed up?'

'Of course I did. He said they were washing up all the time. Usually from gangland killings. Executions and the like.'

'It's why he has chosen to tell you all this now and not then, that's what I don't understand? Anyway, I'll bring that camera in,' he said getting up to leave once more.

'While we're on the subject of people choosing what to tell and when,' David asked putting his hand on his arm. 'Did you once say to me you were a detective police sergeant?'

'I was. In another life, with your father, you know that, why?'

'What do you know of strange creatures that can go through walls; and that click? Police officers, that can be brought back to life, and people wearing masks?'

'Get well David,' O'Hare said reaching across to remove his hand.

David grabbed his breast jacket pocket, 'More I think Detective Sergeant.'

'Phantasm? Classic symptoms. Brought on by stress and suppressed memories of your father coming into your mind playing out subconscious thoughts,' he replied.

'Except my father didn't have red hair, did he?'

Fifteen – 1950s

LUCK CEASED HER SEGREGATION song and looked up from the dirty blackened insulator she was cleaning. Her large eyes pierced the darkness of the tunnel. She thought she heard a train. She looked at her watch. She could make out the time in the half-light. 4 am. Two hours before her shift was to end. She wiped her forehead with the back of her hand. She must have imagined it. The station was closed down for maintenance; and was not due for opening until 8 am. Apart from which, the power was off. She would be burnt toast if it were not. Shaking her duster, she continued cleaning the next insulator singing,

'Look at people answering,
    To the Freedom Fighter's call— '

There it was again. She turned her head to one side better to listen. Standing up she looked round for the nearest escape recess that were set in the tunnel wall. *Had the power been switched on*, she whispered to herself. She should move right away from the track if it had. Several thousand volts could easily jump across to the body, killing you instantly if you were too close.

When she first started as a cleaner on the railway, she had difficulty approaching any track electrified or otherwise, let alone touch one. Being told the power was off by an engineer showing her what she had to do, was one thing: taking his word for it something else. She was not alone there. It was a basic instinct for survival. Like putting the palm of your hand on a circular saw that had stopped; or, putting your face to a glass tank with a poisonous snake, or a scorpion, directly on the other side. When either strikes, you cannot help but react. When she had trained her mind to accept that the power to the track was off, she never gave any other thought to the danger. There were, after all, safety features like alarms that went off a minute before power was restored. There were also warning lights that went from green to red on the sections they worked. All a matter of confidence in a fail-safe system. Satisfied she could hear nothing, she double checked the warning light, stepped forward began cleaning the dirt from the next insulator singing, in a whisper, slower, with one ear attuned should she hear the sound of an approaching train.

'Black, Brown and White American say,

Segregation must fall—'

The scream came hitting her full in the face; and with its following wind, knocked her sideways leaving her scrabbling to regain her balance against the rail line. A dirty odorous wind that had sweet warmth from the mix of thousands of people that ate, drank, and smoked on the platform or in the carriages of the trains. Her scarf knotted round her head became untied threatening to fly off. Holding the multicolored cotton scarf in place, she panicked. A train was about to descend on her at any minute. Subconsciously noticing that the red track light was still illuminated, she calmed herself. But to be on the safe side, she decided to make for the tunnel entrance, keeping as far from the track as possible, though she would be walking into the path of a speeding train if it came, the platform might be a safer option than down here, she thought.

It came once more.

The scream enveloped her. She was in panic and confusion. She could see the platform, but not the train. She ran for the stepped protrusions that would aid her climb to safety. Where was the train? She put one foot on the step, panting in terror. A train she could not see would do as much damage as one she could if it hit her she absurdly thought. The driver of it putting his hands to his face to avoid seeing a body exploding from its impact spraying the tunnel walls with blood and flesh; later to be washed clean by her colleagues after she was gone was a thought she had never considered before. She looked again up at the platform. There was no sign of a train – imagined, or otherwise. Instead, what she saw was a scene that was out of this world. One reminiscent from of her childhood. A page from her Bible. A battle between the devil and God. Satan with writhing serpents to aid him; while God had angels with swords and shields to defend Him. But unlike the battle between good and evil, that was only a line-drawing on paper, this one was playing out for real in front of her eyes. Two creatures. One, possibly a woman. The other, well, it did not look like any devil she had seen in any picture books before. Not that she had seen the real Satan for any comparison. Not in person, only his influence. When this Satan turned toward her, he had no face. A hood framing his face, gave notice of oblivion. A calm oblivion that only death can conjure, with no sign of evil intent only absolution. She rubbed her eyes. Off the ground, between the platform and the tunnel wall, flying, tumbling over each other for possession of . . . what was that with them. The smaller of the creatures was trying to remove a child from the arms of the other. Flashes of lightning were all round them as they came together and boomed like thunder as the two separated from their mid-air tussle.

Further along the platform, two groups of people. Some dressed in white laboratory coats, while others were in uniforms watched. They appeared to be carrying out an experiment. A large transformer on wheels, with cables running from it attached to large metal discs directed at the two creatures was having no apparent effect on them for they continued in this fight for possession. Those wearing uniforms were on their knees beside tubes that were on tripods. Before she had time to work out what they were three of them exploded sending harpoons out over the track taking nets with them. They were attempting to ensnare the creatures as gladiators in Roman arenas might have done before running them through with spears and swords killing them on the ground. Except, in this instance, they were trying to capture them rather than run them through. The two creatures, screaming and spinning, at one point disappeared altogether only to re-emerge once again to continue their fight. The harpoons pulled the nets over them. It looked for a brief moment as if they had them. The men cheered and tugged at the lines, at first with success. One, a man, that appeared to be the leader shouted at them to continue this tug-of-war. He was looking back at some of the other people in white coats, shouting,

'We've done it. Done it by God! The mystery of the universe is ours for the taking—'

Then the tension came away from the ropes. The men pulling at them collapsed back onto the platform. The net glowed red, smoked, then turned black before fluttering onto the platform as charred remains. The creatures were gone, only to appear seconds later. At the other end of the platform, directly in front of her. She cowed away. They could have been of this earth, but Luck doubted it. One, that had the appearance of a woman, was tall with a copper tanned skin. Although a lighter tone than herself, she might have been North African had she been human, where her ancestors, coming from the Gold Coast, arriving in America as slaves in the 18th century were Black. The hooded creature was smaller than her. She judged a couple of feet high – clicking, like one of those Geiger things. To her, he was a messenger from God Himself. She instinctively knew it. No humans fly with the agility of trapeze artistes. And she . . . an *angel*. No doubt about it.

As a member of a Christian gospel community, she certainly believed such existed. Why would they be fighting each other over a child? And why these men, what had they to do with it? The angel had the child by the hand now; a severed rope round its waist gave testament to her held captive. She swung the child away from the grasping hands of the hooded one. Before she could get it to the safety of the platform, the hood swooped in on them grabbed the angel round the waist carrying the two of them forward straight into the path of Luck. She stepped aside. She thought she felt their breathing. The child running along the platform, swinging, released itself as the two creatures veered away from her to disappear into the brickwork of the tunnel. She put her hands to her mouth in horror. When they re-appeared, they came out from between the tracks like champagne corks from bottles. They were spinning and turning, screaming (the sound a train would make coming into a station, its brakes burning against its wheel drums answered her fears as to what she heard in the tunnel). The hood carried on coming so close, she could have reached out and touched him. The shimmering, silvery-white cloaked creature disappeared into the tunnel she had come out from only minutes before. The angel turned away, flying back into the two groups of men. Someone shouted. She thought he said, 'The electro-magnet is overheating, it's going to blow any second.'

Another shouted:

'Fire another round of nets, don't let her go. Throw it! Stop her! We'll take one of them down at least.'

She went among them, still flying. Off the ground she span, turning, outmaneuvering their efforts to trap her. She hissed at one of them that had grabbed her ankle. Turning on him, she tore his head from his body as if it were nothing. The quickness of separation of head from body had momentarily left the man still running before his bloodied person toppled off the platform onto the rails. His head rolled in after him. The eyes open, his brain still functioning, stared in horror before she guessed his lights went out, as she choked back feelings of sickness considering a need to remain conscious and in control of herself for fear of what might happen to her. The tunnel, after escaping what she had first thought were the dangers of being run down by a train, took on a lesser danger from what was happening here now.

The groups of men, seeing what had befallen their colleague, tried to get away losing any further interest in an experiment that had gone badly wrong. The angel suspended in the air, hissed at them, and she was gone.

Luck seizing the opportunity while the men were trying to escape called to the child where the angel had left her on the platform. 'Quickly, come quickly. Come to me.' She must have heard her for she looked in her direction but did not move. She was shaking. She went to her instead. Seeing her up close, dirty, underfed, wearing a ragged dress that had once been yellow her heart went out to her. God, Luck thought, somebody has not had the decency to give her clean clothes. She could have been no more than nine. Fighting back tears she reached out to her taking her hand.

'She's gone. *Get her!* Get that woman back here. And bring the child with her! We can't have witnesses to what's happened here.'

Luck seeing the man coming after her, gathered the crying girl to her bosom jumped off the platform onto the track with her and ran for the safety of the tunnel, deciding that she would rather take her chances with a three-foot tall gnome wearing a silver black suit than to people that would subject a child to what she imagined to be unimaginable carnal atrocities. More for her own comfort than Black equality, she sang running and breathless, all the louder,

'To the Freedom Fighters (shh) call,
Black, Brown and White American say,
Segregation must fall.
Good evening (shh) Freedom Fighter's,
Tell me where you're bound,
Tell me (ohhhhh, little one, you're safe with me) where you're
marching,
From Selma to Montgomery Town.'

A hollow voice of a station official announced over the public address system that: *'Due to signal failure, the scheduled opening of the station has been delayed 24-hours. Will you please make your way to the exits? Attention, due to signal...'*

Louse Sayers dropped the files on Lomax's desk, said good morning, smiled, turning her head to examine the back of her calves, straightening the seam of her left leg stocking returned to her desk. A brave soul wolf whistled. Lomax looked up, the young culprit unseen, but suspected; Lomax pointed a finger.

He carried on his business shuffling through reams of paper. Some had been rubber stamped red: CONFIDENTIAL, 'How in *hell* did he get his hands on these?' Lomax said to himself.

'Louise . . . get O'Hare in here will you?'

The man, according to O'Hare, responsible for the abduction of children appeared to be still out there and not dead as Hoover insisted in his letter to David Weinberg. Whether that man was Spannocs, Lomax, for sure couldn't say. The age of the man was all wrong and that bothered him. Reading further, he felt sick. There were incidences of children turning up dead, in suspicious circumstances all pointing to a syndicate operating on a massive scale. Crimes that should have been solved by the police long ago had recommendations that no action be taken written in the margins. There were rough notes of convicted child abusers as having been questioned, with no case to answer – big names – no more than on the grounds of status and celebrity, released. O'Hare had always insisted to him that there was more to all of this than abuse of minors – as if that were not enough – suggesting some bizarre business motive.

'*Louise,*' he shouted across the office. 'Did you find him?'

He was not looking forward to this meeting.

'Every time that something like this comes to light you get some bizarre idea into your head that, assuming he's alive, one Marco Giuseppi is behind it. Well, I'm giving you the chance to prove it. The case of the girl found at Brooklyn station, has been handed to the Justice Department to be investigated. So it's yours.'

O'Hare removing his bowler hat put it on Lomax's desk in front of him. Lomax picked it up and threw it onto the hook of his hat-stand without so much as a backward glance that it had hooked on.

'And if that little girl had not been discovered; and with the press making an issue out of it, it would not have been, I'm sure. Someone has prompted the department to take seriously what I've been saying for years, which you, rather arrogantly have been poo-pooing!' O'Hare said.

'Poo-pooing? *Poo-pooing!* Is that anyway to speak to your superior? That's the problem with you and all of this; you never understood my position. The Department did not have the resources to follow up these crimes without proper complaints and witness statements.'

O'Hare leant over to him and whispered in his right ear that had taken on the hue of a red rose, 'And they have now? I'll say one name to you, Franklin, for Marco Giuseppi read Frederik Spannocs. These cases have been sitting on record long before the FBI had them. Look at them, NYPD, federal, state, municipal, county and sheriff's offices across the board. Someone has been preventing our investigating of them and I'm wondering if you knew more than you've been letting on.'

'Well, you've got your case officially. So you *fooking* well have! And no, I don't.'

O'Hare laughed. '"So I *fooking* well have". What for an Irish accent do you call that?'

There was silence between the two men. Lomax banged his fist on his desk and cracked a smiled.

'All right, I know you know more than you've been letting on. Carrying out your own investigations on the qt. I've turned a blind eye to all of that. I take it you've debriefed David. Is there a connection with Mexico? If there is, it'll be as well you work alongside him.' He smiled. 'If for not any other reason than you're getting a little too old for some of this.'

O'Hare gave him a look of disdain, retrieved a magazine from his brief case and dropped it onto his desk in front of him. 'Thanks for that. While we're on the subject of age, take a look at that.'

Lomax recognized the magazine. *Forbes*. The corporate journal for rising stars in the business world. It was open at the center-fold, but he didn't recognize the face that was staring up at him. Adjusting his glasses, he picked it up and gave it closer scrutiny. The picture was of a good-looking man he guessed to be in his thirties, possibly Scandinavian. He had a mustache, and slicked back hair, he guessed blonde. The sub headline running with the cover story mentioned that Frederik Spannocs had acquired an interest in an atomic energy research program that would provide cheap electric power. '*Yeh!* And,' Lomax said looked up from the article, 'so, they can do away with coal and use nuclear . . .'

'I know what it says. I'm not here to discuss splitting atoms. That man is Marco Giuseppi. The same man that Hoover says the FBI hold a copy of a death certificate for, and who I suspect built Oceans Galactica from the proceeds of crime. I use the word crime loosely in this context for that suggests Cosa Nostra, what with him being Italian. When it comes to what he's been involved, they at least had the dignity to stay well away. For what this man and those complicit with him, contrary to what J. Edgar says and the corporation he represents are neither good for employment, America, or its moral compass.'

'Well I can understand Hoover not taking up your idea that he is the same man. A little matter of an age difference between the two of you, I'm thinking. A difference this photograph clearly reflects.'

Age was the defining factor for O'Hare. The so-called death certificate for the man known as Marco Giuseppi was always going to be a problem for O'Hare in the persuading of others his true age. This man, Frederik Spannocs, with his 'fashionable' slicked back hair did make him look younger than O'Hare. But of course, there was more to him than a fashion statement. And while he did not look as fit as Spannocs, both men *were* born in 1890. Frederik Spannocs, America's entrepreneurial golden boy was an enigma, and O'Hare's cat may have to be let out of the bag to present the solution to that puzzle.

'Keeps himself fit, same as me. Takes hormones, not the same as me. I don't know. But it is him. I'd know those eyes anywhere,' as slitted as a demon's, he thought to himself. Though to another, they appeared normal.

'Okay. Suggestions as to where we take this?' Lomax said. 'Bearing in mind, Hoover has brought our investigations in Mexico to a close. You are going to have to tread carefully on this one. I can't be seen to be in any way to encouraging you.'

'Well, we know there's clearly a link. Stonercrop mentioning to me that Raynham was either a member or connected in some way with this Order. David's investigations with the IR finding the Order connected with Ocean. Our own files suggesting Tony D'Sotto and Phillip Maddox were one of the same. I didn't know that. Files that apparently should have been deleted. Who is stalking the corridors of power to do all this Franklin? Had it not been for that McCarthyism nonsense and the FBI's counter intelligence program leading to our original inquiries into Stonercrop and Raynham none of this would have seen the light of day. I suppose we should be grateful for small mercies.'

'Well, we're being asked to investigate the circumstances round a girl being handed into social services by a cleaner that was working in the subway this week; electronic equipment being discovered down there that shouldn't have been there which no-one knows anything about. Someone is not doing a very good job of covering their tracks are they. You need find that cleaner, Charlie. Speak with her.'

'I do, don't I? Have you her contact details?'

'Don't know her name. According to services, she was in a bit of a state when she handed the child over to them. Talking of flying angels and creatures going through solid walls. Still, we should be grateful she had the humanity to rescue a little girl some would have turned a blind eye. What we do know is that she's Black . . .'

'Oh, that narrows it down, I don't think . . .'

'With one arm.'

'Ohhh. *Right or left?*'

Getting up out of his chair and reaching across for his bowler hat, Lomax remained seated.

'Something else on your mind, Franklin?'

He hesitated before saying, 'Do you think Hoover's involved in any of this?'

'Even though he insists he has a death certificate for Giuseppi?

No I don't.' He clicked his tongue. 'Wheels within wheels. His term in that letter to David when he refers to "friends in high places" did put me slightly ill at ease at first though, but no. Definitely not. Thought you were at one time. No. Ask me if I think he's being manipulated though.'

'Thanks, Charlie. Nice to know I still have your loyalty.'

What O'Hare could not understand was Giuseppi's grudge against David and his apparent lack of actual bodily harm to himself. What happened to David in Mexico might have been because Giuseppi thought his father had come back from the grave telling all to his son. Of course, it wouldn't have been as ridiculous as it sounds, Giuseppi knew that spirits stalked the earth the same as he himself. That's scary, he thought. Colsson had seen two of Raynham. Two bodies, one and the same. That was more than an illusion. If Giuseppi wanted revenge for the so-called 'sins of the father', wanting the son killed, someone might have to answer to him for such careless shooting. Unless, of course, *they* were his controllers. Another scary notion.

Frank Weinberg had been shot dead after the Seaburg inquiry. He was not allowed to live with what he had seen. A hit could be expected to all those that knew, and from David's perspective, a spiritual passing on of information from his own father, would account for himself being on that death list. That leaves a Clown, a Goat, Fariq Mihalyvich, assuming he is still alive, and me; the only other people bearing witness to that night. As for other paranormal events since, a cleaner with one arm. Frank was right to do what he did when he wrote that report and buried it. As for the creature, he had nicknamed God's Reaper, for its similarity to that of God's angel as described in the first four books of the New Testament, standing in Jesus's sepulcher, as he saw it. The Divine Spirit that did not interfere in the crucifixion of Jesus Christ, let alone the abuse of children, supposedly the one sin unforgiving, excepting Satan (he would have something to say to St. Peter over that, assuming he got beyond the pearly gates). He had given a lot of thought to all of this over the years. None of those thoughts concluded with an answer as to what they were all doing here on earth in the first place. Unless, he wondered as an afterthought, one discounted a possibility of a Second Coming imminent.

But that was only his version of events. Who was to believe Christian faith to be an actuality? As for an angel. Wherever she was, with her track record for re-appearances over the years, he could be sure of one thing, she was seeking sanctuary, not in her place in heaven, but some secret place on earth. 'A tunnel or cave, perhaps,' he absentmindedly said to himself.

He pondered the thought and shrugged the ridiculousness of it off. 'I need to find a one-armed black woman before she ever makes it onto someone's death list.'

'Charlie, I have some more information you might find useful,' Lomax said on the telephone to O'Hare that evening, 'I had a call from the New York City Subway System offices earlier. A woman. She said that they had had a directive by her management from someone high up in one of the law enforcement agencies, he apparently didn't say who he was, but that they would not be allowed to discuss the situation until a formal investigation had been undertaken should we send an agent down to see them. Something to do with using an underage person in the making of the film being prejudicial to any investigation.'

'Film! What *fooking* film? Question being prejudicial! We're supposed to be the Federal Bureau of Investigation, who's above us, Franklin?'

Lomax smiled. His voice, had a touch of irony:

'No-one's above you, Agent O'Hare. You *are* the FBI. Step on all the toes you like. Sort this out and get to the bottom of it, you have my blessing.'

Railroad maintenance had a workshop behind an iron door set into the station's tunnel wall half-way along the platform. O'Hare strolled in asking to see the foreman. An engineer wearing dirty overalls pointed towards another working a lump of metal with a bench grinder. Sparks of red-hot metal sprayed from the wheel. He switched if off when he saw O'Hare.

'O'Hare. FBI,' he said announcing himself. 'Making inquiries of a woman that may have some information of interest to us when they were making that . . . *film*. Do you know her? Where she lives.'

Wiping his hands clean on a rag, he shook his head, 'No idea what you're talking about mister.'

The side of the man's face looked as if it had recently had an argument with someone's fist, from the winning side if O'Hare was any judge. 'Who did that to you?' he asked.

He switched the grinder back on. He looked frightened. He had to shout over the noise of the motor.

'Someone's been asking the same questions as me, haven't they? And not being very nice either, by all accounts. Always painful when you don't know the answer to get them to stop.'

He switched the grinder off once again.

'Look, okay mister all I know is she was black. That's what I told them. Where she lives and what her name is, I've no idea. I told them that as well.'

'Would you recognize them again?'

'And what good would that do me, eh? It's like I said—'

'Yeh! You know nothing. Thanks.'

O'Hare was worried. Whoever she was, they were onto her.

'When are we going to have to start calling you Weinberg–O'Hare, eh Charlie?'

'Don't hold your breath. She won't marry in a Catholic church and Rabbi Vermes said he would only allow my presence for the ceremony in the synagogue on condition I become an honorary Jew for that day. I tell yer, stumbling blocks everywhere.'

'*An honorary Jew!* What in the name of McGinty's goat is one of them when it's at home?'

Father Michael Riley stared at him. O'Hare had a face as straight as a poker player, then it began to crack, first into a smile, then a full-blown laugh.

'All right, all right. I'll buy it—'

O'Hare put his hand on Father Riley's shoulder. 'I've to abstain from eating pork pies for a whole day unless they've been koshered.'

O'Hare carried on laughing. Why had he been so stupid as to ask the man such a question? He waited for O'Hare to calm down before continuing, all the while shaking his head in disbelief. 'Seriously, a civil wedding. She wouldn't object to that if she loves you?'

He was wiping his eyes with a handkerchief, 'We spoke of it. Does seem the only way, I know. She said she'd think about it.'

'Well, it's not as if she wasn't married in a synagogue with her first husband. He was David's father wasn't he?'

O'Hare nodded. 'He was.'

'Thought you mentioned him when I was in the Service.'

'How long has it been?'

'Five years ago I left,' Riley said thoughtfully.

'Any regrets? Leaving, I mean.'

'No. Of course not—' He changed the subject. 'Anyway, are you here for confession Charlie? I can listen if you like, or I can see if Father Holtby is free.'

O'Hare put his hand on his shoulder and started to walk him

into church with him. 'You'll do fine, Mike. When you've listened and deliberated, then if God pleases, Heaven can take me soul, and Ireland me bones.'

The police called to the Church of Magdalena had not expected the murdered man to be a priest. Father Riley had been found by Father Holtby. He had been chained to a church pillar by his wrists. A bloodied silver candlestick on the stone floor was testament to having his bare legs beaten broken before his throat cut.

Detective Warwick knowing the dead man had been involved with the Department of Justice in a previous life, suspecting his killing may have had something to do with that, called the FBI. Lomax, hearing the name, knowing he was an acquaintance of O'Hare's, examined the scene personally.

'I can see where his penis is, but what have they done to his tongue?'

Warwick swallowed. 'Pushed up his arse with the end of a candle, Assistant Director.'

'*Christ!* And how am I supposed to tell that to O'Hare. He's going to be devastated,' Lomax replied.

Sixteen – 1950s

LOMAX HIT A WALL of non-cooperation when he spoke to the New York City Subway System management. They had changed their story. When he queried these changes, they told him he should speak with their lawyers. When he told them the trouble they could be in not answering questions put by an agent of the Justice Department, they showed arrogance suggesting they were above the law in this matter.

When Lomax sought advice from his boss, he said to leave things as they were; and that letters from the Department to individual managers citing them personally for their obstruction may 'rattle' them enough for it to be passed to their lawyers into taking a different stance. In the meanwhile, he should continue the investigation.

Not wishing to draw attention to himself or what he was doing he had bought a season ticket. He knew human nature, what with people being creatures of habit and all that. Sooner or later, O'Hare thought, she was bound to show up. If he were close, he would pick up on her. For what she knew, there was no question, a gunman would lay her to rest before her time. If someone had gone to the trouble to beat up an employee of the railway company for information, they would be serious in this resolve. All he had was a description. Black. One arm. And that would be the same information they had.

Over the weeks, he came to recognize every crack on the tunnel wall of the city subway; every lump of juice extracted gum spat out stuck to the station platform. He saw adverts pasted on its walls, seeing them updated replaced with others. He watched as the *Subway Sun* constantly changed its headline flash:

Go And $ave
Maybe You Can't Get To Heaven
But You Can Live In New York – Crowded Sure!

All of which gave him sore eyes. He persisted. Watching. Endlessly for the woman to reveal herself. He listened for any throwaway remark people might make to their traveling companion. Something that changed, or altered, that might have caught their notice bringing her closer to him before others. By the end of a week, or a month or a day they would become familiar and notice. People with outgoing personalities that did not bury themselves in their own world despite the overcrowded one round them. Where the human spirit to make a friendly casual acquaintance with another, still with them. Cheery souls, O'Hare likened them to.

Six weeks of patient work. A routine that would bore the heart out of a dull-head let alone a thinker. Boredom on a scale unimaginable to those same people that would have felt safe in the tracks they hoped they had covered. Only the single mindedness of a true professional would keep his sanity. A surveillance operation that few could endure, that might never bear fruit.

When it did, with someone asking him the next train to Broadway Nassau, he came close to throwing the whole lot down the drain.

The electric indicator hanging over the platform announced the arrival of the D 6th AV-HOUSTON train. O'Hare, as usual, stood half-way along the platform that would give him the best view of passengers alighting. This train, as all others was nothing special, he having seen it several hundred times before.

'Dat's where I found the girl,' the black woman said to her friend as she stepped off the train onto the platform pointing toward the tunnel entrance. There was pity and anger in her voice.

Barely audible among all other passengers alighting, this one told O'Hare that all these weeks were at an end. He had found what he had come looking for. The concern for him was that if he had picked up on her, others certainly would have. It could be the woman with the pram, the young fellow with the oversize cap on his head, the young couple waiting to board; he could not discount a police officer. She would be in danger unless he acted quickly. He needed to get her away and safe. Going up to her, he was about to introduce himself, when she stepped away from him in surprise, looked over his shoulder. Her eyes open and staring.

'It's alright, ma'am, I'm Charlie O'Hare of the FBI—'

'We know who you are,' the voice behind him said.

O'Hare turned round to find a .38 Colt pointing at his temple. ' *You!*'

A priest smiled, 'Stand aside, Charlie.'

''Fraid I can't do that.'

'Don't want to kill you—'

'And why would that be I wonder? It's not as if you haven't had plenty of opportunities in the past.'

'Step aside from that woman, you're already on borrowed time.'

O'Hare weighed up his options. There were passengers all round them. He needed a panicking mob. 'Help!' he shouted at the top of his voice pushing the woman to the ground while at the same time putting his body between the gunman and her. '*Help! Help!* There's a man here gotta gun.'

No-one at first took any notice. Whether it was because they did not understand, or they were too preoccupied with getting on with their daily lives, O'Hare could only guess. That state, however, did not last. 'He's going to fire. *GET DOWN!*'

A platform of passengers during New York's rush-hour, seeing a priest with a gun, for some reason saw it as bizarrely more dangerous than a street hold-up. The panic started. Shouts of, *There's a priest with a gun*, passed by word of mouth from one person to the next as a ripple from a pebble thrown into a pool. O'Hare knew that the man's options for time, and getting away, were becoming severely limited with screaming passengers running and blocking exits.

The gunman's index finger tightened, and O'Hare saw the movement of its chamber nudge. He held it.

'Very clever. Last chance, Charlie,' he said looking round for a way out. 'Soon as you're down, she's next. One in the mouth will quieten her for all of time.'

'You'll never get out of here alive. Do you think I'm working alone?'

He smiled. 'I've been watching as long as you have; matching you disguise for disguise. All alone, the same as I have. We were educated in the same school, you and me Charlie, even the FBI doesn't have the resources to keep more than one man watching for six weeks. There's no-one here to help you, Charlie. I know it, and you know it. And I can walk out of here with you and her lying in a pool of blood. We both know that and no-one's going to stop me. Now are you going to step aside, or am I going to have to shoot you dead where you're standing?'

At that moment, the door to the maintenance workshop opened behind them.

The man feeling the change in air pressure and with the thought that O'Hare had put in his head that he was not the only agent in the vicinity momentarily altered the position of his eyes. The showing of it gave O'Hare his opportunity. Grabbing his wrist, he twisted it downwards. The gun went off. The bullet ricocheted off the platform hitting the overhead gantry holding the train arrival indicator shattering it sending a shower of glass over them. O'Hare grabbed the woman's good arm, pulled her up, and into the workshop kicking the door shut.

'Hey, what's going on? This area is for maintenance staff only; you're not supposed to be here.'

'Look after her, give it five minutes, call Franklin Lomax of the FBI. Here, here's his number.' He took out a five-dollar bill and wrote it down, passing it to him adding, 'And keep the change.' Then as an afterthought said, 'Did you say you were maintenance?' The bewildered man nodded. 'Only the train indicator needs new light bulbs. That way to street level?' he asked pointing toward a set of stairs cluttered each side of the steps with miscellaneous paraphernalia covered in oil and grease.

The man nodded, a bemused look on his face. 'What in darnation's going on? Hey mister—'

O'Hare strolled purposefully out of the subway and into the street. The sunshine temporarily blinding him. Leaving behind a mass panic of passengers, the 'priest' would have found his way through the mêlée not far behind him. O'Hare was the fox and he would need to be the hound. Moving quickly, he walked into the entrance of a bookshop. Inadvertently taking down a copy of *The Age of Innocence*, and opening it full-in, he began reading with one eye on the page and the other watching through the window.

The 'priest' walked past the entrance to South 4th Street subway opposite. He could not work out if O'Hare were behind him or not. He stopped and looked up. No sign of the man. Angry with himself, he threw a copy of the *Catholic Times* he had been hiding behind on the station platform into a waste bin. Frustrated with himself for balling-up and losing his man, he needed to expose himself, confront him, and damn well kill him! He had got in their way for the last time. He hailed a Yellow cab.

The taxi drew up alongside him. He got in, and after he had said something to the driver, it took off.

O'Hare saw the cab move out into the traffic with the 'priest' looking out of its rear window. He ran from the bookshop, waving one down for himself. A screech of brakes, a Yellow pulled up beside him. 'Catch that cab. Keep your distance. Don't lose him. There's a double fare in it.'

In fifteen minutes, the cab in front of them pulled up outside the Christian Science building on 44th Street, '*Where?*' the driver asked.

'Pass him!' O'Hare looked back to see the 'priest' paying off the driver before walking into the entrance to a building.

'Where?' was his cab driver's repeated request.

'Drop me off over there,' O'Hare said pointing his finger. 'Go down the street, park on the corner; over there by that building we've passed. Wait for me there.'

O'Hare slammed the door closed and the cab moved off. He walked back on the other side of the street to see the 'priest' come back out, look in both directions for any sign of him. Obviously satisfied he was not being followed he got back into his own cab drove off. O'Hare waited a second or two, stuck his fingers in his mouth and whistled. His cab driver hearing him pulled out into the traffic, crossing two lanes testing the approaching traffic's brakes and reactions. Collecting his passenger on the other side of the street. O'Hare got in to an accompaniment of car horns and gesticulating fingers from passing motorists.

'*Same deal?*'

'Same deal,' O'Hare replied.

'Want me to find out where he's going?'

'You can try, but I doubt he's told him.'

The driver called his control and got the answer that O'Hare had been expecting.

'Thanks anyway.'

'Forgive me asking, buddy, but whose side you on, only, that's a priest isn't it? What's he been up to for this cloak-and-dagger routine?'

'I'm the law, and he's absconded with the outing money from the church. It was the old people's day out at the races.'

The driver, surprised at his passenger's immediacy of reply said, 'What a bastard, you can't trust no-body these days. I remember a fare I once carried . . .'

O'Hare pre-occupied and not particularly interested; the one-way conversation with an accompaniment of the sound of an engine at the end of its days (all he could do was nod and smile), settling instead for his own thoughts and where this journey would take him. Out onto the interstate highway the Yellow would keep a respectable distance without drawing attention to the occupant of the cab in front. Driving for a further twenty miles before turning into a new business park at Malaka's Corner, on the Washington DC junction. A single road with no other cars on it, '*Hit the brakes!*' O'Hare screamed seeing a FREEWAY ENDS sign stuck in some scrub-land at the side of the road. The car screeched to a halt, leaving the driver gasping as if he had gone up somebody's back fender.

'What's down there?'

'Government offices,' the cabbie said panting. 'Pensions. Nothing much. He won't be able to get out any other way – dead end. *Fuck me!* man you could have given more notice.'

'So I see. Okay. Straight for it, fast as you can. Overtake them, block them before they get to the end.' O'Hare had his gun out of its holster.

The driver did as asked. He was frightened and began to doubt what his passenger had told him of this 'priest' being the crook he had said he was. Seeing a gun in his hand, he was not prepared to discuss the issue. He did as he was told, accelerating after the other cab. Catching it, he drove alongside it. He figured that at least the driver was someone he knew; seeing him smile at him would stop. But the driver, with a gun to the back of his neck held by the 'priest', stared forward and sped up, cutting across them. O'Hare's driver slammed his brakes on to avoid an almost certain collision as the 'priest's' cab accelerated away from them putting a distance of a hundred yards between them before pulling up outside a building. The 'priest' opened the door and ran for its entrance.

'I don't want any trouble buddy, get out, and I'll be on me way. No charge.'

O'Hare could see the man was frightened. He did as he asked and gave him the cash he promised. The driver looked at the money. Relieved he was escaping what had been a dangerous situation he put it into his inside pocket, nodding at him, pulled away leaving O'Hare to his own devices.

O'Hare, gun in hand, ran after the 'priest' into a parking lot in under the office block. Straining his eyes in the semi-darkness, to see, he made out the 'priest' trying to operate a door with an electronic key card. He walked toward him.

'It's over, Sullivan, or whatever name you're using now,' O'Hare said. 'You're under arrest.'

The man dropping the card turned to face O'Hare, smiling, lifted his cassock, pulled out a gun and leveled it at him, 'Sorry, sergeant. Something personal.'

O'Hare clutched his chest and staggered back falling to the ground.

'Don't tell anyone who killed you when you get to where you're supposed to be Charlie.'

He stepped over him and went out into the open. His cab still waiting for him. The driver wound the window down.

'Everything in order, only I heard a shot?'

'Everything's fine, driver. The shot you heard was from this gun. You won't hear it again.' He pointed it at the driver's head and pulled the trigger. The bullet went into his right eye exiting out the back of his skull. The man's body shuddered stilled. Sullivan pulled the body from the cab letting it fall onto the ground among the parched cactus growing at the side of the road. He looked down at the man and genuflected. He sat in the warm seat and started the engine. He then drove off back the way he came, praying to God for forgiveness that he had murdered two men this day. At least O'Hare would not put the hub of the Order into this place, he thought. That at least would be an excuse for *this* killing.

O'Hare slowly opened his eyes and moved his head. He looked round checking that his attempted killer was gone. Satisfied, he got up and brushed himself down. '*Uh!*' he said smelling his hand. '*Dog shit.* Some killers have got no consideration when it comes to where their victims fall.'

Wiping his hand on the ground, he took off his shirt, then his body armor underneath. He held it up to the light, the outer part showed a neat burn hole. The bullet fell out. He picked it up. *Don't want too many of these as souvenirs*, he said to himself. David was right. And only three layers of silk. He threw it into a trash bin studied his chest. There, marks of heavy bruising. His ribs felt as if one or two were broken, but he thought, little wonder with his torso having taken a punch from a bullet close range. And that was one, big, gun. He saw the flash and heard its percussion. Not many people can say that and live to tell the story. He had become unconscious after, but that was probably more from the shock of the experience than injury. He took a cigar out of his pocket and lighted it drawing in deep breaths of smoke; then began a hot, dusty, three mile walk back to the main road before flagging down a passing motorist, relieved that it was not a cab. He was all out of cash.

Lomax received a telephone call from the Brooklyn station manager to say that one of his agents had apparently asked a member of his staff to contact him on this number regarding them taking a woman into care; and did he know anything about it?

Concerned after O'Hare made the point that an infiltrator was operating within the FBI; anxious to distance himself from any thoughts that O'Hare might have that it might be himself; or if not, knew who, decided to wait for the man himself to make an appearance before interviewing the black woman. When later that day he turned in, dishevelled and in pain, Lomax insisted he get himself to the hospital for a check-over. The following day the interview took place in Lomax's office, immediately called off after what she said she saw, Lomax deciding that the privacy of a hotel conference suite, should his office be bugged, would be a better option.

'No chance of us being overheard here,' Lomax said.

O'Hare was pleased that he was at last taking this all seriously.

'You were saying, "She didn't have any . . ." well . . . is that right?' Lomax asked the woman unsure how to tackle the subject of genetalia, women's, or otherwise.

'Look hon', up until the day 'fore yes'day, far as I know, every woman in der world got one – *including* blackies,' she answered with the look of racial equality on her face. 'Same's we all got red blood, figure. Dat lady, well, she definitely didn't,' Kinsay Luck answered with affirmation.

Lomax worked his mouth and teeth trying to give the impression that what this woman was telling him was believable.

'And this other creature—'

'Der one with der hood and no face? Well, he was trying to get the girl off her. She never had a chance. There was 'quipment everywhere. Flashin' and sparking like. This creature, well it was dragging at her. Short, black shiny bright white son-of-a-bitch clicking like a venetian blind in der wind.'

'And have you watched any out-of-this-world television programs recently? They can look realistic, play on the mind, cause dreams. Only the railway manager said that there was a film crew down there making a movie—'

'Dat was no film, hon' – you need a camera to make one of dem. Dare weren't none o' dat down among all that 'quipment. I maybe black, in somes eyes, thinkin' me down wid der *Joo-Joo* man; or the voodoo Queen of New Orlean'; but what I see is what I saw and what I's saw weren't of this world – no sir, no honky.'

'And no-one's suggesting you didn't, Miss,' O'Hare said looking at Lomax shortly closing his eyes. 'Please continue.'

'Well, dey was throwing nets over dem. There were flashes of lightning, electricity. Dey was stuck, den they disappeared, den they come back. Der noise, screaming, sounded like a train a-comin'.'

Lomax was hastily writing notes with a pencil turning pages without pausing.

'Den day free,' she went on without invitation to continue. 'She had the little girl and den day came for me. The little girl she managed to struggle free and he went right into the tunnel. Right past me. Den gone. It gave me one of the most amaaazin' feelings I ever know'd. Right down my spine it go. Dat was when she went back and tore his head from his shoulders. And serve he right, I say.'

'What did they say when they discovered you?' Lomax asked.

'Didn't hang about. Picked up der girl and ran back down the tunnel as if Satan hisself's hounds were at me heels, her in my arm.'

One arm, O'Hare thought to himself. Holds down a cleaning job; carries a child to safety with one arm. 'What was she like when you picked her up off the platform? In shock, perhaps?' O'Hare asked more for the benefit of Lomax than himself.

'You betcha, mister. Nothing like a child, more like a doll. Or one of dem automatons you do see in the fairground, you know, der ones that move their limbs when you put a dime in the slot. I could do with one of dem,' she said moving her shoulder. 'Though mercy me, my arm is growing bigger and stronger since dat hooded thing looked at me. Stump's getting longer. And I've got movement where I didn't 'ave it afore. Not since the accident when I was making bullets.'

'Bullets!' Lomax remarked.

'In the arms factory. Funny when you think about it.'

'*Funny!*' Lomax queried.

'Yeh, funny. Dat bein' where I lost mine.'

And she would have a fully functioning arm, hand and fingers before much longer, O'Hare thought to himself. Whatever that thing is, it doesn't just bring immortality, it performs miracles on the hoof. That's one clever bastard!

He had not been wrong. Kinsay Luck, with new arm and full hand of fingers, went back to her old job Joannering in bars in the evenings, with her own band.

'*Is she?*' O'Hare said angrily, his face red. 'She might have been with me and Frank 24 years ago when we witnessed what we did. Anyway, returning to what we were originally talking about, David's report on Mexico and all those bizarre events. Two Raynham's where one would have done; Spannocs's yacht blown out the water; Colsson killed in a helicopter crash after being released from hospital he and David were being treated for "accidentally being gassed" by gun-ships bearing CIA markings during a supposed scientific program to control *wood wasps!'* He rubbed his forehead before continuing. 'The priest that shot me *was* in the FBI years ago. Name of Sullivan. Daniel. And if we look deeper,' he whispered. 'I'll bet a dollar to a dime, someone in government knows something of all of this. Unless you're the man that knows it all anyway?' O'Hare put his hand to his shoulder holster and took hold of the handle of his gun more out of frustration than intent.

But intent turned to become intense.

Lomax familiar with the movement and seeing the desperation in his face absentmindedly scratched his forehead; stopping short for, he was looking down the barrel of a revolver. He stayed still fearing that O'Hare might overreact and shoot him. The silence between the two men was overwhelming. Lomax slowly reached out to O'Hare's hand and moved the barrel away from his face. O'Hare instinctively flicked his armed wrist and repositioned it at Lomax's temple.

O'Hare holding his gun to Lomax's head was astonished with himself as to why he would do such a thing, gently lowered it, placing the killing end toward himself on Lomax's desk and buried his head in his hands. He had tears in his eyes. 'I'm so sorry, Franklin. I'm so sorry,' he said looking up at him.

'Forget it, put it behind you,' Lomax said relieved to be alive. 'You've been under a lot of pressure; getting yourself shot and all, well, I wouldn't blame you for not trusting anyone,' he added breathing our more air than he had taken in. 'From what you've told me, coupled with what the Luck woman witnessed, with events reported by David, well, I'd be a fool not to make a formal . . .'

'You might want to reconsider making it official. For the moment, it might be as well we keep this close,' O'Hare said anticipating Lomax's rubber stamping a criminal investigation with paranormal overtones. 'Whoever are at the bottom of all this will certainly use demons and spirits as a canard to undermine us. And while I can live with it, with your position and all, you most certainly cannot.'

'Well, I must admit, I do draw the line at aliens from outer space, as to the rest, I shall make no mention, nor any inclination that any exists in the pursuit of those involved in crimes of trafficking and abuses against children. As for Spannocs being Giuseppi, the directives from my superiors to leave the man be, must stand only as far as to satisfy public interest that he is not involved.'

'Public interest?'

Lomax held up his hand to stay him.

'Putting it as diplomatically as I can – I have done. I have also to tell you that Sax Stonercrop was with the FBI, working undercover in universities, and has himself now gone missing.'

O'Hare shook his head, 'No, no, no, you're wrong there. I interviewed the man personally; I knew him. I spoke for hours with him. I would have known if he was anything other than what he said he was.'

'Well, he was good, I grant you that. Good enough to fool you. And me. Nobody told me that he was one of ours, not until I made my own inquiries, told as much. And yes, he reported on Raynham. *And* the reason he knew Raynham's activities and the Order's approach to him. He also asked his handler if it might be a good idea for him to infiltrate the Order himself. They agreed.'

O'Hare was still shaking his head in disbelief.

'With him likely dead, we've no way of finding out. I'm convinced that newspaper article you showed me was correct, except the part being an accident. Personally, I believe he was murdered while on active service, Charlie.'

O'Hare nodded no, 'There's such animals as double agents, you know?'

'It's a thought that needs to be kept but let me move this on.

Assuming you're not a rocketing nut-zone, and my having sleepless nights wondering what you're going to come out with next, you'll be happy to know I have come to the decision that, without jeopardizing my own career, I concede you're probably right in what you've been saying, crimes against children being known abroad within our government. Whether it's Spannocs, Giuseppi – Bigfoot himself, I cannot say, I'm leaving that to you to find out. All I will say is, I cannot get overly involved other than if I find a child that is in danger, like this last one, I will. Other than that, well, I think you know where I'm coming from.'

'Thank you Franklin, that means a lot to me,' O'Hare said.

'I haven't finished yet.' (He wasn't sure if he was being cynical, but let it go). Opening his desk drawer, he took out two tumblers and a bottle. 'I need a drink, and so will you when you've heard what I have to say.' He filled them half-way with bourbon passing him one. 'Another death, I'm afraid; and one that affects you personally.' He took a large mouthful and swallowed it. 'Father Riley.'

The uncertain news of what Lomax was going to tell him, with that name, put him in a frame of mind that what he would say he would hope to put him off continuing by his own interruption of it. 'Don't tell me he's a double agent too. He was one of ours before he found the cloth you know. A man we should . . . all . . . emulate . . .' He stopped short. Lomax had a look of dread on his face. 'What of him, Franklin?'

'Sorry to have to tell you this, Charlie; but he was found dead. He'd been tortured to death—'

'*Mike Riley*. Dead! For God's sake, tell me you're joking. He was going to marry Sarah and me. *Dead!* Sweet Mother of Jesus. Have they anyone for it?'

Lomax shook his head. 'No. I am aware of what he was to you. Tell me, did he know anything of this business of yours?'

'He heard my confession the other day, that's all. Whatever I might have said to Mike Riley, he wouldn't have broken his vows by repeating them. He would have died protecting the confessional, as he would information he held on the FBI – I'm sure of it, so I am.'

'Not something inadvertent? Weighing heavy on your mind, perhaps?' Franklin asked.

'Wouldn't have made any difference to him, bad thought, bad deed. If they had got anything out of him, it would have been nothing that would have been of use. If it's any consolation to you, it was to do with me marrying out of my faith, that's all. *Sweet Mother Mary*.'

'Well, I've never heard of a priest being subjected to the treatment that was meted out to him before. If it wasn't for what they might get out of him after your confession, it was a warning,' Lomax cautioned.

O'Hare shook his head. If Mike Riley had said nothing, he was stronger in his faith protecting words between confessor and God than he could ever be, O'Hare thought of the man.

'I'm sorry for your loss, but my support comes with conditions. I don't want any more mystery or bull-shit or remarks of what you know, and what I don't,' he said looking at the tumbler taking another sip. 'Only all this inclines me to the view that we have a serious break down in either communications within our own organization; or, we have people working against us and with us at one and the same time; or working against us and not with us; or working against you and whatever you were involved within your dark and distant past life; for ends that are either; of a nature that no-one knows but wants to know more; or, of a nature that someone knows and is not willing to divulge to others; or, a whole heap of people know, but are not willing to tell anyone else; or, *Christ*, something is to happen that is so earth-shattering that we would be in fear of our lives if we did. Do you see the problem that a lowly assistant director of the FBI has to try and run with when he's being pulled in more directions than a compass crossing the north pole; and likely sacked by Uncle John for being too smart?' He stopped for another drink, looked at O'Hare who still had his untouched tumbler in his hand with his mouth open. 'I need to see Frank Weinberg's report of that day in question, Charlie. You know, the one that will make you and your ex-partner laughing stocks. Only from where I'm sitting, until you do that, you are – apart from what I've always thought of you as a man of integrity you would be to me – *exactly that!*'

News of Father Michael Riley's murder had upset him to the point of postponing, for a time his marriage to Sarah. Dismissing the dangers before, but not now, he was not prepared to take the risk of anything happening to her to get at him. She had understood his postponement for the sake of Kadish; he did not mention his true fears, or the mention of a period.

Seventeen – 1950s

For me to exist,
Then God needs inventing.

SATAN 5,000,000 BCE

O'HARE VISITED David in hospital. He had pneumonia and had had to be re-admitted.

David had not been able to comprehend the events of so long ago that occurred with his father and O'Hare. If his own faith could never buy into Jesus of Nazareth being the Son of God, why should he? When Charlie mentioned his father's doubt of faith he was shocked.

'Didn't he seek advice from the Rabbi over those doubts?'

'He spent a deal of time soul searching.'

'Not with my mother?'

Charlie shook his head, 'How would I know?'

'And what were his conclusions?'

'None that satisfied him. All he said was, ". . . and that I have come to that view that all faith in a superior being is baloney".'

'So how did he justify you coming back from the dead? Did he say that it was a stranger that practiced artificial respiration on you? Or that the hooded creature that might have been the Divine Spirit, likely Jesus's, as well as man's, companion at death. The Christian belief that he had overseen the execution of Jesus later seen in a cave after the Man had departed this world; wasn't that recorded fact, not faith? Hadn't he witnessed what early believers in Christianity had?' O'Hare did not answer. 'Because that is what happened. I saw everything. If anyone should have doubts as to their religious beliefs, it's I. And "baloney" would not be the blanket word for doubt that I would use. Christianity–Islam–Judaism is worthy of more than that. Better to remain, *blurred*; down the middle, round the edges; and where religious philosophers usefully maintain common ground that will one day prevent us from killing one another.'

'I obviously cannot speak for your father's choice of word. As to what you saw . . . well . . . we could be certain that Spannocs was there, somewhere. In the walls. Something must have played out a film or recording. I don't know.'

'But it was all so real. A ghost of something going through a wall. A child.'

'I believe the child you saw was the image or ghost of Fariq Mihalyvich's daughter. He wasn't able to save her. Though I heard he had returned to his mother Russia, but no evidence he took his daughter with him. I believe she became an angel, the result of sins against her that wouldn't allow her to pass over without justice or right. The screams you heard were hers. And something evil, Satan, trying to get one over on the Divine Spirit for kicking him out of the club of ecstatic eternity at the dawn of time, for all I know; before getting his horny fingers a-meddling in the 20th-century.' O'Hare filled a glass with some fruit juice and set it down for him. 'There's also the possibility that you hallucinated from the gas. And I'll tell you something else; we never did, your father and me, discount the possibility than it was a conjuring illusion. Your father called in an expert. Unfortunately, Houdini died before he could explain. Changing the subject, and talking of gas, what did the doctor say?'

'Only that my lungs are burnt from chlorine that are likely to cause me problems for a while. But given rest I should make a full recovery. I can't believe Colsson's gone though.'

Charlie swallowed hard. 'Yeh, Franklin told me. Very sad. The helicopter taking him back to Mexico crashed killing the pilot and another agent that was with him. I'm sorry. You two seemed to get on well together. He nodded in the affirmative. Did you ever get that photograph by the way?'

David leant over reaching out for his briefcase. He opened it and took out a folder passing him the picture. 'Charlie. Going back to what we were speaking of earlier, you know what I saw. And if it wasn't an hallucination, is it possible that it *was* trickery?'

All those years before, he had given that considerable thought. Would that have got them off the hook if they had reported it with the explanation that, 'Of course, you're right, Frank, why didn't we think of that earlier, that's how it was achieved, with mirrors!' But he could not. An illusion would be the practical explanation, assuming that all those concerned had been party to it. What value there was in such trickery he could not imagine. Could Giuseppi have pulled off a conjuring trick that allowed him to escape from the law. An exit from the stage of criminality in one town to pop-up and continue in another. A magnificent illusion brilliantly executed and one, which Frank and himself fell for, unable to speak of for fear of ridicule. Could it be that what they had always regarded as irrefutable first hand evidence of paranormal phenomenon had turned into nothing more than sleight of hand? He was convinced that Frank had been right to keep that particular turn of events under wraps, given the reaction to it from his own son was anything to go by and he, with the benefit of modern-day thinking, that there would be an explanation for everything; that anything was possible. For sure, the mentioning of it would have seen them kicked out of the NYPD if it had later turned out to be an elaborate charade to dupe them, the damage would have been done and those responsible would have rubbed their hands together with glee. The only difficulty he had with all of this was his unique relationship with Irinushka; if his assumption was correct, she was the angel and not a figment of his imagination. But. And . . .

Except. . . .

. . . Not David's, aha! And for sure, Frank would not have mentioned that he had seen an angel to Sarah. Her orthodoxy would not allow her to listen to such fanciful tales if they had come from her husband. He assumed Frank's faith, after the event had remained intact, later evidence might well have toppled them. David, so far, had not wanted to admit that, but he was going to have to get used to the idea that it may lead to him questioning his.

'Anything is possible I guess,' O'Hare answered.

David changed the subject. 'How's mother?'

He looked at him and O'Hare knew what he was driving at. His face said it all. He cared for her, he could see that, he could also see he was wondering if she would go through with their marriage with this quest of his still unfulfilled, forever likely bringing back painful memories of his father. 'She's had a lot to put up with, so she has. I wouldn't blame her if she never had anything more to do with me. If it's any consolation I've offered to meet her half way by retiring.'

'Well, if you're doing that for her peace of mind I wouldn't have bothered myself. I've told her I'm not going to let you and my father's work go without someone being held to account for his murder, and if your Spannocs is Giuseppi and responsible, I'll get him, and mother will have to bear it.'

O'Hare saw determination in his eyes. 'If you'll take my advice, I'd give it all up. There's no future in it for you.'

'Did you? Have you? Far as I'm concerned, as a faith we did that in Europe in '39 and look where it got us. Not your precious pope Pius XII would speak up for us – and they *canonized* him.'

'This is not the same David. You'll be fighting shadows. Not human Nazis. Illusions or not, you've seen what this man is capable.

You were powerless against him in Mexico, you will be again. And if you're going to drag race murder into the equation might I remind you of what your people are doing to the Palestinians. What does your Rabbi Hillel say on such matters, "Doing not unto others that you would not have done to you". More. Leviticus 19, somewhere, something on the lines of love not being dependent on liking, more of recognizing everyone's common humanity. If you want a cause, well there's one readymade.'

David should have known better than to bring up religion where Charlie was concerned. For all that, leaving child abusers for someone else to deal with, as far as he was concerned, was tantamount to passing the buck. Israel and Palestine would have to sort its own problems out. He saw his future and could not allow bogeymen to get in the way of that. The photograph of his father and Charlie on his desk, standing together with J. Edgar Hoover gave credence to the respect the Bureau had for both men, and for that, he would continue their work. Whether it was a man named Spannocs, Giuseppi, a career trader in trafficking children for sex, was still, a mortal plain and simple whatever faith. If anyone were to stop him in his inquiries to get to the bottom of all this, the man that would have to tell him would be Hoover, not Lomax, not Charlie, nor Harry S. Truman. As to what he saw, played out with actors to enhance someone's powers against what he imagined would be a mental unbalancing act against an investigator getting too close; using someone within our own corridors of power, would need to do better than that to stop him doing his duty.

O'Hare thought carefully over what Sarah had said to him on the matter of David picking up the baton for his father, 'He has a wife and son of his own,' she had reminded him. 'If he is to continue on this path, he could lose his life as my Frank had.' How he thought he could stop a criminal that clearly had influence in high places by being an agent with the FBI, she had reminded him. 'When you yourself have failed, well it beggars belief.' O'Hare had not been able to answer her. She had told him time and again to let it go and leave Frank to rest in peace, adding that he was a pig-headed Irishman. 'You've a degree in, *You think you know best*, so you do.'

He was not laughing. Neither was she. Continuing in the same vein she added, 'And David has got all this from you. I'm warning you, get our son out of all this before it's too late or you and me, regardless of our engagement to be married, will have to call it a day.'

She went on to say she had had her share of threatening mail over the years. He buried his head in his hands and started to massage his temple, gently at first, scratched the itch he had created. He looked up at her and shook his head, a feeling of resignation was in his thoughts. He was exhausted. Where do I go from here, he thought to himself. He no longer thought he was in the right league for taking these people on. It was a job for someone younger. He took a deep breath. 'You want me to retire.'

She stared at him; her mouth wide open. 'And for David to get a desk job. You can swing that for him I know.'

He got up from the sofa chair he had been sitting in her living room and went to the window. She had a fresh cut lawn running down to a pond with a summerhouse behind. There were fruit bushes to the side of it. The sun was out. Thoughts of retirement appealed to him. David's wife Ruth was potting up some plants. Heavily pregnant, they were expecting their first child in a few weeks. He turned to look at Sarah, not wanting to show he had seen anything in particular. But he had. Casually looking back out the window, beside and slightly to one side of Ruth, a boy, wearing a yarmulke. He had looked at him and smiled. O'Hare rubbing his eyes looked back. He was gone, leaving a shiver running down his back. Another illusion. Ruth looked up at him and smiled in her turn. Not for nothing had he seen that apparition. 'I'll think on . . . of what you've said.'

Eighteen – 1955

He who neglects what is done
For what ought to be done,
Sooner effects his ruin
Than his preservation.

MACHIAVELLI, 1532

THE ATTORNEY smiling at both men left them to it closing the door behind him.

O'Hare looked at the flat document lying between them on the desk. As pristine as the day he and Frank had locked it away from the world all those years before, he worried that Frank might not have approved of his actions. As if another hand was guiding his, he, without further thought pushed it across the desk with the effort of two.

Lomax hesitantly picked it up, looking at O'Hare as if seeking permission to carry on.

'It's what you wanted,' he said.

Handling it reverently, Lomax did not know why, he turned it over first one way then the other. It had a red seal, a piece of cord locked beneath from a time it had been molten, held a metal hasp to the enveloped flap. Its content had clearly not had a reader since the day a clerk holding a stick of wax over his candle had daubed it secure. Looking closely, under the company name in a larger type size of German black letter script, Lomax could make out inked words hand-written and scratched hard into its vellum-like surface with pen and ink that would reinforce its authenticity:

[First Sealed this 3rd day of July in the Year of our Lord 1916. Jonathon Macconey, Attorney-at-Law in the State of New York, USA.].

He made a closer inspection of the words through a magnifying glass that the attorney had left for him to double check any details he might be doubtful of. So far, it appeared Simon Pure. He looked at O'Hare, without more formality, inserted his fingers and broke the seal destroying the written words from the outer surface layer of the envelope from its dermis. Flakes of hardened red sealing wax fell onto the desktop. He blew them away, pulling back the flap of the envelope slipped out the content from inside unfolding them. There were several sheets. He gave a cursory glance over the pages, signatures, and fingerprints, commenced to read from its beginning.

O'Hare, seeing part of his life coming under scrutiny, got up and went to the window. He looked out over the streets that he and Frank had once patrolled as officers with the NYPD. A lump came to his throat. He looked back to see a bespectacled Lomax reading with an unlit cigar sticking out from between his teeth, a match waiting to strike up a flame between the thumb and forefinger of his right hand hesitated over the matchbox in his left. O'Hare turned his gaze back onto the streets that occupied a distant memory from a previous life.

Lomax, struck the match on the side of the box, put the flame to his cigar, drew in several times to secure the glow end, blowing the match out, put the document down on the desk and leaning back in his chair looked across at O'Hare. He was still staring out the window. He could not be sure, but the man looked as if he were wiping tears from his eyes with a handkerchief. He made out he was still reading, went through the process of finishing up once again (this time he coughed), drawing O'Hare's attention.

'And where did you say this has been hiding all this time?'

'Wells Fargo Bank on Macey Street. Me and Frank its custodians, and of course, the attorney acting on our behalf; to be passed to the last survivor of the two of us, onward at his death to the next one of either kin. Assuming we had any. Mother of Jesus, there's some dust in these files,' he said pointing toward the bookcase full of similar documents. 'It's got in me eyes, and up me nose, so it has.' He sniffed. Gathering himself together added. 'Enlightening enough for you, Franklin?'

'That and disturbing. It's an astonishing piece of work. I don't think I've ever read one from any officer to match this. It's little wonder you secreted it away. Those creatures mentioned in this are those the Luck woman described. Whatever are they Charlie?' He shook his head in disbelief. He was not expecting an answer. The reading of instruments of torture hanging up sent a chill through him. As did the boy, stripped of his skin, hanging. Beyond belief that a fellow human being could do that to another. And those crimes, according to O'Hare, the same people involved still being around, perpetuating them still for reasons, he had not managed to get to the bottom of. With this report, and what he had spoken concerning corruption within the government was beginning to have credence. 'Well, I find it commendable that you both chose to disobey an order to protect children that were in danger. With no disrespect to yourself, more so Lieutenant Weinberg . . .'

'None taken.'

'Out of the two of you, the man that had the most to lose.'

'And he did.'

'Of course. And I can see where you have always been coming from. There's got to be nothing worse than crimes of this magnitude being brought before a superior officer for him to do nothing.'

'*Because he was up to his neck in it himself.* Anyone would have done the same as me and Frank.'

'I'm not sure that's true.'

'Wouldn't you? Knowing that children were suffering.'

'Of course I would. I'm not saying it would be any easier for me though, any more than it was for you, or for anyone else for that matter. But I know some that wouldn't to keep their careers intact. But having said that, with the workload of crimes that I have had to contend with in the Bureau over the years, which is to say, I may have inadvertently ignored something like them. Not intentionally you understand. I agree that child abuse doesn't get the notoriety that more tasteful crimes achieve, probably because it's more difficult to prove, especially when it's within families. Difficult.'

O'Hare nodded his agreement, 'Rivers ignored it knowing they were immigrants and social outcasts; the public were not going to bother over. He knew that, as did others. Still do if truth known. Despite that, I'm convinced there's more to all of this than making money from trafficking children for sex. Something sinister is going on here. It has all been going on for too long for it to be anything else. People, Sullivan for instance.' Lomax took on a puzzled expression. 'You've always said Frederik Spannocs cannot be Marco Giuseppi because of the age he would be, well, Sullivan would be his age, give or take a day or two. As I am. All those that bore witness to that original incident have been given the gift of immortality.' Lomax shook his head in disbelief. 'Or, as in Kinsay Luck's experience, her arm is aching and growing. Same creatures, different time, did they do that?'

'I can't buy into that Charlie. Lieutenant Weinberg died, where's the immortality there?'

'Probably because we can be killed.'

'You seem to have an answer for everything,' Lomax said cynically. 'Still doesn't mean you're immortal.'

'Well, how would you describe me to someone?'

Lomax felt embarrassed and turned down his mouth. 'Well. I don't know. Not wanting to offend your feelings—'

'Try Franklin, it's not a proposal of marriage I'm seeking. Be your usual self.'

Lomax laughed, then his face took on a more serious aspect. 'Apart from your liking for whiskey and cigars?' He hoped that would be all, but from the expression on O'Hare's face he knew it wasn't. 'Alright. Since you insist (he cleared his throat). I see before me an average looking sixty-year-old lawman with a slight limp, a stoop, the Grim Reaper with his arm over his shoulder, and an attitude, much like any other old Paddy lawman with which I'm acquainted. Both happy – more often not. There, I've said it.'

O'Hare shamming shock said, '*The Grim Reaper!* I didn't ask you to pull any punches.'

'Well you did ask.'

'And I'm grateful for your candidness. Watch, and eat your heart out, Assistant Director Franklin Lomax of the FBI, you are going on a journey into the unknown,' he said standing up.

Lomax felt that perhaps he had overdone what he had said until O'Hare stopped stooping. He watched him grow upright. His mouth dropped a gasp when O'Hare walked across the attorney's office with a gait of purposefulness before removing a wig of gray hair discarding it to the floor to reveal a head of fresh brown young soft underneath. Charlie O'Hare's anatomical appearance had changed. He had left thirty years on the carpet in front of his eyes.

'*Christ!*' he appealed. 'What did you just do to yourself?'

O'Hare sat down in the chair opposite. 'You won't be condemned for using the Lord's name in vain, Franklin, I've taken His Mother's on more than one occasion. It was one of two entities that done this to us. I cannot speak for others, but I have not tired with the years. All of which, as time has gone on I have prayed is some biological malfunction, but unfortunately, having seen Sullivan, I have to report I'm not alone. I've had to act my age so as not to draw attention to myself, and I'm exposing it to you now for what it is: 65, born 1890, the same year as Marco Giuseppi.'

Lomax did not know what to ask first. This was altogether unbelievable as he gave the only immediate response he could.

'You don't look more than thirty.'

O'Hare laughed and producing an ink pad from his pocket placed it on the desk. Pushing first his thumb, second his index, then finally his middle finger into it, pressing a print of its impression onto the velum of the document alongside another; below his signature taken at the time asked of him, 'Are they the same?'

Lomax had to admit that they were.

'It's the tablets you took when you were in hospital.'

'Come on, you can do better than that.'

'It's a hoax.'

'When you've come to no other conclusion, Franklin, and accept as I have had to, coming to terms with powers that are out of our hands and control, you can live with it and investigate. To my knowledge there are probably five more like me.'

'You're asking me to accept something that's not natural.'

He leaned over his desk, 'No, I'm asking you to accept something that defies explanation. More than me and Frank have seen those creatures. Another chief-of-police, Rivers's predecessor, Dore. Run down by a car and killed for the privilege. A good man. That was after a down-and-out reporter told him a story of Giuseppi throwing a guy into a dock basin with the superhuman strength of Charlie Atlas. He told Dore the man was possessed and that he had seen two creatures, one of them a flying woman. For all we know they may be perfectly natural. Like creation. Natural. Not that we fully understand that as a concept. Someday it may be, perhaps that day has arrived; and for whatever reason, others are actively encouraging their appearances, trying to lock into them for their own ends.'

'Okay, for the moment. You both thought Mihalyvich's daughter became an angel. I have a problem with that. Firstly, I don't believe in God or His offering of an eternal life. Assuming I wanted life in the first place. It's the same old story. Secondly, angels, Satan, Holy Ghost, all written at a time when people didn't know any different. God's chosen by different religions, embellished, iconized to the point where they became living and legitimate, "If it wasn't for a God, we would have to invent him", being a classic line for His reality. If anyone could come up with a different creature. A Martian for instance, a three-eyed blob of jelly, I could give credence. But this *hackneyed* view of what people saw 2000 years ago lacks originality, to say nothing of credibility. No disrespect to your beliefs Charlie, but I don't buy into any of it being God, whoever *She* is.'

O'Hare shrugged. 'Fair enough. Forget God and Bible stories. What if they are creatures from another universe with supernatural powers that were seen at the time?'

'Warmer.'

'Running in tandem with our universe and something has triggered them into showing themselves. From our own future sent to warn us—'

'Warn us of what?'

'Don't know, but the angel, well she's been trying to tell me something. Either I'm not listening, or I can't understand her. Every so often since this first started, I've had relapses of illness, some serious, like the last, that have knocked me back for periods, only for her to turn up in my thoughts bringing me back to the land of the living. It would be fair to say, she haunts me still. I can feel her in my soul; and I can feel when she's departed. Every ailment that had become to cause me problems has miraculously left me after these possessions by her. I fear that the medical profession is going to get suspicious if I have too many more of them.'

Lomax stared at him. There was no doubt in his mind that something had happened to the man. Standing there before him, two inches taller than he was when he came into this office. But, if he had always dressed himself down, it was not surprising. Looking at him in this new light hearing what he was saying, he didn't look his age. If anything, the man was going backwards, senescence speaking.

'You mentioned him looking thirty; that it couldn't be Marco Giuseppi. I'm convinced it is. And because of he's own demon possession, he has been watched. And those being witness to it murdered. I've mentioned Dore, but there were others, that would have known more than was healthy for them. Kurt Runfeldt, one of his own enforcers needed to be disposed of, head removed in Mihalyvich's house after he murdered the man's wife. Twisted a dozen or so turns until the skin gave way. Our Rivers had his head torn from his torso in his own bed after being relieved of duty. Again, who's capable of that? Governor Brent found dismembered and burned wearing what remained of the mask of a Bloodhound. In his case he managed to get away only to be caught later. I suspected at the time that both he and Rivers were involved with Giuseppi. Not the best of friendships in retrospect. Frank and me ran into all manner of villains arresting them only to have them released because they had "friends in high places". Those "friends" would have been Rivers and Brent running their own businesses as a side-line. Our own people, albeit denied by the Bureau, are back in the frame. I've mentioned Sullivan, well there's another. A man by the name of Johnson.'

'*Johnson.*'

He smiled at his chance encounter.

'A coincidence, during the Mihalyvich incident. The man and me happened to buy tobacco from the same drugstore. One morning as he was coming out, and I was going in, I noticed him smoking a Lordhamercy. He happened to be in charge of shipping in the dockyard. According to Mihalyvich, he had little idea of the workings of ship traffic, but a lot more about Giuseppi if warnings he had given the man were anything to go by. He had an inkling he worked for the government. Using the alias Claypole. Anyway, mister Claypole turned out to be Johnson, as I was later to learn. Part of the Johnson–Sullivan double act that recruited me and Frank; and who happened to mention in passing to Frank that he would like his rotor arm returned; the one Frank removed from his car when they were up to no good in the house of Giuseppi. The man that shot me was Sullivan. Minus certain features like hair, mustache.'

'Why do you think you were removed from your jobs and recruited to the Bureau?'

'Apparently for our own safety and well-being. So much for Frank's well-being.'

'Mmm. Interesting. What in *heaven's* name's a Lordhamercy?' Lomax asked expecting some wisecrack answer.

'A Lordhamercy, well, is a tobacco filled clay pipe that is handed out at Irish wakes to guests. In fact, along with whiskey and porter, they are central to proceedings. I had one to go to. Anyway, I says to him in passing, thinking that perhaps he might be Irish, perhaps going to the same one as me:

"Morning. *Claypipes*, eh!"

'Expecting him to say that he was, he replies, after obviously not hearing me too clearly, on account of his accent, what with Yank being inferior to Irish and all:

"No, it's Claypole, and if you want a job in the dockyard you'll have to see the man in charge of the union, Marco Giuseppe." Or words to that affect. So, as you see when I heard the name, Claypole, it stuck in the old head.'

'You put two and two together in spite of the whine from the amateur for three and the cry of the critic for five—' Lomax added smartly.

'*Yep!*'

'So what would an agent from the Bureau be doing working undercover in the dockyard?' Lomax asked.

'Good question. Got his fingerprint though, should I have later had cause to need it. That was some premonition.'

'How did you manage that?' Lomax asked.

'The rotor arm removed from his Duesenberg on the night in question. A rarity motor car even for then. Years later, I came across the same car in the Minnesota Museum of Transport – it's still there. On loan, would you believe, from the FBI. They gave me permission to go over it after I told them I was writing a book seeking famous prints that might still be on rare limos. Couldn't risk anyone at the museum letting the owners know that one of their FBI agents was giving it a forensic going over.'

Lomax interrupted, 'Surely there wouldn't be any trace of fingerprints after all that time. Over the years the car would have been washed and valeted, polished and whatever else?'

'Not on the wheel-jack it don't. That never gets washed.'

'But what I don't understand. Rivers and Brent, if they were involved, why were they murdered?'

'It took me time to figure that one out. I may be completely off key, but it came to me. Something *fooking* big goes on here. They were surplus to requirement, no longer needed. Deeds carried out by despots and the like, not seen in America, more akin to the ancients; in these people's lust for power they saw them as stupid and an embarrassment. Bloodline agendarism doomed them!'

'*Bloodline agendarism?*'

'Every megalomaniac worth his salt has one. Machiavelli knew it. An end more important than the means; that cannot allowed to be watered down by sympathizers that may have their own ideas as to where they should be going. A simple policy that has worked in dynasties up and down the centuries. Mothers, fathers, sisters, brothers, husbands, wives. Use them – destroy them. The king is King. Long live the King.

'Of course, the hypothetical murder of one's own father, makes it all the easier to take out those unrelated that would bring you down in your progress. Our people would be easy pickings, if those involved at the beginning were part of the government. Rivers was a chief-of-police and Brent, a Governor.'

'Doesn't bode well for the rest of us, does it?'

'Frank Weinberg, Christian Dore, Tiber Colsson—'

'*Riley!* Mike Riley,' Lomax added.

'God, yeh. Forgot about him. Thanks for that. Ummh! Anyway, they all died under suspicious circumstances for what I suspect they had seen – or knew. But a more worrying aspect to all of this, Franklin,' he paused for him to take in what he was to say next, 'is that they are going after anyone they suspect knows anything at all of what they are engaged in. Sarah Weinberg, to give but one example. Her son, David another. *Even you!*'

Lomax swallowed. 'All right, I take your point. What I don't understand is this immortality business. Surely, if that was the case, people exposed to these . . . creatures . . . that were murdered should have been immune from death. Your partner for one.'

'As I said, appears we can be killed. No, it's by natural causes of aging that's the worrying part in all of this; and something that only time will tell. Immortality may not be the blessing it seems. Although, "Agent" Sullivan gunning me down, finding later I survived, might think differently about our dying at another's hand not knowing I was wearing body armor. Ah, the wonders of bullet-proof vests, eh! Once he knows that, he could well come for me again. As for Giuseppi, he never made it to the FBI's list of most wanted, or anybody else's for all I know. According to Hoover, apparently in possession of a death certificate with his name on it, obviously a forgery, he never will make that list. At least, not in the name of Marco Giuseppi. The fact is, he can whistle saliva in my face for all eternity, and he knows I can't do a *damn* thing concerning any arrest of him. There's a conspiracy Franklin, and I need to get to Johnson and Sullivan; put the thumb screws on them to get at the truth.' He pulled a copy of *Wall Street* out of his brief case placing it on the table in front of him tapping it with his forefinger.

'What am a looking at?'

O'Hare settled his finger on a picture on its cover. Favorite for Entrepreneur of the Year, the by-line read. Lomax studied it but it meant nothing to him. He'd never met the man.

'Could be anybody far as I know. Do we have his picture on file?'

'We did have. All gone. Along with all the nefarious operations he was involved before he got into child trafficking. The prostitution, his protection rackets, the list goes on. All the negotiated contracts between the NY Dockyard Board Management and his own union during the war years. All gone down the Swanee.'

'So how are we to know Spannocs is your Giuseppi when we have only your word for it?'

O'Hare got up from his chair and went to the window. 'There are others that know; but for the moment, until I get to the bottom of all this, you'll have to take my word for it. Spannocs,' O'Hare said turning back to him, 'has enjoyed a charmed life with others protecting him. I've decided I *shall* retire. The whole world needs to know I've *retired* .' He smiled at Lomax.

'Go on,' Lomax said drawing his words out, 'what comes next?'

'I want you to make me an unofficial honorary member of the

FBI; and for me to keep my badge and gun as mementos in recognition of my achievements. Call it a retirement gift in place of the regular gold watch and chain; and get David from the sharp end and into management before I lose another Weinberg while I get to work.'

Later that day, in his office at home, O'Hare studied the photograph. Far as he knew it was the only one existing of Giuseppi and he had no intention of letting on that he had it. He compared it with the one on the cover of *Wall Street*. And though it was a large screen half-tone, there was no doubt in his mind that the two pictures were of one and the same. Though, he thought the hair, light, probably blonde, no longer black, but still slicked back. The mustache gone, making his lips more prominent now. Lips that would issue a spray of saliva an odor a cross between excrement and bad scent. He turned the photograph into a different light, trying to see something more, but it was enough. David had taken the picture from his hospital bed with his Minolta; and although it was grainy, there was no doubt in his mind as to who it was. Marco Giuseppi, the Great Magician was alive, and to impress and remind David, the blowing out of the sky with a bomb of the helicopter returning Tiber Colsson to Mexico was both easy and successful. For O'Hare, there was no other way. He was going to have to take him head on and assassinate him. He did not intend to bring him to face justice, for there would be none; and he was going to have to find within himself a powerful abracadabra for justice that God was ignoring. The abracadabra that an angel might possess, channeling it through him.

The only people he had heard of endowed with the powers to kill another were from classical mythologies. As a Christian had he that right? As an FBI agent, did he? It would not have been the first time. Vengeance might be His, but by using him she would be using a mortal to carry out the task in His name. Was it against the laws of nature for him to slay in His name? How would she reach a decision to go against natural law that sat so comfortably in the psyche of so many men? Or was it man's inner judgement persuading her? Was an executioner justified in seeking divine sanction when it came to the deed? And, if so, would he turn to God to excuse him? If not a being he had no belief, who? Whom does a non-believer go to for the equivalent of divine justice? And would they have any more authority to give it than God Himself?

If God did not sanction the killing of another by a person that would destroy innocents, He would be condoning His own tablet of sins and the one unforgiving. Assuming he gave permission to a servant for the slaying of another for this crime would He be trying to conceal an evil that he had been personally responsible for by planting it in the mind of man in the first instance? A curious mix that seemed to leave man's abuse of man in no hands, except our own. With no consciousness of good or evil, how can an evil man be brought to book for his actions. Man's justice can only ever declare evil or madness; does not consider God's permission or condemnation. If a man, like Giuseppi, has no conception of good or evil, madness or sanity – he can only be one thing in his faith, a servant of Satan. Whatever the angel's standing in Heaven, she was certainly taking her time. 2000 years. In the meantime, so not to place the Lord in an uncompromising position, he thought, I'd as well ask her permission, to cover meself like.

'But first, a whiskey I'm thinking.'

He dropped the closed magazine onto the table and took his jacket from the back of his chair. Putting it on he went out convinced that he had been right in persuading Lomax to transfer David to the American embassy in London. As to his retirement with conditions, Lomax would let him know.

A wind blew up, the sky darkened. Pages of *Wall Street* fanned one after the other stopping at the double page spread continuing the story from the cover. Another picture, this time, of Spannocs on board a yacht with the name *Galactica III* surrounded by beautiful women wearing bikinis, lace shift tops round their sun-bronzed shoulders, in Florida Keys. A helicopter on the harbor in the back ground, bearing the legend *Galactica II* in gold emblazoned down its length on its deep wax black finish. The face of Spannocs, preoccupied by the girls' idle talk, stopped his conversation, turned, and came forward on the page smiling, then, proofed and set in print, reverted to the same as the other 900,000 copies of the November issue, 1955, page 27.

O'Hare and the angel Irinushka settled into an uneasy relationship somewhere between conjugal fidelity and maternal care. He supposed that she could still be a figment in his mind. The concept of each other kept driving him into a dead-end of confusion, his only apparent escape being not to dwell.

Lomax had not yet decided as to his offer. While waiting, he spent his days burying himself in English history enacting wars of attrition with armies of model soldiers. His life began to take on the role of a parochial country gentleman for which he had always yearned. Growing into the role as an actor would, his personality changed immeasurably from his earlier younger days. Finding himself thinking deeply all manner of human dispositions and understanding less why.

Taking an early morning stroll in the park, wondering who would win the 2.30 at Belmont Park, his mind went back to his younger days when he was a dancer, and to Mary O'Grady, the girl he had pledged his undying love, before their families separated them. He had refused to take up the calling as priest, saying to his father that *he* might have heard the call, but his son was still listening. An hypocrite, his father, he thought, seeing that as soon as they had arrived in America, finding things tough had joined Tammany rapidly moving up its ladder with his fists. Could have been worse, he thought, he might have signed up to the Irish Mob. He thought of his father's brother back in Ireland. Was Sin still alive? He must try and contact his family sometime.

Lunch. Should it be Donheny & Nesbitt's – he had not been there since his illness five years past; and the thought of sausage with mashed potato and onion washed down with Dublin Guinness made him salivate. He went in taking a high stool at the bar. He called after Terry Flanagan, who stuck his head half through the kitchen hatch to greet him (his barman asking him to guess who had walked in). 'And I trust you've had the high stools fixed up. They weren't very safe you know. *And* some English mustard while you're about it, Terry!'

Irinushka never came out with him and he wondered why? He laughed at the thought of her sitting on a bar stool removing a cherry from its stick with her lips sipping at a vermouth or whatever her kind drank. Nectar, perhaps. He supposed that angels didn't have an objection to drinking guessing they could do as they wished. Heaven might be a perpetual church service, but one has to get ones pleasure where one can, he thought.

He wondered over her life. Was it cut short? If she was Mihalyvich's daughter, it certainly had been – and in the most appalling manner (he tried not to put the Latino boy to the back of his mind). As had Frank's for that matter; and where was he, dear boy? They should have both retired together. She had not managed to save him after all he had done for her. Her and her damned almighty connections. If God had long since left, it would certainly explain a lot in this rotten to the core world. Though not everyone comes to the rescue of those that need it most. Even His Son, confused as to His Father's forsakenness had not heard, or chosen to ignore, His crying out for Him. Perhaps He had gone. Maybe He had seen the way things were beginning to pan out with the human race and had plain *foocked* off leaving the Divine Spirit to carry on as best he could.

Enough of this, he thought. Other matters of a more down-to-earth nature had come to mind. A background of the man that would help him to get to him. How he had become the man, he was, for instance. Giuseppi's track record in the beginning might not have been straight and narrow, but at least he was a common to good old-fashioned Catholic criminal that we can all relate at the outset. Something tipped him into depravity and if it wasn't the Lord God Himself, who did?

He finished his lunch and pushed the plate to one side ordering a second Guinness with an Irish chaser. A lifetimes bit on the side with a result of 1-0 to Giuseppi, he thought. That's the sum total for the deviant criminal of the millennium. He left Doheny & Nesbitt's in a better condition than he had five years before.

Twelve years on. O'Hare awarded an honorarium with conditions imposed agreed, with no intention of keeping them. He figured, and Lomax concurred, that as long as he was officially retired, he would no longer be a threat, investigative wise to those that were running this whole unpalatable show. He had once again played out the waiting game, but he was fast becoming impatient, and it was time for him to show his hand, move against them. Children were still going missing, turning up dead. Frederik Spannocs had long gone to earth. He had kept a low profile for twelve years. His company, Oceans Galactica, now specializing in nuclear energy and rocketry was thriving.

Assistant Director Franklin Lomax retired. (Time flies, so it does.)

David returned from London to take up an appointment as Deputy Head of Security and Political Intelligence with the Bureau accepting a placement as a Presidential protection officer. He and Ruth had their son, a bonny boy by the name of Arnold H. Weinberg.

J. Edgar Hoover survived a third attempt to oust him as Head of the FBI by Lyndon B. Johnson. The two previous attempts, first by Harry Truman, the second John F. Kennedy both also having failed; he outlived the one dying May 2, 1972 whilst still serving as 1st Director of the Federal Bureau of Investigation. O'Hare had always admired him.

David and Ruth, Sarah, O'Hare, and Lomax hit when Dutchie's Restaurant they were celebrating a lifetime's friendship destroyed by a bomb left in a suitcase under an adjoining table. O'Hare was in the john at the precise moment it went off, the force blowing him through a window out onto the sidewalk. Sarah got out with minor burns and cracked ribs. No one else in the party survived.

PART THREE

Nineteen – 1997

Kill a man, and you are an assassin.
Kill millions of men, and you are a conqueror.
Kill everyone, and you are a god.

JEAN ROSTAND, 1894–1977

A BOLT OF LIGHTNING struck the ark with all the force that nature could muster, hitting the lid and blowing it open at once setting fire to its contents. Assistant archivist Sister Benedicta Marie, standing over it, took the full force shielding Father Michael Joseph standing next to her by wrestling him to the floor in anticipation of a second Act of God. Gathering her wits, she got herself up taking the fire extinguisher down from the wall. Turning it upside down, she pulled the safety catch and punched the lever setting off a high velocity jet of water; stepping over Father Joseph directed the nozzle into the ark.

'What in *God*'s name are you doing?' he said trying to recover himself. He was having difficulty getting himself up.

She did not answer. The situation must be apparent to an old man, she thought to herself, before becoming annoyed with herself for entertaining such notion. Her heart was thumping; the fire was receding, then went out. She stared into the ark. Part of one of the scrolls damaged. A singeing to its binding. They were fortunate, it could have been a lot worse, the whole of this section of the Secret Library could have gone up in flames with all this material.

A minor moment before she had felt strange, eerie strange. Something or someone had entered her body at one side to re-emerge from the other. A subliminal image exposed for less than the blink of an eye gave her an impression of a partially naked woman with a high forehead. Tall, much taller than herself, she wondered how that was possible, dismissing the idea as a figment of her imagination. Shaking her head to clear the image from her mind, it remained as a moving spot wherever she looked until her brain evaporated it. Her flesh goose-pimpled. An act of God was one thing, but a living soul coming through a barred window like a thunder flash to leave the same way before possessing her was something else. She shook uncontrollably. Father Joseph, up on his feet now, put a comforting arm round her from what he thought was the shock from a spontaneous explosion and fire.

Uncovered by an exploding missile during the Yom Kippur war the ark first saw the light of day balancing on part of a wall among the remains of an ancient Tabernacle, the subject of an archaeological investigation. Urgently needing a safe home the Jewish archaeological team had contacted the Roman Catholic Church in Rome for help. Known for their assistance down the centuries when wars and the like threatened to destroy important documents, the Vatican, taking the view that man was here for but a short time, while history was in perpetuity whatever faith or politics of a nation state were, they agreed without condition.

Covered in dust, Sister Benedicta, still shaking, lighted a cigarette. The blackness of her habit had taken on a faded gray look. She should have worn her coverall.

She should have worn a fire protection suit.

'Are you all right, Sister?' Father Joseph asked thinking that perhaps he should not have admonished her as he had. She had probably saved him from serious burns. She nodded at him.

'Do you want to call it a day?'

She said she would like to finish what they had started.

He smiled at her resilience carried on with their work as if nothing had happened, taking the scrolls placing them on a bench for closer inspection. They had come unrolled from the heat blast, but to his relief they had suffered no permanent damage. The important thing was that they were still legible. He laid one of them out on the wooden table putting souvenir paperweights of Pope John Gregory XVII onto each corner. Their work being to protect articles such as scrolls. Keeping them safe in as dry an environment as possible; not to read them, study them, or bring to the light of the world what they might have to say. But what Father Joseph noticed put the rule, *meant to be broken* onto the front burner of the proverbial. The beginning of its ancient words glaring back at him demanding to be continued.

A student in several languages, English, German, and French. He could speak Russian, from his time as a young priest in Belarus when sent by the Vatican to chronicle Stalin's purges of religion during the late 1930s. Imprisoned, likely to end up being murdered, Pius XII had used his influence on a civil servant, a closet Muslim within Stalin's government, who had no stomach for gosateizm. He signed the paperwork for his repatriation. As Head Archivist in the Vatican's Secret Library, Latin was obligatory. Russian and Old Hebrew were not. He was conversant in both those as a by-product.

What he was reading made it difficult for him not to continue. Slowly running his finger down the lines with a silent whisper, stopping occasionally to translate the more difficult passages before continuing, he was mortified. For this 2000 years-old scroll, not in best condition, written and if true, would turn the Christian world on its head: the multiplicity of faiths rooted in the Man Jesus of Nazareth aligned with that of Satan. Perspiration ran down his forehead at the thought.

He knew this could not be the Holy Ark of the Covenant. That Ark, the aron kodesh, disappeared with the destruction of Solomon's

Temple 422 years before the birth of Christ. Nevertheless, this one did look as if it might have come from another similar. He was preoccupied with its reading when Sister Benedicta interrupted him.

'What is it?' she asked. He had a look of disbelief on his face. '*What does it say?*' she said looking at his face. His mouth open wide.

'I might be completely wrong; and of course it will need to be verified, I hope to God I'm not—'

He gave her a brief outline of what he had read. She thought he was joking. In poor taste, she thought; nevertheless, the Father, not known for his humor when it came to such matters repeated himself. When she saw he was serious her spine tremored. She laid her still burning NO SMOKING cigarette on the corner of the cell window to take a closer look. She was at his shoulder, leaning over the scroll her breath all over it.

'That's the language of Canaan isn't it?' she whispered. 'Jesus Christ Himself would have recognized it.'

'*Recognize it!* It concerns Him. Presented as prosecution evidence at His trial, Pilate would have had no need to wash his hands for. An open and shut verdict would have been given by him.'

Sister Benedicta thought carefully. 'This is Aramaic; we're going to need a second opinion. Someone that can translate this properly . . .' God! She mentally interrupted herself. What was she saying? 'You *are* the expert. Sorry, Father. If what we have here is true evidence, it will be dynamite for any future Christian–Judaism relations. And that's for starters. Isn't there a chance that your translation might be open to a different interpretation? Religious wars are bad enough; I dread to think what will happen when this gets out. There's going to be a world bloodbath.'

Father Joseph had not thought that far enough ahead. The two of them could well be in danger for knowing its content. '*Translation.* My translation might not be academically up to the mark, but there's no altering the coloring of its wording. "Suffer the little children . . ." has never had such a resonance in my book.'

'Look, Father. This is for Jewish academics to pontificate over. Not us. It's none of our business. We'll take a photograph, hand it over to them.'

He nodded eager to be rid of this nightmare.

'All right.' She reached into her bag taking out a camera. 'Spread it out, Father.' He did as she asked. 'The edge is tearing away; see if you can hold it together.' She looked at the digital image in its back-screen, checked that the flash light was signaling, and clicked the camera.

He looked at her. '*Jewish*. Should we?'

'It belongs to them. They wrote it, or rather a lawyer from that time, probably a Sadducee. All I can think is that there was a conspiracy. After all, no-one disliked the Man. This would have nailed Him for sure if the case for blasphemy fell down. God excuse my turn of word. What choice do we have Father, but then to hand it back?'

In the half light, he wiped tears running from the corners of his old eyes. He moved his hand down the cheek of his face. His fingers feeling out the stubble that no matter how hard he tried to shave returned an hour or so later. 'But you're in half a mind, aren't you, Sister?'

She took up her cigarette and turning toward the window stared out. Black clouds had gathered in the sky like portends of doom. A storm was coming. She drew on her cigarette, put it down, balanced it on the edge of the ancient stonework of the cell window ledge, exhaled, then answered him.

'Short of destroying it, yes. If we don't hand it over, sooner or later someone else is going to come across it. We need to make the Pope aware of our findings if nothing else. Let him decide what to do.'

'All that will happen is that the Cardinals will commandeer it.

They will study its implications and do nothing. It wouldn't be the first time the Roman Catholic Church has covered things up.'

'*What!* Fresh evidence for the indictment of Jesus Christ. How is anyone going to cover that up? We might as well kiss goodbye to our religious beliefs and throw our lot in with Satan,' she said.

'No need to go that far,' he said back at her. 'The trial was Him being King of the Jews. This looks like evidence switched from one for another. Something more palatable, that they could still crucify Him for. I must have it wrong. I've misinterpreted meaning somewhere down the line. Mixed up Old Hebrew from its other variants.'

Sister Benedicta knew Father Joseph was not wrong in what it said. The odd word, here or there, that could certainly be misinterpreted, *but* not a whole transcript.

'Tell me you're not that good a scholar, eh,' Sister Benedicta said pleading with him.

He wished he could. But being an expert in Judaism, they sought his opinion from time to time. 'It's what will happen to us in the meantime that worries me. Knowing what we know. They won't allow us to continue with our work, you know that don't you. I'm over eighty, it doesn't matter much to me, but you're still a young woman.'

'Thank you. Not that young though. Thirty-three—'

'*And never been kissed . . .*'

'Uhm . . . I wouldn't go that far either, Father. I haven't always been a Carmelite; but I have a woman.'

He smiled, but not with any expression of sincerity. This dawning was slowly sinking in. He was as shaken as he knew she was. He was all for burning it where it lay. They both stared at it. The foretold Messianic belief from the Book of Isaiah that He was the anointed King never was going to be acceptable to the High Priests 2000 years-ago any more than today. The implication that Jesus accepted by thousands for his miracles and his good works was the Messiah would damn the Son of God (as well as any other Comer) with this enlightenment; He would forever be condemned by man, whether Messiah or Prophet for all of time.

Sister Benedicta was not at first aware of the two men standing in the doorway. Neither was Father Joseph, who was looking for something that would show he was mistaken in what would have been a legal document.

'We'll take that if you don't mind,' the first Cohort said.

Sister Benedicta startled, and turned to see who it was. The white suits they were wearing were in stark contrast to the dimmed light in the depth of the library. She saw they were wearing small red brooch crosses on gray metal shields on their right lapels.

'*Who in hell are you?* This is a secure environment,' she shouted more from fear that their discovery was to be given up than from any material threat from them. 'You're not supposed to be here. *Get out!*'

'We are Knights of the Teutonic Order; and we'll forgo your reference to hell, Sister. The scroll . . . if you don't mind,' the second Cohort said.

'It's not ours to hand over. Who let you in here? This is a secure department belonging to the Vatican?' Father Joseph said rolling the parchment up. He placed it in another box shutting the lid down firmly snapping the padlock in its hasp locking it. 'Now get out before *I* call the Vatican guard.'

When the shot rang out Sister Benedicta did not recognize at first what it was. Or where it came from. She saw the other man with a gun in his hand. She startled at the sound of the second shot putting a bullet into the other knee of Father Joseph. Collapsing, he went the ground, writhing in agony.

'My Brother doesn't see the shooting of a Father as anything more than a distraction. As for a Sister, well, you can make your own mind up from the evidence before your eyes.'

They hauled him to his feet and tied him to a chair. All she could do was stand, immobile, listening to him crying out. She could see both his knee caps were shattered. The gun leveled at him:

'Numbers please.'

Father Joseph was in too much pain to answer.

'You call yourselves Teutonic Knights that you would do this to a Brother of the Church; a Church that gifts you Papal patronage.'

They ignored her.

'Father, we are waiting. Or are we going to have to start on the Sister. We are not playing games here.'

Father Joseph was shaking his head. The pain was intense. 'Leave her, it's . . . 6 . . . 9-2 . . . 4-7 . . . 0.'

The first Cohort tested the lock opened it removing the scroll.

'*Kill him!* And the Sister!' the second said to the first with the gun turning to leave.

Sister Benedicta seeing her cigarette still burning on the cell window ledge picked it up, reaching across, stubbed it out into the gunman's eye as he leant forward in his attempt to place the barrel of the gun to the head of the Father. He staggered back trying to relieve the pain with his hand. None was forthcoming. The eye receded back into its socket leaving a film of white skin to protect any further sight he had in that eye. The other man seeing what had happened took the gun from him and shot Father Joseph in the chest. Turning the gun on Sister Benedicta he shot her.

'We thought you might want to see her; in case she speaks again. I'm afraid the prognosis is not what we would have liked, Mr. O'Hare.'

He looked into her face.

'The bullet had lodged near her heart making it difficult to remove. We managed in the end, but it was a tricky op, and all in the lap of the gods. There's nothing much else we can do for her but keep her under heavy sedation and monitor her,' the surgeon said.

'Her father wants her body brought back to America for burial.'

'Yes, I heard. It's ironic, had she been alive with such injuries she would not have survived the flight from Rome. Her state of suspended animation probably saved her life. And that's something I've not come across before. Usually associated with a body being cold. Frozen even. As near to death as it's possible to be.'

'There are some advantages to being dead?'

'Sometimes,' the surgeon replied smiling. 'Are you, er . . . perhaps a relative or something, Mr. O'Hare? Only I see you're with the FBI. She's not wanted is she?'

'A routine inquiry. Being an American citizen, we would like to know who shot her and why.'

'She was a Carmelite nun, wasn't she?'

'*She is*, still is. Had she been any other nationality, we wouldn't have known anything of this incident. As it is, what with the Vatican's library being ransacked on top of the killings, the Italian police asked if we could help them with their inquiries.'

'Killings? Was there more than one?'

'A Father Michael Joseph, Head Archivist, her boss.'

'Well, it's going to be some time before she is able to tell you anything, if ever.'

'Yeh, I expected that. In the meantime, can we keep our people close by? If those that have done this get to hear that she is here, and alive, a second attempt on her life is likely. This was a determined attack that may well be followed up.'

'Not a problem. Goodbye, Mr. O'Hare.'

Opening her eyes, she slowly became aware of the ceiling. Square insulated sections joined butted together with white plastic rails. Her mind was a jumble of thoughts none of them coherent. A strange smell pervaded the air round her. She did not know how she got here or what condition she was in, but her instinct told her that she had survived something bad. She moved her head to one side and felt something dragging on the side of her face. Wrinkling her nose it was in her nostrils. A monitor of some description was beeping in time with her breathing. Judging by the loom of wires and plastic tubing that ran in all directions, disappearing into various recesses of her body, she guessed she was in a bad way. She tried to speak, but a mask on her face, coupled with a desperately dry throat and mouth made that impossible. She closed her eyes and went back to sleep.

Two weeks following, O'Hare sitting at home drinking coffee, smoking a cigar, read his newspaper. A tragic accident that had happened six weeks before caught his attention. He removed the cigar from his lips. The story, that under Italian law the paper had been unable to publish concerned an eminent lecturer in philosophy and religion from America, had possibly died while on holiday in Italy. It went on to say the car, an Alfa Romeo registered in the name of Dr. Sax Stonercrop, had left the road between the port of Civitavecchia and Rome plunging 300 feet onto rocks below. He continued reading:

> The mangled wreck of the vintage Alfa Romeo Supergioiello coupe, winched back onto the road, was without its driver. The coroner, Calagero Abbatucci, left an open verdict with a recommendation that if the Mediterranean had not given up the body for formal identification proving him to be another after twelve months and one day he would record a verdict of death by misadventure for the purposes of closure and any insurance claims by next of kin of Dr. Stonercrop.

Easing the ash off his cigar into an ashtray, he slowly, quietly, said to himself, *Now I wonder what he was doing there.*

'Have you considered you're compromising your vows?'

Sister Benedicta stood the other side of the Mother Superior's desk. She had been here before. A long time since. Alone. For that is what doubt of faith gives you. A loneliness and bleakness that the direction your life is taking you is going nowhere but into sorrow and despair. Something that novices experience at the beginning; and frequently in later years. She had been convinced otherwise on that occasion. This time it was different. As if Father Joseph tortured and murdered in cold blood was not bad enough, but for her to take revenge by attacking his aggressor, well, she thought, hardly a sisterly act from a Carmelite. She could not say that she felt remorse – for she did not. It was an attack plain and simple with nothing more than revenge in mind. A revenge that for the remainder of her days would inhabit her soul.

The Mother Superior looked into Sister Benedicta's eyes: that she might seek strength for herself from what she had said she had seen. 'And your experience, what of that? You cannot, surely, ignore a visitation by an angel of the Lord.'

'I could have been mistaken, it all happened so quickly. A flash of light, a transparent being, and it was all over. Hardly an apparition worthy of a message of Lourdes. I wouldn't have mentioned it but . . .'

'Your modesty tells me that you wouldn't have; and, but for your speaking of it while coming out of a coma we might never have known, however . . . your wish to now leave the Order. You do know that Pope John Gregory holds you in regard for what you have achieved as an archivist. That's what he was when a Cardinal himself; he knows the importance of such work and what we have waiting to be discovered.'

'Would he have been so interested in me if I hadn't seen what I say I saw? As to the missing scroll and the importance for its recovery, I shall need to be on the outside.'

'*With Papal doubt in your soul!* And you unable to say what that scroll contained, though it did not belong to us,' the Mother Superior said trying to curb her anger at the thought Sister Benedicta had, that the Pope would think so harsh of her for its telling. She took the second or two needed to calm herself before continuing. 'And the rest of your vows. Will you have time for humanity carrying revenge in your soul?'

'He has made no mention as to my soul. Indeed, if such work *is* revenge, it will be for God to guide me. Whether it is in His house or the Department of Justice for the United States, with His help the scroll will be found. All I will say is it's a false document; and the reason I choose to keep its content to myself; dangerous in the wrong hands.'

The Mother Superior gently fingered the folds of the skin on her neck. A nun taking God's work outside into the community was one thing, but for her to take an official role to carry out His work, was unheard of. Perhaps it *was* time to re-think their role when it came to fighting Satan and his evil. God could well be losing the fight, His servants needing to take it to another level, who was she to argue with this Sister if He had plans for her.

'I suppose this is a different world from one I know. Not one I particularly recognize or agree with, but, I cannot say you are wrong. Pope John Gregory was a friend of Father Joseph. They met while studying philogy together at Jagiellonian University and he was as stricken by his death as we all were. The fact that you were working alongside of him at the time reflects his opinion of you; that if you need time out to continue the Lord's work elsewhere, you have his blessing. Whether at the end, you would consider returning to us . . . well.' She got up from her desk removing her glasses kissed her on the cheek, noticing through the window, two black limousines belonging to the Vatican police, spelled out her usefulness for anymore argument, in the light of a decision reached. There was more to all of this than plain research, she thought to herself. 'May the Blessed Virgin Mary be with you and protect you always, Sister Benedicta Marie. An ever-open door of Carmel waits your return—'

'Though my soul be damaged beyond redemption?'

Fading music from The Chiffons, singing *I Have A Boyfriend*, was a bizarre segue to the radio announcement interruption by Gary Delaune, KLIF's normally adroit newsreader:

'I've just been handed a bulletin from our Dallas correspondent . . .' (he switched off his mic looking to his producer for permission to continue). 'I can't believe what I'm reading here,' (the producer rolled his hands for him to run on) '. . . three shots, reportedly fired at the motorcade of President Kennedy near the downtown section, have apparently, seriously injured the President . . . I'm sorry we are checking this out for authenticity (if we've got this wrong, we're off air period, you know that don't you). We will have further reports as and when we have them, stay tuned . . . now a word from our sponsors . . . *Shit!*'

The video showed the date as November 22, 1963 1230 CST, Dallas. Waiting for one of two bullets from the assassin Lee Harvey Oswald's 6.5mm caliber Italian Carcano rifle to find its mark into the head, and out the other side, of John Fitzgerald Kennedy, 35th President of America. And, like any other body made of bone taking on the impact of a high velocity bullet in the right place, succumbing to its inevitability of spreading brains over the back of the car. There was of course, to Fitch, more to this pageant than an assassin; more an iceberg worthy of its salt: a white supremacist two thirds sank in the depths of racial hatred lingered.

Federal agents pursued the Lincoln Convertible, which had

turned from Houston into Elm Street with its passengers, Governor John Connally, his wife Nellie; the President himself with his wife, the First Lady, Jackie Kennedy. She reaching back for her husband's brains now adorning the rear seat valance of the convertible, the realization of her deep-seated fear that such a tragedy was possible had come to fruition. The figure of an FBI agent. One of fifteen in a motorcade of five official limousines was Fitch's own father running alongside the President's car trying to shield him from any further injury. He had failed along with all others.

Fitch freeze-framed the images before resetting the video back to re-wind.

He was fascinated watching this piece of history unfolding before his eyes. He was writing a contributory article for a forthcoming feature to mark 35 years after the event. This begged the conspiracy-old questions. Was Oswald the assassin? Was Jack Ruby, in league with him? Why did they do it? What had they to gain?

All the regular conspiracy theories expounded upon by experts, and more. The reams of paper going over and over concluding the same, nothing for certain, nothing for sure. It was too many, America's greatest unsolved crime and the one that had fascinated him and the rest of the world since.

Everyone knows where and what they were doing the day Kennedy was shot, Fitch of course did not, he was too young. He often wondered how an outcome may have differed had the assassin missed his target. How history might have changed. Or differed had events not gone according to planned ideas of leaders, good or evil, if . . .

If. Such a little word – hardly a word at all – but what power lay in its connotation. He had re-enacted that day by video and concluded that *If* anything to prevent the act would have been possible it might have been prevented, but, not, necessarily from happening sometime. The assault repeated someplace else until the assailant struck lucky.

Determination and persistence are bedfellows destined to pro-create.

He became aware of the clatter of the editing terminals. Two sub-editors were banging out copy in front of their screens. The green luminescent words reflected in their glasses from their computers, mirroring columns of *pseudo*-type matter they were making-up. Banks of television screens attached to the wall of the editing room showed news channels from round the world in all languages with their English sub-titles playing out beneath.

Fitch had 2000 words to get out for tomorrow's edition. Newspapers never sleep; are only ever put to bed. Neither, thought Fitch, do its staff. He concentrated on the task before him. The President of France was visiting, and he was to interview him.

He was acting night editor on duty. His heart always went into overdrive whenever it was his turn on the Rota. Especially when the phone was ringing, as it was now. He got a buzz of expectation from it. It had been ten years since he left NBC News. He was crime and political correspondent. Not bad for someone that should have been a lecturer in politics. He smiled to himself. They could hardly have put him in charge of homes and gardens could they, he thought. He lifted the phone. '*Fitch!* New York Post.'

A woman's voice. Low, slow, and velvety, spoke. A voice a man could listen to for an eternity – assuming there was one to be had. She was certainly taking hers coming to the point.

'Are you, Hamilton Fitch?'

He answered giving her space to speak. She repeated his name, this time prefixing it with a: *The.* 'Yes, *the,*' he said impatiently, 'who is this?' She laughed and he sensed an honest voice. He tried to imagine what she looked like, excited by the prospect that she might have something important to say, seeing as she regarded him the definite article.

'Hamilton Fitch,' she repeated (he did not answer preferring to let her have her say uninterrupted). 'You don't know me. My name is Annie Carter and I work for the Federal Bureau of Investigation . . .' (until she mentioned *that* organization)

'*Miss* Carter?' She did not offer any alternative address. He continued, 'You must be aware that I've turned the FBI down more times than I care to remember, why you have to keep calling me, I do not know, but it's been going on since I was at university. I shall say this once more and that's it, I'm not interested. Nothing personal you understand, but there is no more to be said on the matter. *Goodbye!*'

He was on his way to replacing the receiver, her voice still coming from it as it left his ear, for some reason forced him to listen further.

'. . . tch. I wasn't aware of that. I'm not ringing you as part of any recruitment drive. Something else.'

Lying cow, he thought. 'Well that's as maybe, but I work in newspapers and if you'll forgive me, I've blank sheets of paper in front of me that are screaming for words to occupy them.'

'Mr. Fitch, I can assure you it's definitely nothing to do with recruitment. I'm calling you up because of your track record in certain aspects of newspaper reporting, urgently, and off the record.'

'Miss Carter, I know a little of the workings of the FBI and they do not hold meetings informal or otherwise with complete strangers unless they want something. What is it you want? You have ten seconds.'

'I cannot explain this over the phone, but it's something that will change the way we think of ourselves forever. Do I have a date?'

A date, he thought. This conversation was beginning to become intriguing as well as annoying. He would play her along; find out if she did have anything to say that might be of worth. 'Miss Carter, please excuse my brashness, and I'm not questioning your integrity for a single minute, but I write editorials. I know the way people think.

It's my living. We change the way people think every day of the week, you'll have to be more convincing than that for my editor to break from war, politics, and the anatomical credentials of female celebrities to get him out of the billiard-room, stub-out his cigar, to discuss changes to our way of thinking. Tit-bits over the phone are going to have to sound more stimulating than that for him to allow me to meet you. So unless you have discovered a cream that will make ugly women beautiful, beautiful women intelligent, beautiful, *and* intelligent women less egotistical, goodbye.' He listened for the phone to click down. It didn't.

She had not flinched a single face muscle at his pathetic attempt at chauvinism, for she knew more of the man than he could possibly imagine. A man of directness and integrity that would use throw-away lines to get a person off the phone unless they could sell their story in seconds. She would not be put off by his smokescreen, instead went straight for the jugular. '*More* stimulating! I'm not selling Billy Graham Evangelism, Mr. Fitch, I can do better than that. What in your experience of a world-breaking news story would you think would bring Mr. America away from watching the Yankees. To take his glass of beer from his lips and to put his hamburger down. The national game being suspended. Television networks postponing transmission with no complaints from sponsors. In short, not a single grievance. All that, Mr. Fitch, and with not a whisper of terrorism, violence, catastrophe, or war. Come on Mr. Newsman, take your hands off your cock, and start thinking with your head, for this call is the 1000th after 999 cold ones; and the one that the whole world would want you to answer, call *me* before *I* call others and you become known as the man that said *No!* to Miss Del Monte!'

This time the phone did click off. He looked at it and pulled a face. Without thinking, he immediately tapped the call-back number.

* * *

Fitch came out of the entrance to the *Post*'s office, crossed 32nd Street, going into Fat Frank's Eatery. A feeding station for hacks that brunched, lunched, smoked, and drank coffee when they had less time than five minutes, and sometimes if they didn't. It was scruffy, cheap, unpretentious, and popular. What it lacked in palatable food it more than made up for in its beer. Where the name Fat Frank came from, Fitch had never asked. The guy that ran it was neither Frank nor fat. A Greek from Athens with the name of Elidas Phaedon, who had the handsome suntanned look of a traditional European with the fitness of a man that enjoyed the Mediterranean diet of olives and salads. None of which was on the menu. Here Fitch was to meet Carter.

'Hello, Mr. Fitch, 'ow you doin'?' Phaedon called after him as he came in the door. 'I've had some real bolognaise made up and it doesn't stain the front of your undershirt if you don't splash it down you, ha-ha. Will you be eating? Please come in, come in. *Wine. Retsina.* Beautiful lady to see you sitting at the corner table.'

'I will, and a Bud.'

'Very good, no problem . . .'

'And put some meat with the spaghetti. You know, like the Italians.'

He smiled, 'Ah the Italians, sure . . . Certo, *certo.*' He shouted instructions to his wife. 'Bolognaisey for Mr. Fitch, *presto! presto!*'

'Hi, Hamilton,' she called out to him from the kitchen ignoring the brief oversight of mind from her husband that thought he was boss.

'Hi, Maria,' he called as she turned back through the hangs into the kitchen followed by her husband. What sounded like expletives came from the direction of the kitchen, but he could not be sure if she were practicing English or using her native-tongued Albanian. He made his way to the corner table instinctively looking round to see if any other journalists were here, on the off chance that Miss Carter did have something worthy of listening to. There were a few. He guessed the rest were at the game. He wondered if it would be called off after she had spoken to him.

The table she sat was by a side window with half nets that were half torn, half clean and half up. Maria Phaedon had a spare table with new ones on it ready to replace them. He went over, smiled, and pulled the chair out.

'Miss Carter, Hamilton Fitch, Crime and Political Editor, *New York Post*, nice to meet you.'

He held his hand out to her, which she gently shook using his fingers.

'May I?' he said sitting himself down.

Phaedon was right she was beautiful. He guessed her to be in her late thirties, auburn hair, brown eyes, five foot six, or seven, 120 pounds wearing a large gold cross and chain round her neck. Phaedon came over.

'Your beer, Hamilton. Another, Miss?' Phaedon nodded and smiled as she passed him her empty glass.

He waited for Phaedon to be out of hearing before saying, 'Sorry we got off to a bad start, I was not being obtrusive by purpose, it's not my normal manner, but we do get a lot of crank calls. Have you the copy on you that will cause this world to pause for breath—'

Phaedon returned with a wine. She thanked him and took a sip.

'Forget the spaghetti, Elidas,' Fitch said passing him a bill by way of compensation. He had no wish to spill bolognaise sauce down the front of himself in this lady's company.

'What I'm about to tell you, and what you might see if you choose to follow it up, carries a risk. It would be as well you keep as much of what I'm telling you to yourself, for the moment at least. For your own safety, you understand; not to mention mine.'

Here comes the catch, he thought to himself.

Twenty – 1997

Drop, drop, slow tears,
And bathe those beauteous feet,
Which brought from Heaven,
The news and Prince of Peace.

An Hymn, PHINEAS FLETCHER, 1582–1650

MAX STENNA, Editor of the *New York Post*, figured Fitch was preoccupied by the way he padded round after the morning's postmortem of the previous day's edition. He was waiting for everyone to clear off back to their desks.

'Come in, Fitch. What'd you want? Hurry up, I'm busy.'

Hamilton Fitch hesitated. Stenna was a straight-talking newspaper man that had heard it all. He liked proper news. News that a person can put a handle on, read over their breakfast table without having to think too much. Nothing heavy. But not too frivolous either. Enough for a punter to argue constructively without making themselves sound as if they had just read a rag. Stenna was keen on crime; it sold papers. Politics . . . *well* . . . his jury was still out on that particular branch of journalism. Science was his preferred choice of the three, but only as long as it confined itself to the three important inventions of printing, gunpowder, and the compass. He was keen on classical music (opera in the main); as he was contemporary art, both as listener, and occasional gallery visitor, but not its highbrow criticisms of the subject, telling Ignatius Monroe, the *Post*'s art critic, 'The public want to know if the performance was worth the price of the ticket, not your attuned ear that she might have sang a bum note.

God man, we're talking Renée Fleming here, what next – correcting Webster's. And while we're on the subject, if you want more space, Mr. Monroe, you can buy it yourself. Me, I've gotta sell the damn paper.'

His Holy Grail was sport. The back page was the first a man turned when he collected his paper from the mailbox he constantly reminded his team. Stenna knew the newspaper industry inside out. He was in demand as a speaker on the subject at US Chamber of Commerce symposiums as well as universities.

'. . . But not as important as the advertiser,' he interrupted to answer a media student in her last year at college when she asked if a newspaper had an obligation to educate as well as inform. He had answered, that to run a successful newspaper advertising revenues were number one priority, and that only can you begin to educate: *By stealth, gentle like.*

'While I think of it, have you prepared your interview for the French President's visit? America can do with all the friends it can get right now.' His phone rang. He snatched it up, then calmly answered. 'Morning Mr. Henry.' It was the *Post*'s owner and Stenna's normal Christian name of address for the man. Listening before answering him he replied, 'Can you give me two minutes on that one sir.' He smiled and nodded, replacing the receiver. 'Well!' Stenna said directing himself back to Fitch. 'Spit it out man. You heard how long I've got.'

Fitch bottled it. He was not sure he was ready for what he had wanted to tell him. He decided he needed to do some research first.

'Can I have the keys to the archive Max?'

'You come here to ask me that? They're in the key locker, in their usual place. And put them back when you've finished with them.' He answered with a furrowed brow knowing Fitch had something more on his mind than keys. He would tell him in his own good time.

Fitch went through the *Post*'s predeceased obituary files first. He looked up the name Annie Carter. The name that came up was Ann. He read quietly to himself:

Born 1964 Portsmouth, Kentucky. Mother was the landscape painter Jane Fitzroy; father was a coach with the Boston Red Sox—

Um. Can't be all bad.

Had a brother, Justin. He and their mother drowned in a canoeing accident—

That's sad.

Graduated from the American University with a BA in religious studies—

Archivist at the Vatican in Rome—

No mention of her working for the Department of Justice though, he thought.

Later, passing a newsstand, a copy of the *Fortean Times* caught his attention. On the off chance there might be some reference to a strange or weird woman he bought it. He only found a story of humans that had returned to the sea; that had grown fish tails like mermaids. But nothing of what Carter had spoken of. He was going to have to bite the bullet and speak candidly with Stenna.

'*Fitch!*' Stenna said to him. 'Mr. Hamilton,' he lowered his tone, then hit him. 'I've heard some *bollocks* in my time but this one takes the biscuit. Quite honestly, I would have expected more of you. However, I operate a simple rule in this office. If you wish to pursue *bollocks*, and you've a feeling that the information passed to you, that's *bollicking* weird, and out of this *bollicking* world. Or better, plain *bollicking* mad, given to you by some *bollocks*-cruncher that says they're this, or that, or work for some lunatic *bollicking* organization that's . . .'

'She works for the FBI,' he interrupted.

'I rest my case. Had she been drinking?' Stenna asked as a thought but didn't wait for Fitch's reply. 'You do it in your own *bollicking* time and not the *Post*'s. Now, if it should turn out that this story is true, then, and only then, will I eat my own *bollocks* while you're picking them over with a two-pronged pickle fork, only then will you resume pay-roll time. Do I make myself clear?'

'Perfectly. Two glasses.'

'*What?* Oh! The ones you saw her drinking you mean. And how many did you have? And why didn't you sober up the better half of good sense before coming into work this morning?'

She drove them to Meacham some 200 miles out of Albany. He sat quietly for most of the trip with Stenna's words still ringing in his ears. Was he right? Was he being an idiot? Ordinarily he would not have given such a person the time of day. But this woman, with her soft voice and sincerity had charmed him. He had hoped that she would give more of a clue to her past than her relationship with the FBI. When they stopped at a freeway diner for something to eat, she was no more revealing. And the way she smoked; was clearly not the nun he had read of. When arriving after four hours, Fitch thought the place resembled a residential home for the elderly rather than an establishment that housed Carter's "revelation of the century". A security guard stopped them. She showed her pass.

'Step out of the car and come with me, sir?' the security officer asked him opening the door.

Escorted into a security hut, he was required to fill in some details, stand before a white board to have two photographs taken. One of the pictures pasted to an ID badge that he had to wear; the other, he could only guess at. He figured Carter was more important here than he first imagined, but not so that they were willing for her to take him in without the formality of endorsement that he had gone through. She drove them out of sight of the security lodge and onto a gravel drive that circled a statue of George Washington. She stopped and got out.

'We're here,' she said smiling, leaving him to speculate where "here" was.

He got out and looked round him. Well-kept mature lawns and shrubs surrounded them. At the edges barrier posts of red and white that ran in a half circle from the security lodge down to the house gave an order for entrance and exit. Whatever this place was, it did not encourage people wandering about. He guessed scientists worked here, and if Carter had it right of what they were investigating, they would need to be.

'Are you coming?' she called disturbing his taking in the scenery.

He followed her through a double-fronted door into a large hallway. Here she introduced him to a tall thinnish man with glasses on the end of his nose. He shook hands with them both introducing himself to Fitch.

'David Milligan.' He smiled at Carter before returning his attention to him. 'Glad she managed to persuade you to come take a look at what we've got.'

'*You are?* You may not be when I've finished my investigation.'

'We'll see,' he said. 'Please, come through.'

Milligan ushered them in closing the door behind him. 'I trust you had a pleasant journey, Mr. Fitch.'

'As they go. What is this place?'

'It's a Roman Catholic Research Center for Christian Science; and one of a number of similar round the world partly funded by the country of occupation,' Milligan replied.

'Sounds ominous. Researching what for the government—?'

'No, not the government of the country. Although, they do have access to any research we have carried out that they might be interested in. When conclusions of an unexplained nature are reached. Though, not until those have been finalized.'

'And what do you do with all this *unexplained* research, spin it, make up another Bible?'

Milligan smiled coldly, 'Certainly not. In this particular case, as an example, used to reinforce where appropriate, the Bible. And I use the word Bible in its purely generic sense. Although we bear the name, Roman Catholic Research, we are secular in our findings and conclusions, from wherever and whatever the source.'

Carter turned to them both. This was going to be painful she thought smiling to herself. 'If you'll excuse me, gentlemen, I've work to do. Father Milligan will look after you from here on in,' she said turning to Fitch. 'Let me know when you're through Father.'

'Of course.'

Fitch watched her walk away across the marble floor foyer smiling to herself. She had called the man, Father. Was she the woman in charge here? Was this a monastery perhaps, certainly something bizarre if earlier conversations were anything to go by. An avant-garde religious order that carried out science. Whatever it was, it carried no name on its outside wall or its entrance to give any indication of what went on here. He was beginning to wonder if he shouldn't have taken Stenna's advice in this pointless pursuit of *bollocks!*

'This way, Mr. Fitch. I've something to show you that will blow your mind,' Milligan said determined to put this man in his place.

A mortuary, as he entered, was how Fitch saw the room with its deep drawer fronts from ceiling to floor lining two walls. In the middle, under an operating theater light, a marble slab with a blood channel down each side. Fitch felt uneasy over all of this. Milligan went to one of the drawers pulling it out on its runners. A full green occupied body bag was lying on it. An assistant, standing by, in blue overalls wheeled a gurney alongside and the two of them gently rolled the bag onto it. From there it was removed to the mortuary slab. The assistant helped Milligan lift the body onto it. The overhead light switched on; the body bag was unzipped down its length.

What Fitch expected to see was the image that Carter had put into his head. The reality of the situation was entirely different though. She was right. What he saw did take his breath away. Although Carter's description sounded a fantasy, what was before his eyes surpassed even that. His first thought (as was his last) was that this was a hoax and he prepared himself to say so. Milligan looked at him immediately answered his question without him putting it.

Shaking his head no, he said:

'And if it is, it's one of God's, so help us.'

To Fitch's eyes, this was neither man nor woman. Perfect unblemished skin, untouched from body bone saws and scalpels hanging on the side of the slab, the creature lay before him. Native American in appearance was his best description. Any other thoughts he had for similarity between the known species and an alien ended for him at that slab. If such a thing as this existed, the only thought that came to his mind was of the one put in his head by Carter: as one understood the term, this thing lying here was either an angel, as Carter had suggested, or a hybrid human. She (and he was veering towards that as gender), in spite of her lack of any genitalia, merely added to his confusion. As a woman, neither did she possess mammary glands associated with the female of the species. A cold shiver went down his spine. He stood back unsure of what would happen next. He hesitated. Spontaneous, without thought said, 'Where did you say she was found?'

Milligan was not for any immediacy of answering.

Fitch stared at him and looked back at the body. No question, she *was* compulsive viewing. He wondered if his eyes were playing tricks on him, instinctively rubbing them. His next thought that she was the creation of a Frankenstein-type scientist he had to dismiss. A master of his trade if he were. Although, there were nothing to suggest that someone had reformed a woman from body parts in this instance. He had only seen the film to guess that. A trace from a surgeon's scalpel would be a dead giveaway. The only other thought he could conjure up was that she might be a wax-work model. A closer examination ruled that out. The degree of perfection of skin was too perfect. Unless, this time, a master wax-work artist that wanted to demonstrate his skill using a new process had been employed. If not any of that, what the *hell* was she? How could this have been achieved? And why would anyone go to the trouble to carry out such deception. He stood back and furrowed his brow in thought. 'Do you mind if I take a photograph?' he asked Milligan.

'You can try. Not a good subject. But please.'

His assistant pointed out a corner of the room where a CCTV screen showed the two of them standing while he was getting his camera ready. He looked. Where the girl should have been there was nothing but the gurney with its off-red plastic covering. Nothing of her was visible. When he moved he could see the screen showing the two of them and Milligan's assistant. Nothing else.

He switched his camera on. The lens came forward with a whirr. He held it toward her. He looked into its back screen. Misty-gray. He turned the camera round, turned it off, turned it back on again, and repeated the exercise. Still nothing. 'She doesn't *photograph!* Can I feel her body?' Milligan shrugged permission. He put his hand on her head and looked at the CCTV screen. He saw the end of his arm moving toward her his hand disappearing. He moved it backwards and forwards. She seemed surrounded by a field of energy of some description that negated her image, or any object coming close to its field. He tried to control his instinct not to pull his hand away, but it was too much for him.

'I cannot help but notice you are calling her a woman,' Milligan said.

'Yes. Why do I do that?'

'Because there are only two sexes we are programmed to respond. This one is clearly neutral. We cannot help but choose the gender category we are comfortable with.'

'Then why do you say, he?'

'Ah. That depends on ones sexuality. In your case, you appear to be heterosexual, whereas in mine. Well, suffice to say . . . I am latent homosexual,' Milligan remarked. (Fitch was not going to engage in that subject with a total stranger.) 'It is our opinion he is not of this world. We have settled on the description angel. If that is so, it suggests he is a divine manifestation from God. Again, a God; not necessarily our Christian or any other faith's interpretation. As I said at the outset, and we would not presume to insult anyone's intelligence by playing the Christian card, that he is a messenger perhaps preparing the way for a second coming.'

'I'm glad to hear it,' Fitch interrupted. 'I'm Jewish and follow its natural faith of Judaism where I can. Your faith and opinions mean little to me. Mine, however, remain where they have always been; we do not accept that there was a first coming.'

Milligan felt humiliated reiterating his position. 'Quite so.'

Fitch went on to say that, what he had seen was unusual, a shock, but that he had not reached the point where he could move on from anything more than a reserved judgement that heaven would have to mark its time. He asked again how she got there, and where she had come from.

Milligan felt obliged to tell him, 'She was in the condition you see her now, found in a disused tunnel on the New York subway. The authorities sent her to us. If the public got wind of this, well, there would be, if not mass, certainly panic. There was a need for high security. We offer that here.'

'*The government knows of her?*'

Milligan nodded, 'And as you signed a form when you entered this place, I'm afraid, that to answer any more questions regarding them and their knowledge would put me and yourself in breach of national security.'

'Not much of an answer, seeing as you asked me here, perhaps wanting my opinion.' Fitch said slightly annoyed that he was not to be trusted. He looked back at her staring closely into her closed eyes. He drew in a deep breath, holding it, listened at her mouth. He put his hands on her. She was neither cold nor warm. There was no rigor. She would still be alive, as he understood the condition. All the time he made his examination, he kept looking at himself on the screen trying to see her image. It remained elusive. If someone had fixed the CCTV overhead to show a false one, the LCD on his camera would not. 'Turn her over please,' Fitch said to Milligan's assistant.

Milligan put his hand out to stop the man doing as he was asked.

'What'd you think you're asking. Have you no respect?'

'Have you brought me here for my opinion or not? *Turn her over!* Pull her legs apart.'

The assistant looked shocked.

'Do as he asks.'

With her body on its front, Fitch made a closer examination. Where her anus should have been, it was smooth. As was her vagina. Both showed nothing more than an unformed area of flesh that had not been finished off for either defecation or birth. New smooth, with not a trace of a wiry hair. The model for a human being that the designer was still working on; and gone to lunch, he would continue on his return. But, the *bastard* had not returned to finish his creation.

'Why me?' he asked. 'Why have I been brought here? I'm not an anthropologist. I couldn't possibly begin to contribute on what is before me. This is a freak show, and you're all in on it, the only answer, if you needed one from me, would be a negative one; and why not, for this is no more than an elaborate hoax that I am unable to prove. But given time . . . and possibly a mechanic from the Magic Circle and we can probably crack it between us.' He stared into the eyes of Milligan.

'You question what is before your eyes?'

'Got it in one,' Fitch said assuredly.

'That she may be a messenger from God—'

'*Bollocks* she is,' Fitch said using Stenna's turn of phrase.

'Then there's nothing more to be said. I'll arrange for you to be escorted out of here.'

'Don't bother; be so kind as to tell Miss Carter I'll make my own way back to New York.'

Twenty One – 1997

AHRIMAN LOOKED from the soul of this mortal and beyond, aware that his return to the world of myth and legend would be a reality with God's Divine Spirit knowing of his existence. Cast out since before man walked the earth: a time when the metaphysical divide of matter and spirit separated emerging out into a light of different planes. When gods and those of his kind consigned to other verses away from a new emerging enlightened universe, where order for expansionism of altered physics and knowledge that God, no longer able to control; would ultimately lead to an extinction of the whole of His realm of verse. Ahriman, the last of those capable of fighting back for survival from their state of incorporeal existence His natural laws of physics had spilled over consigning them; and where their future was bleak to the point of dissipation into timeless black obsolescence. With his human given name Satan (how he loathed that epithet), after a mortal written work of half-truths and fiction that ever demanded a scapegoat for human frailties; he had the chance with physical possession to turn it round. Another throw of the dice, with the triple six winner six coming easy.

He might have been one of His such was their similarity of minds. A selling out of souls was how the prophets described him, but it was a certain trade-off needing to achieve those goals presenting themselves here. He wondered at times if he believed he was himself; that he no longer existed; was the Host himself, but when he departed, the spirit was himself once more, his Host carrying on his life, his malignant soul continuing to fire. Since the dawn of man's time, there had been an abundance of contenders, but none that was prepared to forwards the physical world to annihilation in pursuit of their interests, plumbing the depths of human misery and depravity, as this man had. An insatiable lust for knowledge from persons with no understanding for the consequence was his masters and catalyst. As miraculous as creation itself all came together perfectly. And, but for the niggling sprite, the loose spirit, forcing him to seek shelter in this lead-lined building until she herself needed rest (little hopes for permanency she was as old as he), the destruction of God's Divine Spirit would be imminent; and he, a substitute for Him in a man on man, faith on faith world bent on the others annihilation, will affect the balance of this new verse for him not one jot.

A single telephone ring hardly disturbed Spannocs watching from the 24th floor of the head office of Oceans Galactica overlooking Staten Island. When it rang once again, he turned and walking to the other side of his desk sat down and picked it up.

'Mr. Spannocs, morning sir. The name's Mahon. You called my office . . .' the voice continued without stalling.

Spannocs stuck an unlit cigar into his mouth, taking the phone from his ear as the voice tailed off. He absentmindedly flicked at his gold cigar lighter. He was in no hurry.

'*Kilkenny International.* Hello.'

'*Kilkenny.* Is that right. I don't think so. My company *is* international, Mr. Mahon. Whereas yours, is American operating internationally. There is a difference. How can I help you, Mr. Mahon?'

'Major,' Mahon said put out at the way the man addressed him.

'That's the second misrepresentation you've tried to pass off on this call Mr. Mahon. Major is a rank in the armed forces. As far as I am aware you no longer serve either with the British SAS, or any other force for that matter.'

How in God's name did he know that, Mahon thought. He was all for putting the phone down ending their conversation, but he was not in the enviable position of having money in the bank to do that. Instead, he thought this was another of those *mother-fuckers* he had to deal with from time to time. He would allow the remark to go over his head. A brief outline of this contract left on his answer-phone was, like any other at this moment in time, important to him. He was overspending capital faster than it was coming in. The need for mercenaries on the world stage was declining. Nobody wanted to pay for specialist soldiers anymore, preferring instead to use heavy-duty thugs from security firms with no brains that could work a trigger for half their pay.

A product of the English establishment, Michael Mahon had been educated at Eton. Following his father into Sandhurst, the Guards, he went on to train in the SAS where the war in Iraq called on him for his specialist skills. Mahon and his two-man team were to assassinate Sadam Hussein. Discovered wearing the uniform of the Republican Guard after a tip-off by either the British government or the Americans; after a change of heart by both governments to keep the man in power, were captured, having their fingernails removed in the time-honored fashion with the dispensing of an anesthetic. His friend, Captain Pat Beamish, brave, but not psychologically strong, died from trauma. Taken down from a revolving fan attached to a ceiling after two hours, no-one realized he had died half-an-hour into the torture. Mahon never received an apology from the British government for their change in politics resulting in their capture. Surprisingly, Saddam Hussein did, through his second cousin, Rafi Daham Al-Tikriti, Chief of Iraqi Intelligence:

'We are not all as uncivilized as some will have you believe, Major Mahon. There's more politics to this war than will ever be written in your *Times*. We are all of us victims in the game.'

They gave Beamish a funeral with as close as one could get to being with full Iraqi military honors. The remaining two released into the hands of the Americans at a secret military exchange between the two countries (there was no mandate to take Sadam Hussein out). Mahon betrayed by his country of birth, went to live in America.

'An honorary title, Mr. Spannocs. And one my people freely afford me. It was well earned.'

'In the world of tin soldiers, no doubt. However, I am unimpressed by titles; I shall call you . . . *Mahon*. Take it or leave it.'

Mahon felt bankruptcy was looking to have a better taste than eating off this man's table. However, he persisted with the humor. 'Whatever, you say Mr. Spannocs.'

'*Mr. Spannocs*, Mahon? You may call me Prince Spannocs. For that is what I am. Prince of Darkness, ha-ha-ha.'

Fuck me, the man's off his trolley, he said to himself with his hand over the mouthpiece of the phone. He was beginning to lose patience. 'Look, you want me to transport a person that's in a coma, I believe? Are you sure you need my services for something as mundane that a private ambulance service could provide, *Prince*. I don't mind, but it's your money.'

Spannocs smiled to himself. Lighting his cigar, he drew in the smoke, exhaling answered. 'I've always believed in getting a simple job done by experts, and to that end, it tends to be done satisfactorily; and you get a task without having to think too hard getting it fulfilled, Major Mahon. Do we have a deal?'

This change in manner took Mahon off guard. He was beginning to think differently about the man. What he said made sense, though there was no such thing as a simple job. The time for it to be called that was after it had been completed. The world's battlefields, full of corpses, were testament to the complacency of an 'easy job' commanded by officers' disregard for the fuller picture.

'*A million dollars*, Major.'

What did he say? 'For driving an ambulance. What hospital did you say this was?'

'Not a hospital, Major. An establishment belonging to the Roman Catholic Church. A woman, ha-ha-ha.'

Mahon was puzzled. This was bizarre. 'You're not serious, right—!'

'A woman. I want her. The building is crawling with cameras and sound sensitive equipment. Sniffers that can identify the presence of your body odor. Cut yourself on any of the razor-wire surrounding the grounds and it will blood type you analyzing your DNA in minutes. All of it linked to CIA Security and Surveillance in Fairfax County. Don't let the appearance of the establishment allow you to take your eye off the ball, Major, for it will mix-and-match you in less than an hour.'

'And how do you know all this?'

'Because my company installed it. It's the best in the world.'

'*Your* company. And how am I supposed to get a person out of there if that's the case? If they've got what you say they have, they'll know as soon as I piss on the road outside?'

'You're not getting paid to *piss*, Major. But you will disappear at the jobs completion. From your company, your country, everything. This is to be a one-off last job for Major Mahon.'

'A one-off last job. Are you out of your mind? I've a company to run. Alright it's not making a fortune, but it gives me a living.'

'No. I am not out of my mind as you so crudely put it. Let me spell it out for you. You're 42 and over the top to be playing soldiers. You are suffering physical and mental problems from old campaigns. Iraq and Saddam Hussein did you no favors. You made fundamental errors of judgement; put your trust in people that led to your double-crossing by the British government. Had you been ten years younger you would not have made such mistakes. In short Major, one more operation is all you're good for. I am offering you last chance saloon. I can personally guarantee your government or anyone else for the remainder of your days will not bother you. You can disappear off to Thailand, or wherever, and *fuck* yourself blind for the rest of your life with the cash.'

Mahon listened to what Spannocs was saying and knew he was right – he *was* over the ridge; and finding it hard to make decisions that would have come easier a few years ago. His reactions were not what they were. The world was getting smaller, and politicians had to re-think their involvement in other countries. Modern conflicts involving terrorism could not be fought with armies. Negotiation was the new watchword. The corporate world was where the new business was. Organizations like his were turning to shopping malls for work. He could not cope with that. Spannocs had offered him a way out and he would take it.

'A *million?*'

'Dollars,' Spannocs replied. 'There will of course be a penalty clause should you not deliver. One that's personal to you. I do not want your organization involved; this is a one-man job.'

'Naturally. But I shall require a quarter up front, win or lose.'

'That's not what I had in mind, Major. The money's not a problem. Should you fuck-up . . . . your soul is mine.'

Mahon thought for a moment then laughed. 'For a million dollars Prince, you can see my *arse.*'

'I'll have a bank draft sent out to you by FedEx this morning.'

The phone went dead. He smiled. 'Over the top, am I? I'll have you, you arrogant *bastard!*'

Twenty Two – 1997

Thou canst not see my face:
For there shall no man see me, and live.

EXODUS 33, v. 20

FITCH FELT LIKE SHIT. He had a headache belonging to three people. Nauseas, Groggy, and Queer. His eyes felt as if they had been strobed by a car engine timer for hours on end leaving him with the all-round feeling that an elephant with attitude had trampled over him. That aside he felt okay – he was at least coming round, until he saw a face he recognized. He remembered and took a swing at her. She sidestepped him and he missed her by a mile. He had no strength in his arms. He tried again, but she grabbed his wrist.

'I'm not the enemy,' she said to him.

'I'll be the judge of that,' he snapped back.

He remembered leaving the Roman Catholic Research Center on foot. Hardly through the gates he had earlier driven with Carter, past security onto the street when two guys jumped him, roughly pushing a needle into his arm. He remained conscious but lost the use of his muscles. He was bundled into a car and driven off. Then an accident. Guns fired. The black chauffeur shot in the forehead. The man had automatically reacted turning his head round. Fitch saw the hole. A perfect dark ring with a blood line round the outside. There had been an explosion, the car engine locked and he and the driver went through the windshield. There was blood everywhere. He guessed some of it his.

'It's as well we came for you when we did, none of this would have happened if you hadn't told your editor you would take unpaid leave, and where you were going. I did warn you to keep it to yourself. Did you know your office has more bugs than a flea circus?'

'Occupational hazard. All newspaper offices have them—'

'Yes, planted by other newspapers; and not by the people I have in mind. And if all that wasn't bad enough, I've had to kill someone.'

'Are you and that Father Milligan of this *fucking* planet? Never mind a waxwork, what about me?'

'Oooo! If you're going to use that language, *I'll* put you out. If you only knew it, I was talking about you. The Father and me probably saved your life. Some gratitude wouldn't go amiss. And as for any "waxwork", well, you've seen her, if there's nothing further I can say to convince you she's genuine, let's leave it there shall we.'

'Genuine! *Bollocks* she is.' Her face glowed red. 'If I'm not mistaken, your lot got me into this mess in the first place. If you were so concerned, why didn't you take me to hospital?'

'It would have been too dangerous. We arranged for a doctor to examine you while you were still unconscious. Not ideal we know. Superficial cuts and bruising. Nothing lasting. You're alive; in a bed recovering, what more do you want? Anyway, there's someone that's keen to meet you.'

'Who's that then, the *Marshmallow Man*?'

He put his head into his hands and passed out.

When he came round, she was gone. At least he was feeling better. He got up off the bed. Looking round, she must have left him when he fell back to sleep. Good riddance. Whatever they shot into me, he thought, was powerful stuff, no question. If there was going to be any more trouble he needed to be ready for it. He would need to get himself moving. He looked round the room. There was a bathroom in the corner, and a fridge. His mouth was dry; the latter would be more useful to him first. He opened it finding a carton of orange and half a bottle of lemonade. He mixed them together, shook them up and took a swig, then sat down in an arm-chair putting the bottle on a small table, following it with his feet and waited. A copy of the *New York Post* caught his eye. He reached across and read the headline to its lead story. It took up the front, second and fifth pages. It concerned a company called Oceans Galactica headed by its CEO name of Frederik Spannocs. He had heard of him, who had not? Internal Revenue had recently raided their offices. Shortly after, five of his employees had died in a fire. The paper's date was July 27. He looked at his watch. July 30. He had lost three days of his life.

A knock at the door. Manners dictated he remove his feet from the table.

'Come in,' he instinctively said wondering if he had the right to make such an invitation. A woman wearing an orange apron with the picture of a glass of stout printed on the front poked a head round the door, smiling said:

'*Hamilton Fitch?*'

She had a voice that sounded like a dentist's receptionist inviting him to take a turn in his chair, 'Mr. O'Hare asks if you will join him for dinner?'

'*Dinner!* And who is this, Mr. O'Hare you refer?'

'Why, this is the gentleman's house, sir.'

'Well, I'd as soon leave his house, if it's all the same to the gentleman.'

She smiled. A smile he figured that that was not about to happen.

'If you would follow me.'

He reluctantly conceded. Down a corridor, she showed him into a study. He guessed the man in question; the one standing against the fireplace across the room, studying papers was Mr. O'Hare. He placed them on the shelf over the fireplace when he saw him. He had a ruddy complexion, red curly hair, and an enormous smile. He came toward him, introducing himself with a large open hand saying, 'Hamilton Fitch, I'm delighted to meet you at long last.' For some strange reason he felt at ease in this man's company, putting the feelings of anxiety he had behind him. He reciprocated.

He judged him to be in his forties. His clothes, English in style and cut, fitted him well. His suit, he guessed from the twenties. Expensive? Certainly. He knew enough of Jewish tailoring to know the difference between off-the-peg and bespoke. Quality shouts. The only troubling aspect of him was that he was wearing a shoulder holster over his open waistcoat, a varnished and polished grip of a Smith & Wesson .38 showed. This man was clearly the business; and dinner, as far as any interruption was concerned, would not end in his blood being spilled.

'And you are?' Fitch said hesitantly.

'Me, *thir*. Well, *thir*, I am the man your grandmother minded when she changed your name to Hamilton Fitch, telling you, "Have nothing to do with anyone from the FBI bearing the surname O'Hare, with the first name of Charlie".' He smiled allowing Fitch to take in what he had said before continuing. 'And the same that was your grandfather's partner in 1920, and your father's in the fifties. And now, I expect you'd like a proper drink after your ordeal, Arnold . . . *Hiram* . . . Weinberg.'

Fitch stared at the man; his lips tight closed together. This world has become a mad-house, he thought. I would be safer in an asylum, than out here with these people. An angel was one thing, but this man who professes to be who he says he is, with connections to my family, taking it on himself to put words into the mouth of his grandmother, albeit words, given what he had told him, of a truth succinctly put, had gone too far. Max Stenna was right.

'Do you know something, O'Hare?' he said refusing his offering of a drink. 'Since I got from my bed yesterday morning I've been surrounded first by religious idiots making attempts to insult my intelligence, attacked, shot at, thrown through a car windshield, all before being put back to bed. And not my own I hasten to add. An Irishman, or a bad actor, which purports to have worked alongside my grandfather, and not content with that as a lie, tacks on my father, has abducted me. Can I take it I am free to leave, or are there any more surprises up anyone's sleeve for me?'

O'Hare pushed the drink back at him with a strict authority he was not expecting, 'Assuming you do not want a repeat of what happened to you earlier, I wouldn't advice it. Whiskey, *drink*.' Fitch took it. 'Very good. Now believe me, when I tell you that none of this has anything at all to do with me, or Annie Carter, a woman incidentally, who was only trying to protect you, please, take it to heart, because it's the truth.'

'So how in hell were you both the partner to my father, and his before him? Eh! Tell me that. You'd be over a hundred. Do I look a Patsy? And this Carter woman you speak of, and her *box of tricks*, you'd better find her a theatrical agent before another gets her name on his books. Charlatans all.'

O'Hare lost his temper. 'Go. Leave. I'll guarantee you'll be gunned down before you get ten steps from here.' Fitch laughed shaking his head. 'Think I'm joking. They've murdered half your family already. They won't have any qualms about you. Didn't you read your own newspaper? Work it out. The CEO of Oceans Galactica, one of the wealthiest men in America, made his money from crimes that the likes of John Gotti wouldn't touch. Trafficking children for sex. He knew your grandfather, knew your father, and murdered them both. He also knows me. All of us lawmen. All trying to bring him to book. Two words newspaperman, child abuse. And if you want to tack on, *with a government department's blessing*, as a rider, you won't be far from what me, your father, and your grandfather believed to be a conspiracy.'

Fitch was taken aback. This man, his manner, his determination, forcibly to make his point, clearly was an honest broker. He looked him in the eyes. They seemed to hold more images of a past he could ever say to convince him anymore of his sincerity. A newspaperman he had called him, and a newspaperman, until he knew different, he would remain.

'If what you say is true, why? Why would anyone want to defend child abuse? And a government department. Are you mad?' He shook his head considering what department that might be. O'Hare did not respond. 'Have you see this woman? Were you behind that? What has she to do with all of this? Unless you were looking . . . did you think that I might be the one; who would uncover a fraud that you had been unable to? A second opinion.'

O'Hare turned toward the fireplace taking a cigar from a box on the shelf above it. Putting it in his mouth, he opened a box of matches, took one out and lighted it. Placing the spent match into an ashtray, he took three heavy puffs ensuring it had taken, satisfied, he turned to face him. 'Let me tell you what two of your forbears knew before they were murdered for the knowing of it.'

'All right, all right, all ready. But was it necessary to insult my intelligence using the wiles of an attractive woman to entice me?'

'Ah, Miss Carter. Don't let her hear you say that. She wouldn't approve. But yes, I must agree with you on that point. But would you have listened to anyone else in the first instance I ask myself?'

Fitch shrugged. 'Probably not.'

'Point made. Let me tell you something of Annie Carter. When our path's first crossed she worked for Archivum Secretum Vaticanum'

'The Vatican Secret Library.'

'Quite so. Events had reached the stage where we needed more than witnesses for me to convince those above me to listen to what was going on. Witnesses murdered for what they had seen were becoming a rare breed. Thankfully, they didn't get all of them.'

'Hang on a second, what are we talking about?'

'An archivist, her boss, and she came across a scroll in an ark while cataloging the evening in question. A scroll that if they had interpreted it correctly, according to her, was dynamite; forcing the world to re-think religious faiths.'

'So what was in this scroll?'

'She didn't say. Wouldn't say. The night in question though, her and Father Joseph Donne, the Archivist she was working with; and arguably the greatest authority in the translation of ancient documents anywhere in the world, accidentally stumbled across it. While they were discussing what to do with it, two men dressed in suits wearing brooches; she thinks red crosses, came into the cell they were working, armed, demanding they give it up to them. Father Donne refused. They shot him dead before turning their weapons on her. She attacked one of them, so they shot her too. Twice. Then escaped with the scroll. When paramedics arrived, she was in a coma and needed surgery. Suspecting it was Mafia, the Vatican asked for our help, seeing as we were world-wide experts.' He smugly studied his fingernails before continuing. 'It was clear that her life was in danger for what she had witnessed, so we got her out of Rome back to America. They know she's still alive. And likely able to identify them in the future, may well come for her again.'

Fitch waved his hand at him. 'Wait, wait, wait. You're saying these men stole this scroll. And she wouldn't say what was in it. But *they* knew?'

'Apparently. Don't ask me how. The only others that knew, and that was only after she told them, is the Vatican, and for who she was, they took her at her word, took an executive decision, ordering her to take a vow of secrecy over any content pending its recovery when the 21st Ecumenical Council would decide how they will make any findings known to Jerusalem before returning the scroll. As for Sister Benedicta Marie, with her hospitalization back in the States, the story reached our ears and along with coincidental links and happenings that I have been involved, and of course, your forbears, she was immediately put under the protection of the Justice Department, where she has since been co-opted by us.'

'Wait a minute; you've got a sister working with the FBI. A nun?'

'A Carmelite. Both for her own safety . . .'

'What . . . as padre in residence?'

'Yes. *No.* Annie Carter *is* the Carmelite Sister, and our religious adviser.'

'*What!* And I suppose you're going to tell me the Pope gave her his blessing.'

'Not if you don't want me to, I won't. But yes, we did get the approval from John Gregory. That might give you some indication as to how serious the situation is we find ourselves. The important thing you need to understand is that although these men called themselves Teutonic Knights we suspect they were from the Order of the Most Divine Third Circle, a scientific religious breakaway currently in vogue in the world of celebrity and those with more money than sense. We believe it has a darker side engaged in scientific research, that may have something to do with that scroll and far beyond anything man has ever considered before.'

'They've created a waxwork.'

'No. And it's not her they're after,' O'Hare said.

'You keep saying "they". You still haven't answered that question. What have "they" to do with a government department?'

'Simple answer, we don't know. Someone, somewhere in government is controlling this. I've got one or two names. I think bit players. Who they represent, I've no idea. But they are buried deep without any presidential knowledge, we're sure of that. And the man known as Frederik Spannocs, the one you read about, the CEO of *Oceans Galactica* is part of it. Has been since the off. A man the same age as me. A hundred. As I am now.'

'You are a hundred?'

'You wanted to know how come I could have worked with your forbears, well that's how.'

'How in *hell's* name are you that age? Oh, I've got it. You are another wax-work; re-incarnated the other waiting in the wings. You and her were both put under suspended animation to be thawed out when technology caught up able to defrost you.'

O'Hare shook his head from side to side, but considered in her case, the likely prospect, only her ability unable to project an image of herself put that hypothesis beyond reach. 'Get a good picture of her did you?' Fitch pulled a face that might have said, Good point, well made. 'Thought not,' O'Hare said. 'And how old is your grandmother?'

'She doesn't look fifty!'

'And I'm not frozen. Let me go on. Frederik Spannocs was me and your grandfather's number one suspect for child abuse and abduction in the early days back in Manhattan. His given name, Marco Giuseppi. The man responsible for the murder of first your grandfather and your father, before going on to take a pop at your mother. And whether you like it or not, you're next.' Fitch had a look of shocked disbelief. 'Yes you. And you needn't look so surprised it's true ask her. Anyone trying to end his filthy trade or knew of it. The man is evil, wealthy, vengeful, and in league with people that I believe have an interest in some bizarre experiment. What I can tell you is that *Oceans Galactica* bought into an atomic energy research facility some years ago. They never applied for a license for plutonium enrichment production, which means they have something else in mind. We think there is a link with that woman you saw and whatever science *Oceans Galactica* are involved. And, co-incidentally, there is another link with Oceans and the Order of the Most Divine Third Circle. On every occasion for at least the last eighty-odd years, there's been serious cases of child abduction linked to this man or his organizations, all hushed up. And Spannocs has made a fortune from it. And that waxwork, I believe, is an angel trying to protect them by intervening. Naturally, this not being good for Spannocs and his business, he is looking to take her out. When you mentioned suspended animation you were not a million miles away from the truth, but I've seen her active. As have many others. But the nub is, they are trying to capture something else that is coming to earth using her as incentive bait.'

Fitch shook his head from side to side once again. All this was too much for him. 'And what is that?' Fitch asked dubiously.

'Short, wears white robes, no face . . . and clicks. Don't ask me why it should do that, it could be a reaction to earth's gravity, whatever. It glides in low. No strings attached. They've tried roping it, netting it, throwing copper bands connected up to machinery out over it—'

'And I suppose you're going to tell me you've seen that as well?'

'As did your grandfather, and your father. And if you can live long enough, so will you.'

Fitch was having trouble listening to this man. Addressing him in a way that was more in keeping with a father than a man he had met off the street, so to speak, had clearly made an impact, bringing him back to his first question.

'Can I return to your age?'

'I'm not some weirdo that happens to wear well. Something happened to me back in the twenties that caused this. But I can be killed (he patted the grip of his .38). Frank Weinberg, your grandfather, might have been sitting here talking to you had he not been murdered. Whether your God intentionally brings these conditions of the flesh or not, I cannot say. But if this thing is what I believe it to be, I cannot see that he would have bestowed that same gift on Giuseppi. Something else did that to him. *Satan*, perhaps. Some go through life with God in their hearts. Some with the dark angel.

'If He has been round fighting for our souls since the dawn of time, it cannot be unreasonable to say the juxtaposition with Satan would have the wherewithal to bring on his own brand of immortality. Assuming that what I am suffering is not old age. And if it isn't, it's from God, and not the latter. I cannot see that someone engaged in crimes as depraved as Spannocs is would get his immortality from anywhere else.' He hesitated. Giving a name for the entity had been easy for him. He had fallen back on religion to provide the answer. He knew it was a compromise – a cop-out from an informed questioning world. Saying the name sounded fantastical. With accusations of religious paranoia likely placed at his door. 'As for the other, the entity I speak, best I could come up with was the Divine Spirit. As in the Holy Trinity.'

Fitch shook his head. 'Oh no, not in my faith it won't be.'

'Well, if you'll excuse me, if you were speaking to me of events such as I've witnessed I would hear Judaism from you; when I speak, you'll have to listen Christian from me. I don't know how else to put it that would make any other sense. Whatever your father and grandfather thought they saw, made not an iota of difference to their faith, if it had, well, they never mentioned the fact to me. We were investigating cases of sexual exploitation of children. Giving something a name was a long way down that list. Far as I'm concerned, you can call it the spirit of Moses, for all it matters to me.'

'I won't be calling it anything, but as a point, how do you know this entity of yours is not a model on pulleys and wires, and that you haven't been seen off?'

'In truth, I don't; in reality, with witness records of this entity performing trapeze gymnastics for the last eighty years, it's hardly likely to be anything else. And if you're going to be argumentative in the matter, when it comes to the paranormal, God's as elusive as any – materially at least – I notice you don't question His existence. I happen to believe in the Holy Trinity, one of whom, or all three, if they are one of the same; that are capable of dispensing both good health and immortality; with the resurrection of man to a better place after death. A condition, if I'm not wrong, Judaism still subscribes. *Bet Ha-Hayyim*, as an example. And if you want further proof I can show you a woman that coming into contact with its power, having lost her hand in an accident, having it totally restored. Think about that. Whatever they are or not, no-one on *earth* can bring that on. And someone is *fucking* with them to use newspaper parlance and they are getting angry. Angry enough for—'

For some reason, the man had stopped short. Fitch did think about it. In fact, he gave it great deal of thought. O'Hare looked like a man that had more going on in his brain than two heads might cope with. He was having this conversation at the gallop. It was if he did not believe any of it himself; needed someone to explain what he thought was happening. Then walk away and forget it all. If scientists O'Hare referred were seeking to capture spirits for scientific investigation that would be one hell of a story. But what was he thinking. If what O'Hare had said were true, how in hell would he ever convince Max?

'Look, don't take my word for it, ask Sarah. Ask your

grandmother. Frank may well have told her of what he saw, assuming she's not . . . *in denial.*' She had cut herself off from him years before. Carrying a human trait, not yet recognized by psychiatrists that people unnaturally old, like himself, would have the world turn their face against them as if they were the living dead earthbound. He shuddered at the thought. Was he such a creature?

'I will.'

O'Hare nodded. 'A battle is brewing for possession of earth between good and evil. Only unlike ancient stories, where Satan gets his arse kicked, this time, with a little help from his friends, the good side might throw in the towel. Likely had enough of us all.' O'Hare's face strained with bitterness and anger that had put years in his soul. 'I've said it before; I'll probably say it again. The one sin nonredeemable in the eyes of the Divine Spirit that it sees, as young minds in the image of God in need of nurture, will bring an apocalypse down round our ears. And if my opinion is worth anything, its beginning.'

'It's the religious nonsense I can't get my head round. Talk of angels and spirits. If I did believe in what you're saying, how am I supposed to convince others?'

'You don't have to convince anyone. Those that don't need convincing know – the instigators. Everyone else is superfluous,' he leaned forward to him, 'including newspapermen.'

'But why me?'

'I would like to come out and say, it's all for your own protection, but I would not be entirely honest with you. The attempt to abduct and murder you, take you out of the equation, means that you most definitely need protection. It's for your grandmother's sake.'

'Again you may be wrong.'

'Marco Giuseppi sent you a birthday card threatening to kill you before you made your Bar Mitzvah. Fortunately, he failed. But only because your grandmother was so frightened she moved out and changed your name. Did she tell you the reason? Or did she use some excuse, the Ku Klux Klan for example, forcing her to leave being responsible for your change of name. I love Sarah, but her keeping back from you the truth will be the death of you. Giuseppi wants the last of the Weinberg's written from the face of the earth as an hors d'oeuvre. Sarah's never forgiven me for the deaths of your grandfather and father because of all of this; I'm not prepared to lose another one of your family if I can help it. It's in your court. I wish your forebears were here to tell you, but they're not, and Sarah, as I said loves you too much. But there is another reason. Your heritage. May be the catalyst for an answer to a complex situation. You being Jewish might be upsetting the applecart.'

'How so?'

'Not sure. A hunch. Still practicing?'

'Well, I'm not orthodox if that's what you mean, more, reform I guess.'

'Well let me get one thing straight, it's important. Those of us including Sister Benedicta Maria . . .'

'Her married name to Christ, another example of taking religion out of this world into the unknown. A virgin birth, yet another.'

O'Hare gave him an old-fashioned look, and shook his head in disbelief, 'It's faith, *David!* Belief. Another's . . . con-vic-tion . . .'

Fitch interrupted. 'I'm not David.'

O'Hare stared hard at him. His face, a calming expression looked gently out at him holding O'Hare's attention long enough for him to recognize it was no imagination. He had returned a smile, before he gently faded away. 'Did I say that? I'm so, so, sorry, Arnold.'

O'Hare was embarrassed. The thought that he was his father moved him more than anything he had said so far. His outburst could not have been orchestrated. This man was clearly sincere in what he believed. He had inadvertently linked a passing of time with the future. His.

'Hamilton.' He was getting name confusion once more. 'What I am trying to say is that we all have dubiety of faith from time to time. None of which is going to rest easily with any of us. If it helps, put them in a box and mark it PENDING. No need to lock it. You won't be struck dumb for your doubts. None of this has anything to do with the world's written version of the Word of God. Whoever He may be. What an individual chooses to believe; well, only they can answer that; not subjected to the dictates of others on the matter. There's a catastrophe in the making here, whether anyone wants to call it an apocalypse or not. But you can be sure of one thing, global warming it is not. This is the Book of St. John the Divine writ large, about to be acted out.'

'That's still Christian New Testament, I told you I cannot subscribe to your version of faith.'

'Bible! Christian!' O'Hare gesticulated; the palms of his hands uppermost. 'Apart from one originally written in Hebrew and the other Greek, they're both as old as the other, both with their salient points, both interminably linked. Look, it's my view Revelations should be with the Old Testament along with all your stuff when the Bible was first collated. It's not about our individual view of our own end. When called to account for our conduct we will all be up on similar charges no matter which faith we have chosen or been born into. This entity I speak of, this angel, this devil, they all exist. Somewhere. All faiths have them. Why are you so surprised that they are real? It's what your life is based. When whatever it is that's out there decides to call a halt to the world, it is my belief that your faith along with my own will be no better than the next man's.'

Fitch thought good and hard once again. When Annie Carter (or should he call her sister), first approached him, she said she had a story that would change the world and our perspective of our place in it. What worried him was if he were to say no to this man, carry on his life, how he would feel, when faced with the consequences of what he was laying before him doing nothing. He had seen a creature that defied all the known laws of nature lying on a slab in front of him.

'Look, faith or not, whatever is going on, dragging an alien in from another world whether a mythical heaven or not, I should think would appeal to a whole heap of people wouldn't you? If the alien turns out to be the Divine Spirit, do you think that God is going to let that happen without consequences for the rest of us, angels, and sinners all? I've prayed that they're all figments of my imagination, but they're not. If something on the lines of a Divine Spirit does exist; that only recognizes love rather than twisted faction's intent on destroying young minds, it may decide to put an end to all of us. And if it does get a *shitty-on* our universe could well be returned to a time before science's name for what we call the "big bang" quicker than we can say, "Forgive us O Lord, for we have sinned by association by ignoring the plight of our children".'

O'Hare made compulsive arguments. For all that, he was, at the end of the day a newspaper man. Arguments about the end of the world were as old as the world itself. People with placards round their necks with various nigh dates plied the streets of New York on a regular basis. More often than not, down at heels, advertising for the next crack-pot religion prepared to pay them a couple of dollars an hour for the privilege. He would be surprised if they were not contributing to a pension, and paying taxes, such was the continuity of the work. There was no questioning someone tried to abduct him. Whether they had murder in mind was another matter. The only abduction he could remember was that carried out by O'Hare himself. There was no question he was an old friend of his family; he knew too much to be anything else. For all that, it was not his job to go tilting at windmills for what may turn out to be no more than criminals; and that he was more qualified to report their activities than to bring them to book. He also had his grandmother to consider. Of course, he would speak with her about O'Hare, but at 93, her mind may not be as sharp as it once was. Intriguing though all this was, he was not the man for the job.

Twenty Three – 1997

SARAH WEINBERG'S reaction, given the circumstances, was expected. All past disappointments she had come to expect from the FBI continued. Her family had been let down by them; and although none of that was to do with O'Hare personally, his contribution of *bloody* mindedness had done nothing to alleviate her situation. Two generations of her family caught up in his and their obsessions for what. Nothing but death and misery to them while he had come through it all without so much as a scratch.

She completely lost control at Ruth and David's funeral – or what was left of them to bury. Two full sized plain wooden coffins covered in black sheets, where one would have been sufficient for what remained, her only consolation.

'Lord our God, we turn to You once more to cry out our longing of all men and women for a beginning of the wholeness we call peace . . .' She recited the words along with the rest of the mourners. But for the first time in her life, she wondered if there was a God out there or within them to hear their cries; when Rabbi Len Levi calling for the resurrection of the dead imparting the message: *Blessed art Thou, O Lord who callest the dead to life everlasting* . . . was the point she completely lost it. She tore at her clothes before collapsing in screams and tears leaving David and Ruth in the hands of *hevra kaddishah*. She was to spend the next two weeks in the David Ben Gurion Hospital with financial assistance by the Department of Justice dispensed to her at the behest of O'Hare.

Arnold Weinberg was seven when his mother and father were murdered. He became so distressed he went into himself, not speaking, staring at the ceiling rocking backward and forward like some caged animal. Sarah made up her mind there and that she would change his name, bury his faith, and move them out without so much as a forwarding address. She became paranoid telling O'Hare it was Nazism at work and not a vendetta being played against the male side of the family (as he suggested), for (and this is where O'Hare's take on the reason took a turn from hers), being a Jewish cop (while O'Hare considered the chase against those responsible being carried down the Weinberg blood-line a generational threat to person or person's unknown's long-term objectives something they needed to bring to an end for reasons only they could know).

'You can't be serious?' O'Hare said after she had screamed out her intentions to him.

'That serious!' she replied. 'I'll show you how serious I am.' Taking hold of the overcoat from over her grandson's arm looking at the label under the jacket hook. 'Change it, change it, I will . . . to this!'

O'Hare read Abercrombie & Fitch.

She did not calm down, in spite of his protestations, declaring she no longer wanted anything further to do with him and the people he represented.

As good as her word, she packed up and moved her and her grandson out of Albany to the East Coast. He was devastated at her decision but accepted it along with the reasons she offered. He had not heard her name mentioned since.

Twenty Four – 1997

AS IF IT WASN'T bad enough for Fitch to miss covering the goodwill visit of the President of France; but to then go missing for three days without telling Stenna, well, dereliction of duty with the words, *Monumental proportions of bullshit; and are you trying to take me for a complete idiot?* followed. After he spoke his mind, Fitch casually mentioned his abduction. His one redeeming salvation was that he did look as if he had, and for that, Stenna gave him the benefit of his considerable doubt. He added that he hoped his temporary insanity subsided and that he would return to his desk asap.

'A woman in a coma that couldn't be photographed. If I didn't know you better, I'd say you'd cracked. But I do, you probably haven't . . . but having said that . . . my first inclination, assuming I'm stupid enough to have one at all, is to run with what you've said you saw. I will stick with your story, Fitch . . . until, that is, one or the other of us comes to our senses. I pray it will be you, for you have entertained me quite enough in this matter. And do something with yourself, get yourself cleaned up, get a shave.'

Stenna went out of the subs room returning immediately. Fitch had counted to seven.

'We appear to have two schools of thought here, Fitch. One, you've seen something you can't account for; and B, they found someone gullible enough to dump this rubbish on. It is my opinion, that in all probability you have been duped. And for the respect of our readership, I am duty bound as editor of this esteemed rag to demand you look closer into it before you select a single letter from its case setting it in your stick. Even the word, Story, might be more in keeping with its sister of Tale, the backbone of children's books the like of, *The Hat And The Cat*. Having said all this, Fitch, I must admit to a degree of curiosity. This Charlie O'Hare fellow. Did you say that he'd worked with your father?'

'Apparently.'

'Wasn't your father FBI when Kennedy was assassinated?'

'Apparently. Although, having listened to you addressing his son in the way you just did, it doesn't sound as if he was much good at his job either.'

'Guilty by association then!' He changed his tone. 'Didn't both of your parents die in a chop-house fire?'

'It was a bomb . . . in a restaurant if you don't mind,' Fitch answered annoyed at Stenna's flippancy. 'I didn't know until yesterday when O'Hare told me. My grandmother mentioned it was a fire. He was with her when it happened. Both he and my grandmother survived. My parents did not.'

'Apologies. Must have been a bit of a shock finding out it was deliberate. Was it directed at your family, or was it Cosa Nostra trying to make a point with the restaurant proprietor?'

'She said us, went on to say that I should have nothing to do with O'Hare as he and bad news had an historical relationship within our family'

'Um. Sounds like a wise woman, this grandmother of yours. You'll be taking her advice then.'

He had not gone into the full story over the shooting, preferring to keep quiet for the moment, in case it had been a set-up. He was still not a hundred percent that it had not been for a purpose. Stenna put him on night duty hoping either it would keep him out of harm's way, or he saw some sense. He felt that perhaps he should have shown some of that from the start.

The day subs- had gone home leaving him a heap of copy to look over before he would wander down to the press room to oversee borough news changes. He was feeling in control and beginning to feel better about things; more able in himself to start questioning what he had witnessed in that woman and how they might have carried out such trickery in plain sight. He supposed that O'Hare could be right in his thinking of keeping him close for his own safety. But that was not the point. Someone must have known his connections. He hoped that he and Carter *were* on the side of Superman and not Lex Luther. What had he said was his name for the people on Luther's side when he asked him? *Walsinghams.* Government people. Buried deep somewhere in its fabric. Interesting, he thought.

When his phone first rang, his mind being otherwise preoccupied, he had not heard it. When he did, the surprise made him snatch it up. It was Johnny Bingham, the *Post*'s field reporter.

'HAM!' he shouted. 'That you, Hamilton?'

Knowing the nickname they had for him was more out of colleague affection than insult he nevertheless wished at times for some other title, but it had stuck, and he resigned himself to it. 'Do you have to keep calling me that? What'd you want, I'm busy?'

'Busy you say, you're going to be. You'd better get down here – African Queens. It's not pleasant. In fact, it's not nice at all. Contractors working down the Hudson on that new dock, you know?' He didn't wait for him to answer, rambling on, 'A dredger dragged a whole heap of kids up; all bound up in chicken wire and weighted down. They couldn't have been there long, someone's panicked and dumped them, I mean – you don't use chicken wire unless you want the crabs to do away with the evidence. *Christ*, what am I saying? Get your arse down here, Ham, I can't handle this alone.'

His voice was cracking down the mouthpiece of the phone. Fitch felt a chill go through him. The Bingham's of this world do not usually overreact, but he was sounding hysterical. '*Fucksake*, Johnny, calm yourself down. What are you going on about? Slower, start again.'

'You deaf? Children, hundreds of them, murdered, dumped. The media world and its wife are surrounding the area, grab Mike and get down here, quick like!'

The phone banged down.

Fitch grabbed his leather jacket from the back of his chair, slung it over his shoulder, ran down through the office shouting:

'Somebody get hold of Max. And a cameraman quick – Mike working tonight?' he shouted at Dave Davidson, sports sub-ed.

Davidson looked up from his desk and nodded.

'Go find him. Get him to follow me outside.'

Davidson jumped up out of his chair in front of the screen he was working sending copy sprawling across the floor.

'In the car park, two minutes, and someone wake *Max* up.'

Sports writer Jude Johnson was on the floor picking up Davidson's copy while Davidson himself was screaming out Mike Crawford's name through the office door into the next section. Crawford casually strolling up the corridor with a tray of coffees in paper cups spotted him.

'Camera Mike, quick,' Davidson shouted. 'It's Ham; he wants you to go with him. He's down the corridor.'

Crawford dumped the tray of coffees on political and foreign correspondent Heinz Oakey's desk spilling the top level of the liquid over copy extinguishing a still smoking cigarette hanging from its ashtray before following the direction of Fitch's voice.

'What's the *fucking* rush?'

'Come on, I'm gone,' Fitch called from beyond the corridor.

Crawford ran through reaching out for his camera and recorder Davidson passed to him as if it were a baton in a running race. Fitch, with his foot jammed against the elevator door, was holding it open.

'What's on, Ham?' Crawford shouted stepping into it as Fitch moved his foot releasing it.

'Would you kindly refrain from calling me Ham?'

Fitch, Crawford, and Davidson arrived at Greenbush, a bend on the Hudson river that had once housed a sixty-acre industrial site; given over to up-market waterfront dwellings and marinas for those good at sums on New York's Stock Exchange. A section of the river reclaimed was half finished. Within fifteen minutes of them having arrived, the area resembled a circus coming to town. The site choked and cordoned off with police incident trucks, had replaced the normally active diggers and earth scrapers. Overhead an NYPD helicopter buzzed, its floodlights danced over the river. Police launches were loud-hailing private boat owners warning them away. Fitch cursed that he hadn't got here sooner. They found Bingham close by, one arm outstretched against a wall throwing up.

'See if he's alright, Mike?'

'Can you see the dredger he mentioned, Dave?'

'Over there,' Bingham said calling from the ground pointing. 'Someone said his name was Larry King. Not that we're going to get to him they've closed the site down. Men in suits everywhere. And you know something, no indication that any of them were police. Before I had a proper good look, they threatened me with a kicking if I didn't leave. Gave me a taster in case I had any doubts. Nice of them I thought,' he said nursing his ribs. 'I saw enough though. Went back under the wire. Those kids, you know, didn't look any older than . . . *kids*.'

Crawford made his way to where Bingham had pointed to the dredger. He clicked off as many long-distance shots of the dredge area as he could before official launches got in the way.

'So where are these men in suits Bingham mentioned?' Fitch asked.

'If they were where he said they were they're gone. Looks like police have moved in,' Crawford replied.

Bingham standing upright was wiping his mouth with a handkerchief.

'Did you get what you want, Mike?' Fitch asked.

Crawford nodded. 'All in the can.'

'Just heard Chief Gojke's calling a press, we'd better go, see what else is afoot here.'

Under pressure, Chief-of-Police Edwin Gojke forced to call an emergency press conference on the hoof, still not fully briefed by his senior officers over what had taken place. Standing in the side door to a police incident van calling for order. He was trying to do the best he could over a situation he had thus far mostly heard second-hand. The gathering press instantly fell quiet, leaving the clicking off of cameras flashing as he spoke the only sound heard. Nobody envied him his job this night. He gave a brief account of what they had discovered before they bombarded him with their questions.

'Look!' Gojke shouted, 'let's not over-egg the situation. A couple of skeletons have been recovered, that's all you need to know at the moment, *Goddammit*, I don't know any more myself yet, give me a break.'

Harry van Diemen NBC shouted out to him. 'Well I've pictures showing thirty or so children that have been sheeted-over lying out on that pier over yonder. Ambulances are standing by, presumably waiting for forensics to finish before they take them away. And that's more than a couple of skeletons, Ed. What have you been told to say, that it's a Stone Age burial site?'

It was clear that Gojke was not going to contain this. He was out of his depth and knew it. He put both the palms of his hands in the air to quieten them. 'Please, please, ladies and gentlemen, let's all calm down. Let's get our work done here first; we'll have a fuller report when we know more.' He hoped they would be satisfied with that as explanation for the time being. It wasn't.

'Chief Gojke.'

A woman's voice. He looked up.

'There's a rumor doing the rounds that this will be covered up, as on other occasions. Similar incidents to this have occurred across many States. Are you aware of that, or have you been approached to put the lid on this as others have?'

His face drained. He had not heard of any other incidents. He was certainly not part of any cover-up, if that was what she was suggesting.

'And what organization are you representing, ma'am?' he inquired.

'Annie Carter. I'm with the FBI.'

Gojke choked. He smiled thinking to himself that that was all right. If the Feds didn't know what was going on here, he could refer any questions they might have to the Department for Justice. 'I would have thought that if you are asking questions of previous incidents that involved conspiracies to divert the course of justice, you might have other lines of inquiry more appropriate than mine.'

Fitch's ears pricked up. Hearing the name and recognizing it, he looked round for her, but she, buried in the crowd was not visible to him. He would make his presence known to her instead. 'Chief Gojke. Hamilton Fitch, *New York Post*.'

'Yes, Mr. Fitch. I can only take one more,' Gojke said looking round at the rest of the news media.

'You must be aware that children do go missing from time to time—'

'Happens on occasion.'

'Immigrants, Mexican, as well as other minority classes that perhaps shouldn't be in the country in the first place. Forensics may well clear up some of the cases here. However, that is not my question. Is the NYPD operating a policy of ignoring cases of missing and child abuse because people in high places are involved?'

Gojke had heard questions of its type before, and although not being particularly aware of other States having problems with missing children, he was ready for it. 'Let me assure every one of you here, indeed the public at large, that missing children wherever they come from, are not discriminated against under my watch. The government operates a policy of diversity, so do I. Differences between people, whether cultural or nation makes no difference in the eyes of the law. Neither does it to the mayor's office. Does that answer your question, Mr. Fitch? . . . *Right*, this is definitely the last . . . yes . . .'

'How's the drag operator bearing up?' shouted Bingham.

'That woman, the one that said she was from the FBI,' Crawford mentioned to Fitch as they walked away from the press conference. 'Strange that she was down here don't you think? Almost as if they knew something was taking place before it did. Her question where she mentioned conspiracy, odd don't you think, seeing as who she was supposed to represent? I'm thinking it might be a good idea we take another look round that site before the trail goes cold. Never know we might find the guy that dragged those kids up. What did you say he was called?'

'Larry King. But let's try not to get any broken ribs in the process, eh.'

Making their way to the other side of the man-made harbor, they hung round the working site waiting for someone to come out that might know where the man concerned was. They did not have to wait long. Two men in yellow and orange bib and brace overalls, with the company name, Acme Pollock Construction printed on the front emerged from the light of a portacabin, until the door closed, and they became silhouettes against the city lights shining across the estuary. Wearing leather work boots, carrying tin lunch boxes they came toward them.

'Either of you two Larry King?' Crawford called to them as they approached the security gate that accessed the site.

'I am,' one said. 'Who are you?'

'We're press, need to ask you a few questions about what's happened,' Fitch added.

'I've said all I'm going to say to the police,' King replied.

Fitch caught him by the arm as they started to go by. 'Can't you give us a minute?' King stared at him menacingly. He released his arm. 'I'll pay for your time.'

'You go on Abe; I'll deal with this. See you later.' He turned back to Fitch. 'How much?'

Fitch only had a ten dollar bill on him but said a hundred. King put his hand out.

'*What's this?*'

'The rest tomorrow.'

'I don't trust no-one where money's concerned.'

'I'll pay you tomorrow; that's a promise.'

'Ha-ha-ha. You must take me for a sucker,' he said walking away.

'You got children, King?' Fitch shouted after him. 'What you saw out there tonight, that was no kick in the park for them.'

The man stopped. He did have. And they were never more on his mind than this day.

'A son, two girls, what's it to you?' he shouted back at him knowing what this man was getting at. He had spoken with the police; not once did they ask if he had children; or had showed any sympathy for what he had seen; this man had hit a raw nerve.

'Well, think about them and what happened here tonight. Can you sleep with that on your conscience, you can help them talking to us? I said I'll pay you tomorrow and I will,' Fitch repeated.

'*No!*' he shouted across to him. 'And it will be a long time before I get one. And I don't need you to remind me of what's occurred here. Look, we can't talk here. I'll answer your questions, but I need a drink first. There's a bar over there,' he said pointing some distance away.

The three of them sat down while Crawford got the drinks in, passing tins round.

'Thousands of tons of shale and mud have to be dredged out of there,' King said answering Bingham's question of what was involved. 'We're working day and night until this happened, now all shifts are canceled until further notice. If I hadn't put the drag in there, another day, and they wouldn't have been found for hundreds of years, if ever. I'll tell you what though, Mac . . .' King took a tin up, pulled at the ring, gulped on the liquid Bud, '. . . you always wonder what you'll drag up next when the grab goes in,' he said wiping his mouth with the back of his hand, taking another swig. Sweat had started to form on his forehead as he drained the remainder of his beer. 'I'll have another of those.' Fitch nodded at Crawford to get another round in. 'Mostly dumped cars, with the odd dead dog or cat thrown in for good measure, but this – this is as bad as it gets. Whatever went on here is pure evil. This is going to haunt me to my dying day. I feel sick to the guts.'

'What did happen?' Crawford asked.

He took a tin from the front pocket of his bib, opened it, and taking out a rolled cigarette lighted it inhaling the relaxing smoke. 'I was on the floating crane barge, out there where that police launch is, when the grab went in tipping itself to one side. I pulled it out and dropped it again winched up quickly hoping to release what was holding it. That usually does the trick—'

'It clearly did,' Fitch replied hardly noticing a motorcycle that was pulling up a little way from them.

'You betcha. The grab comes up in a burst of water and black stinking mud. That was when we see them. Bodies of children all mutilated and pulped together like they'd been in a mincer.'

'How many did you reckon?' Bingham asked.

'Hard to tell. Dozens I shouldn't wonder. All bailed together. Some wearing small dresses. Hour or so later, this bunch of suits turns up telling the night site boss to drop the drag back into the river. Said it was important if the work were to continue, what with us being on contract and all; that was when the company said we would be advised to say nothing.' He looked out across the river. 'Still, looks like they arrived too late. The police are here and thank fuck for that. And if you guys have your way, it'll be all over the papers by morning.'

'Would you recognize them again?'

'Not particularly, no.'

'Hey! Bring that back,' Crawford shouted. He knocked the chair over and chased after a snatcher that took his camera from the table they were sitting at. But Crawford was not quick enough, the man was on the back of a bike, its rider dropping the clutch, leaving them in a cloud of dust and exhaust and Crawford to wonder what the hell had happened.

'Someone's not mucking about here, are they?' King said. 'Time I made tracks; I think. Don't want any more trouble today talking to you lot.'

'Thanks for your help; I'll get your money tomorrow,' Fitch said.

'Forget it,' he said. 'I got a conscience for what's right and wrong.'

The following morning Stenna called the three of them into his office. He was annoyed that his most experienced reporters had not been able to get a corroborated story from anyone other than the man known as Larry King. That worried him. A request from the police asking them to hold off printing any story over the previous night's incident until they had finished their investigations gave him further cause for concern. A simple press statement of events to put the public at ease would suffice was their only response. Newspapers and television were responding to an official press statement from city hall that contractors dredging the Hudson had uncovered an archaeological site that looked to be an early human settlement.

'So this dredger operator,' Stenna asked. 'Why did the police say they had not interviewed him when he said they had?

Bingham piped up, 'Yeh, I do.'

'Well. Would you like to tell me, or am I going to have to drag it out of you,' Stenna said quietly.

'They said he was traumatized,' Fitch answered instead.

'*What!* An hairy-arsed heavy plant operator, traumatized! Come on. And you,' Stenna said turning to Crawford, 'had your camera nicked. So no pictures. I'm surrounded by . . . idiots!'

Crawford smiling took an envelope from his file of notes and dropped four A4 color pictures in front of Stenna.

Bingham turned to Crawford. 'Where did you get those?'

Crawford took out a small snappy-Fuji camera from his pocket. 'They only stole the Nikon, not this one.'

'That was a fair exchange,' Crawford said.

Stenna turned to face them. Three were of a net hanging from a crane that had been lifted from the river. It was not brilliant, but clear enough to see the subject matter. The fourth picture was of the pier. Laid out were bodies, some covered and some in bags. He breathed out deeply. His team had come up with the goods. 'Victoria!'

'Yes, Mr. Stenna.'

Stenna saw Fitch with the photograph in his hand. He was studying it closely, a look of sadness on his face.

'Get me the mayor's office.' She smiled, dialing a number waited for an answer. 'And Vicky . . .' She looked back at him her hand over the mouthpiece, '. . . don't take busy for an answer. If he won't come to the phone tell him Max Stenna is going to put a story to bed that he won't be comfortable waking up to tomorrow morning, with pics. *Hamilton!*' Fitch looked up at him, at the same time replacing Crawford's picture down on the table. 'You *okay?*'

'Yeh . . . yes of course, why shouldn't I be?'

Apart from letting Mayor O'Connell know that he was confused as to why city hall had decided to turn the discovery of a number of dead children into an archaeological burial site, Stenna also proposed to combine the resources of the New York media and let the public know of their suspicions (he was being diplomatic in his appraisal).

O'Connell denied knowledge of what Stenna was talking of making some excuse to get him off the phone with an, *I'll call you back, Max. I implore you not to do anything you might later regret.*

When the return call came, Stenna called Fitch's team in to listen, putting the phone on speaker:

'All a bit of a mix-up, Max. Police said that a number of items removed to the city museum meant the contractors could carry on. Great news, eh! We've got a site of historical importance in town. That should bring the tourists in. Anything else I can do for you?'

'Yeh, Mayor. You can send me the name of the government department dealing with all of this.' There was a silence. He could hear a conversation taking place in the background. When he came back on the line, he apologized for the interruption. ''Fraid we can't answer that, Max. Apparently there are complications. And those pictures you sent my office?'

'What about them,' Stenna replied sharply.

'Someone official came said they want the negatives from you. From national security. You know what it's like with bureaucrats. Touchy people. You can't publish or run a story over anything your staff might have seen or any witness statements you may have. Surprised you haven't had a visit already.'

'Be careful, Mayor, there's such a thing as the Freedom of Information Act. I'll implement it if I have to.' Stenna put the phone down. He looked at Fitch. 'Well, you people seem to have stirred up a hornet's nest. Did you say that an FBI woman with the same name you met recently was in the crowd at that Gojke fiasco?'

Fitch nodded.

'And do you know why?'

'Got a good idea.'

'My office, Fitch. Gentlemen, good work, I'll speak with you later.'

Fitch filled Stenna in with everything that happened to him during those three days he went missing, along with his meeting a man with the name of O'Hare. He went into details of the abduction and the killing of his abductors.

'Didn't think you believed me.'

'Surprising as this may sound, Fitch, I did,' Stenna said. 'Not at first, but as soon as you mentioned *Oceans Galactica* and its CEO, well, I've heard stories before. If you wish to investigate this under-cover and look into these people, you have my backing.'

'Not sure I'm ready for any of that, Max. But thanks anyway.'

The following day King turned up at the *Post*'s offices asking to speak with Fitch. Stenna sat in on the conversation. King went on to deny all knowledge of what he had told them the evening before, going on to say:

'Archaeological sites are being discovered all the time in this business.' He got up to leave. 'Sorry to have wasted your time, don't bother me no more.'

When he left, Stenna looked at Fitch, 'There you go. Someone's nailed him up good and proper. Nice day out there as well,' he said wandering over to the window and looking out. 'What the *f—*'

Stenna's phone rang. Fitch picked it up. It was Victoria. 'Ask Mr. Stenna to take a look in the car park,' she said. 'Only . . .'

Before Fitch could pass the message on, Stenna watched Larry King opening the door of a brand new Ferrari parked in the executive auto space. 'Anyone know who owns that piece of flash King's about to nick?' he said turning to Fitch.

Fitch joined him at the window, 'What do you *reckon* a dredger operator earns, Max?'

'Give him the benefit eh, he might have won last night's sweep,' Stenna replied.

Fitch's view that it might not have been impossible for the man to fall lucky changed the following day when a large yacht turned up in the *Post*'s car park on a trailer. He was in reception when two fit young women, manicured and polished, dressed in corporate colors, wearing sashes called asking for Max Stenna the editor. He had apparently won first prize in the Wooden Indian CoffeeCo competition.

Stenna came down. Suspecting a set-up, spoke quietly to them at first, before giving them their marching orders. 'I don't enter competitions, and certainly don't drink coffee. *Now get out of here!* And tow that Gin Palace back from whence it came.'

The evening of the same day Stenna received a call at his home from, that, *FBI woman*. She apologized for calling him so late, going on to say that they were concerned for the welfare of Hamilton Fitch. So concerned, they had been forced to take him into protected guardianship.

'Are you serious? What the hell's "protected guardianship" when it's at home? First, it's a woman with an absence of . . . Bubs! And —'

The line went cold.

He immediately called Fitch but all he got was his answer service provider. He put the phone down without leaving a message with the intention of trying again later. He did not bother. He guessed he would be wasting his time. The time waste was confirmed when Fitch did not turn in for work the following morning. Stenna sent out a missing person's report to Borough Queens South, NYPD. Within five minutes, his phone rang. He snatched it up.

'*Hamilton!* Where the hell are you?'

'Max. Any chance you can tell our people to refrain from pouring coffee into my ashtray putting my cigarettes out,' Heinz Oakey said calling from further down the open office, adding; 'I'm tired of being persecuted by members of staff because I smoke.'

Stenna impatiently sighed, telling him that no-one was persecuting him and not to be a *fucking* nob-head adding whilst at the same time looking at him through the offices. 'I've more important things to do than sort out petty aggravations, do it yourself. Now kindly get the *fuck* off the line, I'm expecting an important call.' Still holding the phone he waited for Oakey to clear before trying Fitch's number once again. This time he got through. A recorded voice answered that the line had been cut-off owing to non-payment of his bill. 'Oh, Hamil-ton—' He paused for thought, and began to worry over one of his staff; and for the first time since he had been in the job as editor-in-chief of the *New York Post*.

Fitch had seen something in Crawford's photograph that would resonate mentally with him for the remainder of his life. He wrote to Stenna, apologizing for his sudden absence asking him if he could be temporarily relieved from duties for six months. Stenna informed the *Post*'s human resources that Fitch was investigating a story that would necessitate him being out of the office for some time; and that he was to continue on full-pay. He called a meeting with the staff that had been involved with the Greenbush incident showing them a confidential directive from the Department of Justice sent to him asking to keep the story under wraps while they investigate possible conspiracies with local authorities. He was annoyed that once again someone was dictating what could, and could not be published in his newspaper until he read the preamble:

> The version of events that had recently taken place regarding abuses of minors purporting to be an archaeological find within the vicinity of the Hudson river would, for the time being, need to be kept on hold.

After which the statement continued:

> A complete non-event approach would be appreciated by all concerned and hope they could be relied upon to allow the unorthodox investigations that are now taking place be allowed to continue without the *Post*'s proper concerns for news of national importance, for the time, infringe those investigations.
>
> *Chas O'Hare*

Before his staff had any chance to shout the usual, 'Press freedom', 'Cover-ups', and the 'Like' (with the thought that Fitch's life might well be in danger without beginning to understand why), Stenna pre-empted any argument saying that he had no doubts as to the authenticity of the directive and the genuine spirit in which it was sent and that he would (he held his fist up threateningly), comply with its request expecting them to do likewise.

Twenty Five – 1997

MICK MAHON PEERED across the space between the gate-house and the building. Dressed in black, wearing a balaclava, he waited for his eyes to accustom to the dark. He was away. Zigzagging and crouching – fast. Unbelievably fast. He could make a hundred meters in fifteen seconds in this stance, stop on a dime – freeze frame and drop to the ground unnoticed at the first sign of an enemy. He listened while still watching. His heart thumping. His eyes pierced the darkness anticipating opposition. There was none. With his heart-beat back under control, he was up and away again. Not quite as good as he had been, but good enough. The security guard never stood a chance; his arm round his neck, the knife went in with only a hint of resistance.

If CCTV security at this establishment was as good as Spannocs had said it was he must be in and out with the girl before they – whoever *they* were – realized he had been and gone.

Inside the building, he quietly closed the door behind him and removed his backpack. He placed it on the floor in the center of the foyer. In front of him, to the right of the wide staircase, was the red door that Spannocs told him would lead to the girl. He opened it and hurried along the corridor, through a second door into what looked like an operating theater. A bank of drawer fronts, he guessed holding bodies, was in front of him. He shuddered before studying the name labels.

A camera set high in the corner of the room sensing his movements reacted. He heard its hum but ignored it.

Angel of the North. Putting on blue rubber gloves, he inserted his fingers into the drawer handle and pulled at it. It came out on its runners faster than he expected. Putting a knee to it, he arrested it. The body shape was in a green plastic bag. He had seen enough of those in his time. Pulling a mortuary trolley against it, he rolled the body onto it wheeled it out into the middle of the room. He unzipped it to check the content. This had to be her, he thought. Spannocs had described her as being Oriental in appearance. He looked into her face. She was certainly that. A fur skin cloak at her feet, he imagined placed there for some bizarre comfort ritual. He shunned the logicality by the person for someone that was clearly dead. Lifting his foot, he kicked the mortuary drawer closed, opening the door pushed the trolley back down the corridor he had entered allowing it to roll under its own momentum for the last seconds, before running in front of it and turning the door handle, guiding it as it went passed him. He steered it out into the foyer. Another camera whirred following his shadow. Showing it two of his fingers, he went out into the night and loaded the bag into his Jeep.

Ten minutes later and Mahon was back on the road. The Jeep cruised gently but powerfully, its four-liter engine giving off a masculine hum of reassurance, reminded him that he had pulled off this last job successfully. He smiled and looked behind him. The body-bag laid out on the rear seat covered in its fur was secure. What was so special about this one, he wondered that Spannocs was prepared to pay such a high price. What he saw of her face he could tell that she had once been beautiful. Was still. Her luminescent skin gave the appearance that she might have been Asian. Mongol, possibly Russian. Wherever she came from it no longer mattered. Would that bother Spannocs, and what he might have in mind for a beautiful, albeit, deceased girl, if he were necromantic? Everyman should have a hobby.

He stopped the Jeep on the mountain road and got out. Below, the Roman Catholic Research Center for Christian Science, ringed with floodlights negated the light from the stars in the sky above them. A full moon made an occasional appearance from partially shrouded clouds blown from the surrounding hills. Night creatures were the only sounds round him. He shuddered for a second time that evening, putting it down to a chill in the air. He could see the building more clearly, his eyes accustomed themselves to the dark. Vehicles were moving. No doubt, he figured, with the realization that they had been broken into. Amateurs. He would need to act quickly though. Removing the radio transmitter from inside the Jeep, he extended its aerial flicked a switch [ARMED], another [READY].

Inside the building, the back-pack on the floor in the foyer clicked once.

A light on the transmitter in his hand illuminated an orange [FIRE] recess. He gently pushed down on it, passing through its point of resistance.

In less than a second, a white flash illuminated the sky in the surrounding valley below. When the explosion came, a second later, it rocked the building. Echoes from the sound, as an endless re-play, went across the hill valley diminishing at every rebound as distant thunder. In more seconds, the ground floor of the west wing of the building engulfed in a fireball. Flames ripped upwards through the ceiling into the second floor blowing out windows as chewing gum bubbles over-inflated from lips of children. Black acrid smoke billowed through the shattering glass. Alarm sirens howled until the heat from the inferno silenced them. Streams of smoke poured through the pan-tiled roof preceded the flames that bursting upwards, the explosion from the flames of which illuminated the night with the brightness of orange red before settling to a sober ember glow.

Mahon could make out the wailing siren from a distant fire engine doppling, but they were on a wasted journey. The incendiary had done its job destroying any evidence that it was he that had been there. He got back into the Jeep. Taking a last look at the inferno below him, he muttered to himself, *Mix and match me to that if you can!*

With his heart pumping, he put the Jeep into first gear and dropped the clutch mercilessly. The vehicle accelerated aggressively into the night, its four wheels spinning left a cloud of dust and stones in their wake.

On the rear seat of the Jeep in the still zipped and closed body-bag the girl opened her eyes. She looked first left, then right, before closing them again. The zip pull slowly slid down its track with no hand to guide it.

Mahon felt another cold shudder, this time down his spine. Turning the heater up higher, he drove on, oblivious to the fact that his mind no longer had the capacity for structure of thought or reason, drove off the road into the valley below.

Inside an unknown government facility housing more than pension records, a bank of computers downloaded the last known movements of Major Michael Mahon, ex-military intelligence, ex-British SAS: automatically defaulted his file [DECEASED].

Barrack room gossip at Kilkenny Cats HQ was that their boss committed suicide. The company did have financial problems.

Twenty Six – 1997

'NO MR. SPANNOCS, I can assure you we haven't found her . . . Yes, I know you're offering a reward, but she's still not turned up . . . yes, yes. *And* I do know you're a friend of the State Governor, but it doesn't alter a *damn* thing, I wish it did. When we went back to recover the driver, or what was left of him, he was alone. If there had been a girl with him, well, she's gone . . . look we've combed the valley. Although, she could have gone into one of the mines down there. They go for miles. I'll check 'em out . . . All right Mr. Spannocs, I'll do that, but no-one could have survived that drop, she would have been as incinerated as he was . . . hello, hello. *Ass'ole!*'

Sheriff Winfield Bell slammed his phone down.

'*Carson!* Where the *fuck*'s he gone?'

An oversize wet-with-sweat under the armpits of his uniform, the man appeared in the doorway to his office. A cigarette stuck between the deputy's lips moved in synch as he spoke.

'You want me, Sheriff?'

Bell stared his deputy up and down with incredulity. Any resemblance between this man and an officer of the law for the county had to be coincidental. He shook his head consoling himself with the thought that the rest of his team (he used the term loosely), were not that much better turned out. 'Take the truck and that idiot Woods and go back to where that Jeep went over the other day. Someone is keen to find that other passenger. Suggest you have a look round the mines. And don't get yourselves lost; the county can't afford another search party. Chances are if she's still alive, you'll find her down in one of them.'

His deputy protested.

'What, today? We've searched; and anyway it's Derby, I'm meeting the boys at two, it's one o'clock now.'

'Yeh, sorry to interfere with your social life, Carson, but today would be preferable.'

'Okay, Winfield, take it easy. What's the rush? Wouldn't tomorrow be better?'

'It's Sheriff to you, and my *rush* is that some guy with trouble at arm's length is giving me grief that can as easily rub off on the rest of you. If you wouldn't mind, do as I'm asking. And let me remind you, if you'd been doing your job properly in the first place, we wouldn't be in this mess.'

'Wasn't my fault. She was probably snatched by someone.'

'*Snatched!* You were supposed to do that. Who else would remove a dead woman from the scene of a car accident? She wouldn't have wandered off, dead or alive, if you'd stayed with the vehicle. We couldn't get two bodies out of that valley at once. What were you doing while we were away that's what I'd like to know?'

Carson changed the subject. 'Could be she wasn't dead in the first place. Maybe the accident woke her up.'

Bell sat back at his desk, buried his face into some paperwork. He spoke while reading hoping that his deputy would go. When he did not, he found himself forced to answer. 'Yeh, and my prick's a bloater. Not out of that canyon she didn't. Would you get on with it, I'm busy.' He persisted and Bell wondered if he was merely taking the piss or was genuinely thick.

'Well she could still be alive, there was that report that someone had heard something wailing in the canyon. They reckon it was a ghost. Could have been her calling for help.'

Bell had a look of resignation. Ever since being lumbered with the title sheriff in this one-shit town he had been surrounded by imbeciles. If not from his own officers, then it was from people he was supposed to be serving. He was not only getting it in the neck from the governor, he had got some nut ball name of Spannocs on his back. Crooks all of them. He was beginning to wonder the importance of this girl that so many were interested. He'd heard she'd walked away in the confusion after that fire up at Meacham at that church place. To top it all, as if the governor hadn't been bad news enough, an agent from the Feds turns up telling him to let them know if he comes across her and not to tell anyone else. A woman out of her mind, walking into Cheyne County, he thought, with the establishment she came from being over a hundred miles away, off her head or not, would not be able to wander that far in six hours. As to how he was supposed to recognize her from the rest of the fruitcakes living hereabouts; if she did manage such a distance was the next question he asked himself. He had seen no need to mention to Spannocs that other people were also making inquiries as to her whereabouts. There could be more than one reward here. He looked up from his paperwork and tried a different approach to his deputy. He spoke softly.

'Forget ghosts; let's see what we can do to find her. She might have family that are concerned for her safety. Though what she was doing in a body-bag in the back of a Jeep is anyone's guess.' Carson turned to go. He called him back. 'While you're about it, tell that partner of yours to have a wash. He smells like a month old collie bag waiting to be changed; and that aftershave he's wearing is doing nothing for him and this office. It stinks in here.'

Cheyne Ridge Valley was a dust bowl of intolerable heat. Temperatures in the high 40s hardly cooled by the winds eroded its landscape. Clouds of sandstone swirled round the valley, wearing exposed rocks smooth and shrub bushes sparse. Often visited by natural history scientists studying the ability of the region to sustain mammal life in such a hostile environment, Bell imagined NASA could do a lot worse using this as a potential site for a practice Mars landing. For the most part the sand dust, composed of light granules, stayed in the valley. More often than not it was drawn up the sloping side of the ridge to be blown out across the town leaving a brown stain on anything it could get onto and into. If you were not indigenous to the county it would roughen the skin on your face raw leaving it feeling as if you'd had a once over with a wire brush. It got in the eyes and ears. If it caught in your mouth it would catch you unawares when you least expected it, causing teeth to snap painfully together when eating. And as for round the foreskin, well, the least said about that the better. All of which made no difference to the two deputies that were standing on the ridge 200 feet above the valley floor with the wind howling. Known locally as Furnace, and with some added sun, Cheyne Ridge recorded more cases of skin melanoma to the faces of those living there than anywhere else in the State. Wearing flat plastic orange goggles to protect their eyes the two men; with handkerchiefs covering their mouths and noses, began their descent to the last resting place of the Jeep.

With the wind trying to pull them off the side of the ridge they carefully picked out a path down onto the valley floor towards what remained of the vehicle below. Shouting at each other to make themselves heard, the relentless howl from the wind sounded like someone blowing continuously through lips that were too far open. Once they were over the thrust of the ridge the wind pushed them inwards preventing them from falling. This was as well. With one of the deputy's being out of condition, while the other nursing a hangover, they might never have survived the climb descent.

At the bottom, the Jeep was still upside down from when they had last seen it. Its front wheels out of line, its track-rod ends stripped from their sleeves. The metallic green of its body-work was giving way to a dusty brown that would soon blend in with the surrounding landscape. In the quietness of the valley, it gave the impression of a derelict ship. It looked as if it had been there for years rather than days. Woods pulled the door open and peered inside.

'Eerie in it,' he said. 'Glad it wasn't me driving.'

Carson pulled the handkerchief down from his mouth spitting out a mouthful of grit. 'You said that last time. There's nobody there. We'll have a quick look down the mines.'

'I'll take the Lucky Silver you the Moab,' Woods said.

Carson thought for a second suspecting that his partner had seen him off. But he figured that one mine being as good as another, what the hell.

'It'll be quicker doing one each, we can get back to the fair sooner,' Woods added. 'And I'll be able to get it on with Masie Maddison before her old man's gets back from 'braska.' Carson looked at him shaking his head. '*What?* She likes me company—'

'She likes sucking cock, and not particularly fussy whose. You happen to be flavor of the month. Though what yours are like cramped up the way they are in sweaty underpants that haven't seen a bar of soap for – how many months has it been? – has gotta take an acquired taste to new heights.'

'Well that's where yer wrong, 'cos I washed 'em last week see. Anyway, she ain't like that,' Woods added. 'Least she's living. Not like that Alison woman you found dead up in her barn last fall.'

Carson looked at him hard, 'Shut your mouth up about that. You hear me, or I'll shut it for yer.'

'All right keep your dick in your holster,' Woods replied. 'At least it was me that saw you, anyone else . . .'

'She was on the game when she was alive; don't suppose she would have had any objections what with her being dead an' all. Anyway, if you'd been watching properly you'd seen that I couldn't get her jeans off her, so I couldn't get into her – not properly anyway. It don't count.'

'All right, none of my business,' Woods answered.

'Yeh, well— Right, we better get started; meet back here in twenty minutes. And keep your radio on.'

Woods was glad to be out of the heat. Both mines were dark and cool. Since the mining company gave up maintenance to keep them from collapsing, they had also become dangerous. Support timbers loose threatened to come down without warning burying anyone unfortunate enough to find themselves under them. Tommo, for instance. Held up the liquor store, hid out at Lucky where he opened his last bottle of beer before that part of the mine he was sleeping caved in snuffing him out. Woods pulled aside the corrugated iron sheet supposedly put in place to keep people out. Next to useless, he thought. Somebody had been in here recently. A coke can and an empty pack of Camel lay on the ground inside the entrance. Probably the same person that had spray painted UNLUCKY TOMMO in red on the metalwork in front of the name LUCKY, painting over SILVER. He stepped into the gloom flattening the cigarette pack under his boot. His radio crackled.

'Copy . . . copy . . . Al. Found anything yet?'

'Give us a chance; I've only just got here. And cut the *copy* crap,' Woods said into his radio switching it off from transmit. '*Pervert!*'

'Roger that,' Carson replied.

'I'll Roger you, yer prat,' Woods replied under his breath.

Carson clipped his radio back on his belt and switched on his torch. He began walking down the passageway. His ears picked up the sound of animals scratching. Hesitantly he bent down in the darkness and felt for a stone. Standing up he threw it hard toward the sound. It clattered as it hit the rock wall before ricocheting against what sounded like wood. Pit prop, he thought. The squeal from rats protesting made him shudder. He worried that one might come racing in his direction taking a bite out of his leg. Stooping down he picked up another stone dropping his torch. Bending to retrieve it, he picked it up. It went out. *Fuck the thing*, he whispered to himself, shaking it – it came on. Relieved, he pulled out a cigarette, stuck it in his mouth, lighting it carried on further into the mine. Another sound stopped him. That was a fucking big rat, he thought to himself.

He strained to listen. Could it be her? He was certainly looking forward to finding a naked woman. Dead or alive, he would have his way with her. Worry was, if it were not her, who in hell could it be – Woods, perhaps? 'Come on, baby. Come to daddy,' he called out into the darkness. Moving it quickly from side to side, he shined his torch bringing light to as many of the dark recesses as he could. His heart was beating fast, but there was no sign of any woman. 'Woods, that you? Woods! Al. Stop fucking about, Al I know it's you!' The bastard's creeping round after me, he thought. He stopped shouting and decided he had had enough go back. He heard the sound once more, further down this time. It sounded like water dripping. He called out. Why didn't Woods answer? He called again, still nothing. It sounded like someone was sipping water. Pulling his radio from his belt he pushed transmit, but all he got back was static. *Damn.* He tried again. More static. *Right let's sort you out once and for all.* He pulled his gun. The sound of sipping moved away the further down the passageway he ventured. A realization that he had come further into the mine than intended entered his head and he was no longer sure he knew the way back. Whoever was here, they could have it. He was leaving.

Woods, not generally overly concerned with Carson's well-being, nevertheless realized that having not heard from him for two hours was going to have to do something. Having finished searching Moab, he made his way to Lucky Silver calling Carson on his radio as he went. 'Dave! Where are you, Dave? We gotta be getting back. Answer me, Dave.' He switched to receive it crackled. That should not be happening, he thought. Not with these sets. He tried again but there was no response. He stepped on the iron sheet shouted into the tunnel. A dull echo returned. Switching on his torch, he went in. Bending down to pick up a cigarette butt, he sniffed at it. It was one of Carson's. He called out his name. Nothing, he went deeper, reasoning that a voice as close as round a single corner in these mines would die away to nothing. 'Carson!' he shouted. 'You down there?' He listened, but all he got back was a dull echo of his own voice. He tried his radio once again. Switching to receive this time, he heard a noise half between static crackle and frantic heavy breathing. That could be Carson, he thought. It would not be the first time he had left his radio on transmit while at the same time pulling himself off dong in hand in some dark recess unseen. Although, if he had got himself into some trouble, knocked out, unconscious maybe, he was going to have to call for back-up whether Bell was in favour of the idea or not.

Carson hurried along the passageway his feet picking purposefully among the stones and rocks toward the sound while at the same time calling Woods's name. If that was the sound of breathing quite possibly it was the woman, he thought. An excitement went through him. When he came upon her, she was on her knees and hands drinking from a pool of water his excitement, seeing her, was beyond all expectation. A fur across her back and shoulders turning him on.

He shone his torch onto her back not noticing that she cast no shadow.

When she turned in his direction, he had not expected the look she gave him; a mix of terror and peace came over him. Both recognizable human emotions were vying for supremacy as to what he should be correctly interpreting in that look, he settled on terror. For what he saw in her soul over-rid the beauty of the woman. The light from his torch reflecting green from her eyes. A luminescent dark green not of this world. The terror, as quickly as it had come, washed from him. He became confident.

'Hello girl,' he said to her excitedly. 'I've come to rescue you. You stay the way you are,' he added. Her immediate rescue not foremost in his mind seeing her down on all fours in this position of female submission. It was not to last.

She stood up and as if reading his intentions moved away from him, several yards behind the pool she had been drinking. It did not involve the locomotion from her legs, or the sway from her body. Turning round once again, she looked at him. He must have been mistaken for she surely never floated. He was a man that commanded respect in his women. Usually from the end of his nightstick. She would not mess him round. He reached into his belt and withdrew it, walking towards her, he smacked it in the palm of his hand repeatedly. He knew how to deal with disobedient children, a woman would not be any different. He ignored her seemingly magical ability to move backwards while appearing to stay in one place, putting it down to a trick of the light from his torch he had put down. When she did it again, he got annoyed. She would not make a fool of *him*. Walking quickly toward her, he took hold of her by the neck his fist grasping at her flesh that stretched slipping from his hand before resuming its shape, leaving him struggling to regain balance, his mouth opening in terror. This was no trick of the light. He cursed and made another grasp for her. This time she stayed where she was. He brought up his night-stick striking her hard across the head. He felt the resistance. She was rigid, and how he liked them. If she was not dead before, she was now, and back on the floor on all fours. He unbuckled his belt and loosened his trousers. He would have his way with her, fuck sense into her vacant body with no-one to see him. And he would come back again, another day, when the feeling to do it came over him once more. A dead woman would be good for a week in this chill air he thought. He began removing the fur from her body exposing first one shoulder then the other until . . . feeling at her breasts.

'What!'

Where they should have been, there was none. Carson pushed her onto her side. With horror, his eyes, drawn down to her lower body; to where her navel should be, there was nothing to indicate she had been born of a woman; lower still; her vagina was nothing more than smooth skin. He screamed out, what was before him sent his heart racing. She had no place for a man to enter. He turned to run but it was too late. She was up and on him, his trousers round his ankles. A face that had once shown beauty was hideous. He struggled but knew he was powerless.

A surge of deadly energy from the universe channeling from her hands entered his body sending out a visual vortex of power through his brain blowing out the side of his neck separating his head from his torso. Such was the force nothing, but a mess of flesh and arteries connected to soft blackened tissue was all that remained. His soul, part of this world and another, felt the pain of being inside an iron container with flames licking round it, where, in spite of his efforts not to touch the sides his flesh seared turned black. Without the mercy of death, she carried his version of this world into another where it continued to see and feel by proxy his body forever in torment. Carson had found hell.

Woods, not especially fond of Carson, did not make what he saw of him any less of a shock when he came across him. Sheriff Bell was not so confused. He had not believed a word that Woods had told him, arresting him for his murder. That Carson was a pervert, Bell could not deny, and nobody was going to miss him, especially the kids up at the orphanage, but murder was murder and Woods, in the absence of anyone else, was in the frame. What troubled Bell was what Woods had done with Carson's head, to say nothing of the weapon he had used to remove it leaving a burned black flesh opening. With not the means that would leave a body in the shape Carson's was in, Bell thought about planting one, so convinced was he that it could not have been anyone else but the man. But what in *darnation* could Wood have used that would be sharp enough to take a man's head off. Something that a County Sheriff's Deputy would carry in the execution of his duty. A sword, perhaps? Hardly US issue these days. A Swiss army knife? That didn't fit the criterion to sever heads either. Not unless someone had a calling, and a couple of hours to spare. All his talk of a woman becoming mist vaporizing into the mine's rock wall when he had come across Carson, Bell was having none of. He wanted Woods indicted for first degree murder and he would have it.

Accompanied by Daniel Sullivan, Spannocs landed by helicopter close by the entrance to Lucky Silver. Sheriff Bell was waiting for him. He showed the three of them to the entrance to the mine offering to lend them his radio and torch. Spannocs declined, telling the Cohorts to stay put, he would go alone. Entering the darkness of the entrance, unseen by those outside, he transmogrified into a spirit more suited for another world than this one. He could not afford to be carrying his human shell. If she were here, and he was in no doubt over that, having seen the body of Carson and hearing Woods's version of what had happened to him, she would tear Giuseppi to pieces. He felt her presence. He knew her signature. Her ability to cloak herself was limitless. She was part of the minerals. He smiled to himself. He would trap her here. She would interfere for the last time in the affairs of the human race. An interference, not hers to make, she would be sealed up for an eternity. She might think that the human race, with all that it suffered from war and famine, that still had faith for a God that was not prepared to lift a finger to help them, would one day aid her in her ambitions. How wrong was she, with thoughts that a God would step in bringing order to a world falling into decay by its own hand. *And they call me evil; blame me. Arrogant hypocrites!*

Spannocs the man came from the mine to see Sullivan set a detonator inside a lump of nitroglycerine before putting it into a box. Making himself scarce behind a rock alongside Bell, he screwed the wires to its battery pack. Spannocs stood out in the open, looking as if he was overseeing the operation.

'What's he doing? *Heh!* Spannocs you better take cover. You'll be in serious danger of never having to take another shit,' Bell said laughing.

'Watch and learn!' Sullivan said smiling.

'Yeh! Blood and guts blown up the side of the valley. Should paint a pretty picture. A good lesson to learn.'

Why Spannocs, the ass-hole wanted to kill himself, Bell had little idea. He had other problems on his mind that would soon be resolved. That of the murder of Carson by Woods. The blowing up of the mine would take care of that, leaving no possibility for a forensic examination. He would tell the coroner that when he found both men they appeared to have had a fight. He would tell him that he knew that both men were sweet on the same woman and must have argued the matter to the point where one had murdered the other. He would mention a non-existent Bowie knife he had seen beside Carson's body, buried in the mine. Two deputies, both dead and all for a bit of arse-candy known as, Masie Madison.

Sullivan flicked the switch.

The explosion partially sucked the air from his lungs. The thump to his head and chest was as if a truck had run over him. With eyes partially closed from the dust, Bell looked over the rock that protected him. He could see the hillside was still there, but the mine had collapsed in on itself. He stood up and looked in the direction he had last seen Spannocs. Another arrogant arsehole to meet his maker, he said to himself. He turned to Sullivan. 'That's the end of him,' he said laughing. 'I think – mebbe you're going to have to seek employment elsewhere, mister. May I suggest safety adviser to a mining company?' He laughed. Brushing down his uniform, he became aware that Sullivan was tapping him on the leg. *What now?*

Sullivan pointed to the where the mine entrance had once been. Casually smoking a cigar, Spannocs, with not a scratch on him, not a piece of torn clothing, nor a hair out of place, was smiling back at them. Bell's mouth dropped open. How could anyone have survived that?

Spannocs came over, a revolver in his hand. Spinning the barrel, he passed it to him.

'Your turn for some Russian roulette I'm thinking, Sheriff. No rules. You put it to your head and pull the trigger. Five-to-one against,' he said affirming with a nod of his head.

Bell smiled at the same time looking at Sullivan as someone to share the joke with. Then seeing Spannocs was serious, feebly protested; tried to make a run for it. Sullivan grabbed him from behind holding him in a neck restraint. Spannocs placed the gun to his head. Bell was sweating, struggling, and protesting.

'Sorry about this,' Spannocs said before pulling the trigger. 'Nothing personal you understand.'

Sheriff Bell was three parts cremated when the helicopter with its passengers took to the sky. It was the third pull of the trigger that did it for Sheriff Bell. With odds down to 2–1 against, falling to evens, it was only a matter of time. An acrid smell of black smoke along with scorched flesh wafted across the valley. Sullivan would know that there would soon be nothing left of another that knew, *A little too much*, Nathaniel.

Giuseppi found it amusing that the man Bell had tried to frame for the murder of one of his deputies – later acquitted for lack of evidence – became the new sheriff. *There's good in everyone if you look for it,* he said to himself. *Even me. Can't take the soul of an innocent man can I, Spannocs?*

Sheriff Alexander Woods sniffed what was left of Masie Madison on his fingers, smiled, then went inside his office closing the door.

Twenty Seven – 1997

Fie, thou dishonest Satan!
I call thee by the most modest terms;
for I am one of those gentle ones that will use
the devil himself with courtesy.
The Clown to Malvolio:
SHAKESPEARE: Twelfth Night, IV, ii.

FOR SPANNOCS, to be celebrated by members of the organization he had founded; a club of successful, degenerated, hard, and heartless men and women; some of the most corrupted souls the world, to say nothing of America, was to be honor indeed. The Lord's Flies had soaked up his evil as a dried out sponge crying out for water, an honor indeed. They were still difficult for him to comprehend. He would like to have taken the credit for the perversion that had generated such wealth, but he could not. Its success was all due to bad people using his name as excuse. And all the time, another spirit, one that imparted love, and knowledge, brainwashing the human race into believing he was cast into hell for the world's evils when man was as equal to him as any when push came to shove. He could teach them nothing. This quest for His knowledge would bring them to His door, and if he knew only one thing, their end of time was imminent. And not his problem.

He had merely promulgated the perversion allowing them to live with themselves. With crimes difficult for the authorities to contain, without people within the fabric of their own government encouraging its continuation, his Host had built an empire. And while they had their own agenda, he had his.

A good name the Aryan Farmers Association; and one that appealed to a particular breed of American. The right-wing gun-toting wealthy whites that did not give a damn for blacks, Asians, Muslims, Catholics, Jews, Native Americans, and anyone else that did not fit in with their brand for white supremacy and arrogance. Why that should be was another difficulty Spannocs could not comprehend. Their hatred for what they called 'gays' was another. That new generation that 'came out' spoke of 'limp wrists' and 'camp' mannerisms. Some considered them an alternate sex (they should look at where he comes from). But they were not above having 'liaisons' with them. That was all right; that was supremacy over those considered inferior. *Or underage.* Mostly. A child from another race of their own species – all too much for him to take in. Animals were not excluded; and though the other man could not make big bucks from them, he would secretly video them indulging in this perversion if they crossed him. Later to show them performing at one of his private movie theaters before blackmailing them. They had a lot to lose. Mostly wealthy high profile people or celebrities, he would take them for everything they had, leaving them with destroyed lives and no other choice than to self-destruct; husks of their previous selves. Such was the enormity of feeling that humans could indulge in bestiality went unreported. No journalist, no editor, no proprietor would risk exposing people of such status for fear of losing in a court of law for slander or libel. Sexual depravity of that nature does not exist in modern times, unlike pedophilia, hard-wired into some.

When it came to searching for those with similar aspirations, www.ayranfarmers.aux was the web site to visit from the innovation that was the Internet. With computers, operating from *Oceans Galactica* only reached by subscribers it was out of reach of the authorities looking into their activities. Child trafficking was the crux of his business with its profits ever swelling the coffers of the company. The wealth it had been allowed to accumulate was for a reason. Frederik Spannocs knew it, as did others behind the veneer of the government's state pension service. Power was needed and it came at a price. The energy required to worm-out the secrets of the Universe and its Creation, less than that needed for time travel, was never going to be a legitimate expense that a country's government, let alone the world, could finance from the tax payer. He had been encouraged in his work. They were ready. It was time to destroy all those associated with him in his past. His manservant and lover among them. He would be sad for that.

Spannocs stepped from the onyx-green marble bath – its neo-Romanesque style designed by the Italian architect, Giovanni – into a white bathrobe held out at arm's length by his manservant. 'Thank you, Tony. Are arrangements in place?'

'They are Frederik. Your clothes are laid out in your dressing room.' His voice was quiet and unhurried. 'Will there be anything else?'

'I'll call you.'

D'Sotto turned on his heels.

Spannocs watched him salute his head in his familiar manner. His locomotion as ever slight of angle off vertical. He stepped from him between two marble columns. His shoes, tapped with metal, rang on the tiled floor echoing before muffling away on the sumptuous carpet. He would miss him. They went back a long way.

The house had forty rooms. More than his house in Mexico that had other purposes, already destroyed, explosive engineers were busy rigging this one similarly. Spannocs watched as Tony appeared once again before going past the bar area down some further steps that would take him outside and across to the garages, there he was to fetch the Bentley RT Turbo for the last time. Too easily recognizable by law enforcement agencies, watching, he was sure, for it to take to the sky, the hangar close by housing his helicopter, an Agusta A109C bearing the legend *Galactica II* in gold emblazoned down its length on its deep wax black finish, was being lifted by a scrap dealer's grab. He made his way into his dressing room, opened a gold cigar box, and took out an Havana. He snipped the end off before sticking it in his mouth. A decanter of absinthe set on a gold tray earlier by D'Sotto beside of it. A single goblet, solid gold placed alongside the decanter, might have been the Holy Grail itself. He went to a drawer in his dressing table and took out a red box. Opening it he removed a syringe. From a drawer below he removed a small bottle. Taking the syringe, he carefully drew off the liquid from it. He leant forward opening his legs, injected half into one of his testes, the remainder into his other. A small tear, from the sting, ran from the corner of his eye. He still had some human attributes. Satisfied, he drank his absinthe and lighted his cigar. Puffing gently on it he stood in front of one of his more erotic works of art began masturbating.

'Tony!'

D'Sotto entered the dressing room to find his master still half-dressed staring at the bronze sculpture of Donatello's David. On loan from Museo Nazionale del Bargello Museum in Florence, his master had considered purchasing. The gallery had set an asking price of twelve million dollars thinking he would no longer be interested. They would have to go higher if they wished to retain the national treasure though it was to be destroyed along with the rest of the house.

Spannocs turned towards him.

The sight of Spannocs's erect penis brought a dryness to D'Sotto's mouth and lips. Dampening them with his tongue he said, 'Let me help you with that, Marco.'

Always he had preferred his former name.

Going down on his knees, he opened Spannocs's dressing gown. Taking his erect penis in his hands, he took it full into his mouth.

Spannocs closed his eyes. Tilting his head back began pumping down D'Sotto's throat. Going further and deeper, he felt the warmth on the shining end. Gently pushing, he was going into raptures from the ecstasy of a bodily function yet to explode. Resisting for as long as he was able, he ejaculated, quietly saying, *Buonanotte old friend*.

Tony D'Sotto collapsed onto the floor gasping for breath, his hand clutching at his throat. His mouth, full of his master's golden fluid he had come to enjoy, was burning him from within. Looking into Spannocs's eyes, seeing no look of malice on his face, he smiled and whispered:

'We did well for immigrants, Marco. You and me. Good days—'

Spannocs with a trace of remorse nodded. 'We did Tony. You did.'

D'Sotto smiled closing his eyes.

O'Hare had got to hear that a large number of *important people*, were gathering for a party to honor Spannocs. He had persuaded the powers that be that it would be a bust something on the lines of the Seager Investigation all those years before that Frank Weinberg was involved. In this case, they were child sex offenders rather than a corrupt Mayor of New York. At long last, someone had taken notice of him, and agreed. He hoped that he was not to suffer the same fate as his ex-partner.

'He's driven off. It's a Bentley. Red,' O'Hare said closing his cell-phone. He turned to his team. 'In you go, and remember, when that hell-hole in Mexico got blown up, it took three good men with it. Be careful that he hasn't got the same planned here.'

He watched from the side of the road as they put a length of optic cable with a camera on the end through the mailbox slot in the door.

He was right to be cautions. One of them signaled back for the bomb disposal team. They sent a robot to the front door of the property. Firing a single shot into the key lock the door blew wide off its hinges. One of the men, dressed in an anti-bomb suit went in to disarm the first of them. Minutes went by before he returned dragging a body with him out through what was left of the front door. He put a thumbs-up to O'Hare, then returned to deal with the bombs. O'Hare looked at the body on the stretcher. He recognized him immediately. He looked, if he was not dead, that he was hugging it close.

'Get forensics.'

An incoming G-mail on Carter's laptop alerted her.

She and O'Hare were driving to Becland County where they were to meet Fitch who had gone on ahead. He had been keen to see this man and his organization first hand. They were not but agreed to his going.

'Well. You going to tell me or not?'

'Better stop the car first,' she said.

Bringing the car to a stop, he took the laptop from and began to read:

ATTN. OF: FBI Assistant Director, Charlie O'Hare.

FROM: County Forensic Officer, Austin, Texas. (Dr. Alison Cunningham)

DISEASED (If known): Tony D'Sotto (ID reference O'Hare [as above])

SEX: Male Caucasian.

NATIONALITY: American National.

PLACE OF BIRTH: Sicily, Italy.

DOB: 1888. Appears to be some mistake here, as this would make him around 117. He does look it though. Dr. AC.

CAUSE OF DEATH: Primary: Hydrogen cyanide poisoning plus one other.

ATTRIBUTED: Mouth, throat, and stomach show combination mixture of approx. 200mg solution of cyanide and human semen.

CONCLUSION: Speculative.

OTHER: For a fuller version refer. #000789A/12.

It was the attribution that did it for him. He pushed open the car door, stuck his head out and began vomiting onto the grass verge alongside. He then got out, and with one hand up against a tree, with his head down, brought up the remainder of the contents of his breakfast onto its exposed roots.

'*Prussic acid!*' he said between urges. 'How in the devil's name did he swallow a cocktail like that?' He wiped his mouth with a kerchief, then returned to the car.

'I can't imagine, anyway, feeling better now?' she asked.

He nodded.

'*Come on then*. We haven't much time. Let's get out of here, or we'll be late for lunch.'

Spannocs was welcomed at the Becland Diamond Conference Center with a rapturous roar from the crowd that had gathered by the side of the red carpet to greet him. For this was the home of the Texas Branch of the Aryan Farmers. The whole of his organization was here to celebrate him. He had driven himself. He could not help smiling and nodding at this show of affectation from business colleagues and associates, for this was a glittering array of some of the wealthiest mavericks, whores, perverts, and child abusers that were ever to assemble under one roof. He was the man responsible for their wealth and they knew it. Shown to the center of the top table he took his place and surveyed the gathering, all the while smiling and nodding at their clapping and hooting that had become their trademark until called to order by the Master of Ceremonies for the evening. Benny the Ponce dressed in red livery with gold braid, black top hat, introduced the first act.

'Ladies and Gentle . . . *men* . . .'

Not all of you, I'm sure, he said as an aside.

Roars and guffaws of laughter.

He held up his hand for silence. 'One of the finest examples of shape-changers in the business. Ladies and Gentlemen, allow me to introduce to you the most delightful and effervescent artiste in the business of what we call transvestic, and what the world of thaumaturgy . . .

Oooo!

'. . . described as, the miracle of the disappearing todger with accompaniments.'

Though she could be a woman, he said as another aside.

Laughter and cheering.

'Not to be taken too seriously though . . . all the way from Austin . . . Little Miss Poppet Tupper, Trannie to the Stars . . .'

And who wouldn't?

Hooting and whistling.

Poppet Tupper on stage to the left of the top tables came on smiling to cheers.

'Thank you. Ladies and gentlemen, you're so perverted,' he said pulling up a leopard-skin dress above his crotch to reveal a full set of male accoutrements to loud applause. 'How's that for a luster cluster? Swallow these Benny, for you've a mouth big enough.'

Woooah.

Using his fingertips, he pushed the whole lot up inside himself.

There was a gasp from the audience. Removing his matching leopard skin top hat, he took a bow as a full-on looking woman.

'Thank you very much ladies and gentlemen. More later. For the moment I should like to give you our guest of honor, Mr. Frederik Spannocs, founder of the Aryan Farmers Association, and host for the evening.'

A standing ovation came again, this time continuing for a full five minutes before Spannocs held up his hand for silence. The applause died away.

'That's what I call all things to all men, Poppet Tupper, ladies and gentlemen, the thinking man's confusion,' Spannocs responded to his wave from the wings.

They clapped on.

He returned, bowing, disappeared stage left into the wings of the drapes that hung to the side of the top table.

'Every one of you has been given the opportunity,' he said holding up his hands for silence, 'to make money you could only dream of before you joined me on the dark side.' He laughed.

They joined in his merriment.

'We are to embark on the greatest show on earth. We are to align evil and good and show there is no difference from Satan's version of both to that of man's so-called God.'

The laughter ceased. Some felt this was getting a little too heavy.

'Because, you dregs of humanity . . .' he reached behind him and picked up the gold metal tube he had placed there earlier. Unlocking it he took out a scroll waved it in front of his audience. 'Evil is the power that all men aspire. Evil. Not a word we should be afraid of, eh. Because, ladies and gentlemen, the so-called Holy Trinity or – with the discovery of this 2000 year-old affidavit I am in possession – might better describe them as the Holy Dynamic Trio, departed the building the same time, leaving the other Prince to vapor away.' He looked from one to the other of them. 'Who am I referring? . . . Well, Satan, of course. The original shining light cast out for standing up for himself. And the first to admit that he could not exist were it not for God. This did not mean he was prepared to be His servant.'

The audience were showing signs of nervousness.

'Let's talk of this parchment that refers to His so-called, Son. Let me tell you something of that, and they liken me to it, pretender! Deceiver! Jesus of Nazareth enjoyed parties, keeping the company of whores and money men. Some people at that time called Him a glutton, a drunkard, a friend of sinners – and much else beside. Well, ladies and gentlemen, that was only the half of it.'

He held up the roll of parchment.

'"Suffer the little children to come unto me", has never has such poignancy since this discovery. As most of you here are, or have at one time or another indulged, so did He. He was a *pedophile!*'

There was a roar of disbelief.

'Oh, yes. The evidence is here for all to see, in this scroll. If you had been the Creator, and you had him for a Son, how would you feel? Well, I'll tell you. For his effrontery, He let Him suffer and die right there on that cross; left the world with Satan, the true Prince of the Universe, to try and do a better job with mankind.' He paused. 'And do you know something, ladies and gentlemen, His absence from the top table, with the world the way it is, is clear for anyone with half an eye to see.'

There was silence. They looked at one another with incredulity; and an uncertainty came over them regarding his mention of the content of a scroll.

The Ponce, sensing a mood change, tried to inject some light heartedness into the proceedings by offering up a toast. Spannocs squeezed his arm. He had not finished.

'With no-one to answer to, you can do as you please. Now

doesn't that make you feel a whole lot better. No guilt. No conscience gnawing away at you. That's got to appeal, doesn't it?' He took the drink from the tray and held it up for a toast. 'He'd forgotten something when He *fucked off*, leaving the keys to the workshop with instructions for anyone to read it if they knew how.

'I couldn't have done it without you all. Anyone here read Greek; and would care to translate the greatest lie God ever concealed from the world?'

He hesitated. Part of the scroll was missing. A small piece torn off at the corner, gave him cause for concern.

Benny the Ponce, sensing his mood, took control. With a smile on his face he held up the notice board.

FREDERIK SPANNOCS

THE NEW PRINCE OF DARKNESS

The world of sin, that so many were comfortable, shown evidence that Jesus Himself might be one of them, stuck in their craws, and for the first time, thoughts of being cast alive into a lake of fire and brimstone had been put into their heads. For wasn't he the one, above all others, that knew their fate. The terror would begin.

Spannocs smiled to himself. The world and its striving for knowledge had created for him power beyond any he could have imagined. He had outgrown his Host, leaving science to take him out. These people, superfluous to those plans, were doomed. This gathering is going on a journey with no future. A journey that will see none of their DNA carried into another life for processing for their next generation, he had the power to destroy their children and their souls. The only acceptable pact between good and evil: God and Satan were upon them. He thought He had got that right when He said:

To be carnally minded is death.

Not that there would be any mystery over *their* demise. It was remarkable that none of them could see what was coming – it was

431

there for any with half an eye. The gathering of seven-headed ten-horned beasts was at their door, that is, after Internal Revenue had the first portion of their souls. When books he held passed over, a hasty transfer of assets and funds would take place: to no avail. They might try and bury them in off-shore accounts, which would solve the problem; it was their primary assets however, that would be the problem. Their spending money. The school fees, the homes in Martha's Vineyard, their yachts on the Keys. There was their social standing among their peers. Suicide would be their only option. The rest of them imprisoned, executed in some States for their crimes. Any remaining, hell would take them!

They halfheartedly cheered him when he made his good byes. They were never to be part of his plan. As he had often remarked to Tony, it's what separates the *punks* from the *spunks*. And where was he, Giuseppi wondered; where; and he wished him here with him with a passion?

Ahriman manifested into the surrounding mist regaining form. A rattlesnake, wriggled in its death pangs at his presence, releasing from its mouth, to escape, a small rodent, to make good an escape. Cheyne Ridge Valley in its namesake County was at its season where blistering hot days became freezing nights, the differential changes to temperature turning everything it fingered damp to wet; but Ahriman the angel, was in neither a time nor world where vagaries of weather troubled him. No more than did his infection of the mind from the body warmth of his human Host; the man, Ahriman all but had any further need of. For Ahriman, having managed to cloak identity from others of his kind – who would condemn for a further 600 millennia his near and good as extinction – was to give it back destroying the multilayered world of man and spirit; from this edge of darkness; the fundamental matter from nonexistence, he would summon anti-matter reversing this universe's time and verse; wipe the slate clean. The one gift – forever elusive to those of his kind – the bringing of everlasting life, was never going to attract to his cause the following that God enjoyed. But he was working on it.

The known closest touching link between Man and his Creator, the Divine Spirit, the Order of the Most Divine Third Circle were reaching out for His seventh gift, with little thought for what they were arrogantly researching that would always bring his kind into the fray. For Man's pursuit of that dangerous knowledge, Ahriman had acknowledged to himself with all like-minded spirits of the mist, those incapable of handling, in spite of their powers, was for reasons he could only put down to apathy to rise up, would remain elusive to them to their end.

Further off, among scrub, the rodent shaking twitching its nose after its miraculous escape looked on at the apparition, its tiny mammalian brain never having evolved to hazard a guess at what it was seeing, rolled over on its side kicking its legs died from a heart attack never being able in its genes to pass the information for future generations to build on.

Over the District of Cheyne County, two earthquakes of moment magnitude scale nine-point-two, the second a millisecond behind the first hit. Their epicenter, a mine named Moab. The devastation to the landscape immediately reconfigured becoming a crater half a mile wide leveling the town to sea height. The evacuation of air returning to low-pressure became a hurricane, tearing up its main highway destroying anything remaining that managed to survive the first onslaught; the sky taking on a blood red hue from the Furnace's sandstone.

'You summoning up demons, Sister?' O'Hare asked Carter laughing, after feeling a shudder through the wheels of the car.

Spannocs sensed a temporary weakness. His mind had gone. He had to appear casual, putting his falling against a table, disturbing those seated, knocking the table and spilling their drinks down as an accident. As quickly, recovering his previous self, he apologized. Something he had not done since his childhood days of surplices and choirs. A time of innocence and one before his own abuse where the stiletto would rule, okay! *Over-indulgence of the spirit*, he added snarling at them. Someone called to him. He recognized the voice as that of Bernard Ritchie, one of those people that had the ability to irritate no matter the ills your flesh was host to.

'Rich! Always a pleasure,' he said straight faced trying not to look too bored.

The man shook his hand pumping it vigorously, 'Great do, Frederik, you could always lay on a bash. And the people. There must be everyone that's anyone here,' he said looking round the large ballroom. 'Have a drink with me.'

Spannocs smiled. 'Well, not quite, but nice of you to say so. I'll pass on that drink though. If you'll excuse me, enjoy the rest of your evening.'

Ritchie never could take a hint and caught him by the elbow.

'How's Mexico? Still got the Pyramid?'

'No, I've had it moved,' he sighed.

'And your manservant, what was his name Tony, er . . .'

He did not answer. Something was troubling him. The tear in the scroll.

'Come on, Frederik, there's no need for you to treat me like that, have a drink. *Alfonse! Alfonse!*'

An immaculately, well-presented dinner-jacketed brick shithouse of a man with a shaven head came over, a tray in his hand, with an attitude Attila the Hun would have approved.

'Alfonse, a drink for Mr. Spannocs. What was it? I

remember . . . absinthe, I believe. Alfonso-o-o baby if you wouldn't mind.'

Alfonse gave him a look of disdain and looked to Spannocs for approval to drop him. Spannocs touched him on the shoulder to calm him down.

'Thank you, Alfonse, absinthe will be fine.'

'And don't forget the cigar, *Al-fonso*, babe,' Ritchie shouted after him.

Spannocs smiled at Alfonse. 'It's all right, the man's a *wanker*. I will have a cigar though,' he laughed.

Ritchie laughed with him assuming it was one of those throw away remarks made between friends. He put his arm over Spannocs's shoulder. 'We'll be right over there, *Al-fonso!*' Ritchie said directing Spannocs to a table in the corner pulling a chair out for him to sit down. 'There's something I've been meaning to mention. I've been having trouble getting through to your manager.'

Spannocs had had enough. He got up to leave. 'I haven't time for this, I've business to attend.'

Ritchie put his hand on his shoulder to prevent him leaving, 'The point is, Frederik . . . let me say, that thanks to you I've made my fortune and want nothing more to do with the business. I have a new life; don't want to be involved with this anymore. You've a bad reputation when it comes to certain circles and the children's high school . . . well, you know what I mean. Not that I've any truck with you personally,' he said looking at him seriously.

'Glad to hear it. The thing is Ritchie; it doesn't quite work like that does it? When you came to me, and wanted into this, I promised you that I would get the law off your back and give you a new life. In return, you promised your allegiance to me. When I said there would be no leaving, didn't you say to me, that that wouldn't be a problem, or didn't you?'

'Yes, well, that was when things were different, I've money now, and I know a lot more about you. You see, Spannocs, I've enough on you to put you behind bars for a long time, so you see the boot is rather on the other foot. And I'm not the only one.'

'What you see and what you perceive is entirely different from my perspective. You cannot up and leave. As for blackmail, forget it. Where would your family television show be if it were to leak out that you were trafficking immigrant children? Then there's your interfering with children from Sunday school. Ah, yes. I know everything; and everyone connected with you. I made it my business; you see.'

'Don't threaten me, Spannocs. I've enough to wash you up first. You've more to lose than me.'

Spannocs flicked his fingers. 'I don't think so . . . *Alfonse*.' The man was on his way to his table, the tray with the absinthe in his hand. 'Alfonse. Would you mind? This man is beginning to annoy me. Take him down and break his neck or something, will you?'

'A pleasure, sir.'

Alfonse placed the tray on the table lifted Bernard Ritchie up from the table and manhandled him enthusiastically to the top of a flight of concrete stairs below a sign reading FIRE EXIT. He lifted him up, turned him round, and kicked him down the steps. Following him to the bottom, he gathered up his unconscious and broken body and threw him out onto the side-walk where he lay like a rag-doll. He walked back up the steps interlocking his fingers in each hand, cracking the joints as he went.

Spannocs felt strangely ill at ease not able to understand why that tear kept coming back to him. Something was amiss and it had nothing to do with his conversation with Ritchie. Perhaps it was his inner soul. Normally he was not aware of it, switching his personality from one to the other with hardly any consciousness that it was happening. He felt as if he was two people. He would of course continue to enjoy his human pleasures this evening, worry about the other later.

The band was playing that infernal *Shaft* theme; the audience amply lubricated with drink were applying themselves enthusiastically to its rhythm. Aryan Farmers were still coming up to congratulate him. Shaking his hand. Thanking him for their successes. Patting him on the shoulders, their previous uncertainties gone. He was obviously still popular, in spite of what Ritchie had intimated. Tight lipped and with the slightest of acknowledgment to them; needing a change of scenery, he walked toward a group of hostesses that were congregating at one of the bars. Surrounded by men with personalities and manners that would not pull a hound in a dog pound, he ordered them away one at a time. They laughingly protested until they saw his face; made their excuses.

Alone with the girls, dressed in the scantiest of clothing. Harlots. They were a fantasists dream. Wearing theatrical costumes, thigh-length boots, they appealed to his sense of the dramatic. A Redheaded girl, that he was particularly fond, stood among three others.

She knew who he was, but he had tried this time round. He was better looking than usual. Blonde slick-backed hair tied into a ponytail with a black ribbon, his half-tanned skin and well-cut gray suit, marked him out. His lips still on the corpulent side, his tongue long; and no bad thing when it came to his performance of cunnilingus, she thought.

'What are you up to Ahriman?' she whispered continued, 'can I get you something pretty?'

Costumed as a Southern paddle ship's card sharp's good luck moll, her emerald green costume decked in baubles and fringes, with her hair piled high on her head appealed to him. A matching green choker with a pearl in its center completed her regalia. He smiled at her. A leering expression that would send a chill through any normal woman, but not her, for she came from the side-lines of another verse, a place overseen by their own Gods; she was not fazed.

'I should say that you could all get me something before the night ends,' he said looking round at the rest of the girls that had heard their conversation and were becoming interested.

'Think you're fit enough to pleasure all of us do you, Ahriman?'

He nodded his head up and down as an automaton. He had isolated Spannocs's mind, but not his animal instincts.

'How are you, Hilda? Haven't seen you since Eva Bron's bash – still sporting the plaited hair I see – sorry about the Fuhrer, but he was getting himself into deep water for even my ego to stand and go unchallenged. Don't tell Eva it was me that forced him to take that capsule.'

She smiled at him. Her waxed eyelashes gave a permanent expression of surprise.

A handmaiden from the Roman period interrupted them. Her hair blonde and ringed. A toga dress cut to her waist revealed the top half of her bust. She had been the lover of Pablo Sauno, the infamous torturer working on behalf of Pope Innocent I, and a temporary ally of his for his good works against Christians during that period.

'Don't listen to him and his over inflated prowess, girls. He's been crowing the same old story up and down millennia. I'd be surprised you could raise it at all after all these years.'

He laughed. 'I may not be able to—'

He stopped short, looked round. She was here, here among them. His sanctuary compromised, Ahriman was gone, and the girls knew it, leaving Spannocs alone.

Spannocs shook his head continuing where the Possessed Ahriman had left off. 'And you over there, what's your name? I haven't seen you before,' Spannocs said wondering what had happened to the last second. He was looking at the back of a girl dressed as a North American Indian. She had long black hair with a tribal war-band on the top of her head. Round her waist, a belt, slung with a hunting knife that he thought he had seen somewhere before.

Invisible to the world, Ahriman staggered towards a wall putting his hand out to steady himself. Part of his being was still Spannocs's; and although he still had his own powers, recovering from the transition, he realized that Spannocs had inherited more of him than he had intended. How long he would possess them, would only be a matter of time; he worried that they may be enough to save him from her initial attack once she saw him for who he was.

'She's not with us,' the Southern belle said. 'Are you, hon'?'

The Redhead turned to Spannocs. 'Someone from another past, perhaps? You try to keep secret, one of your previous conquests, *Ahriman?*' before stopping herself from saying anymore when she recognized it was not him.

He was trying to recall where he had seen a knife like that before.

She turned to face him, then looked sideways at the Red Indian.

'Mmm! Get her,' the handmaiden said. 'Playing it *cool*, are we *squa?*'

'Bitchy,' Spannocs said. 'There's plenty to go round.'

Hilda looked at the other girls and smiled.

'Yah, the big boy he's taking all four of us on maybe, yes!' she smiled. 'By the time he's taken two he'll be all burned out. One more is not going to make any difference to the rest of our pleasures I'm thinking, yah! We can always get them elsewhere later.'

They laughed at him but Spannocs was becoming anxious. He sensed things were not as they should be. 'Enough of all this talk. *Champagne!* Champagne for all. *Alfonse!*'

Alfonse looked up from the hospitality bar he was attending. '*Champagne*, Mr. Spannocs? Coming right up, sir! And for the ladies?' he asked; but the sisterhood misted away, until only the *squa* remained, then she too was gone. Alfonse rubbed his eyes, putting the disappearance down to drink.

Spannocs's sense of ill ease had not subsided. Something was amiss. Perhaps it had been that damned Ritchie. He would be dead, why was he concerned. He had not felt like this before.

Alfonse approached with a trolley of ice buckets with bottles sticking out from them, 'Champagne sir,' he said hesitantly. Looking at him he thought Spannocs's eyes were slanting at the corners, though, again, it must be drink; he had helped himself to one or two more than he should have. 'Your champagne—'

Spannocs turned and kicked the trolley over on its side. The bottles of champagne hitting the floor exploded spraying wine over those close by. People dancing immediately stopped to see what had happened. Like a ripple on a pond, it quickly spread to others until the band, playing *Campdown Races*, ceased, their instruments stopping one at a time, in various states of disarrayed notation until all fell silent. Everyone was of an expectation that something was to happen. Something serious.

He knew it. There could be no question in his mind. She had dematerialized, going through solid rock, to come again as an animate spirit from his past, albeit a different time. He needed to find her. He began attacking people dancing:

'Where are you *squa*, where the *fuck* are you? Show yourself!'

He pushed a couple into another couple, who in turn blamed them. The two men started to argue and turned to fighting. It quickly spread; the Diamond Center was becoming a battle zone. Some thought the cause was Spannocs running amok tried to restrain him, wrestling him to the floor, but they were no match for what he had become. A change they had never seen before. He was throwing them off him as if they were rag dolls, attacking them one after another.

They were beginning to realize the price they were paying for their depravity turning on him with a vengeance, hitting him with chairs and glasses; and anything else they could lay their hands on. Still he came at them, hitting out at them with his fists when he stopped. Some thought he was getting his breath back, but they were wrong. He strode back to where the harlots had been; a faint trace of her sitting on a stool was all he could see of her at first. When she materialized out from the dark matter, he saw her fist tight wrapped round the handle of that knife.

Ahriman fought for control of himself; but drawn back to his host by his remains that his form was absent and needed if he were to break from this verse to save himself. He took another option. One that might destroy Giuseppi, as it did the one before.

'*You!*' He screamed. His voice boomed in the night as from the inside of a forest. The word vibrated the crystal chandeliers above bringing part of the plastered ceiling crashing down to the floor. Silence, utter soundless. He stared at her, '*Who – are – you?*'

Those that were still conscious tried to escape. They stumbled round falling over each other. Their faces featureless. If anyone minded to notice, they would have seen their watches had stopped. Time for them no longer had any relevance. Darkness enveloped them with a blanket of suffocation that the predawn of the universe was familiar.

She turned to face him. Her voice deep, echoed as a boom of thunder:

'*I'M YOUR NEMESIS, AHRIMAN. DON'T YOU KNOW ME?*'

'You have mistaken me for another,' he said. 'For I am, *Frederik Spannocs! PRINCE OF DARKNESS! THE CHOSEN ONE.* Did no-one tell you? Your Master. He's gone. And *YOU!* . . . *YOU!* . . . Are a freak from a cave, the *Mother of All Harlots*; your powers are useless against me.'

Her statuesque half movement came toward him. He turned and walked away. He had no need to take her out. Time verse would see to that. The download to shift between them was his. He could step into it and out of it, leaving her in this place, as a tired, earth-bound angel to face her fate alone. To age and fade away as all mortals will. He laughed the laugh of an audience watching six dozen clowns in a marching circle, kicking the one in front up the arse; blaming the one behind.

'*NO! IT IS YOU WHO ARE POWERLESS . . .*'

Her voice resonated from her mouth into the walls of the building. A shining blade in her hand hanging in front of Ahriman's face shook him rigid with the realization that his powers were not what he thought they were, left him frozen where he stood.

'*MY KIND SHALL FOREVER BE YOUR NEMESES,* for I am one of the *SEVEN ANGELS OF WORMWOOD: HIS ASSASSINATOR!*'

Fitch ran to the door of the Diamond Center. He was immediately constrained by a security guard who hearing the rumpus upstairs, quickly released him to see what was going on.

God this is some party. Whatever are they on up there? Fitch said to himself running after the guy. Sensing something wrong, he looked back. A fireball that came from nowhere roared after him cutting off any chance of his going back. *Oh, no*, he said to himself, *The last moments of my dying day are upon me*, he said to himself looking for some means of escape before the heat overwhelmed him. A ticket entrance door, a corridor to his left, was open. Sidestepping into it, he watched the fireball turn the security man in front of him to ash. His black form frozen, for less than a second, before it disintegrated into dust falling to the steps.

*   *   *

A flashlight illumination that appeared to come from a camera caught Spannocs in the face, his eyes reflecting a trace of his Possessor. Within a split of time known physics was not yet able to measure, came an explosion of magnitude energy. With Spannocs and Ahriman one, and with the confusions of minds, sensing that portion of time remaining neither able to react within it, the angel's knife came down slicing a piece of his arm away. The leached fluid that should have been blood black and thick; burned into the floor giving off an odor of acridity. In a moment of time still available, they were gone.

The security man, having shifted into another time, entered the dance hall, seeing what was going on turned, taking the stairs three at a time in a bid to escape ran back down after sensing the imminent collapse of the building, fell instead dead from an apparition of mist that entered his body before exiting out the other side, and would have done the same to Fitch but for more luck than judgement. Fitch came from the ticket office, hesitated, returned to its safety. Something had gone past him temporarily interfering with his vision that might have pre-emptied a migraine attack if he was having one, which he was not, as he watched the man collapsing on the stairs into a heap of burning clothing and flesh. All that remaining, liquid mush in a suit, leaked down the steps.

Ha-Shem, Adonai, Fitch murmured, relieved he had avoided a second fate.

With a population of 6500, the town of Becland in the State of Ohio; with the intensity of another sun, that quadrant portion of the earth shook the shook with an intensity of two stars colliding; became a white explosion of heat, leaving every living soul between the ages of one second and infinite years incinerated where they stood or lay. The top blew off the gold tube leaving the scroll inside charred remains. When the second pass came, earth time defaulted to its norm leaving people to wonder later what had happened to some of their population; why some had perished when others had not.

When a mixture of dark matter, matter, and anti- – what O'Hare was later to learn being the equivalent of a mini 'big-bang' – unable to re-occupy its space in any time, expanded, giving reason to the theory as to why the universe kept getting bigger; or, as O'Hare was to later comment his version of the scientific theory: *The genie, once out of its bottle, is too fat to return, so it can't.*

Twenty Eight – 1997

THE NEWS REPORT interrupted O'Hare's left foot toe-tapping the floor pan of the car he was driving in time to Frank Sinatra singing along with the Count Basie orchestra, *My Kind Of Girl*, on KTSU 90.9 FM from Houston, Texas when he slammed the brakes on skewing the car to a halt, stalling the engine.

'Not now, please, God. No!' he said banging his head on the steering wheel.

'Charlie, you'll get us killed,' Carter said picking up her laptop that had slipped forward out into the floor well between her feet.

'Listen! They're talking about Becland.'

. . . the Becland Diamond Conference Center was hosting a private party when it exploded. Emergency crews are moving into the area, but reports coming into us say that the Highway into Becland, no longer serviceable, is hampering them in their efforts. We have not, yet, been able to find any witnesses to substantiate this news report. A police statement issued at 1245 said that they have put traffic restrictions in force that include a 30-mile exclusion zone to air traffic. Relatives can contact the authorities by phone . . .

'*Hamilton!*' was Carter's next words.

O'Hare re-started the Chevrolet, pushed the pedal to the floor and gunned the motor along Interstate 30 East Highway towards Becland in a state of anxious desperation.

The realization in his mind that Fitch might no longer be with them after having gone into the building brought him panic turning to terror. Why should he be alive when so many others were dead? Once more, an O'Hare had survived while a Weinberg had perished serving the Bureau. The thought came into his head that he was going to have to pass to the last of their line, the aged, infirm, and bitter Sarah Weinberg, the news.

Arriving they got out of the car and looked up at the building. All the windows had been blown out. Large cracks in its exterior fabric ran to the ground threatening to topple what remained.

'Sorry sir.' the armed Marine said. 'No-one's allowed in. Orders of the State Governor.'

'Sorry soldier. This is my case. Stand aside,' O'Hare said holding his warrant ID out.

'And the lady?'

'She's my sister. Come on, Annie.'

Hardly daring to believe that Fitch could be among this carnage they went in. There were bodies, and parts, strewn over what had been a dance hall. O'Hare, not wanting to move in case he stepped on the remains of Fitch, hesitated. Carter nodded at him and took the lead. With a flashlight in her hand, they went carefully across the floor looking at heads that had faces; and some that didn't, searching for any they knew, both knowing it would only be one. All round them were charred remains. Carter took a cross and chain from her handbag, held it towards the scene, closed her eyes and genuflected.

'No good praying for any of these. They were souls lost well before we ever came here, Sister,' O'Hare said angry.

'Habit,' she replied putting it away before carrying on with the search. 'In the event the evil is still hovering.'

The skin on some of the bodies was perforated; tightened black across what remained. Framed bones of one fell to dust when O'Hare touched it with his boot, instantly pulling it back in horror. He had never experienced a man's rib-cage fall in on itself before. The hair on some heads had melted like pitch tar. Stuck to exposed skulls looking like freshly painted black gloss paint still wet. O'Hare was getting more and more despondent. Everyone they came across would be one less before the inevitable remains of who, he had come to regard as his *son*, would offer himself up as a further victim. He wondered if this were how a nuclear war would end the world. He should have brought in the Geiger counter out of the car when he arrived. Not that it would have protected them. They had come through a rain of debris falling from the skies. A useless piece of information telling them the amount of Becquerel's their system's had ingested before they died from radiation poisoning.

Carter recognizing the look of a man on the verge of trauma by bad news quietly said to him:

'Pray Charlie and keep looking. We'll find him.'

He was not convinced that prayer would be of any use. Another useless gesture of faith. '*Hmmm!* It's not finding him that's bothering me; he's here somewhere. The problem I have is the Catholic keeps floating to the surface, while the Jew sinks; the O'Hare's keep living, while the Weinberg's perish. A familial curse.'

If this was his philosophy, she found it contemptible; as to his feelings of him being responsible, she angrily said, 'It's Satan's curse on us; not yours.'

He looked admonished, and she felt pity for him. She moved away to continue their unhappy quest when, glad of the distracted interruption, something caught her attention. '*Charlie!* Come take a look at this.'

Please no, he thought to himself.

'Look at that. That's some knife isn't it? Is that its handle shimmering, look? And what is that alongside of it, meat, bread?'

'Don't touch it,' he said. Carefully picking it up with his handkerchief, the shimmer from the handle faded before his eyes as if he had earthed it. There was a small piece of flesh on the floor where it had been. Part of an arm hacked off. He remembered Tony D'Sotto carrying such an injury. He also recalled who owned a knife like this. He looked about him. Seeing what he was looking for, he strode with purpose to the other end of the building and began studying a gaping hole in an outside wall. It was smoldering round its edges. He reasoned what had happened here saying to himself, 'It's as if she's gone straight through after him,' he said feeling the broken plaster and brickwork; 'taking a piece of his arm off first.'

'*Who?* Who are you talking about, Charlie?'

He looked at her standing beside him. 'You know who. She was up his *arse*; and this is Armageddon's beginnings, so it is.'

Trapped behind the wall of the Guys and Dames washroom Fitch had problems. He had not been able to release his arms. A roll of toilet tissue that had been against one wall was jammed across his mouth preventing him from crying out for help. The opposite wall pushed hard up against him from the explosion prevented him from moving his head. He had had enough listening to this *Charlie O'Hare* going on and on and how he was going to broach the subject of his demise with his grandmother. With one mighty effort he kicked at what remained of the wall from his legs, blew the roll from his mouth and screamed out:

Emergency teams, as well as the FBI and CIA arrived. O'Hare passed on his findings, organized them as to what they should do. Government forensic operatives in blue suits and masks were bagging up body parts, taking photographs, filming; all with an ease, to Fitch, that they had done similar before.

'Damn,' O'Hare said catching his foot on an object he failed to notice lying on the floor as they were leaving.

'What is it?' Carter asked.

'Think I've stubbed my toe on a brick.'

From the air, Becland looked like a war zone. Fitch asked O'Hare if any of this was avoidable if they had acted sooner. O'Hare replied that he doubted it adding, 'If the authorities had listened to me twenty years ago it might have been.' He went on. 'There's going to be a need for a cover-up, you know that don't you.'

'*Why?*'

'Well, apart from us being at world's end, there not being anyone round to buy your paper, a meteor would have hit Becland, with questions asked where it came from and how it managed to evade the eyes of astronomers, which is going to cause the government to keep its cards close for damage limitation purposes. The possibility of this being a nuclear strike by a foreign power with our likely retaliation being foremost in the public's mind. And if there should be anyone round to buy your paper, the government would have written your story for you. It will say that 300-odd people died. And that'll be it. Silence.'

'And how'd you imagine they're going to get away with 300 as an answer for something that had caused so much damage?' Fitch asked.

'An act of mercy by the Lord! That should sucker most. They'll ring fence it with a hundred mile exclusion zone. No-one leaving or entering. Likely declaring dangerous levels of radiation.'

'Like Chernobyl,' Fitch said sarcastically.

'Exactly like Chernobyl, only unlike Becland, Ukraine had a nuclear reactor to blame it on.'

Twenty Nine – 1997

Two loves I have of comfort and despair,
Which like two spirits do suggest me still:
The better Angel is a man right fair,
The worser spirit a woman, coloured ill.

Sonnet 130: SHAKESPEARE:

O'HARE DECIDED TO INVESTIGATE administrative (annex ii-38) section pen.gov from a distance. A government department that size handling the United States pension's service was not only above suspicion; but had security second to none. No-one seeking a life of anonymity and obscurity could find a better home. Whether you were FBI, CIA, or the President himself, access to the building without authorization was nigh impossible. An extremely well thought out piece of subterfuge in the choosing of such an establishment could not have been bettered for those wishing to hide their activities. How could he, how could anyone, turn up and expect to walk in asking for people by name that had always been denied; but that he may be able to recognize, on the pretext that they were not bureaucrats or public servants, but career criminals with an agenda that was protecting a weirdo child trafficker for a prize that physicists would die for. He would be asking to have his American citizenship stripped from him and deported to Ireland for his trouble. He had sought the man that attempted to kill him buried in its bowels that knew his former police rank and name, before apologizing for shooting him. Daniel Sullivan. Whatever this man was planning, along with others; bearing in mind what was occurring, was clearly coming to a head.

He had never been able to admit, even to himself, that there were such people as those he imagined that had the authority to walk corridors of governance with power of life over death. To say nothing of how such a secret organization managed to conceal itself for so long. Since he and Frank Weinberg first started to investigate child abuse, they little realized that bad research involving investigating the paranormal was taking place. Summoning up spirits from another world was never going to be good news if those concerned did have the moral justification. It was clear that this Order had connections with the Teutonic Knights, giving them the potential to access ancient records held in the Vatican's Secret Library; no doubt passed to them by complicit priests, nuns, and others currently members of the Knights today. That would take the Order back at least 1000 years. Before that, at the time of the Carpenter of Nazareth's crucifixion, all manner of sects became established, one, the Order's likely predecessor. In an attempt to bring some sense of order after having seen what amounted to an alien standing over the body of an executed Christ, in the tomb of Joseph of Arimathaea before their faith in the coming of a messiah speculated from witness evidence that it was the Divine Spirit; may well have set some on the road to speculate what it could tell them if they interrogated such a creature, person, spirit, or *alien*. Times passed would not necessarily have made them any less intelligent than those of us today. The basis for such sightings would have needed the writing of the New Testament to bring order to troubled minds by writers of the day. Matthew, Mark, Luke, and John, to mention but a few.

The one small clue as to those inspired to run with this two millennium baton. The one chink in an otherwise perfect undercover operation was when Sullivan's partner, Nathaniel Johnson, arrogantly asked Frank to return his rotor arm. That one slip, occurring to him later, had condemned Frank to death. Selected to oversee the Seaburg inquiry into the affairs of Mayor James Walker because of his other pet hate: corruption, Frank had given them the perfect opportunity to take him out putting Cosa Nostra in the frame for it.

The realization that our own people had a team; that were in the business of bringing a spirit world to earth; financed from the suffering of minors with the detriment to human life a consequence, made him sick; that such people might use the excuse: end justifying the means, to sleep nights; would put Satan himself in depravity's shadow.

Since returning from Becland, he had difficulty in sleeping. For the last seventy years, the memory of two small children had particularly haunted him. Even though he knew she was more than a ghost in his head, he, could still not be sure it was not Irinushka, the daughter of the Mihalyvich's. He had assumed it was, as they never saw her again after they raided Giuseppi's house to rescue her from the atrocities against her and other children there. To discover such crimes had been a fluke; one he was still having trouble bearing the memory of after seeing such instruments of torture. His searing revenge for what they had done, he had had to bury deep within himself if he were to retain any sanity to being them to book. If by some divine intervention she had become the angel, she certainly did not look like any six-year-old grown to maidenhood that he was familiar. If she wasn't Irinushka, then an angel had come to earth, causing havoc to the human race seeking out Giuseppi, bringing heaven or hell down round them.

When she had needed sanctuary from chasing Giuseppi, Spannocs, or whatever he's calling himself it had clearly taken something from her that she needed to recover or re-generate. She would have found it too; had some idiot of a mercenary not decided to abduct her. Whatever Giuseppi had paid for his services was not worth his losing his head over. Unable to return to that particular retreat due to its structural damage and leaky roof; a headless war hero a clue that it had been her if one was needed; she was after Giuseppi with a vengeance.

He had often wondered to himself why he had used the female gender where an angel was concerned. All he could say on the matter was that it was because she looked female. Which he supposed was fair enough. He had never questioned before that she was anything other after all, it was perfectly normal for humans to put pins in pin boxes, and buttons in button boxes. All shades of skin tone; Jew, Catholic, Muslim; male, female; heterosexual, homosexual; angel, and demon. Of course, if she were the daughter of the Mihalyvich's she would be female. Why should any elevation to the divine alter that? Or had she had attained a plane where it was no longer a requirement. Would that follow for the rest of us too? Again, it was always going to be difficult to talk of someone that did not have a sex gender. Not without it sounding disrespectful and cold. She deserved that much at least, assuming she cared for human feelings any longer.

She never did show feelings or compassion toward him. An emotion, if she had once been one of us, would no longer be a requirement. A piece of ineffectual human baggage in the world of souls. Although, that did not necessarily follow, for she had the capacity for violence. Seventy years she had left Giuseppi in peace. Why had she decided that he was earth's public enemy number one now? And not before time. He guessed with Giuseppi's bash in Becland, that she invited herself (it was the knife that synched it, that and a piece of his suit material sticking to a large slice of flesh found on the dance floor forensically matching the waistcoat he had not worn that evening recovered from the wardrobe of his house) and taken the fight to another level. A level that would destroy the world.

Better late than never; better never late, one of his mother's sayings. *Don't leave child abuse in the hands of authorities to act against*, His.

He laughed quietly to himself. The same dream, for all these years and she had shown neither acceptance nor rejection: love, hate, happiness, or indifference toward him. Continually with him. She kept coming. Taking something from him. All he had to offer her were his opinions based on a long life of experience. Which ones? All of them, some of them; discarding others. He could not be sure, except when she departed, she left him exhausted with temporal thoughts playing over in his mind. He supposed that he should be honored that he was the object of her attention, being able to provide what she needed. A stand-in surrogate God.

Sweet Mother of Jesus, any other Irishman would get a leprechaun for luck, what do I get? A *bloody* angel!

Two am. He decided to get himself up out of bed. Sleep was going to be out of the question there was far too much going on inside his head. He put on his dressing-gown and slippers and made his way into his study. There at least he could take his mind off her. He would read. An early morning nightcap, perhaps, to dull an overactive brain. He poured himself a whiskey and sat in his armchair. Turning on his reading lamp he put his feet on the table and picked up a copy of the English Civil War. Opening it to its book mark on page 297. He took two mouthfuls of liquor and settling himself down began reading:

With the arrival of spring 1651, the English turned their attention once more to Limerick reopening their siege . . .

'. . . *bloody English!*' he said unable to concentrate.

Feeling that he should have got up earlier, he would not have gone through all these thoughts that he had gone through time and time again. He looked at the page of print before him and set the book down. He would have liked to share what he knew with someone else.

It would have made her haunting of him more tolerable. Like a wife perhaps. But it was not to have been. The only other woman he had ever wanted to marry was Sarah Weinberg.

And they speak of the luck of the Irish!

Tears began to well up in his eyes and a shiver went down his spine. The dream or the reality of her was arriving in his soul to pick him over. *Where do you think all this is heading?* His voice had a hollow ring in the semi-darkness. *Don't you ever stop to consider your actions? Aren't you accountable to someone? We* fooking *well are!*

'YOU'RE GOING TO DESTROY THE WORLD! DAMN YOU!' he said out loud.

He was angry and sweating. His throat had a burning sensation. He spoke again.

'Not everyone in the world is a child abuser. Couldn't you settle for those you took out in Becland? Are you on a crusade for your own personal salvation or, for, *His* will?'

He went quiet. He had been through this emotional roller coaster before, each time it had taken more from him. Whatever she took from him, was wearing him down, until she killed him off only to resurrect him with life anew. He feared immortality more than death.

'Are you listening to me, lady? How much longer?'

His voice carried out into the half-light of the room before stilling; an awareness that he was talking to himself came over him. His breathing rate that had increased with his anger was beginning to abate. His heart-rate returning to normal if you were in your twenties – but *117!* She was:

'Damned well keeping me alive,' he shouted, swearing under his breath as she left him, screamed out after her, 'I can drink meself to death you know! I'm from a race of people well adept in the art!'

She was gone. Whatever she had come for, she had taken from him, and sleep would come easy to him.

The entity! He's trying to stop her! They are going to capture it as I first thought!

The idea she had implanted in his head hit him as a bomb-shell.

Early morning still dark. The latest special edition of the *New York Post* was put to bed (probably for the last time). A thin pink newsprint copy. Free. For this was the government's response for civil order. With the clock ticking down to human annihilation its banner headline, composed by Max Stenna himself, the *Post*'s editor-in-chief read:

KEEP CALM,

EMBRACE YOUR DIGNITY,

AND REFLECT.

WE – *ARE* – AMERICANS;

GOD'S CHOSEN PEOPLE

With its by-lines:

THE GREATEST NATION OF PERSONS

EVER TO HAVE IMPRESSED THE EARTH

WITH THEIR FEET

In view of the current situation, O'Hare had at long last agreed to allow Fitch to see his grandfather's version of events from that day in

1920. With a probability that there was nothing to lose by allowing him to read both he Frank Weinberg's versions of events, he had handed it over.

Fitch took the opportunity of reading and taking notes from the manuscript that he had before him. He would not accept an inevitability that the end of the world was at hand, but in case . . .

Lost in thought over the notes and statements made by his grandfather and father; and to a lesser extent, those of O'Hare (his views, expressed verbally to him more than occasionally had been consigned to memory), he failed to notice a white suited assailant come up on him. His shirt sleeves rolled up the needle going in his arm had been easy. He shouted clutching at the scratch, but the effectiveness of the drug came home immediately. Collapsing unconscious he toppled from the office chair onto the floor. A second man, similarly, dressed helped the first drag Fitch from the *Post*'s offices. Coming round several hours later he sensed he was in a plane. A second scratch to his arm and he was unconscious once more.

O'Hare had taken the call on his way to collect Fitch. The President had agreed that he, Fitch, and Carter should attend the meeting of the National Council planned for the following day at the Pentagon.

'Who the hell is this and how did you get my number?'

'Oh Charlie, I'm disappointed in you. Did you think we were amateurs? The point is your angel is on the loose. How she managed to get herself out of that mine, well, she did and Spannocs underestimated her abilities. Not to worry, it won't alter anything.'

'Well, whoever you are, you're clearly worried over something otherwise what other reason would you call me up, unless it's to chew the fat over the old days, Nathaniel.'

O'Hare taking an educated guess plucked a name from the air from a list of suspects with the power to support Spannocs in whatever they were involved; and the only other one of two, excluding Spannocs himself with mortality equal to his own.

'You're very good Charlie. You haven't lost it.'

'What'd you want?'

'We have Fitch, or should I say, Weinberg. I would like to say that Giuseppi doesn't hold a grudge against the Jew, unfortunately, he does. You see it was either the Weinberg's wiped from the face of the earth or the O'Hare's. Personally, I was in favour of the latter, running backwards and forwards to Ireland was always going to be a challenge to take out a few bog villagers for you to see the point and back off. But it wouldn't have made any difference. Your Sarah Weinberg is testament to the care you showed her family. Have you seen her lately by the way? Oh yes, sorry, I forgot, she won't have anything to do with you anymore. I wonder why that should be. She's a broken woman, Charlie, and she blames you.'

'Don't try and turn the situation round, putting guilt on me for what you and your fellow perverts have been wallowing in all these years. My conscience is clear. As for my background, you should have done your homework more thoroughly. My family were farmers from Wexford County; and the real reason you didn't take me out was my father's connections with Tammany. They would have destroyed you along with Marco Giuseppi if anything had happened to me. You couldn't take that chance. Local Mafia, who knowing a son of theirs from Sicily had crossed the crime line, would have joined forces with Tammany to curb his activities. So get on with whatever it is you want to say, because whatever happens to Weinberg, you and your outfit of sickos are dead men walking.'

There was an interval. O'Hare was well aware that as long as they had Fitch hostage there was not much anyone could do. All he had was threats. When Johnson answered, it was with confidence as to what they were.

'Fine words admirably put Charlie; but of no consequence to the people I represent. There is a bigger picture here. When we speak of end justifying means, it's well meant; and to the business in hand; and the President's options to pull the world back from the brink of a nuclear winter that will see nothing living left on earth for the coming 10,000 years except cockroaches and yourself, for I count you among that Dictyoptera.'

'I've seen enough to form an opinion as to what your happy band of mad-men is. You think that you can capture a spirit—'

'Not any spirit, Charlie.'

'God's Divine Spirit. You think you can summon up and capture what is out there without a fight. You've seen the destruction that an angel and Spannocs have caused in doing that. Oh yes, Nathan. That was something you hadn't planned for. A little bird told me what Spannocs tried to do with her and a mine in Cheyne County. She wasn't supposed to emerge from that one was she. Except she did, and you've a problem. You can't expose Spannocs with her on the loose. Or, wait a second; it's not Spannocs is it? It's what possesses him that's of interest here.'

'The most feared and deadliest in the universe, you're right on. And he knows you. And there's a deal on offer here. The chance to take your immortality beyond the realms of a chained earth of knowledge into one of expansive understanding. Have you any idea what that can mean? The secrets of creation, time, multiverses, all revealed in spectacular Technicolor. Secrets that man has always dreamed and we have it within our power to deliver. What'd you say? Won't you join us?'

'What then for man, when he knows everything, put their feet up and pour a beer. You and your egg-heads don't get it do you? You've no idea what you're getting yourselves into. Have any of you given a single thought as to what you are playing with here? Two opposing spirits. You've seen the devastation that one and a minor can do, what'd you think is going to happen when Creation locks horns with a cloven hoofed meddler?'

'But they've met; nothing happened.'

'They have, I'll grant you that, but the devil has managed to conceal himself. You are being taken for a ride by a known deceiver. He's not only going to see you mad-men off, he's going to take the rest of us with you. Let me tell you a story. One that was too hot to be included in the Bible because of its God-fearing manifesto limiting our options when it came to sin. Written 500 years after the death of Christ. I can't use Bible- speak but it refers to the Divine Spirit. God's enforcer. Roughly translated it reads, if you've stepped out of line, you go through him head first. By the time he's finished prodding you with red-hot pokers, pulling your bowels out forming them into a tail, tearing your lying tongue out with pliers, breaking every bone in your body until you look like a demon, you'll then be ready to join all other transgressors in hell. And lest ye forget, Satan did not build the place, God did. The black angel was expelled there. So think on. Have you been a good boy, Nathaniel?'

'Fairy tales. I'm sorry for you, Charlie. Unfortunately for your team the powers that be have sold our research to the President. And he believes it is our job to save the planet; his option, at any cost including Satan over its destruction of mankind appeals.'

'And it'll be my job to bring you in whether that happens or not?'

'And with no law to back you.'

'I'll kill you!'

Thirty – 1997

JUDAEA–CHRISTIAN BIBLE, HAHUM Ch. 1, v. 2

THE PRESIDENT read the remaining confirmation handed to him by his Pentagon aide; for the first time since his inauguration, felt the full weight of responsibility of office.

> . . . as well as which, our submarines have uploaded programs from the mother computer to all her children instructing them to begin counting down for a Doomsday scenario for 12 hours as at 2105.15 GMT.

His hand was shaking as he read the order that was of his own making. His choices were narrowing. 'Very good, and I suppose mother will smack their bums should they disobey her . . . tell me Peter, how is it that British intelligence are light years ahead of us when it comes to US naval shipping movements . . . forget that? Doomsday minus twelve, eh!' He took his railroad watch and chain from his claret colored waistcoat pocket. A gold Rolex passed down to his father, who in turn had it passed from his; winding up with himself. He reached for his glasses from his desk holding them up to his eyes. 'Eleven hours, 55. *Shit!* That's hardly time to have a decent dump,' he said biting his thumb hard on its side.

'Of course, that will need to be agreed by the Security Council –

retrospectively in this case. It may not be to their liking. Here's the box. Are you sure about this sir?'

A tin box put together by John F. Kennedy, for such an event as Henry Clancy found himself. NOAH'S ARK contained printed documents requiring no more than a signature for the saving of time. When you've only four minutes, what's the point in wasting them? An order for any remaining missiles to target American soil: a modern slant on the salt-earth policies carried out against ancient countries by foreign invaders preventing them from growing crops after they had left (if America were to go down in a nuclear holocaust, the North American continent would be unavailable for any take-away business). He hovered over the last page of the protocol, a gold fountain pen in his hand its top dangling from his lips. As Commander-in-Chief, he had ultimate power to override the National Security Council – *in writing*. Though, what use that would be when the world had destroyed itself was lost on him. The more gung-ho of his military leaders, expecting him to pronounce an immediate nuclear strike, regardless of what those idiots were up to in Alaska, would not hang round for any of this twelve hour nonsense, but would, metaphorically have their helmets on, fingers inserted up their arse holes; likely taken to their bunkers. What he had been unable to get his head round was the nature of all this destruction. Becland. Well, that may have been a one-off, not a town of any particular significance. Why should seismic activity begin there before moving on to Russia, China, Iran, North Korea, Israel, and Palestine? This couldn't be anything other than design, surely. If some crackpot's mindset were to seek earth's annihilation, they certainly knew the right people to involve; he would be playing into their hands if he were not careful. His decision making faculties with the consequence of getting them wrong shifted up a gear in his mind. His finger was on the button, perhaps he should let it hover awhile. The choice offered, with circumstances the way they were, agreeing to *Oceans Galactica* offer of help; that they had an answer, if it did mean criminals were involved, was blackmail for sure, but until a better solution presented itself, he would run with them.

'Of course I'm not,' he said angrily. 'Perhaps someone else could be persuaded to make that decision instead of me . . . *eh!*'

He searched his logic for a third way out of this mess. He scratched a brief note under his signature blotting the ink dry. All he had to do was have his meeting with the Security Council and tell them what he had done. And if his logic did not kick in, what did he have as an alternative.

He reached across for the purple phone from among the rainbow spectrum of others, telling his waiting war gaming programmers to stand-by for further instructions. He asked his secretary to put him through to the British Prime Minister.

'*David Monkswood*, sir. I have Henry for you,' Ross said.

Taking the phone from his secretary, he told Monkswood that he intended to align their computer time clocks to launch a full scale first-strike on those countries one minute before the Russian deadline.

'I shall, of course, honor the alliance made after the Second World War of defending London, Ottawa, Canberra, and Wellington from any hostile attack before any other. A feeble gesture, I know.'

'Thank you Henry. I was hoping it would not come to that, but I can see any other alternative as down to zero,' Monkswood replied. 'You are of course aware that New York was part of that post-war alliance.'

He knew that, and a single tear welled up in his right eye and ran down his cheek for its knowing. He would not brush it away. 'Confidentially, David . . . do you think there is any possibility that earth could be under an alien attack instead of something man-made?

I could cope with this better if it were.' There was silence. 'That'll be a no then.'

He thanked him for all that the United Kingdom had done for America with their special relationship, blessed the country's Queen, and quietly said, 'Goodbye David, may God go with you.'

David Monkswood replaced his telephone, and made a note in his diary:

> I have never before come across such a true statesman as the 42nd President of America, the man known as Henry Clancy Montgomery III. One with Christian values; and that this world would be hard put to replace; under such pressure that would resort to make a statement, with the sincerity that he had; in the hope that earth was under an alien invasion instead of one from another human's hand.
>
> DAVID MONKSWOOD, Prime Minister, UK.

As President of a country, Henry Clancy Montgomery III, would ordinarily go out of his way to appease the nations of the world to get the message across, that America was, though not always in its past, a respecter of secularity and race. This was to fall on deaf ears. What should have helped the President in his ambition to take the heat from a likely nuclear attack was the counter value destruction on homeland America itself in order to convince them of his sincerity. To demonstrate to Russia and China of his commitment he had directed missiles on three major cities in America. They acknowledged his stance but could not promise a peaceful resolution to hold off because of it. New York was to be part of that package of his policy for self-destruction. Putting that forward as a promissory solution to the Security Council as his intent would see blood on the carpet; literally, his.

Carter was half through a cheeseburger when her cell-phone rang. She had ignored advice from FBI security staff of a volatile situation that was developing on the streets. She figured that with the world on the brink of destruction, the last people to turn the lights off and close the doors would be a multinational business; no doubt having their own arrangements for the safety of their customers. She had queued for fifteen minutes in a line at the drive-thru with other like-minded people, no doubt, she reckoned like her, wondering where their next meal would come from.

The caller was Father Milligan and he sounded over-wrought.

'You aren't going to believe this.' He had not waited for her to ask. 'She's back with us. Her that's caused all of this. I'm going to have to give her up, they're threatening—'

At that point, the signal between the two phones failed. She thought she heard him mutter . . . *like a* fucking *homing pigeon,* but she was sure she was wrong. Throwing the remains of her burger into a trashcan, she called O'Hare telling him the angel had returned to Meacham, and that she would have to go there first.

The Bell helicopter touched down onto the lawn of the Roman Catholic Research Center for Christian Science; or rather, that part of the building unaffected by the bomb planted in its foyer; not dressed in scaffolding and sheeting awaiting rebuilding completion. An ugly crowd were gathering round its perimeter at its landing.

'Can you stay?' Carter shouted to the pilot over the noise of its engines.

He cut the rotors to a slow chop.

'No, too dangerous. Think they want me plane. Call the emergency number and I'll come back for you then.'

He had a Glock in his hand as he was speaking waving it toward the side screen in the event that someone tried to sneak up on him.

She nodded, knowing that if things took a turn for the worse, he would not be able to pick her up at all, leaving her invitation as special envoy at the Pentagon in jeopardy; and O'Hare to convince them of what was happening, and why, without any benefit of her religious input to help him. She thanked the pilot and closed the door. He lifted off before she had time to get fully clear. The down draught took her breath away.

The mob, seeing it take to the skies, decided to take it out on her, and began pelting her with stones from outside the razor-wire fence. Armed security watching her run toward the building threatened them by firing over their heads holding them at bay for long enough for her to get to the entrance door. Milligan was holding it open for her. He slammed it shut and locked it as she went in. She was breathless and turned to face him. Smiling at first, her expression changed when she saw the look on his face; he was not the same man. He was unshaven, disheveled, with all outward appearances of a man that had started down the road to unfaithfulness. He was a mess. Her normally respectful manner toward him changed as a result.

She spoke angrily to him. 'I hope to Christ you haven't done anything stupid, Father.' Her call to O'Hare confirmed what she had thought from the beginning. He reckoned, as did she, that the angel had not yet finished with this business. Her safety was in their hands.

Milligan's expression was one of bemusement. She had never spoken to him in this manner before and it had taken him off guard. He walked off in the direction of the laboratory muttering, expecting her to follow. She did.

The room smelled of fresh paint. The light was dimmed fluorescent blue (was that an improvement, she thought). She saw the gurney with the angel lying on it and she despaired. Reaching into her shoulder bag, she took out her rosary and attached it to her skirt belt. She did not know why she had gone to the trouble, but when she had left the convent, she had a clip studded onto it by a leather-smith for such a purpose. She dropped to her knees and bowed her head fingering the beads. Aptly, it was a Wednesday and prayers for the Descent of the Holy Spirit were in order; this was getting more and more bizarre. 'Was she like this when she came here?' she said to him.

Milligan was playing with his fingers. He shrugged but did not answer. He hoped she did not think he had done this to her.

Carter wrapped her fingers round the angel's wrist and gently caressed it as if to pass life to her. Although death was not their original conclusion for the state they had first encountered her, she certainly looked as if she had succumbed.

'God, what's happened to you,' Carter whispered.

She looked ghastly. Her skin, tight to her skeleton (she assumed that was what it was, so corrupted was it), was torn away like paper that had got wet. Crow black bruising round her eyes, shoulders, and arms gave the impression she might have gone ten rounds with a professional boxer with hands tied behind her back. She remembered that when the three of them had seen that impression in the wall at the Diamond Centre, O'Hare assumed it was hers. By the state of her now, he may not have been wrong in that for estimation. If her endeavours to put down this evil had done this to her, it had come at some cost. They had not given it a second thought at the time as to what damage she would be doing to herself. It was plain now. The realisation came to Carter that spirits in the world of matter were as susceptible when it came to violence as mortals. And if she was not hard-wired for self-restoration or self-resurrection, she was as doomed as the rest of us. Death with corruption to dust of the body its inevitability. She looked up at Milligan and wiped the tears that had run down her cheeks. 'How long did you say she's been here?'

'Found her this morning. I stayed overnight. With all this going on, I had nowhere else to go . . . apart from which . . . well, you know, there are *fucking* armed mobs walking the streets looking for any excuse to attack people that might be responsible for what has gone on. Throwing bricks and stones at windows, well, you saw for yourself. They beat up one of our security men trying to prevent them storming the building; they would have killed him too, had not a response unit shot two of them dead. What have we *fucking* come to, Sister? This is a Catholic institution supposedly bringing science to faith.'

Thought I heard him right when he spoke of homing pigeons.

'I don't mind telling you, I no longer hold onto the beliefs I once did Sister. Dressed as we are, we're open targets to those that would do us harm.'

She was annoyed at Milligan. Turning his back on his faith; admitting that he did not want to be dressed as he was in public until she remembered that her own clothes for the Carmelite Order were in her shoulder bag. She had not given it a second thought since she had first got involved in all of this. 'Look, can you stay with her a little longer, Father?'

'Until they break in, and start attacking—'

'*What is it?*' Carter startled.

He was looking down at the angel pointing, 'She's . . . *changing!* Look!'

Carter stared down, fearing what changes he was speaking. She put her hand to her mouth. Her skin, previously showing signs of ageing was processing to that of a new-born baby without the accompanying puppy fat. The translucency of the epidermis showed clearly blood vessels, previously unseen, and to all intents and purposes, non-existent. Non-functioning before, they were now pumping life-giving oxygen saturated blood round her body. All signs of bruising and tearing to the body appeared to be repairing. Looking down at her navel, she thought she could make out the faint trace of the formations of male and female organs, but after looking closer guessed she was mistaken. She was still. Her eyes closed, and with no other body movement, lifeless, she would remain an enigma, a woman that had passed over, a messenger from God, she had died here on earth.

Milligan was afraid. Uncertain whether she was for good or ill. He looked at Sister Benedicta. Her eyes closed, her hands together, on her knees, an almost indiscernible whisper of a prayer he recognized:

We beseech Thee, O Lord, in Thy mercy, to have pity on the soul of Thy handmaid; do Thou, Who hast freed her from the perils of this mortal life, restore to her the portion of everlasting salvation. Through Christ our Lord, Amen.

Seeing the Sister like this, he felt ashamed of himself for ever doubting that, whatever this was before them, with the simplicity and convenience for the name angel they had imposed on her for want of one more scientific, she was clearly not of this world, but from somewhere greater, and with the munificence and glorification of God she was returning. He went to his locker picking his habit and crucifix up from the bottom where he had dumped them earlier and put them on. Going down on his knees beside Sister Benedicta Marie, he silently wept.

Despite the one-way, tinted, triple bullet-proof windows, Carter could hear a storm picking up beyond. She felt the same feelings of atmosphere she had experienced in Vatican City when that lightning bolt struck the ark. She startled. A clap of thunder shook the building rolled endlessly across the landscape without diminishing in sound volume. What she thought as having been an act of God was repeating itself, and she wondered if it was His portent for an end to this world. She was contorting. Carter was afraid, and with these fears, she put her hand on her head, as much for her comfort as for her own. Each contortion seemed to be resonating with every flash of lightning and roll of thunder. It was as if she was in direct communication with Him. His voice inaudible and unintelligible to us. She had gone through stages, from what Carter supposed was a body rotting in the ground to new life; resurrected. If God had no hand in that, she dreaded who did. Unless, not an angel at all as they had first thought, but a being that had the capacity for life-after-death reconstruction. A human species from our future that had evolved. Or more frighteningly, from another place—

Her body had given way to a shimmering silvery white.

'Jesus,' Milligan uttered. 'She *is* the Son of God.'

'Is she?' Carter said as an afterthought, that they might have stumbled on a primordial gene buried deep within us all; that some have the ability to trigger for self-preservation. In an effulgence of brilliant light their closed eyelids could not shade, she was gone; and Carter's primordial gene theory followed her into the aether.

'*Where?*' Milligan asked.

She bit her lip and shook her head. 'Back from where she came from I guess.'

FBI rescue pilot, Baxter 'Spider' Webb brought the Bell fast over the ridge, dropping his machine into the valley, leveling out, continued low to the ground all the time fighting with the cyclic stick against the buffeting storm that was testing the Bell's structural fabric to the max. Regaining the line, he cruised on to his destination. ETA twenty minutes, if I don't hit base level first, he thought.

She had called his emergency number and no matter the danger, he would get her out and to the Pentagon no matter what. Did the powers that be consider the worsening weather, he wondered. Probably not. But FBI stood for Fidelity, Bravery, Integrity; with the unit he belonged, its Hostage Rescue Team with the given motto, *Servare Vitas* (To Save Lives); with his immediate boss for this operation being his indomitable new deputy assistant director Charlie O'Hare who, he would give nothing less than a hundred percent. He had not known flying weather to be so bad, often grounded for better. Below him, Cheyne County. A notorious fly zone given to rising hot air currents and winds at the best of times, but this, tonight, had it with bells and double clangers – and some. A storm of this intensity was how he imagined the end of the world. A turn of phrase banded round, not something he necessarily subscribed; although, he was of the opinion that it could be nothing more than a natural phenomenon never before experienced on earth. Not by man. Solar. The earth's magnetic field switching from north to south. Its iron earth core surfacing even. All things were possible. Turning on his ground-lights, he picked out the main highway following it closely for the next forty miles picking out the occasional mammal scuttling from one side to the other as he passed noisily overhead disturbing their feeding, or any other habits such creatures carried out in darkness.

Carter and Milligan watched as Spider began his descent. The sound of the helicopter's arrival brought the mob round once again, only unlike before; they were better prepared this time. Hitching ropes to the fence tying them to the fenders of four-wheelers and the like they were pulling the electric surround support uprights from the ground. Security firing over their heads was having trouble getting them to back-off as Spider touched his plane down. Seeing them driving forwards and backwards, retying the ropes to the surround, with time against them, he threw open the door politely shouting to them to, 'Come on, move your arses!'

They did not need a second invitation. Getting in they strapped on their seat belts.

'All set? Hooked in?' Spider asked.

Carter and Milligan nodded. He powered up the engine lifting off fast leaving their stomachs on the ground. Thank God for small mercies, Carter thought to herself swallowing from the temporary nausea, as the plane began a slow circle to gain direction.

When the fence gave way, the mob surged forward. Under the plane, they began shooting at them. This time, having exchanged their previous assault weapons of stones and small arms, they had brought in heavier weapons. The helicopter was fifteen feet from the ground when the screen hazed over obscuring Spider's field of vision causing him to re-negotiate his options. He dropped the plane slightly, recovering stability. Too low. A guy jumped up, caught hold of one of the wheel stanchions, and began swinging on it. Spider knew immediately what was happening and how easy it would be to bring the plane down unless he took evasive action. Taking the plane higher, rapidly moving direction, he tried to shake the idiot off. And he would have done, easily, but for someone in the mob launching a Laws missile at them jamming the main driving rotor gear. The helicopter lurched violently to one side. Milligan in the outside seat put his hand up against the side screen to steady himself leaving Carter leaning heavily against him and clinging to Spider; and with nothing better to do, begin screaming.

Spider fighting with the controls as the plane moved first one way then the other, hit a tree. The rotor, tried to defoliate it, losing first one of its blades, then the other. Trying to keep the plane horizontal, knowing he had little chance for recovery, he activated the plane's Mayday switch before the plane tipped sideways hitting the ground. The electrics shorted out, hissed glowed red, ignited the fuel that was spewing under pressure from its fuel tanks. There was a short delay, silence. Those of the mob that were savvy, smelling aviation fuel, knowing what comes next, ran, leaving some brave, some stupid, liberally sprinkled and primed by the accelerant to burn alive in the fire ball that followed.

FBI Flight Controller, Wendell Dieterlin contacted Fed office, Berkeley, to say that O'Hare's flight code name, Daemon Crush, had gone off the radar following a Mayday. Director Louise Sayers called O'Hare at the Pentagon informing him.

'I'll give you . . . too old, you Irish *soak* . . .' her reply in answer to his patronizing remark after her suggestion that she would carry out a rescue and recovery mission.

OVAL OFFICE, WEST WING, WHITE HOUSE

The President looked at his watch once more. It caught on the gun holster hanging loosely round his middle. He uttered an oath normally reserved for male accoutrements, turned its face toward him. He imagined the hour hand twelve hours hence less the four minutes replacing it into his waistcoat pocket.

'Remind me again, Peter. Why does a man with a boxer's nose, and hands like shovels need a Magnum . . . eh? Never mind.'

His aide had to admit he did look ridiculous with his holster to the front. If ever a man was not in need of a weapon for his own defense, Henry was such a person. His loyalist of staff (he included himself among that elite), might prevent the man having the authority from pushing the red button to bring life on earth to a certain and dramatic end. The toughest of men cannot stop a bullet; a pistol could be Henry's last line of defense when he and his assailant are the only two men left to play the game and his finger is at the point of press or restrain; assuming he passed his first test with the Security Council.

'Umm. And this, *Irishman* . . . what did you say he's called?'

He reminded him.

'He would have to have a name like that, wouldn't he? Wait a minute, though. I think I have come across that name before. Get me his file. Anyway, as I was saying, like I need to chew the fat with yet another from those damned emerald isles. I'm not standing for re-election you know, assuming there'll be another. Do I need keep reminding you it was the first Montgomery that was born there; *not* the third?'

'Says he has evidence that the government has been shielding crimes for the past hundred years in the pursuit of a scientific theory; that are the direct result of what is happening.'

'A hundred eh. I take it he's talking historically. Is he a *scientist*? Only Ocean's working on that. He can't possibly add anything to what they're doing.'

'No, he's not . . .'

'Any argument he may have will be flawed up against theirs.'

'He reckons you've a crisis he can put his finger on, explain it, and possibly prevent the world from destroying itself.'

'Can he convince the Ruskies? Or the North Koreans? That'll be a good trick if he can. All right Peter. For the case you've made, I'll indulge him. Though what the chairman of the Joint Chiefs-of-Staff is going to make of me dragging in an outsider . . .'

'He's got a team—'

'*A team*. We've got a team. If the earth has come off its axis won't Ocean's be enough?' He had got himself angry. He was going to have to calm down. 'You said he's with the FBI; highly regarded is he?'

'Er, yes. Well, er . . .'

'Er? Spit it out man, what's "*Er*" you're referring?'

Arse, Ross thought. This is going to get worse. He bit the bullet. 'By all accounts he's an honorary member—'

'*What?*' The President interrupted impatiently once more, 'The Ivy League? The New York Yankees? The IRA? The Institute of Raving Lunatics? *Who?*'

'An honorary member of the FBI.'

The President stared at him. The man was taking the piss. Perhaps the pressure of the crisis was cracking him up too. He was glad of the gun in his holster. He was going to have to use it on his secretary before reaching for the red button. 'You're pulling my dick, Peter? Who the *hell* has the authority to make people up to be honorary members of the Justice Department – *ER?*'

His secretary breathed out deeply better to draw a good lungful of air to build up his adrenal reserves. He had hoped that the President wasn't going to ask that particular section of O'Hare's credentials. He should have known better. He closed his eyes before gasping the words at the same time trying not to make them sound like a question:

'J. . . . Edgar . . .*Hoover!*'

Carter could not comprehend what was happening. She was burning. Everything was burning. Stinking fuel, rubber, plastic, clinging to her flesh. She should be experiencing agonizing pains from such an horrendous accident instead of which she felt nothing. She guessed she must have died. Not a surprise, seeing much of her time on earth was devoted to life after death. What was a surprise was someone tussling with her. She cried out, 'Who the hell is that molesting me?'

Having roughly dragged Milligan out, laying him on the grass, Spider concentrated on getting Carter free. She fought with him, punching his back with her closed fists until he said, 'It's me, you silly woman, keep still I'm going to drop you in a minute.' Pulling her clear from what remained of the helicopter, with her over his shoulder, he tried to make the Center building. With a Glock pistol in his free hand, he fired off several rounds into what remained of the mob that were threatening to come for them. To have survived a plane crash, only to be murdered on the ground was not how he saw things. What he could not get his head round was how in hell the three of them had survived after being drenched in burning aviation fuel.

Security, seeing the pilot's dilemma, came out from the Center with heavier weapons. Milligan was up now, and the three of them, made a run for the Center's library block.

Milligan lost no time in praise for the Lord. Immediately making his way to the chapel, kneeling before its altar, he prayed for forgiveness for his doubts of faith; thanking Him for an angel of mercy, He had sent in their hour of need.

Spider was wondering if there was an airfield close by he could commandeer a plane. If Carter was going to get to the Pentagon, he was going to need another miracle.

'Say that again, Annie.'

'A woman must be your age,' Carter shouted above the noise of the car's engine in serious need of attention into her cell-phone. 'Looking like Katharine Hepburn; wearing a straw hat, drove into the grounds in this convertible Pontiac. God alone knows how old it is. Anyway, says to the leader of the mob surrounding the Center that we were wanted by the Kluckers Grand Wizard for questioning and that we were to face his court. Then hang us.'

'Louise, you say?'

'And drives like one mad bitch; excuse my language; the pilot is throwing up out the window as we speak.'

'And they let you all go, just like that?'

'You betcha! Made us wear white hoods over our heads with nooses round our necks; chained together like a gang, holding us at gun point she led us out to the car as common criminals while the mob jeered us.'

O'Hare was laughing, 'And the angel, what of her—?'

'The beast won on points. . . . She's no longer with us. And I believe I have witnessed the resurrection and rising of her soul to the Kingdom of Heaven.'

He mulled over what she said to him. If she was Irinushka, well, he thought, they had gone back a long way the two of them. If she had been earthbound, and for whatever reason forgotten, at least she would be at peace. And sad though it was at least random devastations caused by the two of them clashing with each other round the world would cease and he could deal with Spannocs without her interfering.

WAR ROOM, PENTAGON, ARLINGTON, VIRGINIA

Commander-in-Chief, President Henry Clancy Montgomery III feared the coming of such a day as this. A nightmare crisis, and one he had reached a decision. A decision that was unique in the annals of human history; unlike any of his predecessors had had to face, let alone make. The President of the most powerful country on the planet, earths demise with the name of the most powerful man on its surface alongside its date; engraved on a copper plate. A potted history of man on this planet the last 600,000 years in a strange mathematical language hopefully needing an alien genius to understand. Nevertheless, a fitting epitaph for his and his predecessors' achievements and failures in finding a solution to live in peace with his fellow.

Malmstrom, Montana, Minot, North Dakota, Wyoming; the United States missile sites stacked up, were all counting down. A first strike counter force of various warheads followed up by Minuteman ICBMs. Hundreds. Megatons of TNT equivalents all within half a day of light blue touch paper and retire. *Launched in anger*. Not how Henry saw the situation. More. Part of his failure. Man's shortcomings sent from earth; carrying its final message finite; and read beyond. And for the benefit of whom? Another species that might learn the lessons of mankind's folly. Fat chance. If it lives, purple with three heads with a tail or not, it will always compete against its brother whatever part of the universe it emanates; with its own eventual destruction (a bad example lesson well learned), assured.

Seated round the large oval polished table each side of the President members of the Department of Defense and National Security Council. Closest to the President, Janet Fox, his personal secretary. A woman in her fifties, plain, intelligent, she had been with him since, well . . . a long time. The Council made up of the Navy, Marine Corps, Army, and Air Force, each engendered with the same mindset: to give cold, calculated advice to the President for his options in the event, in this instance, world war three should break out. Options they would not have the time to pontificate over. He had dug deep into his soul trying to make up his own mind as to what he should do for the best. If he were wrong, it would be an error of judgement he would not have to live with. If he was right, well the luck of the Irish, even though his ancestors were three generations removed.

He formally introduced everyone, primarily for O'Hare's benefit. The Secretary of State, the Defense Secretary, an NSC advisor, the Director of National Intelligence, CIA, the Chairman Joint Chiefs-of-Staff, and the Pentagon Chief-of-Staff: all to indulge assistant director, Mr. Charlie O'Hare (forgetting to mention he had been elevated as Henry had learned during his investigations into the man). Missing, for the moment, was Carter (should he mention what she was), co-opted into the FBI as special envoy (His Holiness held her in some regard; who was he to argue, excommunication was not an anachronism as far as he was concerned).

'Ladies and gentlemen, I don't need to tell you we have, and I cannot overstate the case, a crisis that has the potential to destroy the world.' He nodded at O'Hare who acknowledged the use of his words. 'A crisis, all major players are blaming on America . . .'

'No change there,' Fox interrupted.

'However, before I get into that, I would like to mention that I had, after advice, an approach by Oceans Galactica. Without going into too many details, they informed me they are carrying out a scientific evaluation as to the likely cause. They came up with oscillating gravity.'

The meeting looked at O'Hare thinking he had muttered something. He had a blank expression on his face when they did. Thinking they were all mistaken, the President continued:

'With that in mind, I agreed for them to continue their research.' He looked round the table before continuing. 'This man,' he turned in O'Hare's direction pointing to him, 'thinks differently, however. Although I have made it clear to him they may have our only option in their hands, which is, to prevent the world from engaging in a war with human annihilation at stake; and with a shelf life of less than a day for that to happen, my choices are limited. As you are all aware, Oceans Galactica is a well-regarded company; one I was happy for them to continue in their mission. In the meantime, with the equipment they apparently have at their disposal, they can pull any missiles off course destined to land on this country. And to help things along in my deliberations, believing we have a weapon of mass destruction that's gone awry, Russia, China, and North Korea are set on doing that. And that ladies and gentlemen is the state of play to date. I have to tell you that Oceans Galactica has not got back to me as to how they are proceeding. Assistant Director O'Hare, we should like to hear what you have to add.'

'Thank you Mr. President. First off, what I will say is that behind this homely and cuddly company that is Oceans Galactica lays a foundation of child abuse and pedophilia, not only in this country, but across the world.

'The organization is colossal and has generated hundreds of billions of dollars for a single objective. A crackpot, dangerous, scientific experiment that will break through time to get to living entities from an alternative verse.'

The meeting went hysterical with laughter and incredulity suggesting that O'Hare was either drunk, mad or both. He continued unabated.

'From evidence gathered from sources over many years, this magnet, for want of another description, known as AG-MX-960 is located at the disused Air Force base White Bear currently on lease to Ocean from the Defense Department; and has been since the end of the cold war. And sir,' O'Hare looked at Rodgers, 'has nothing to do with the defense of this country.'

'What have you got to say?' the President asked General Rodgers.

'As you've stated sir, they have been working on a weapon which can pull enemy missiles out of the sky; none of which has anything to do with his ludicrous suggestion that they are interfering with time and other universes. This is pure conjecture on his part, science fiction, never proven; and without going into our defense policies with an FBI agent I cannot say more than that; these are matters of national security.'

'Which have gone down the tubes. Mainland security is their business every much as it's yours.' He turned to O'Hare. 'Rodgers may be right in his castigation of you over creatures, it does seem highly improbable, however, that aside, the interference with time you speak, how could that bring on destruction the world is facing?'

'Best answer, don't know; best guess, anti-matter meets matter;

worst case scenario, and what's happening now, nuclear powers believe America is about to launch a first-strike.'

'Well, that part of it is right, that's for sure,' Rodgers cut in, 'his suggestion of matter and anti-matter, there has always been this mix in the universe, at least in earth time. What has prevented this clash of opposites from destroying us is that there is not enough anti-matter to make any difference to that balance. His science is all wrong there, from that point of view, Mr. President, he is not the right man to advise us.'

He ignored his defense secretary's remarks. He pulled his railway watch from his waistcoat pocket. 'In nine hours and twenty minutes our missiles will make a first-strike on Russia, China and North Korea should another one of these "devastation devices", as they are calling them, goes off anywhere else in the world. Can anyone here guarantee that that won't happen?'

'From my perspective,' O'Hare answered, 'no; and we can expect another anytime soon.'

There was an eruption round the table. Members of the council stood up, knocking papers to the floor, laptops over, waving of fingers. The Director of National Intelligence asked the President if they were wasting their time attending a meeting he had clearly reached a decision regarding a first-strike.

'Gentlemen, gentlemen, ladies, please. There was me thinking that you were all in favour of war-mongering and taking out as many with us as possible when we go down. Oh yes, we will go down. Well let me tell you. Given the time, I had little choice! Sit down, shut-up and listen up. General Rodgers, since you leased these people White Bear; apart from pulling missiles out the air, do you know if they are up to anything else?'

Rodgers looked round at everyone. He sighed. 'We were approached by Ocean's scientific division, I believe they're called the

Order of the Most Divine Third Circle, they wanted the facility for research. They gave me a brief outline of what they were doing with this weapon of theirs, and we issued the appropriate licenses. We naturally assumed, as with any other company involved with the defense industry, that to ask too many questions would jeopardize their corporate integrity. We let them get on with it—'

'And a name like that suggested weapons science to you? Never mind. Let me tell you,' O'Hare interrupted angrily. 'This piece of machinery is purely and solely for the purpose of bringing creatures or spirits from beyond the veil of the universe into our own; with devastating consequences as you are witnessing. And they haven't switched the *bastard* thing on yet!'

'Bourbon, more like,' Rodgers interrupted. 'And you've had too many by the sound of things.' He looked to the President, 'Mr. O'Hare is known for his love of whiskey, sir.' Laughter went round the table.

O'Hare not joining in their mirth, his face stoical waited for the laughter to die down before continuing. 'I use the word spirit, for they have been seen, by me personally, and apart from having some resemblance they are most definitely not us. And this government, that has a civil service department buried within another, namely the pension's service, is not only watching for these creatures; knowing they exist; but are encouraging their arrival using Oceans Galactica to bring it on disregarding world peace in the process.'

The President interrupted. 'Well that's a serious accusation against this government. I hope you're not suggesting that I know anything?'

'No sir.'

'Glad to hear it. And what of this suggestion Ocean made regarding oscillating gravity. Could there be any truth in that?'

'I wouldn't trust anything an organization that Frederik Spannocs is CEO, had to say.' O'Hare said shaking his head.

'Apparently, Mr. Spannocs died recently, Mr. President,' Rodgers added.

'How convenient,' O'Hare interrupted. 'Will he be away long?'

'Okay gentlemen enough. Let's get on with the job in hand. I think as a matter of urgency we'd better send some people to Alaska, take a look.' He turned to the chairman of the Joint Chiefs-of-Staff, 'I believe the Seals are on stand-by, are they ready to go?'

'Whenever you are, Mr. President,' Tom Villiers replied.

'Go to it Tom. Let's get something constructive done here.'

TEN MINUTES IN

'Assuming you're right, Mr. O'Hare. These spirits or aliens,' the President looked round the table for reactions. Seeing none, he continued. 'Personally, I cannot accept anything so fantastical. But, having said that—'

'*For God's sake*, Henry. Are we to swallow this rubbish?' Jocasta Siemens, the NSC adviser interrupted. 'Spirits! Aliens! What next – the angel of the Lord?'

'Funny you should mention him,' O'Hare interrupted. 'Let me recount to you all events of 1920. October 27 to be precise.'

Siemens sat back heavily in his chair, folding his arms in a manner that suggested that this would be good.

THIRTEEN MINUTES IN

'You expect us all here to seriously believe that something that came from God is responsible?' director of National Intelligence asked.

SEVENTEEN MINUTES IN

'Well, if that's your scientific opinion, explain to me how it is seismologists from round the world haven't recorded any? Russia for starters. They are of the opinion that we attacked because they are rogue states we've lost patience with,' O'Hare put it to Barry Betambeau, the President's scientific adviser. 'And while I do, up to a point, agree that the earths tectonic plates are constantly on the move; this is destruction that I can account.'

TWENTY-FIVE AND A HALF MINUTES IN

'What, that that man dead, Spannocs, was hosted by an evil spirit on the lines of whom we know of as Satan? The man has done a lot of good for this country. If it hadn't been for his wealth, we could never have, well. The point is Oceans Galactica has the wherewithal and technical ability to move the earth back onto an axis that will stop this destruction. Surely we can excuse whatever else they have been involved in,' the President said to O'Hare aware of his need to play the devil's advocate here.

FORTY AND A HALF MINUTES IN

'Mr. President.'

'What is it Janet?'

'The assistant director's – *secretary?* She looked first at O'Hare then the President. 'She's outside.'

'Show her in, Janet. Mr. O'Hare, would you like to—'

O'Hare got up and opened the door. Carter was standing up outside, but only just. She looked as if she could do with a shower, a change of clothes, and 24 hours sleep.

'Would you give me some time out?' The President waved him excused. '*Annie!* You okay?'

'Something intervened out there. I don't think I've ever—'

She staggered, held onto the wall, and began sliding down it. O'Hare grabbed her stopping her from hitting the floor. She was on her feet, but her legs were jelly. Several from the meeting helped him.

'Janet, help her up and take her to the guest wing will you; and ask the doctor to attend to her. *Gentlemen, ladies*, we can spare ten,' the President said.

ONE HOUR AND ONE MINUTE IN

'Sister Benedicta Marie from the Carmelite Order,' O'Hare said introducing her to the meeting.

She smiled at them, looking at lot better than she did when she first arrived.

'Well I am when I wear the sack-cloth. Miss Fox has kindly put it on a warm wash for me. Loaned me her jeans and T-shirt. Thank you.'

'Yes. Sorry for the slogan,' Fox said smiling. 'Purely coincidental.'

'Oh I don't know, *Nuns Do It Out Of Habit*, appropriate under the circumstances. Please, as I am out of dress, I answer to Annie Carter.'

The mood that had once been suspicious of O'Hare with a nun alongside him co-opted to the FBI warmed. If he was an untypical FBI agent, she certainly was not their conception of a sister belonging to such an auspicious order as the Carmelite.

'You worked in Rome? Wondered what you had to do with any of this, Miss Carter,' the White House Chief-of-Staff, Admiral David Fairfax-Grant asked continuing, 'The Vatican, eh?' He looked round the table. 'They're taking it seriously. After what Mr. O'Hare suggested was the cause of all this, suppose they would, what with their record on child abuse and all—'

The President thumped the table, 'Right, I'm going to stop you right there.' He turned to his secretary. 'Strike that last statement of David's from the record, Janet. *David!* a word. Outside please.'

The Admiral turned to face the President. He knew he was out of order and was to be reprimanded for it.

'We've known each other a long time, you and I. You don't talk that way. We're all under pressure here. What Mr. O'Hare and Miss Carter have come here to tell us, well, we might have our views. But you seem to have taken it further with doubts as to O'Hare's credibility: that he might be a fantasist – a nutter. Well, let me tell you, I have seen his file. He has spent a lifetime with the FBI; and before that, the Department for Vice with the old Bureau of Investigation, and apart from reports from various heads of department of stubbornness and insubordination, the record shows the man's commitment and sincerity to the law is above question. In spite of what we're hearing from this man, he comes to this table well recommended, as does Carter. They are people of integrity and honesty. Ask yourself. Why would a man with his reputation come here and talk the way he does if there was not something in it. As for Carter, I will not have accusations banded round the table that have nothing whatsoever to do with her.'

'My apologies, Miss Carter,' Fairfax-Grant said when he came back to the table.

ONE HOUR FIFTY-ONE MINUTES IN

'. . . Far as I know, there are probably five or six other people that were there that suffered the same fate as mine,' O'Hare said. He took a handkerchief from his pocket and wiped a tear from his eye. 'Annie would you please continue.'

She stood up as O'Hare sat back down.

'Gentlemen, ladies. Let me recount to you events of Wednesday the 8th of October 1997 . . .'

THREE HOURS TWENTY MINUTES IN

'Aramaic . . . yes. Fortunately, but not so for Dr. Artur Siefert; otherwise known as Father Michael Joseph. He studied ancient documents from all over the world; considered an expert in the field. The Teutonic Knights, two errant members – for I still believe the organization to be noble – that removed the scroll, knew of its existence intended to expose it untested to a world for an end that will serve no useful purpose.' She went to her briefcase taking out a large manila envelope. Opening it, she removed a photograph of a scroll holding it up for them to see. 'There were others with this one that was 2000 years old; giving the impression that if one was that age all were. Fortunately, for us, this was not one of them, and again, fortunately for us, neither was it complete. A piece of the parchment torn from the corner and found in the ark after the removal of it and the murder of Father Joseph was enough for us to carbon date. The science showed the writing and the lamb skin it was written to be around 150–300 years after an event it was to be attributed. Supposedly written as witness statements by a high priest, and two Pharisees that opposed Jesus and His teachings threatening their authority. The impression to be given, that had Pilate *not* washed his hands, leaving the verdict for others to deliberate, instead of throwing the case out for lack of any real evidence, would have been submitted condemning Him for its content. In short, the high priest and the two Pharisees swore written evidence that they had seen Jesus of Nazareth carrying out acts of indecency against very young girls. And although the Romans and Greeks were not adverse to taking boys for sex, it was not Jewish practice; considered condemnable. Here was a Jewish trial brought against a Jewish citizen by Jewish elders because He got under their skin. Of course, as I said at the beginning, that was never their intent. The scroll turned out fake; not for an event 2000 years before, but to convince others into believing that what they were doing would be a forgivable sin today.' She looked into the eyes of those seated round the table, looked toward the President. 'Whoever engineered that document, Mr. President, was a deceiver of the highest order worthy of Satan himself. And the ramifications of its publication without the benefit of science debunking it would have rocked monotheism to its core.'

The President was mortified. The idea that a blasphemous document, though fake; that men were prepared to make public against Jesus made him feel sick. Whatever faith those responsible were, it was beyond the palus. Reminding himself of the Old Testament book of Nahum; if he could have written one line as an addendum it would be, *And His adversaries drowned in their own blood,* he would be happy to die a worthy scribe. What was happening on earth being a direct result of that blasphemy occurred to him: that God was capable of returning the earth to a barren planet was an idea he had never questioned before. The Lord's past anger confined to plagues of locus and the like. But why would He wait 2000 years before exacting this for revenge on mankind.

'What became of this scroll?' the President asked angrily.

'Its remains, along with the gold holder it was encased, were found in the Diamond Center at Becland.'

'Destroyed in the explosion?' the President asked by way of confirmation.

'No. Forensics says it spontaneously burst into flames before. My only regret is that Father Joseph died with the untested belief that Jesus might have interfered with children.'

FOUR HOURS THREE MINUTES IN
Outside the Emergency Operations Center's window there came several rounds of machine gun fire followed by an inaudible voice shouting through a megaphone.

FOR HOURS TEN MINUTES IN
Hector Dove, Presidential butler came into the room with two female

waitresses from the kitchens and began laying out the table with food and drinks.

'Thank you, Hector,' the President said adding, 'Given the circumstances and the situation, would you instruct the staff that those wishing to leave and return to their families may do so.'

'I could try, but I know what their answer will be. All excepting one, that is. One of the gardeners. She tried to stop an intruder coming into the grounds. I'm sorry to say she took a bullet from him before our people managed to bring the gun-man down.'

'Which gardener, Hector?' the President asked.

'The young Filipino. You probably didn't know her, Natalie. She came here—'

'With her mother. Yes I did. Thank you, Mr. Dove. We'll take a break here, I think. Please excuse me. I need to speak with my staff. Help yourselves to refreshments.'

FOUR HOURS TWENTY MINUTES IN

'Is this gathering prepared to accept what I am saying is the cause of all this, or not?' O'Hare asked angrily.

The President looked round the table at his Chiefs-of-Staff. They were sullen. As the President of a secular nation, he considered himself as God-fearing as the next man. Of course, he was aware of Revelations. He had personally read of the last battle between good and evil. Armageddon. The eve before the Day of Judgement. All faiths had their own version for the same scenario. The question was, for him, if the Order of the Most Divine Third Circle, as O'Hare was suggesting, were playing games with a man that was this new 'Satan' and nothing done to stop them, the price could be an acceptance of the Order's new world order with 'Satan' at its helm. A dictator. A Hitler. A Spannocs. The only other way was to take the one chance that O'Hare was suggesting, and the President would sell it as Good

v. Evil; God v. Satan to a Christian America with the one redeeming feature message that mankind would be able to look their Creator square in the face knowing their souls and consciences were intact as they died off. He hoped that would be adequate, but it was some awful goddamn decision to make.

'Distrust for other faiths and religions were always likely to be the end of us. We didn't need the wrath of God to point that out; He must've known we were capable of that on our own account. Why is He putting us to this test if He thought there was hope for mankind knowing the rest of the universe will tick along nicely without us? I've heard all I want to hear. It's decision time. From the perspective of where the buck stops, I am responsible; I know that, I'm not about to walk away. Some may think that Presidents of America have a protocol for out-of-this-world events that will keep us all safe and secure. Well I can tell you,' he turned to Carter, 'if you'll excuse my Latin ladies and sister, when I say it's *bollocks*; that I am referring to that part of misalignment for what should be in our heads. If a President doesn't know something is going on, it probably isn't. In this case, Mr. O'Hare, I most assuredly did not; and I will accept that you were right, and it did.'

He was fumbling for an answer that he assumed would easily come to him. O'Hare and Carter had offered up arguments that to all intents and purposes had not the world come to the edge of destruction as it had, he would have thrown them out personally. Most of his own people had poured scorn on them, and he could not blame them for that. They were tired of listening to what amounted to fairy tales. He gave it one last shot. 'The idea that a government department had planned this for as long as you say, well, investigations have been carried out and found—'

'Nothing.' O'Hare interrupted adding, 'What people though, Mr. President? Whenever I offered to go in there, a bureaucratic door was slammed in my face. Whether you like it or not, you've been sitting on a conspiracy. But these people have had plenty of practice concealing it. You were not the first. Hopefully, you'll be the last.'

'But it's the *department for pensions for God's sake*,' he shouted across the table at O'Hare. 'Not a nest of *doom-makers!*' His phone rang. Fox retrieved it, listened, and replaced the receiver. The President was still waiting for O'Hare to answer him before he realized she was waiting for his attention. He calmed himself before asking, 'What is it, Janet?'

'Commander of Navy Seals, sir. They've come under a sustained attack by opposition forces at White Bear. They're hopelessly outnumbered . . . his words, not mine. They have had to retreat.' Not for humor did she smile.

The mouths of his Chiefs-of-Staff curled down.

'Before the cock crow, thou shalt deny me thrice,' O'Hare said without thinking.

'*Fuck-off!*' the President said angrily, then whispering added, 'We're at DEFCOM 2.5! What more can I do?'

'That'll be two or three, Mr. President. There isn't a—'

'Don't correct me, Fairfax-Grant,' the President snapped. 'Break I think, a break. Mr. O'Hare . . . I'll have words with you. In private.'

'I'll give you a scenario,' the President began. 'During the second world war America and Europe fought against German National Socialism. Why such a political idea needs enforcing by despots and genocidal maniacs is beyond me, but what do I know. The point is we won that war. Every memorial to those that died, every poem, prayer, gives the view that death is preferable to living with evil, do they not?' O'Hare nodded his agreement. 'Hitler *was* evil; at least, that's the general consensus of sane opinion. For better or worse though, he had a vision. What's theirs and how do we stop them without us all destroying ourselves? They've made up some cock-and-bull story that our Seals, our *Seals!* would you believe are Russian Navy come to stop them doing what I've ordered?'

'Putting the world back on its axis.'

'Don't know how they've the gall to attempt to take one of our submarines on. Fortunately for them our people were following my orders not to make a bad situation worse.' He hesitated. 'I need evidence, O'Hare. Before I take this any further. Evidence mark me. Do that for me O'Hare, if it fits with what you've said, I'll send in the Marines.'

'To my way of thinking, part of the solution lies at the offices of the administrative (annex ii-38) section pen.gov building. I need to get in there. Something that has been denied me for years.'

The President nodded his head. 'We won't. be letting them know you're coming this time.'

O'Hare re-entered the room with the President after what seemed like hours but was nearer fifty minutes. He looked at Carter and grimaced. The President had the look of a man that had struck dread and was to mine it with broken fingernails.

'I apologize for keep saying it, but this coming to a decision has caused me a degree of heart-searching that no man should ever have to make and one which I wish I didn't.' He looked at O'Hare hoping against all the odds that the man was right. He made a noise in his throat before resuming. 'I hold that office that demands me to make a decision that cannot be delegated. We have clearly come under attack by our own people. I can see that we have been misinformed, lied to even. I have concluded that their intentions are not in our interests. I need hard evidence. Mr. O'Hare is of a mind that he knows where he can get it and I have agreed with him that he should do that.' He drew breath after impatiently swallowing a mouthful of hot coffee that Fox had put down in front of him, 'If that evidence does turn out to be as far reaching as Mr. O'Hare says it is, I shall immediately send in our Marines. With that in mind, I have made the decision to run with Mr. O'Hare and his team and trust they have the necessary tools to do the job. I shall speak again with Russia and China telling them that we are having problems with some of our own people asking for more time before they consider launching any attack on us. I will inform Oceans Galactica that the government considers, with this act of aggression against the Seals, saying they thought they were a foreign force as laughable. If none of that works, black and burnt on a pile of radioactive earth, I shall feel a whole lot better knowing we didn't give in to people that might be holding us to ransom. But of course, it will be academic. None of you here will be able to see what a great President I was and the decision I made.'

There was muted laughter. Not all followed his line of thinking; nor willing to make their voices heard. They had no answers.

'Ladies and gentlemen, thank you for your input,' the President said looking towards his Joint Chiefs-of-Staff. 'Organize what you need. Consider the situation war. And sister . . .'

Carter looked up at him wondering what he had in mind for her involvement for war.

'Perhaps you can put your other hat on, lead us in a general service for any faiths here feeling the need. The Meditation and Prayer room is at your disposal.' He turned towards O'Hare. 'I will speak with you before you leave.'

'Before you do, Mr. President,' Colonel Lennox of the 3rd Battalion the 49th interrupted, 'should it be necessary, I should like to personally lead any op you feel is necessary sir.'

Following the President down a corridor and into another office full of staff handling phones, he went to a desk opening a drawer. He took out a folder, handed it to O'Hare.

'Here. For our mutual enemy in common. His emergency number should the situation go tits-up. There is other information in there. Sensitive. Mark me; it's for your eyes only. Guard it with your life.' He held his hand out to him and O'Hare shook it.

'Last time I heard his voice was his calling me to tell me that he needed to speak with his grandmother. He mentioned to me some time ago of what he had seen at African Queens; that it had been a turning point in his life; and why he had come in with us. Was it that bad, Charlie?' Carter asked of him.

'By all accounts, it was. Fortunately, I wasn't there to see it.'

'When I introduced myself to Sara Weinberg and told her who I was, she angrily asked to speak with you. When I told her you weren't there, she put the phone down on me.'

He read the sickening message of condolence she passed to him, resulting in O'Hare and her having their first conversation in over twenty years. She had changed. The tears she had shed since the death of Frank, and David, had drawn deep lines of anguish down her face. She still had nothing but disdain for him, he could see it, understood, and could do nothing to turn the clock back. And, but for Carter's training with the FBI it could have been hatred bordering on her murdering him. For that training gave Carter the skill to carry out that single shot from her Magnum into the engine of the car that came straight for her after they had abducted Fitch first time. Bound and gagged on the back seat, and with the car traveling at the speed it was, she would soon have joined him, but . . . for the soft-headed bullet she fired into the car's engine block stopping it dead in its tracks. With her second shot, going through the driver's right eye exiting out from behind his ear, leaving him in a pool of blood across the hood; and making Fitch's abduction the shortest in history; to allow this particular Weinberg to survive the longest in years of his family's three generations on the male side. Whether, after the experience, she would ever be mentally the same again, to O'Hare, was debatable.

He told Sarah that her grandson was no longer helping the FBI and was back working on the *Post*. She made nothing of what he regarded later as a pathetic statement, and after all that had happened, equally pathetic timing.

O'Hare made a call to the *Post* after leaving Sarah; to satisfy himself that Fitch was safe and out of the frame. It was a pointless exercise. Stenna told him that Fitch's desk chair, found on its side with his computer monitor smashed on the floor behind it, and with no sign of the man, he had hoped he would have given him an answer as to where he was, adding, 'Not that it matters much now, with the human race following dinosaurs on the road to extinction.'

Continuing with the ear-bashing, he blamed him for involving the best journalist he had ever known, the FBI still exploiting him (he did not believe O'Hare when he told him this latest absence was anything to do with them), put his phone down on him, settling down to write a last story to those who cared and were still left working, in particular, Wall Street: that the CEO of *Oceans Galactica*; and the man they had sucked up to over the years, Frederik Spannocs – who had gone to such pains, with their help, to persuade the American public that it was as legitimate a company as *Gideons International* – *but*, was in fact, nothing more than an organization that made its money from pedophilia on a global scale; and, following O'Hare's estimation, that the likely reason the world was on the cusp of a nuclear holocaust was for what they were doing. He added notes from Fitch's scratch pads; something that he would not normally do without confirmation as to their source, contenting himself with the man's well-worn mantra, *This is* kosher *, Max. Would I tell you a lie?* before topping the story in 9- and 7-line typeface of Grot 9 respectively, filling the front page with the banner headlines:

NOT FOR GOD OR AMERICA,

BUT FOR SATAN AND HIS WORLD

OF CORRUPTED SOULS!

FINANCIAL MARKETS TURN THEIR

BACKS ON CHILD ABUSE

With a new front-page plate processed and locked onto the press, he 'sacked' himself as editor of the *Post*. A self-sacrifice that gave him little pleasure. Taking his coat and laptop from his office, he walked out onto the machine room floor where the rumbling of the press was starting its print run – likely – the last newspaper in the world. Its #1 machine-minder passed him an initial copy to check. He took it, scanned the pages, nodding at her after ink-pad stamping it, PASSED FOR PRESS. Kate Parr smiled at him, breaking with tradition removed the first edition origami-style hat from her head and plonked it on his. He returned her smile, kissed her on the cheek, left the press offices to go out into the darkening, lightning streaked sky where civil disorder and the gun were now King in New York and the World; to get himself drunk and much, much more.

Thirty One – 1997

Alas, regardless of their doom, the little victims play!
No sense have they of ills to come, nor care beyond to-day

ODE ON A DISTANT PROSPECT OF ETON COLLEGE,
Thomas Gray 1716–71

'IS THAT YOU CHARLIE?'

'He's here; I'll get him for you. Who is it calling, please?'

Agent Harry Fen signaled O'Hare that there was someone for him.

'——ise Sayers, from the New York office . . .'

He passed O'Hare the phone, '*Louise Sayers* . . .'

'Hello, *Louise*. Thanks for returning my call . . . I need another favour.'

'Could be your last. What is it?'

'Let's hope you're wrong. Listen, this might take some organizing. New York Tammany owe me. Assuming any of them is still alive. You're looking for a man name of Toomey Sin. Last heard of sitting at a desk in the Union Theater, Madison Avenue, East 33rd Street. Looks like a gipsy . . .'

'Relative of yours, is he?'

'*Fun-nie!* Tell him I sent you. Listen carefully to what I'm about to say.'

O'Hare backed by a team of heavily armed FBI agents burst into the offices of administrative (annex ii-38) section pen.gov building after crashing heavy vehicles through its concrete and wire fence surround.

Two security guards and a girl attended the reception area. They gave themselves up at the sight of armed agents. The agents removed their communication devices discarding them into a fire bucket. A swift disconnection of the switchboard from the computer by a sharp blow from one of the agent's short automatic rifle butts put paid to that as a passer of information tool, sizzling after going through its screen. Obtaining the codes to operate the elevators, they escorted them from the building.

O'Hare reading the occupant manifest of the building nodded at his team to follow him. They took both lifts and stopped at the top floor. The doors opened. A large office that had been used as a call center before they had all been sent home to their families. This can't be right, he thought. He went back into the lift. One of the elevator buttons wasn't numbered. He pushed it but it didn't do anything. He thought and quickly pushed the top one at the same time as the unmarked one. The elevator moved on up. They exited at its floor ran down the corridor following O'Hare who signaled one of the agent's eyes towards the wall alarm.

Getting the visual, he smashed it. The bells went off, along with the building's sprinklers.

'*Fookin' 'ell.* Forgot that was going to happen. *Sorry team!*'

'Yeh, right!' one was heard to say pulling his jacket collar up.

O'Hare continued to run down the corridor under sprays of water until he saw a door marked:

SPECIAL SURVEILLANCE OPERATIONS
NO ENTRY TO UNAUTHORIZED PERSONNEL
(INCLUDING FBI & CIA)

Cheeky bastards! O'Hare said out loud. There was an eye-scan lock to one side. A ramming rod in the hands of one of the men instantly made it obsolete. They pushed past office staff answering the call of the fire alarms coming the other way. O'Hare frantically looking for a door that he might recognize, finding it immediately:

OPERATIONS DIRECTORS
(Dr. Nathaniel Johnson, Univ. of Pittsburgh).
(Dr. Daniel Sullivan, Univ. of Ohio).

He hesitated at the last name nodded to the agent to kick the door down. The office was empty. They went out. Another. Next door to the first:

PENSIONS ADMINISTRATOR

That door opened unaided.

'Search the rest of the corridors. Anything unusual, that you think may be booby-trapped, call me first. Harry, you stay with me and guard the door.'

When they had gone, O'Hare went through the files and paperwork that Johnson and Sullivan had accumulated over the years. Skim reading some, at the same time discarding others. Coming across an old clown's mask he discarded it into the waste bin. He found references going back to him and Frank's time working the beat on Manhattan's Lower East Side and melancholia flooded over him.

He came across notes and letters. Mostly pasted cuttings in note books with recommendations and references to Johnson and Sullivan. Their involvement as undercover agents in the dockyard to keep an eye out for communists, radicals, saboteurs, and the like under the deputy head of the Bureau of Investigation, J. Edgar Hoover. A reference to a paranormal event, written by Commissioner Dore. Of how they had broached the subject to Hoover, who passed them on to a government agency called – O'Hare whispered the words to himself – the *Order* . . .

An immediate interest toward Marco Giuseppi
was to be shown. Marco Giuseppi, head of the
Dockyard, Ships & Rigging and Allied Workers'
Union whilst at the same time, two officers
from New York's 7th Precinct were to be
prevented from investigating the abduction of
an immigrant family's daughter. Her
disappearance has to date remained a mystery.

Not her murder, he said to himself. He continued reading:

The officers concerned taken on board for the
purposes of keeping them close and under
control . . .

. . . keep officer O'Hare alive . . . Tammany
connections . . .

He looked heavenward, 'A muse of a thought, father,' he
whispered. 'Your membership did give me some consternation over
the years, but on that one point, I think I might owe you one after all.'

What he came across next sent a chill through him. For the killer
of Frank Weinberg was not as he had first thought at the time as
Marco Giuseppi, or someone with an axe to grind following on from
the Seaburg Inquiry, but someone else. Likely, the same person that
had blown-up the restaurant they were in that had killed David. He
read on.

The powers that be within the FBI should be
allowed to think O'Hare had exaggerated what
he had seen. In all event they should be
encouraged not to take him seriously; also, it
would not do for both of them to be removed,
suspicions of conspiracy etc. Weinberg was not

to be a player. A Jew. He should be
discredited and taken out with blame falling
on others for his death. Suggest a test of
loyalty for Dr. Sax Stonercrop . . .

The murdering double crossing *bast*— He continued:

Stonercrop should be recruited to the FBI for
his knowledge of cults and the paranormal. As
an academic, he could be turned. It would be
useful for the Order to have an infiltrator in
their midst with such knowledge . . .

. . . recruited and given status of CEO . . .

. . . the entrapment of an Entity to reach out
and pull in among us for the knowledge of
creation it possesses would propel man to
heights of unimaginable possibilities: The
Seventh Gift is within reach. Stonercrop would
be a hundred percent with them in that
endeavor . . .

. . . imperative that the name Teutonic
Knights be disassociated from the Order . . .

. . . the authority heading the organization
into this scientific investigation is
Operations Directors Dr. Nathaniel Johnson ,
Dr. Daniel Sullivan, formerly of SSO . . .

Special Surveillance Operation, O'Hare said to himself. *Nice to know Roswell's still alive and kicking.*

. . . both immune from prosecution; any

attempts made to implicate other person(s) are
also immune . . .

Are they? This organization does protest too much, methinks,
O'Hare thought to himself. He rifled through more paperwork
coming across a folder marked:

ORDER OF THE MOST DIVINE THIRD CIRCLE

He quickly opened it. Most of it referred to memberships,
recruitment, accounts, and names. He would go over at his leisure
later; time was not on his side; all except for one brief paragraph
drawing his eye:

. . . in the event, a full denial to the
Vatican that any other person(s) were in
anyway responsible for the death of one, and
the near death of another of their library
staff. (We are not yet powerful enough to take
on the might of the Roman Catholic Church
should they act against us) . . .

His thoughts turned to Frank and another death; when Lomax
had shown O'Hare a photograph, in a buff envelope, removed from
Frank Weinberg's clothes after being gunned down, planted on him
by a Rabbi of all people, he had shook his head saying, No way. A
calculated, disgusting, and shit-faced touch after his murder, and one
that he determined would avenge no matter the price to his own
reputation and freedom. Prior to the revealing of that photograph he
discussed with Lomax that Frank had probably been the victim of a
gangland execution the result of his work with the Seaburg Inquiry;
that picture changed his mind; he never thought for one minute that
anyone would sink so low as to hypocritize the man that had done so
much to protect vulnerable children using planted indecent material.

Lomax agreed. He tore it up. Such attention to detail involved more than the two arseholes working out of administrative (annex ii-38) section pen.gov. No longer concerned with his own wellbeing, more that of Carter and Fitch (oh yes, they had him all right); 'Person' or 'Persons' made this a very dangerous operation for all concerned. Assuming, of course, in the light of events, any of them were going to survive the apocalypse of a threatening third world war. If he were going to face these people, he needed to put thoughts of 'Immunity' with all its implications to the back of his mind, as he would his determination to kill those concerned in all of this. He took a deep breath to control his rage.

'*Sir!*'

The three post-stick notes attached to each other, overlapping on the telephone reminded him of those that were #1 on his hit list. A message from Stonercrop to Johnson and Sullivan by way of a reminder.

```
Daniel. Telephone conversation from Father
Milligan to Sister Benedicta Marie tapped. The
angel has been taken into divine custody.
Whatever possessed the form of Spannocs has
departed. Go ahead with replacement. The most
despicable person Spannocs can think of that
he would give up the ghost for would be a Jew.
We have him with us. The Jewish curse will see
an end to him. See you in Alaska. Nath.
```

'*Charlie!* Are you there?' Fen called down the corridor looking for him.

'What is it, Harry?' O'Hare shouted from the office.
'Another door.'

He put all the paperwork and notes in an historical order that the President would not have to spend too much time studying.

Having done that he sent facsimiles to the Pentagon's dedicated phone line.

Another foot fall, that door too separated from its hinges. Behind was another looking as if it was made of solid lead. It had a handle. O'Hare turned it gingerly, it opened, and he stepped forward inside, gun in hand. The room was in semi-darkness with no windows. The walls were black. He put his fingernail to the part closest to him and scratched at it. Soft. As he eyes became accustomed to the dark, he saw what he suspected and came for seated at a desk surrounded by papers, books, old telephones, teleprinters, and answer phones. He looked at him. He was different. He looked his age. The hair on his head, hair that had once been blonde in an earlier life, was a sparse dirty yellow gray. His face wrinkled and dry, his eyes hollow, lacked any expression. To O'Hare, if the man were to lie on the floor with his eyes closed he would pass as dead. Which he guessed he probably was. Count Dracula was alive not very kick-worthy.

Giuseppi rose from his chair, a slow labored exercise. He looked at O'Hare, a comfortable smile, as if he was an old friend. For a moment; and only for it did O'Hare feel a hint of sorrow for what a man becomes when steeped in so much evil. But, as he had earlier in life learned, situations are never what they at first seem; that lesson had not by-passed him. He recovered from that sympathy he had for him.

'You could have knocked, sergeant!' Giuseppi said quietly. 'I would have opened the door.'

'And when was there ever a requirement for a good man to stand on ceremony to Satan, eh?'

Giuseppi shuffled his feet. With the difficulty of age, he lifted his head.

'I fear you have mistaken me for another, sir.'

'No. I don't think so. So what are you doing here, I ask myself? The situation in Alaska too cold for you, or is it you've other plans?'

Giuseppi laughed. An echoing sound that made the office walls vibrate. He took on a serious aspect.

'You surely know me better than that. Whatever are you suggesting, Sergeant O'Hare?'

'Well, it's no longer the Angel of Death that's at your arse, she's gone. You were used to attract whatever's out there for others to capture. And up until now, it's worked pretty well. I must admit, it took me a little while to work out, but it's come to me. It was not coming to save children at all. The incident on the Brooklyn subway told me that. It totally ignored her distress. The Divine Spirit was coming for you and the angel was getting in its way. Sealed up here in lead, with her gone, you'd be in trouble, there'd be nothing preventing it getting to you once you emerge into the light of day. And that's your current demise old son. That was never part of your remit was it? Bet you haven't told your master's that have you? They think they have you up there with them in Alaska. Which, they have to a certain extent, but only enough to fool the Divine Spirit to come for what remains. Bit more magic. This world is on the verge of destruction and ripe for a take-over from you. Revelations will end Chapter 17: .. . *and God will give up his kingdom to the beast.* That how it goes. And those idiots up in Alaska,' he were shouting now, 'have no idea what they're doing. Oh yes, they'll have their knowledge all right, but on your terms.'

The two FBI officers, not used to confronting a man of advanced years, lowered their weapons, before standing easy. Giuseppi seeing his opportunity made a move. O'Hare saw it:

'*Keep him covered!*'

No sooner had he spoken, then a distortion of air came away from Giuseppi leaving his body collapsed onto the floor, taking him off his guard. A shape of an ethereal being moved to the side of him, though invisible, it told him what was taking place. Keeping the gun he had in his left hand still aimed at the vacant body of Giuseppi on the floor, he jangled a small gold cross he had with him into the space he guessed the spirit was occupying. It funneled upwards and came down over the body of Giuseppi. The body slowly moved as O'Hare slammed the lead-door closed.

'Constrain him, Michael. And when you've done that take him outside and rub his nose in some dog shit.' Fen looked at O'Hare in amazement. 'Only joking. Not a bad idea though, eh, Marco. Give me his cell-phone before you go. We're taking you to Alaska for a little holiday. Get up, get your hands up, and face that wall.' O'Hare nodded at one of his armed agents. '*Do it!*'

'Leave it out, Charlie, he's an old man. What harm can he do us?'

Giuseppi was smiling. His wrinkled face anticipated further deception from his box of tricks.

O'Hare went over and pushed the agent aside. He shoved Giuseppi hard against the wall, kicked his legs apart and shouted hard at the agent to come over while he held him.

'Search him. Don't look in his eyes.'

The man ran his hands over Giuseppi's body removing a gun from inside a shoulder holster. He continued down his legs and felt something. He unbuckled his belt and pulled Giuseppi's pants down.

Giuseppi turned to the agents, 'Your boss wants to give me a blow job. Help yourself, Charlie.'

Taking a stiletto from a thigh knife sheath the agent handed to him he said, 'No thanks, saw what fellatio did to Tony D'Sotto.' He looked at the knife and smiled. 'Um. Take the man out of Sicily, so you can. But you ain't goin' take Sicily out of the man,' he said roughly pulling Giuseppi's hands behind his back. Handcuffing him, he pulled a black bag from his pocket and put it over Giuseppi's head.

'Do you know what you're doing?'

'Oh, yes. Returning you back from whence you came you piece of shit. That's your old man for you. Take him down,' O'Hare said shaking with excitement. 'You had a secret, and no-one knew it. Well it's out now, so it is.'

Giuseppi laughed, 'Ah, but do you know which one it is, Charlie O'Hare?'

'No. But I know enough and *is* will suffice. Whatever he tells you,' O'Hare said turning to the agent, 'keep that bag over his head. And agent . . . give him a change of clothes. Put him in one of those nice bright orange jump suits I want to make sure that the person seeking him doesn't have any difficulty finding him.'

Giuseppi struggled like an animal as they led him down the fire escape stairs that came out onto a secure area. He had a van ready waiting for him. If the angel were in the wings, she could have him and let the world descend into chaos. On that point, he agreed with the President when he said, 'Better for mankind to be written from the face of the earth with its soul intact, than for it to risk eternal damnation with daemons, Mr. O'Hare.'

Going back to collect remaining paperwork, O'Hare heard gunshots. At first he thought it was a *car back-firing*, but not for long. He ran down the back fire stairs; all nine agents were lying skewed on the steps at various angles in pools of blood. He pulled his gun out, but it made no difference, two men stepped out from where trash bins concealing them in a dark alcove, were on him before he knew what was happening.

Dressed in white suits, wearing crosses, both armed, they pointed their weapons at him demanding he drop his gun. Encouraged by the description, and dangerous nature of these men from Carter, O'Hare immediately complied. With a shield of white skin over his left eye where she had stubbed her cigarette, this man, with all the attributes of a dangerous animal cornered, he feared likely the worse of the two of them.

The other stepped forward to him.

'You Charlie O'Hare?' He nodded without thinking. 'You've been living on borrowed time for interfering in matters that do not concern you. There's an overall picture that has to be considered, and your shadow is bringing bad light.'

O'Hare's anger at seeing his agents slain in such a brutal fashion caused him to lose it.

'*Who in* hell *are you people?*' he cried out before his voice muffled by a piece of toweling jammed against his nose and mouth by the 'cornered animal', the snub of the barrel of a gun pushing against it silenced any further utterance from him. The bullet exiting the rear of his neck ricocheting from the concrete block wall behind with a zing he did not hear – the only response to his demand for an identity.

'We need to contain him quickly if our work is to come to fruition,' the first cohort said. '*Interfering fools!*'

Giuseppi removed the bag from his head. He was failing fast. The surrounding air full of spirits were taking up elements from his corporeal existence at a rate of declination that would see his powers pass to other manifestations as a virus eager to take on his mantle before the two could isolate him. Only fire from the House of God would cremate permanently that angel which the Lord banished without thought for the consequences.

The cohort's stood watching the aero engineer at his work. Ignoring the warning from the man that looking at its arc would damage their eyes, they watched as the cracking and spitting from rods enclosing the steel surrounded lead container, amidst choking smoke was near completion. Breaking off wires of spent rods from his hastily carried out work the man closed the gas bottle valve down.

'That do?' the engineer said wiping his hands on a piece of rag. 'No-one but Houdini; not the devil himself; will escape from that.' He smiled at the two strangers in white suits that had first approached him in his workshop hangar. He had told them he and his family needed to get out of town with all that was going on; but for some strange reason he had cheerfully helped them in their quest; that and the small gold bar offered as payment; assured that the man in the orange jump-suit had been dead for many years now, needed preservation. He watched as they fork-lifted the box onto a waiting plane before collapsing on the ground, with the words:

'God will welcome you,' ringing in his ears from the man with no name given, overridden by penalty from the man in the orange jump-suit recently sealed up.

'Yes sir. All dead, sir . . .' Agent Harry Fen answered the President from the pension's administrator's office. 'Including the . . . umm . . . *assistant director*. I'm sorry, sir. There was nothing to be done. They came—'

He waited for what seemed to him a lifetime, heard the President say, 'Oh, my dear men.' Not sure how to put what else he was to say; knowing that his next remark, with the President's obvious expressions of grief being an open wound, would reluctantly rub in the salt:

'I shall see to their removal as soon as the police are finished down here, sir. *Shall I?*'

With the bodies taken to a morgue, Fen called up Carter asking her if the President had heard from Oceans Galactica yet; as given the massacre that had taken place, he had authorized a team of Marines to be led by Colonel Lennox to be sent to White Bear immediately and that, given the circumstances he would like her to accompany him and them.

She had interrupted to ask, '*What massacre? Charlie was supposed to call telling me when it was go for Alaska—*'

'Didn't the President tell you?'

'*Tell me what?*' she screamed down the phone.

Thirty Two – 1997

Cromwell, I charge thee, fling away ambition:
By that sin fell the Angels.

HENRY VIII, Act 3

WITH ITS GLOBAL POSITION, the United States Air Force base White Bear; last occupied during the cold war, was ideally located. Once home to America's missile attack fighters, primarily for purposes of taking down the Soviet Union's air defense systems in the event of an invasion of Great Britain through Norway's narrow side door corridor. Another army: the Order of the Most Divine Third Circle; sentinels for an elite team of scientists intent on hacking into, by electromagnetic radiation, the brain of a spirit. Not any old spirit, nor any old seance: this modern Order had moved on since its birth 2000 years before when first they had crudely begun to spirit-rap God into revealing Himself, confess all, and explain to the 'animals' as to how He did it. Science had the technology to water-board Him into an explanation of His wonders of physics (known and not); with the Order on the verge of whipping up time/verse to reveal the composite mythological Father, Son, and Divine Spirit as true entities, using ultimate sin for finance, and lore Satan for bait, they were within a gnat's cock width of ousting Stephen Hawking off the No.1 slot of Master of the Universe.

Arriving in a Globemaster at Eielson Air Force Base, Fairbanks, Carter, Colonel Lennox, with Sergeant Brantlinger, and a pioneer team of marines transferred to a Sikorsky taking them on into a blizzard welcome that was White Bear. Hitting the Alaskan white landscape under a cloud of swirling ice from the planes vast rotor blades hacking into its freezing air, the exhaust from the engines blasting ice and snow into drifts of dirty slush, the doors were flung open. Marines fully armed with ancillary weaponry jumped out onto the snow. Two tracked Humvees, driven out from a transport plane ahead of them was readied and waiting. With heads crouching down against the blizzard, Carter, Lennox with two accompanying marines got into the first vehicle, while Brantlinger and his team, the second. Making the most of the blizzard to cloak their movements, they headed in two opposite direction, Brantlinger with orders to skirt the rear of the base, while Carter and Lennox drove their track straight to the front entrance where a force of para-military soldiers was facing them. While this was going on, Lennox's main thrust of his 1000-odd marines held back with their heavier weapons waited an order for an assault, when it became necessary.

The Order's army of para-military did not look as comfortable as they first did after seeing the Sikorsky. Outnumbered by the visitors awaiting orders; looking on at more marines than would be used as security at a Reganesque last night performance of Frank Sinatra Live at the White House, the officer in charge, carrying more stripes and decorations than was suited for fashion, was speaking on his radio hand-set as Lennox approached.

Wearing a uniform he did not recognize; challenged by the officer in charge as to what right he thought he had bringing all this heavy weaponry to intimidate a private company that had the President's blessing, Lennox spat in the snow told him, 'This base is the property of the United States Government and we're here to secure it, with or without your bloodshed, open those doors and get the *fuck* out of my way or I'll personally be using your arse for some kicking practice.'

At that, the para-military officer, seen by his men as a disciplinarian and bully, considered his standing in front of those same men, showing more concern for what Lennox might do to him than his men think of him, as all bullies worthy of their salt, telling his men to stand-down and drop their weapons.

'Thank you.' Lennox issued his order. 'You two, gather them up and take them in—'

'You can't do that,' the officer said trying to gather up some lost authority, 'we're employed by *Oceans Galactica*—'

'*What!* Dressed like . . . *fucking* Nazis.' Lennox spat in the snow once more. 'Get 'em out of 'ere. And . . .' Lennox held out his hand to the officer, 'your radio!'

Relieving him of it Lennox switched to transmit and announced to whoever was on the other end who they were (if they didn't know with CCTV covering the surround), and what he expected them to do next.

Carter, still mourning the death of O'Hare; with the thought that Hamilton was being held by these people; likely as a bargaining chip should things go wrong, was struggling with her conscience. She had never worked with the military before, if she ignored method training employed by the FBI, who had an altogether more subtle approach to problems, and with no concept of the military and their methods close up, it came as a culture shock to her. She hoped for an avoidance of killing. Judging by the no nonsense approach that Colonel Lennox was demonstrating; knowing he was certainly the right man for the job, she would not hold her breath as to how that might be achieved.

Colonel Lennox was taken aback when he first heard that a Carmelite nun had chosen the FBI for a 'sabbatical', until hearing what she had been capable of then changed his perspective of the woman (and for nuns in general for that matter). Clearly, these were talents they found useful. Her capability for halting a moving car by shooting the driver in his head and saving one of her people – *a passenger in its rear seat for Christ's sake* – from abduction. Apparently, that same man, a journalist, this time successfully abducted, was hostage once more.

Not a military officer to question orders, Lennox had found it bizarre what the late assistant director of the FBI had told them; and how these people had brought the world to the edge of nuclear war, was a mystery to him. Bringing to justice people involved in child abuse, was not something he ever imagined he might be involved. Not in any military sense anyway. In this case, by default, he was at the cutting edge of all that O'Hare had persuaded the President needed doing. If the prevention of these people carrying out an experiment was instrumental in bringing the world to the edge of the end, he was certainly the man to take them down.

Although he had the fire power, the responded conformance of his order, the other side of those doors, surprisingly took him back. This might be a cake-walk after all, he thought. The vast bomb-proof doors slowly slid away to reveal a secondary set twenty feet inside the first. His driver handed him the site plan. He studied it, passed it back, nodded issued the order to, 'Move forward.' The Humvee set off with a judder and a roar from its engine, setting down a cloud of exhaust in its wake before coming to a halt. He looked at Carter. She was looking anxious. 'You okay with all of this, Miss Carter?'

She half smiled at him.

'Please Colonel. Call me Annie. Charlie did, among others,' she smiled at the inappropriateness of O'Hare's more forcible words; 'it'll give me some comfort if you'd do the same.'

He returned her smile, 'Annie it is.' The secondary doors slowly slid back to reveal the hangar illuminated by enough energy to light up New York at Christmas. 'Into the jaws of hell,' he said moving forward. She looked at him in horror. 'Sorry, I always say that when I move out.'

A voice shouted, 'DOORS!' as they went through.

Lennox looked back to see the outer door close leaving his back up marines outside and the four of them inside; isolated.

'That's far enough,' a para-military soldier inside called to the driver putting his hand up for him to halt, 'stop right where you are and shut your engine down.' The driver looked at Lennox for permission to take an order from this man. Lennox nodded at him. 'All of you get down and come with me,' the man added.

Lennox had no choice than to do as asked. The four of them walked into the edge of the central hangar, the officer in charge, armed with an automatic rifle waved the direction they were to take. Lennox ascertaining a means of escape, with thoughts of getting any guns off anyone, turning tables would have be put on the back-burner now. The hangar had been re-equipped with levels of walkways in the center, banked with rows of computers at ground level; and what looked to Lennox to be a petrol-generator the size of a small house in one corner. Two giant coils that would not have looked out of place in a sub-way power station sat on the ground beside of it. Scientists in white coats were everywhere; clipboards in arms, some at computers, all gave to Lennox the appearance of a serious experiment being underway.

'Who are these people and what are they doing here?' Stonercrop asked the para-military soldier covering them with his weapon.

'Colonel Lennox and the President would like to know why an attack on Navy Seals took place, and who instigated it?' Lennox interrupted. 'Two killed, six injured. Would that have anything to do with you? Whoever you are.'

'I'm Dr. Max Stonercrop, head of science for the Order of the

Most Divine Third Circle; and nothing to do with the military. My understanding of the incident was that they were a Russian Task Force attacking us.'

'Your military incapable of distinguishing Russian uniforms and flags from our own?'

He did not answer, instead turned his attention to Carter.

'You're Sister Benedicta Marie aren't you?' Stonercrop asked.

'And how the hell do you know who I am?'

'Oh, I know you, good to see the Pope taking this seriously enough to honor us with his envoy,' he said holding his hand out to her. 'Dr. Max Stonercrop.'

She ignored his overture.

'You expect me to shake the hand of people bringing the world to catastrophe; that sanction the abuses of children, probably responsible for the killing of Charlie O'Hare. My capacity is firstly that of an FBI agent under orders from the President; and his Holiness's envoy, second. Both of whom demand the release of us and the surrender of this establishment and whatever distorted science you think you're engaged in here.'

He smiled, '*Charlie O'Hare!* I heard. A sad loss. I knew him in another life. My condolences.'

'You seem to know more than is good for you.'

'Let's say, a little bird told me,' he replied. 'As to bringing the world to the point of catastrophe, you're right; and your next question, yes, we have Hamilton Fitch too. We need someone to write our history books. Anyway, enough of this,' he said turning to one of the para-military guards, 'kindly take them down to the cells until we decide what to do with them.'

Carter felt the butt of a rifle in her back, along with Lennox and two of their marines, they were unceremoniously marched to an elevator. A slamming door made her turn round. A see-through door to a Plexiglas portable cabin. Inside, a body, unconscious. She broke away from their keepers and ran towards it. The one that had the best chance to stop her had his legs kicked from under him by Lennox. Despite this the para-guard caught her, taking her back, his arms round her waist, her legs off the ground kicking at him, she saw that it was Fitch. In this position, they forced them into the elevator with the others, descended down before stopping to she imagined was the lowest level. From here, taken down a service tunnel to some cells, Carter and Lennox locked in one; the two marines in another opposite.

Lennox had his face sideways jammed against the steel bars looking down the corridor. 'They're working on something down here. Did you see the end that has collapsed; that had building work alongside?'

'If you don't mind my saying, Colonel,' Carter said angrily, 'I'm more concerned with what's going on up there and what they have in mind for Hamilton.' She bit her lip desperately concerned for his welfare.

Lennox, one step removed from this woman's emotional state of mind, saw the end of the collapsed building as a means of escape.

Late afternoon, the military hospital morgue at Washington DC became a blaze of white light unsurpassed by anything before seen on earth. Witnesses later likened it to a white-out of snow shined on by thousands of camera flash bulbs fired simultaneously. Questioned later, no-one was able to ascertain with any degree of certainty where it had emanated. Causes offered varied between temporary blindness from having eyes open to those that had theirs closed from the shock of light. Whatever they were consensus was that a hydrogen bomb had been dropped somewhere in America. Though no measure of destruction seen, consoling themselves it was too far away to have any effect on them – yet. Despite this, people continued with their looting and rioting, figuring, there was nothing to lose.

If the light outside was powerful it was nothing to that inside where if anyone had been alive would have felt a rush of air. By the time life had re-emerged from being on hold, all still, as a morgue should be once more. Still that was, until someone starting kicking the base of the draw front he was being held prisoner inside.

Each man in turn hearing the kicking of bare feet on cold metal, realizing they were not alone, hearing shouting, joining in the chorus, added their own voice. Working out that by jerking the body backwards and forwards in the container considered the last resting place bar one, they found they could inch forward until they emerged out into the half-light of the morgue room that had no staff in attendance.

The door of the aircraft opened, and O'Hare jumped out onto the ice. Coming towards him were a group of marines headed by a sergeant.

'BRANTLINGER!' the man shouted his name in a salutary manner taken by surprise at this unexpected arrival. 'SERGEANT!' He added offering his rank. 'You're *Charlie O'Hare* aren't you? The man mandated by the President to oversee this op. We were told you were dead.'

'As you can see—

'Where are we at, Sergeant?' O'Hare asked.

'Colonel Lennox and the nun . . . she one of yours, sir? He nodded. 'There inside the complex; we can't get to them,' he said pointing to the hangar. 'Looks like they've been taken prisoners.'

'Are they in danger . . . of course they are, what am I saying? I need to get in there, Sergeant, can you help?'

'Well, I've reconnoitered part of the site, after speaking to someone earlier. Guy living local, civilian, used to work here apparently; a Scotlander chappie. He reckons the reason the Yanks pulled out was because of an earthquake back in '64. Big by all accounts. Anyway, there was big damage to the area, huge fissures in the earth and the like,' he pointed to what was left of the airstrip. 'Reckons the whole area, where our planes are parked, "crystallized sugar on a bowl of porridge". Whatever porridge is when it's at home. Anyway . . .'

O'Hare stamped his feet, 'Solid enough to me, but I'm only 180lbs. Carry on.'

'. . . the upshot is; there's a way in, courtesy of that particular Act of God. Through a fissure. Brings you into the basement, by all accounts.' He waited for O'Hare to say something more. He didn't. 'If you would come with me sir.'

'Good work. Lead on Sergeant.'

'Handful of men please,' Brantlinger shouted to those standing round. 'I need light weapons, ropes, rope ladders, ice-axes, pitons, screw-gates . . .'

'Brantlinger! *O'Hare?*' Lennox called out seeing them and several marines breaking through the end of the corridor.

'*Charlie!*' Carter shouted seeing him at the same time. She had tears in her eyes when they came up to the cell door. Reaching out, she had to touch him to reassure herself that it was he. 'They told me you were dead . . . they've Hamilton. I don't know if he's still alive.'

'Annie!' O'Hare said. 'I'm here; I'll take care of things from here on in.'

'She's gone. Evaporated in a ball of white light.'

Lennox nudged Carter in the arm. She looked at him and looked in the direction he was showing with his eyes.

'Stay right where you are. Seeing as you've gone to all the trouble, you can be my guests for the remainder of the show.'

'Max Stonercrop, as I live and breathe; so does he.'

Nobody noticed when it arrived from nowhere to arrive outside the hangar doors. Standing on its end, its steelwork as the skin of a chameleon changed its appearance to the white of the hangar door it stood beside. Inside, waiting, scientists with O'Hare, Lennox, Carter, and Stonercrop watched to order. An orange jump-suit was the first they saw as an hors d'oeuvre for the formal presentation of the magic that was to follow. A life size faded photograph. A faint dirty orange image appeared on the gray steel-work on the inside of the hangar door. It became brighter and clearer, until, 3-dimensionally formed, the body with its weight unable to remain attached to it slid down the door like rotten tomatoes thrown haphazardly against it. Ahriman fell forward to the floor. Fully shaped, two white-coated assistants helped him to his feet. O'Hare was astounded. Somehow, this creature had managed to reduce his molecular structure of one material: the metal door, to less than that of his own. Known physics for such an achievement was an impossibility that would have been earth shattering to the world of science without him pulling off any other trick.

He appeared to O'Hare older than he had been when they had first confronted him. His head hanging forward. The energy that he had summoned to organize his atoms to pass through the steel had clearly taken a toll on him. His hair long, lank, and thin. His face and arms looked as if they belonged to someone 200 years old run flat by a road roller.

Enter his next trick.

Like a pupae to a moth he was metamorphosing; growing younger before their eyes. The chains they had bound him fell away as if they were cooked spaghetti. He turned and smiled at them. The creature, a composite of Spannocs, Giuseppi, and something stinking; with his programmed human mind and sense of humor murmured to them:

'I'm getting *far* too old for this.'

All O'Hare could do was stand and stare. He was changed. He was not Spannocs, but neither was he Giuseppi. His only link to both men, his slick-backed blonde hair with the black ribbon tied in a bunch.

'He's his own magic, you know. This your man, Charlie? The one your angel is seeking.'

'She's not my *angel*. She belongs to another. So if you had any designs on her, you've had it, she's returned from where she came from.'

'I don't think so. Giuseppi has shown himself, she'll come again, only this time she'll bring the other; and we'll be ready for both.'

'Ready for what? You do know they'll destroy all of us, don't you? What's the point of that?'

'Why, we are going to break into time, bring to us those creatures that have created us.' He smiled. 'An experiment that few will be privy to live through. In fact, I will go so far as to say, that no-one witnessing what is to happen will be permitted to leave passing on their message. We're on the cusp of a new order here.'

'You're mad,' Lennox suggested.

'A stock response from people that cannot see beyond the end of their noses, Colonel. The same observation made of people seeking to break new ground, as Francis Galton; and Hitler, his believer and much derided practitioner of the science. A science that to this day still holds credence. *Darwinism.* But I cannot expect a mere soldier to understand the intricacies of the universe.'

'I will not disagree with you over Darwin,' Carter interjected before Lennox headed off at a tangent knocking six bells of shit out of the man; 'but I don't think his observations extended to wiping out people considered inferior. And how, pray, is that going to further the cause of eugenics; that is what you are speaking of, isn't it? Asking it to explain?'

'We shall not only be seeking their knowledge; we intend to procreate with them.'

She laughed. 'You're not *serious*.' The look on his face showed he was; the expression of insanity recognized from earlier days when the Carmelite administered to the sick, as well as the insane, was that he was also serious.

She tried humoring the man. 'Well, I've not seen one, but the *other*. If you are expecting to breed with them, you are no doubt aware; there is a mechanical flaw to that process in her. How do you intend to get over that?'

Colonel Lennox looked at her in horror. Creatures! What in hell was going on in this place? His remit was to fight, take prisoners; it had all gone wrong. Had it been Carter's intention of allowing their capture, though how she managed that, when he had taken charge had bypassed him? *This is a madhouse!* he muttered for them to hear.

'*Artificial insemination*,' Stonercrop announced casually.'

'And the giving of birth?' O'Hare added.

'*Caesarean section.*'

'What's to be gained?'

'A hyper-breed of humanity; without its frailty. Of course, he has to steer clear, in case she gets a sniff of him. You see they are both identical, only biologically do they differ. Separate the two and she is confused. A clever precaution don't you think, Charlie? *Miss Carter*, you are a welcome spectator. I'm sorry, your faith is about to be shattered. Your expertise is superfluous here. As I explained to Charlie some time ago. He never listened. Religion and faith in an Almighty by prophets and religious leaders from the time – fundamentally disbelieved by them – was encouraged for the power it gave them. You know, Charlie . . . it never ceases to amaze me how much has been written. Whole libraries full of the stuff. Such a small word with such power. Of course, the interpretation of *faith*, for the convincing of the masses is complete and utter trust in something that has no logical proof. I can never understand how so many swallowed it, but they did. They do. And all based on a human need for something greater than themselves. Until that is, 2000 years ago, something did happen that turned faith into a reality. An incident recorded, written, passed down to people that would secrete it. The Roman holiday. The genocide by their judiciary, without trial, of Jews, Christians, anyone that had witnessed events of the day; telling others what they had seen.'

O'Hare interrupted, 'What they had seen was the Holy Ghost. Recorded, according to the five gospels in the New Testament. What's to add to that, pray?'

'That God and He's angels are a superior race of human beings; and not what religion tells us to believe them to be. More importantly, He is not singular, but one from one verse; other Gods and spirits equal to Him in others.'

'And where is the proof?'

'We are about to prove that now,' Stonercrop answered.

O'Hare shook his head.

Shcch!

The sound issuing through Giuseppi's teeth was loud and chilling. His words, toward Carter, tightened O'Hare's fists, brought blood and anger of years to his face:

'Another Harlot of Babylon from a nest of crawling maggots. Pussy suckers all. Does the Pope still bring gifts of dildos? Multi-coloured strapping. Does he film you while you're in your cells working them up your fellow Sister's privates for the entertainment of his Cardinals?'

O'Hare put his fists up and came forward to knock the son-of-a-bitch's head off his shoulders. And he would have done had not one of the para-soldiers grabbed him from behind.

Carter smiled shaking her head at Giuseppi, then turning to O'Hare said, 'Thanks Charlie, but there is no need. He bears all the hallmarks of being possessed of Satan. Who else could come through a solid door like that? Now exposed he will be relegated to 665 when the angel comes for him.'

'And when that happens, we'll have them both,' Stonercrop added.

'You've to do better than that. The world has moved on. Do you think that God is interested in personal human behavior?' She turned to Stonercrop. 'Another race? Quoting words from Revelations. I don't think so. Old Clooty there is taking you for a ride.'

The Ahriman Host rolled his head and looked toward the heavens, snarling.

Carter laid the rest of her hand.

'And the thought by him that Our Lord Jesus Christ was supposed to have been engaged in pedophilia because of a badly written scroll, in the hope it would convince a modern world of its truth was a joke,' she continued; 'that someone who had an axe to grind over Jesus of Nazareth's popularity would use to convince, again the modern world, that it might have been used as evidence at His trial. An insurance policy to ensure His execution in case Pilate lost his nerve condemning the Man on nothing more than flimsy accusations, that He was engaged in insurrection against Rome.

'And you passed it to someone to smuggle out of Italy. Who did you pass it to before faking your own death? Crosses on an ancient element background that would have afforded them protection, for they were his people weren't they. Satan's cohorts.'

The Ahriman Host continued to roll his head toward the sky.

'Why could you not read Aramaic?' Carter said to Giuseppi. 'Those cohorts of yours, saying they were Teutonic Knights, were nothing of the sort. How would they have known such a document, found in the middle of nowhere existed if they did not know Satan had not written and planted it in the first place, before someone informed the authorities that a Tabernacle uncovered in the desert would be worth investigating. As long as it wasn't the Israelis, who of course would have known immediately for what it was. Anyone knowing Jewish document layout protocol would have spotted immediately. Getting it into the Vatican for safe keeping was clever, I grant you. You orchestrated that with precision. But you let yourself down again, your cohorts left part of it in the ark; big enough to be carbon dated; it's no more than 1800 years old.' She leaned forward before anyone had time to stop her, grabbed his hair, pulled his head back and spat in his face. She could see the pain in his eyes was immediate and intense. She did not need a cross at her bosom for what she was doing to him. It was within her heart, burning into what passed as a soul.

He held his head back and began howling like a wolf. The terror that was emanating from him from those standing close crept into their bodies making the hairs on their arms stand rigid and the back of their necks turn cold. Outside, across the Alaskan tundra, the horizon darkened; the clouds rolling, sent lightning searing through to hit the earth, with a following thunder that shook the hangar. He was growing smaller as they watched. The para-solider, no longer interested in holding O'Hare, released him, and tried to get away. But he, as the rest of them, was unable.

'The angel won't find me. I've thousands of years of practice avoiding all of them. While she's looking, the entity will be theirs.'

Carter let the hair on his head run through her fingers as he went toward the ground. She smelled the dressing coming from it, turning her own head away from the smell, urged. Regaining her composure, she came again with words uttered with venom: *As is usual with you, deceiver, you have your own mandate:*

'And I saw thrones, and they sat upon them,

And judgment was given unto them:

And I saw the souls of them that were beheaded for the witness of Jesus,

And for the word of God,

And which had not worshiped the beast,

Neither his image, neither had received his mark upon their foreheads,

Or in their hands;

And they lived and reigned with Christ a thousand years.... . Arsehole!'

She dropped his head down on his chest as if she were throwing a stone to the ground.

'Annie!' O'Hare said feigning shock. 'That's hardly becoming language for a Carmelite.'

'Becoming enough for an FBI agent?' she asked angrily grabbing his hair once again.

'Well, I suppose, I will allow dispensation.'

'I'll take it.' She pulled his hideous face to her own, 'Hear that, *arsehole!*' she repeated back into Giuseppi's face as he slipped from between her fingers leaving clumps of his hair in her hand that then began moving. She stood back in horror. Her hands in front of her. She snatching at her fingers trying to remove the creatures the hair had become. Black maggots crawled over her hands and wrists falling to the ground as she slowly removed them. He was gone, and he had taken Charlie with him. All that remained of him were the pupae on the ground, and she drew back in horror once more, the sense of who she had been speaking coming upon her.

O'Hare faced him. Disaffected from all round him, this Ahriman–Giuseppi was duplicating himself at a rate that was nauseous; and O'Hare found himself traveling down through centuries, wondering if it would ever cease. For if it didn't, was he destined to follow him to the very beginnings of time itself? Where accepted science separated from religious creationism: one 12000 million years before; the other 10000 years; and where the possibility that their two verses, each a victim of their own given hype co-existed in their own time with no knowledge of the other. To O'Hare, he hoped at least to end this at the latter though it would be a denial of his understanding and for the first time in his life, he understood he had never settled on an answer he had passed over. Would his religious faith overcome the science?

The images kept coming. Gratefully spared from what he looked like in reality. The shock to the system could well be permanent, similar to that of the Divine Spirit, seeing and not living beyond the experience. If his watch sweep hand was correct, he was traveling into a past.

A tabernacle before him, each side, a man in a white suit, their hands gesturing him to enter; to follow Ahriman–Giuseppi. Assuming that time flowed from past through present to future; and not the paradox of future through present to past he forged his plan. He knew that past and present being real, that only the future is not; therefore, he was going from present to past; the other paradox that anything he carried out in both times would flow in what he understood as forward, he determined, towards the future. He followed him inside to be confronted by hundreds of the same man moving past him. Each identical to the one before, *doppelgängers en masse*, they kept coming in a dizzy line-up of similarity.

When the line-up ceased one, fixed in front of him like a picture, began slowly moving back as if they were individual frames on a film strip, that he found himself studying each in turn. Each fixed and smiling, laughing, as he moved onto the next seeking out the man that had been instrumental in the worst cases of child abuse, child abduction, child murder, mental and physical torture that humanity had ever had to bear. An insurmountable task he knew it to be, as did the instigator of such diabolical evil. He stood facing him. His hand shaking, trying to hold his gun steady. A man in a white suit beside him laughed.

'Ah, but which one, Charlie? How can you possibly know? Behind the mask is you, take out the wrong one, and you'll be repeating the exercise to the end of your death time. *A hell of your own making!'*

As close up to Ahriman–Giuseppi's face as he could stand O'Hare began reciting:

'Mrs. Puggy Wuggy has a square cut punt,

Not a punt cut square.

It's round in the stern and blunt in the front,

Mrs. Puggy Wuggy has a square cut punt,'

over and over, faster, and faster, until Ahriman–Giuseppi, bemused, began to play the game.

Repeating the rhyme up and down the lines, through centuries, frame by frame, laughing, reciting, and falling over the words, tears in his eyes, until O'Hare was satisfied.

When he pulled the trigger, the images of the man came together like a pack of cards before disappearing. Born 1890. He looked his age. Standing before him, was Giuseppi the younger, his Host departed. A gangster, a union boss, mobster, psychopath, child trafficker.

'How could you be so sure?' Giuseppi croaked. The bullet entering his Adam's apple also went into his voice box. '*How hhhhh?'*

A small hole, the size of a dime, ringed with a black bruise, leeched blood. The back of his head, the nape of his neck, a hole, big enough to put a fist in, surrounded by brain matter, bone, and blood. He spun then went down.

Stonercrop, with the para-soldiers pushing them in the backs with their weapons, forced them all to the inside of the hangar where the equipment, readied for the 'experiment', attended by scientists and assistants in white coats, were frantically working. Despair for Carter. On his knees, with Giuseppi standing over him, smiling, with a gun to the back of Fitch's neck, execution-fashion, caused her to scream.

'There are no other choices here, Charlie.'

He had reappeared, as if by magic, '*Charlie!*' Carter shouted seeing him talking to Giuseppi. 'For God's sake, can't you do anything?'

His life or your co-operation,' Stonercrop said. 'Think of it. A world with the ability for its people to move between verses. The exploration – the infinite knowledge gained – would be mind-blowing. And Charlie, you can come with me on this. Join us. You can share in this quest to uncover the greatest truth that will ever come this way again. All you fought against, surely has its own rewards. If the means to an end was ever in need of being justified, this is one.'

'Umm. You make a compelling argument, Stonercrop,' he said seeing Fitch in the position he was in; 'I'll say that much for you.'

'Thought I'd get you round to our way of thinking in the end. Always hated Jews with a passion, you know – Giuseppi won't be disappointed.'

Stonercrop was smiling. The culmination of years was to reap rewards for infinitesimal knowledge and the creation of a new world order. An order that many had spoken of, but never had the power to achieve. Lower orders of government knowing what they were came under a strict regime of secrecy on pain of death overseen by Johnson and Sullivan. The upper echelons, his bosses, he knew neither their names nor where they came from. He had never meant to outline his plans, leastways, not to O'Hare. But with the world on the brink of destroying itself; and with this base, nuke proof and them inside with the means to sustain themselves for six months, a year, he no longer saw a need to keep his powder dry.

O'Hare was puzzled. Giuseppi was still standing. *What was that all for?*

'Think of it, Charlie. One race of humans that all think scientific; have the same aspirations; Illuminati: keepers of the secrets of all ages, the inauguration of all religions that will practice Orphism without the hindrances of Judaism and Biblical Christianity . . .'

O'Hare clapped his hands. 'Wonderful . . . and so *original.* And I suppose a population of Illuminati of no more than a billion people on the earth at any one time?'

'Two actually.'

'Many as that? And who might they be after your new breed of hyper-humans that the human race would benefit from the removal of those not quite up to the mark I wonder? Let me think. I know, we can start on . . . let's get the disabled out of the way first. Mentally retarded. You'll have to be a bit careful yourself there. White skins only. Check out your ancestry on that while you're making up your list. Unclean, unsavory, poor, educationally lacking. How am I doing? *It's all been tried before!* Doesn't anyone read history books anymore? Hitler was Illuminati you know, along with his SS, though, they were only initiates; and they would have gone. One small chink in that particular brand of armor for a population of such intelligence . . . someone will always be brighter – and duller. The lesser on the intelligentsia scale will be every much a demand on resources in your new world order as those unfortunates are in ours. There's your new breed, which will soon become bored and tire of you. It's all relative you see Stonercrop; I'm surprised you hadn't thought it through. Unless . . . you have, haven't you?'

'If it weren't for our people you wouldn't be in the position of being able to criticize me. You small-minded Irish gipsy.'

'Steady on, no need to get personal. You're mixing me up with . . . Sin.'

'*Sin!*'

O'Hare's thoughts were in another country. Another time. His ancestral family.

'And where are the rest of your Illuminati, I wonder?' he asked, his eyes searching the hangar, studying faces, before seeing a smoke-black one-way window further down, two levels up, showing the shadows of Johnson and Sullivan behind them.

Before Stonercrop had the chance to answer, a vivid white light that illuminated the hangar struck.

She came in through the vast shut down metal doors as if they were draped mist.

Missile- and bomb-proof doors that once gave war planes shelter to the runway outside, never designed to deny access to a spirit world might as well have not been there.

The sky cracked. The son of Woden could not have delivered a greater rumble of thunder across the Alaskan wasteland; bringing with it a blizzard as an accompaniment. She brought part of it in with her. The wind-driven ice shaping itself round her, giving those that saw an impression she was a Christmas card design model. She hung in the air, her hands in front of her half clawed, looking as if she would spring on anyone at any moment that made a false move. Turning her head slowly from side to side, she sought someone. Seeing Giuseppi, bound, on his knees, she was confused. She sensed him in another person. He did not seem the same one she had been chasing down all these years; that always seemed to keep two steps ahead of her. Too far from a world she had once inhabited, her remit had differed from what it had once been. The Prophet was to suffer and die for a greater effect, while she, abandoned by default was to wander the earth until the Comer took her back. The role of guardian hard-wired inside of her replaced by a different mandate. Life should not corrupt its off-spring – it should cherish and nurture. A world that traumas and cheapens is destructively challenged. A losing battle constantly having to seek solace and goodness to carry on milked from a human spirit. Two thousand years had taken their toll on her; she would have to decide.

The succession of lightning strikes, accompanied her, illuminated the smoke-black window in three flashes resembling a strobe light revealed two men to O'Hare. One seated, the other next to him, standing. O'Hare guessed if that was Sullivan seated, the one watching proceedings alongside of him with a clipboard in his hand was Johnson.

The screech from her was ear piercing as she moved forward to take the one she had come for.

'*It's a trap!*' Carter screamed at the angel.

A double edged sword appearing from nowhere was in her hands. Going through the Plexiglas cabin, before Giuseppi had chance to move a muscle against Fitch, she wiped his head from his shoulders in a single blow. No head. She looked round. He had gone, returned, his head back on his shoulders.

The Host had returned.

The sword at his feet, Ahriman–Giuseppi, snatched it up in his hands laying it across Fitch's neck.

Fitch tensed at his imminent death by decapitation. A Biblical form of execution used against infidels, only . . . *He was not one!*

Ahriman–Giuseppi stood his ground he would carry out his

threat to the last of the Weinberg's. Stroking the flat of the sword gently to the back of Fitch's head, better for him to strike his head off true, he pulled back his arms. Looking up at O'Hare, smiling, laughing. O'Hare could do nothing but pray the angel would come again to remedy this desperate situation playing out before them. She was gone again. As was the Host.

With time, past and its future, neither Giuseppe nor O'Hare had any awareness, he, Giuseppi dropped the sword. It fell to the ground ringing. He staggered back with a look of utter bewilderment. The bullet that had not come from the present came into his frontal lobe exiting the back of his head blowing his brains against the cabin, which executioner and condemned hostage – their extraordinary relationship – should have concluded for the latter, instead of which the former, was finalized.

Something in the back of O'Hare's subconscious spoke the words *Because you spit when you speak*; replayed themselves repeatedly as a continuous loop of recording tape in his head.

A tomb deep underground below remaining graves alongside a hypermarket in midtown Manhattan; the last resting place of the tribe known as Algonquin; two men, side by side, wearing white suits attracting not a speck of dust shuddered initially for no apparent reason, assuming any witness to the event were there to look on, before a hole appearing in each of their throats would have given them part answer; vaporized, the tomb collapsing in on itself; crows, absent since 1920, returned; struck up their choruses in the trees surrounding its car park began nesting.

Hamilton had remarked to Carter, after, and first when he exposed to the presence of the angel had said she reminded him of what Queen Orithyia of the Amazons might have looked like. '*Why?*' she had gone onto to ask, he answering that that would have accounted for her not having a vagina. Carter, finding his remark in bad taste made the comment:

'I take it you are likening her lack of any natural genitalia a sign of some "perpetual virginity" to make such a statement. You know that Herodotus called the Amazons Androktones. *Killers of men!* Tread carefully Mr. Reporter; else she'll have *you* for breakfast.'

He looked suitably chastised, nonetheless, could not prevent smiling at the thought.

In this place, to Carter, the angel needed neither natural nor earthly accoutrements that separate the female of the human species from its male counterpart. She suffered none of the vanities that a makeover industry might bring to her. She had a beauty all of its own. Her long hair had a tone Carter could not easily put a name to (monastic life removing the need for such products), that fanned back tumbling over her shoulders. Her skin sheen unblemished color light brown. Off-white teeth bared inside her slightly open mouth. Her eyes were those of a tigress. She was pure blown angel in human form. *Charlie*, she said to herself. *You had who you thought she was so, so wrong.* A human child cannot transcend to angel status of this likeness. She was clearly not the little girl abducted all those years before that he and his partner Frank Weinberg had sought protection for.

More from sense of wonder than devotion to worship, Carter put her hands to her mouth as in prayer. If she required a visual interpretation by one of the seven angels and their seven vials from the Book of Revelation's, Visions of Doom, this slayer of the Mother of Harlots would be as good a starting point as any.

She . . . was . . . *awesome!*

Whoever thought of crossing her was going to have to think again. They would have no conception of what they were taking on. Until confronted by her when they would have understood too late.

Their heads torn from their shoulders instead of an expected sexual fantasy played out with them for their pleasure. For if accounts were partly correct, and she was what the High Priests transcribed her to be, one of two angels in Christ's sepulcher: an angel overridden by God's will to save the Son of Man before He 'gave up the ghost', it was little wonder Stonercrop's Order were so keen to bring the world to its knees for knowledge it possessed. And *she* was the messenger turned bait, Carter could not imagine what was to come in this place.

Written in the Bible, as sin beyond redemption, was not for nothing. The problem was the human race would suffer for its complacency. Carter recalled minding St. Matthew's account after the crucifixion of Jesus, of earthquakes and temples collapsing. This was more than a few temples. The destruction at Becland was just starters when she confronted something. And clearly, an angel interfering in God's world was not acceptable to Him whatever her reasons. Perhaps O'Hare's thoughts that divine intervention was attempting to bring her back into the fold might hold substance. Although, finding that as a theory, however intriguing to her, she was still out jury-wise. If she was the conduit the Order had sought to bring whatever was out there to earth; the Holy Ghost, Divine Spirit, call it what they will; likely the most powerful Being, at least in O'Hare's version of his space–time continuum; judging by the scientific equipment in place they had every intention of capturing something, head scanning and whatever other sick plan Stonercrop said they had for breeding with them.

Was it close? With a world fast closing in on all of them. Darkness descending for reasons other than the time of day or season. The roar of thunder, along with the deteriorating earth, resonated through her body. As the pages of a book, blowing in the wind, one upon another that would return to the first paragraph, the thought that time itself going backwards came to her – and prayed she was wrong. As Sister Benedicta Marie, Carter found herself reciting the first Book of Moses:

In the beginning God created the heaven and the earth.
And the earth was without form, and void;
And darkness was upon the face of the deep.
And God moved upon the face of the waters . . .

The Supreme Being was returning earth to dust and to what it once was: an empty cold timeless vacuum, without so much as dark matter to hold it together. *Would He fade into faithless obscurity?* she asked herself.

Hamilton, with the thought still being operative inside a head, to his relief, still attached to the rest of him, implanted by Carter of her description as to her being 'a killer of men', dared to glance into the large video screen erected to the left of his shoulder. Hanging from the metal roof trusses it appeared to be showing a live link. He guessed, You Tube. This was too big an event to be contained to those here. The CCTV camera had captured an image of something. A sylph-like impression in the snowflakes that surrounded her left no doubt that image manipulation was not at play when he had first laid eyes on her. She was not there. To him she looked as if she knew what her business in this place was. *He* guessed forgiveness for any of them was not in her mind.

She moved forward and stopped. A universal gasp from those here for ulterior motives went out. No doubt, wondering if Stonercrop had control of what was coming from this particular Pandora's Box. Whatever they thought, it was too late the clicking had started. Something's eternal trademark entrance echoed from the roof beams.

The look of the creature was a surprise to Fitch when it entered the hangar. Where the angel came in at two meters, it was no more than a meter. If they were an item, they would have looked awkward. But they appeared to be two different species. She, human in appearance, assuming *she* was best definition for a creature that did not have the usual anatomical attributes; the creature – to make the comparison with a character from the Sci-Fi film, *Star Wars*, was Yodaesque. He laughed. And without seeing under its cloak, no way of knowing if, it, like her, had a sex. But any talk of sexual differences was a human perspective; postulate. What was in front of them here was two species. And he, brought up with the teachings of the Torah, could never accept any implication that any of this was to do with Jesus as the messiah and all other implications for angels and the like attending Him at His crucifixion. O'Hare had told him that he himself was not necessarily on that particular road to Damascus, it all being too simplistic given 2000 years of story-telling. Only Carter, employed as an archivist within the Church of Rome, had held onto her faith that these creatures are messengers from God and that their acceptance of their faiths should not compromise that of Hamilton Fitch. And, with the name Satan banded about, regarding that other creature, that clearly had *his* own agenda to take over the world, he thought his time was up. For there is a paranormal occurrence in their midst which he could not deny. God and the Devil! He remembered O'Hare saying to him, that where Christ built a church, Satan would have his chapel in its yard. Present circumstances seem to bear that out.

What concerned him wasn't its liking to the sound of a curtain opening or closing, but the sound of a Geiger counter. The entity might be measuring the degree of radioactivity it was exposing itself to entering this alien world. Which, of course was ridiculous; but the thought that it was generating a lethal dose to everyone within range was not beyond the realms of possibility. Bringing an unnatural life span to all those exposed? Perhaps this Order, instead summoning up spirits, should have had a scientific reappraisal of where these things come from relative to the cosmos before any of this. And it wouldn't surprise him to learn; for them to discover that it wasn't some mythical finishing school for those that have passed over waiting to be re-born; where the white bearded God sits surrounded by celestial music poring over a drawing board with a pair of architects dividers in his hand; more a space in time commiserate with a black hole. A slot in dark matter that would be toxic to any space–time traveler entering for purposes of exploration – dying rather than the other way round.

There was to Fitch what he could only describe as a wind of electrons moving between them. He never pretended to be scientific. Her hair flowed away from her as if by static. The entity was not part of it. In fact, Fitch hadn't noticed, but it had left the stage leaving the angel and Satan to fight it out between themselves.

Stonercrop's scientists and technical experts were concentrating on their work stations. They appeared to be waiting for computers and instruments to reach a level that they would move in from. One of the men, a clipboard in his hand, pen in the other, was moving between computer and recording screens checking on figures. He seemed to be anticipating where the entity had gone and when it would return.

With the gravitational pull of AG-MX-960, no-one was going anywhere soon. The angel sensing what had happened was onto it. Coming down at him with an ear-splitting scream. She was tearing at Satan's head trying to get inside him. Came the clicking beside her. It was attempting to pull her off him as in the past.

What the . . . ! O'Hare said to himself. *Have I got the wrong person on the right side here?*

The Order's engineers released a stream of data from one computer into another much larger one. They were unfazed by what was occurring, or what was happening. As far as they were concerned it was pure scientific mechanics. Divine Spirit. The Man. The Harlot. Held fast. A metre in height. To O'Hare's eyes, He looked no more Biblical than a garden gnome. Wires and connections over his unhooded head revealed a face with two eyes and no other facial features.

O'Hare looked away.

Carter looked away.

Fitch, despite his skepticism, did the same.

Illustrated science fiction artists all tend to interpret the look of a creature from beyond the stars regularly. Whether one of these artists had seen one, or it was the product of a commercial artist's imagination, one could never be sure, O'Hare thought. Whether they had or not, he was not going to go checking the look of one out anytime soon, and he hoped that Carter and Fitch were feeling the same. Was Divine Spirit a go between representing Satan; as well as God, was another thought that went through his mind. Did He have a vested interest in keeping Satan on-board?

O'Hare seeing the main power unit to the computer and fearing a nuclear catastrophe from combining spirits with gravitational magnetism of these strengths attempted to disable it with a fire axe hanging on a wall. Sullivan, seeing him, coming from nowhere, pulled a revolver on him.

Fitch went to his aid.

'Stay where you are, Weinberg. A journalist is supposed to report news does not get involved in its outcome. Still placing Weinberg's in your firing line I see, O'Hare.' He turned to Fitch. 'Did you know he was responsible for the deaths of two of your family? Perhaps I should take revenge on behalf of the family by killing you,' Sullivan said. 'As soon as you involved a reporter from the *New York Post* I put two and two together. They used you, Weinberg. To trap

Frederik Spannocs. Except, they didn't know that Spannocs was a servant of the State as themselves. Not on the wrong side – for there isn't one – but on another, eh, Charlie boy. Drop the axe.'

He let it fall onto the concrete floor where it clattered.

Sullivan lowered his revolver.

Fitch nodded at O'Hare, who kicked out at his wrist knocking the gun across the floor. O'Hare made a dive for it. From his prone position on the floor he picked it up and pointing it at Sullivan put pressure on the trigger; but the sound of the generator bursting into life distracted both men. When O'Hare looked back, Sullivan was gone.

O'Hare shrugged. Sullivan wasn't a million miles away from being right, he thought. He should have quit as soon as Frank was murdered. He should have had the good sense to know that he couldn't outgun the State. But he was where he was, and that was an end to it. AG-MX-960 was a remarkable piece of kit (he had to admit that) but had no place in this world with what they intended it for – not now, not ever. This was science too far. A strange part of him decreed that if God leveled by man's science, it was for Him to either accept it or put more science between them and it. He had always reasoned that was the case after every scientific advance ever made, except the part that would forever remain elusive, creation itself, and who was behind it? He would destroy it.

Fitch noticed that some bright spark had the audacity to hang a notice on the front of the giant magnet:

GOD'S REPRESENTATIVE ON EARTH

BROUGHT TO YOU WITH THE SCIENCE OF THE

ORDER OF THE MOST DIVINE THIRD CIRCLE

Given a different set of circumstances he might have laughed. All they needed to add was:

SPONSORED BY PEPSI COLA AND COLONEL SANDERS

and it would have been farce complete. Here was the world hanging by a thread, and these lunatics were opening Pandora's casket with arrogance, ignorance, and self-aggrandizement.

The video crew sensing something seriously dangerous happening were in no mood to hang round any longer than they had to in spite of Stonercrop's protestations that they had no need to worry. They didn't believe him. Knocking him to the ground in their rush for the exits they pulled trails of wires and equipment over. The angel was on the move away from the entity as Ahriman floated away from the two of them in a breeze of encapsulated celestial light. She appeared to be considering her next move.

O'Hare seeing what she was attempting tried to stop her, too late. Carter walked forward and pulled one of the connections from the entity releasing it from AG-MX-960's force field. *What was she doing?*

He screamed at Fitch to get her away.

Fitch grabbed her. But it was too late, she had pulled him in. Darkness fell over the hangar as if a heavy duty black cloth the size of the universe had descended on them. O'Hare knew, *knew* that it had taken them. The Divine Spirit's showing as a mortal size was not comparable to its actual one. Larger than man's imagination could ever get its head round; and with its ability to move round and across the universe and the rest of what might be out there would have been no surprise to anyone with a modicum of intelligence. They were gone in a flash of white light and a click. The both of them.

Into a world of chaos and disorder; where the ingredients for the recipe for the creation of life and its potential for good or ill are but a thin line; where the Chef of His interpretation of dimension can spoon his mixtures of particle matter to create His own unique life form adjusting it at his experimental whim. All juxtaposed with a smidgen of a time–shift far enough apart not to spill into the next. Except, occasionally and opportunistically, over a 10,000,000,000 human year time flow a saucepan boils over spilling a cooking cabbage out onto the kitchen floor, where it assumes hierarchical status as that of a king.

Fitch was looking at her. She smiled. Was he dreaming? Standing next to them was interfered light of a creature. The remains of a cable trailing from her hand were severed; with the other end, a probe attached to the side of Its head. It tried to shake it off but couldn't. All round her, Carter was unable to estimate, mirrored millions of herself. They came from all directions. All dimensions. They both collapsed alongside of each other onto the hard, dusty concrete floor, the cable in mid-air attached to something invisible fell to the ground free.

As Fitch was helping her to her feet, she saw and screamed, '*Charlie! Behind you!*'

Sullivan. Coming up on O'Hare, dropped a box over his head, pushing it down hard on the top of his skull.

O'Hare put his hands up to remove it, but it was stuck fast. He heard the movement of a clock winder taking up the tension of a coiled spring into a tight circle. He felt the tightening of a steel band round his forehead. It was slowly pulling his head round. With nothing more than a hair trigger holding the explosive coil, he knew what would happen when it was released.

'Goodbye, Charlie. Nice to have worked with you these past ninety years—'

'Stop it, stop him. *Hamilton!*' Carter screamed.

O'Hare, with Sullivan's gun half in and half out of the man's shoulder holster fired haphazardly; at the same moment, Fitch punched Sullivan hard on the jar, knocking him to the floor. The stray bullet from O'Hare's gun struck the center of Stonercrop's chest shattering his sternum on its journey. He staggered with his hand over the blooded fatal wound, falling over the keyboard of the computer's console sending the last stream of data into its memory before passing into its hard drive. The information uploaded, it turned itself off, ejected itself from the terminal.

Hamilton found a lever on the box, ceasing its movement, carefully removed it from O'Hare as Sullivan got to his feet and tried to run. O'Hare seeing him getting away snatched the box from Fitch, chased Sullivan and jammed it on his head saying, 'I owe you this one.'

The spring firing mechanism inside exploded and the box fell away from his body. Sullivan, his remains in two ill proportioned halves lay still. The box, which half a minute before had been on his own head began vibrating taking Sullivan's head a full six feet across the floor and away from his lower body before its spring relaxed.

Stonercrop fell backwards from the console collapsing on top of the larger part of the body that had been Agent Daniel Sullivan, born 1876, died 1997; the son of Irish farming stock, from Wexford County, Ireland.

O'Hare looked round for the other he was sure was there. But for Nathaniel Johnson, there was no sign.

Whether the Divine Spirit came back through the wall, clicking as some 'thank you' for what they had done, or, it had made a mistake in its direction home, before disappearing back through the wall, O'Hare could only flippantly muse. But understanding basic physics in regard to electric wiring shorting out and flammable substances close by what the likely outcome would be next. AG-MX-960 had caught fire, with inflammable material enough to blow the place to smithereens; they needed to depart this place.

'Let's get out of here,' he shouted at the team.

Fitch grabbed Carter by the hand and ran. O'Hare went to the computer console, kicked the bloodied body of Stonercrop out of the way, pulled the plug off the external hard drive and put it in a case. He ran and dived out through the door after them into the Arctic wastes of Alaska. Still running he followed Fitch and Carter. The three of them heading for the door of a Sikorsky. Colonel Lennox and Sergeant Brantlinger were waiting for them.

The pilot, seeing the first explosion take the roof off the hangar, didn't need a second invitation to lift off. He looked back to confirm that his passengers were on board. The giant rotors one after each other began their circles from their power units, and gently, lifted the aircraft from the snow. The pilot lowered the front of the cockpit towards the ground turning the aircraft until he found west, powered the craft forward with as much lift as he dare without stalling. He was clear away before the second explosion blew the entire site back to whiteness.

'*Man*, I could murder a whiskey,' Carter said to the two of them.

'And I could do with one of your cigarettes,' O'Hare said.

He listened as the satellite dish worked its signal the shortest path to Russia. It rang. He prayed he had the right number. When it was answered the voice listened to him introduce himself. There was a pause, before to O'Hare, the person considered who he was hearing the message, 'Says his name is Charlie O'Hare. Returned from the – *Dead!*'

Bezukladnikov took the phone from his secretary.

'And what did St. Peter say? Go back and pay for the repair of the bar stool you broke, and you can come in. *Ha, ha, ha.*'

O'Hare smiled to himself before continuing with respect for the man's office. 'Good morning, Mr. President. You saved my life, are you in a position to move up a gear and do the same for mankind?'

The man's voice tone changed, 'We're engaging with you in world war three here, Irish. Only Henry can save you, *ha, ha, ha*. Nothing you or I can do to change that for a situation, unless you've a better idea. I think the words, to use the American vernacular, *we're all stuffed*, is appropriate, don't you?'

'The sky is clearing, and the sun is once again rising in the east, isn't that enough, President Bezukladnikov?'

'Your Henry has one of our submarines in his backyard. Shouldn't be telling you this, but any advantage for a first-strike by him has been lost. Old Russian proverb for him Irish, *For a mad dog, seven versts is not a long detour*, ha, ha, ha.'

'And one for you, Sergei, *America will go to hell and back for a bag of coffee!*'

Bezukladnikov thought long and hard. Inhaling his cigar, he nodded to his defense secretary while speaking with O'Hare, 'Don't I know it. Listen. We seem to have an impasse, Charlie.'

'Stalemate is the word I would have chosen for this game, so it is.'

'So we do, so we do. You are not wrong. Though, I do have it on good authority that Henry's ICBMs are sited without their warheads. If that is the case, it is a dangerous game to play at this stage – even for him.'

'Can't help you there, Sergei. Might have, might not. Don't know the man well enough. Wanna risk it?' He added after a pause, 'Rules for engagement are psychological in the main, as you know well. *You've* played the odd hand of poker, if you suspected such a hand how many kopeks would you stake to see it?'

Bezukladnikov thought good and hard for a second time this day. '*Ha, ha, ha.* You make good argument, Irish. Always did. Tell Henry, I'll stand down, but no mistakes, eh. One force move—

'Will we meet again before we both retire, Comrade?'

'Can you find your way to Ireland?'

'Ah! Praviy! *The Emerald Isle*, eh! Where Irishmen are sober for as long as they're clutching a blade of grass preventing them sliding off the earth.'

'You better believe that, Sergei. Thank you. *Do svidaniya*, for now, President Bezukladnikov.'

Thirty Three – 1997

SISTER BENEDICTA MARIE was at a cross roads. Her life as Annie Carter, still a Carmelite; and fully paid up member; special envoy to Pope John-Paul II; special adviser to the United Nations' Ecumenical Society of World Religions; and Religious Consultant in waiting with the FBI was about to revert to her old life, and she worried. Heading the party across the tarmac of Kennedy Airport, dressed in the cloth of her Order, with a cigarette dangling from her lips, a bag hanging from her shoulder, a laptop part tucked under one arm, and a cell-phone to her ear; was speaking a conversation to the caller that was clearly not asking, *Have you had a nice holiday?* by the tone in her voice. The call was damage limitation from St. Peter's representative on earth to followers of a religion that numbered a billion souls; that were questioning all faiths. And she, unable to accept her vocation in likely tatters, was having none of it, aware that her disagreement was ex-communicable to the mind of the man that was inspired by her playing a royal flush against a full house with this woman, when she chose to lay her cards on the table saying, *I shall begin again, Your Holiness.*

Fitch had a worried look on his face, 'About your relationship, with my grandmother,' he asked O'Hare with an idea in his head that he might have been his grandson. 'Was there anymore in it than that?'

'Don't worry, son. You're still *kosher,*' he had answered. 'I might be a lot of things, but your grandfather, Frank never had any need to consider a bill of a divorce against Sarah where I was concerned.'

Hamilton, born Arnie H. Weinberg of Jewish mother and father was *halakhically* all too aware of his identity; although not circumcised, was still the son of Ruth, his Jewish mother. He had argued with O'Hare, that his repudiation of Judaism did not mean he had severed all links with the Jewish community, only that he was Jewish with a belief waiting to be found. O'Hare, hard wired in Irish mentality, studied him greatly, furrowing his brow. He would have to come back to that some other time, reminding himself he had glanced Pandora's Box and was not going to help Fitch's 'waiting to be found' anytime soon.

His grandmother referred to the last resting place of his mother and father as *Bet ha-Hayyim*. When he had asked what she meant by that expression, she had replied that one day he would understand. He had not understood her when she had whispered, *Long life* at his parent's grave. And he never did get round to asking her what she had meant, he didn't have to. As he grew older, he learned that death is an important part of Judaism. But with the violent death of his mother and father, he no longer had time for Judaism as a faith, and that his God had turned His back on the constant suffering of man against man.

Fitch asked O'Hare what Carter knew to be true.

'As I see it, Satan is a creation of God and as essential to order as He Himself. You cannot have one without the other. Annoying though it is, for an angel, thwarted by God's own, beggars belief, but who am I to argue with Him. I'll tell you one thing though, when my time comes and He asks what I did, I shall proudly stand up and say, "Something. I *did* something. Where were You?" There, and damn be to me for saying it.'

'And will you ask Him to explain?'

'No explanation necessary. He's given us a taster of Armageddon, that's good enough for me.'

The Sikorsky hovered over the desolate house.

'There's another plane down there,' the pilot observed.

'Take her down anyway,' O'Hare replied.

Fitch stared out the window. Someone was standing by the plane. A heavy set guy dressed in a suit that wasn't quite right for an environment forty degrees below. He had a heavy automatic weapon in his hand. He stared up at them through dark glasses. A small glint of the sun through heavy black clouds reflected off the lenses.

'Looks like we've company, Charlie.'

The pilot looked at O'Hare again to check that he was happy. O'Hare nodded and they touched down.

'Stay here,' O'Hare said; 'keep the engine warm. Come with me, Weinberg.'

They walked towards the cabin. Passing the stranger, he pointed and nodding at them indicating the doorway of the single floored ramshackle hut used by Indians in that part of the world. Signs of hunters were all round. Traps, fur boots, a half broken sledge with dog traces that had seen better days twisted and worn through. One fully operational, with huskies sleeping haphazardly round it. A well-dressed woman wearing a fur coat came into the doorway. She looked O'Hare's age, fifty or so. 'Who are you?' he asked slowly.

She hesitated. He looked familiar. 'Irinushka—'

'*Mihalyvich?*'

She nodded.

His lip twisted. A tear tried to well up in his eye. He wiped it away with the back of his hand. 'I believe I am the man responsible for failing your family; and I should like to apologize—'

'No need,' she said leading the way into the hut, a domicile that looked as if it served for everything. It was colder inside than out. Fitch shuddered. Irinushka went to a cot that stood in the corner. A wicker arrangement made of heavy grass stranded and broken. A baby, lying in it on a fur was crying. She picked him up. 'Is this what you came to see?'

'I don't understand,' O'Hare said. 'She's given *birth*. How? *Show me!*' She passed the baby over. He gently took him, instinctively clutching him to his own body as paternal protection. He was warm. He looked for the birth cord. When he found it, his brow furrowed, and his mouth opened slightly. His body shuddered with this miracle of resurrection he held in his arms. His thoughts went back to a time, one he would never forget, and those he held responsible. Getting himself together he said, 'He is beautiful though,' passing him back said, '*Latino?*'

'A second chance for a life cut down; unable to pass over; an infringement on God's will that cannot interfere in the affairs of man. He is as bound by the laws of the universe as the rest of us. Shamanism is very powerful, Sergeant O'Hare. It has no boundaries to the point that it can override Gods.'

All these years O'Hare believed that, the angel he took as Irinushka was she; and at the end, that's what she was, a ministering spirit. Get an idea into your head, he thought. As for Irinushka, with the same faith as her mother Oona, as all North American Indians – a Shamanic. Born of powerful spirits. The few, blessed with abilities to cross boundaries imposed by Gods to reach Gods, summon them, put right wrongs that had gone before. And he, a simple bog Irishman of Roman Catholic persuasion, had allowed his imagination to run away with him. Out of curiosity, he turned back to ask what had become of Fariq her father, but she was gone, along with baby, and the stranger wearing dark glasses.

'And we've been given, all thanks to her, a second chance, so we have. And *she*, as the proverbial Connie Lamar, *You just can't keep a good woman down*, and all that, has triumphed—'

'And though she was not who you thought she was, but an angel with her own agenda,' Carter interrupted.

He shrugged. The crossover line between the forces of good and evil had not escaped his notice and Carter didn't pursue the point.

A suited man, wearing a trilby hat interrupted them. His hand was out towards him.

'Mr. O'Hare?'

O'Hare turned to see who was speaking to him. 'I am. *You are?*'

'Nathaniel Johnson, Special Surveillance. You have a hard-drive in your possession. I have instructions . . .'

O'Hare smiled, 'Of course, you are. It's right over there in my suitcase, Nath. I'll get it for you.'

He turned quickly, picking up the suitcase, walked away out through Kennedy Airport's departure lounge door leaving Johnson with his mouth open wondering how he thought he was going to get away from him this time in an airport that was not yet fully operational. Closing the door behind him, laughing, O'Hare started to run toward a Bombadier Learjet, decaled with the Irish trefoil; at half engine power on the airfield's grass surround. He climbed its steps.

A team of security chased after him.

A stewardess, wearing a tight fitting two-piece dark green uniform complimented with an orange pillbox hat; with one hand on his shoulder and the other on the door greeted him. She passed him a glass of malt whiskey, 'Compliments of Tammany New York,' she said. He cheered her. Necking the gold liquid, went inside the plane.

The stewardess smiled as Johnson and security came closer and closed the door on them. The engines increased revs and the plane gently turned and taxied to the center of the airfield where it came to a halt. With a roar from its twin Honeywell power unit, the pilot released the aircraft's brakes. The plane shuddered. Its jets screamed, and it was away off down the runway lifting up into the direction of a setting sun; leaving behind a trail of heat haze in its wake before the astonished eyes of security.

Fitch returned to the *New York Post*, with the story of his career. One that would never see the light of day as it stands. But he will cut, stet, transpose, edit and redraft until something resembling a manuscript might be published as a science fiction novel. But he would never forget, the enduring snappy-Fuji photo Mike Crawford took of a little blonde curly haired girl, part decomposed, trapped in a haul net being dragged from the cold waters of the Hudson river that evening with her hand holding tightly onto the arm of her teddy bear.

Intrigued with the woman in the furs; and with more questions than O'Hare would answer, Fitch, Editor-in-Chief, asked permission of Stenna, Chief Executive of Media Groups Newspapers, if he could employ the services of a detective agency to trace a family possibly living in Russia connected with events.

'Not more *bollocks!* Fitch,' he answered; then seeing Fitch raise his fist at him continued, 'Only joking!'

He read the report. An accompanying photograph attached of a woman he saw with O'Hare in Alaska, confirmed to him it was she. She looked no more than fifty, though records showed she had two grown children, four grandchildren, as well as an adopted boy; that should have put her in her eighties. The report showed she worked in sales for a failing medical equipment company in Omsk supplying surgical goods for hospitals and medical services. Rising to become overall manager in charge, she bought out the company. Concentrating in the making of disposable syringes, the clean needles demanded by doctors and medics carried the trade name OONA, finding also markets in China and India. The report went on to show that her father, Fariq Mihalyvich was still alive.

He answered the question O'Hare had wanted to put to Irinushka.

BIBLIOGRAPHY

Oxford History of the American West,
Edited by:
CLYDE A. MILNER, CAROL A. O'CONNOR,
MARTHA A. SANDWEISS, N.Y.,
Oxford University Press, 1994

Alistair Cooke's America, ALISTAIR COOKE,
Alfred A. Knopf, N.Y., 1973

Judaism, C. M. PILKINGTON,
Hodder & Stoughton

A Prayer for a Deceased Woman,
ROMAN CATHOLIC CHURCH,
Catholic Online

Marching 'Round Selma, ANON, 1965,
Negro Spiritualist Online

Civil War – The Wars of the Three Kingdoms 1638–1660,
TREVOR ROYLE,
Little, Brown, 2004

Philosophy,
SIMON BLACKBURN,
Oxford University Press, 2005

In recognition of:
STEPHEN HAWKING (*decd.*),
Master of the Universe

www.ingramcontent.com/pod-product-compliance
Lightning Source LLC
Chambersburg PA
CBHW010630100726
47900CB00011B/2770